The
HISTORIAN
PROJECT

A TIME TRAVEL CATASTROPHE

NELL GAVIN

Acknowledgements

Many thanks to Leslie Mort-Kane, Sue Kovats-Bell and
Alice O'Donnell Sullivan for their suggestions and contributions

A grateful nod to Jacinda Ardern and other leaders at every level
who lead, or have led, with empathy

CHAPTER 1: WASHINGTON, D.C.

Avid was a few minutes early, so he stood at the crosswalk and waited for the stream of protestors to continue past him, marching in the street toward the National Mall where they would all gather for speeches after the demonstration. This march was just one of many, as people took to the streets in protest across the country. They did this even as a pandemic raged around them and thousands of people died of COVID-19 every day after being cared for in hospital hallways, filled to overflowing, their corpses stored in refrigerated trucks. It was a challenging historical period from any perspective, which was why Avid was there.

Another unarmed Black man had been killed yesterday in another city, and the country had erupted, once again. Avid had worked fourteen of these demonstrations in the past year, and was scheduled to work two more in the following week. It had become routine.

He checked the time, noted that Terence Jackson would be approaching now, and searched the crowd for a tall, bald Black man wearing a bright yellow nylon jacket and a COVID mask, holding a sign that said "Black Lives Matter."

There he was. The yellow jacket made it easy for Avid to spot him. Terence was arriving right on time, with his girlfriend marching beside him and holding up a sign of her own. As Terence moved past, Avid stepped off the curb and slipped into the crowd of marchers, positioning himself just behind the man so he could clearly watch the action unfold, walking immediately alongside the four white supremacists who would kill Terence Jackson at 15:12 hours on March 14, 2021, a few minutes from now.

Avid did not carry a protest sign as he marched. He did not establish eye contact with the white supremacists. He did not shout catchy slogans along with the crowd, and he did not interact with any of the people who surrounded him. He was only there to observe and report on the actual murder, not the march leading up to it. It was not Avid's job to report on the crowd—other members of his team were positioned at various points along the route to do that. And he did not have clearance to interact, so he ignored everyone but the four white supremacists and Terence, making certain they were never more than a few feet away.

Avid had prepared for this event by studying the contemporary news stories and scanner footage of the protest demonstration before he could "interview" the witnesses a little less than two blocks ahead of where they were marching now. He knew which of the marchers belonged to various white supremacist organizations, and he knew which belonged to Antifa, the anarchist group of self-proclaimed anti-fascists, who viewed themselves in this situation as the guardians of the protestors. He knew which white supremacists and Antifa members were pretending to belong to the opposite group to either get close enough to monitor the opposition, or to incite violence and commit destructive crimes they would later blame on the other side. Both groups were highly aware of one another and kept a tense distance, watching each other for signs of disruption or trouble, prepared to step up and take action the instant it occurred.

That trouble would arise in five minutes and fourteen seconds when Terence would twist his ankle in a pothole. In this explosive atmosphere he unfortunately would stumble and accidentally push one of the white supremacists, who would then lose his balance and react. The two men would exchange words, which would escalate into shouting and pushing. The offended man and his three companions would grab Terence and drag him into a nearby alley where three of them would pummel him with their fists. The fourth would stab him in the heart with a knife while Terence's girlfriend watched, screaming.

Avid's assignment was to attend this upcoming event and upload his observations immediately following the attack.

Avid Burhan was a Historian who was assigned to the United States, Twenty-first Century Racial Unrest Mission. Last year his team had had a busy summer attending Black Lives Matter protests like this one, and recording violence, looting and murder as it cropped up in various places throughout the United States. The perpetrators of violence were all identified in the historical records and tagged by name, political affiliation, and background information, even though contemporary law enforcement could not identify many of them and would never arrest them. Twenty-eighth century scanner records

2

knew exactly who they were. These people all thought they'd escaped detection, not knowing that there is no such thing as "historical privacy," or that they would be held up, by name, as a shameful example of what not to be long after they died.

Avid's team consisted of Historians who all had facial features and skin tones that did not suggest any particular race or ancestry to make it less likely that they would become the target of violence from anyone who was inclined to attack people of a specific race. Consequently, the white supremacists who walked beside Avid found nothing overtly objectionable about his appearance or his demeanor. Neither did the Black marchers who were scanning the crowd for threats. In fact, they all only barely noticed him, which was the Mitigators' intent. When an assignment involved twenty-first century racial unrest the Mitigators deliberately sent light-skinned mixed-race Historians who appeared to be neither White nor Black nor Hispanic nor Asian nor Middle Eastern because they enjoyed a neutral position that did not draw anyone's attention or, with any luck, anyone's ire. This allowed them to safely mingle amongst, and sometimes interact with, the event participants whose thoughts and actions they recorded.

Avid Burhan wore a burgundy hoodie with "Washington" imprinted in yellow across his chest. He wore an N-95 face mask in deference to the COVID-19 pandemic, even though he was genetically immune to the virus. He was tall and of indeterminate Eurasian ethnicity, with short, wavy, medium brown hair and skin the color of coffee mixed with lots of milk, not dark, exactly, but not quite "Caucasian white." He was a well-built man who appeared to be in his early thirties, and who had a wiry but muscular athletic build that suggested he worked out, or was involved in sports.

He had his hands in the front pocket of the hoodie as he marched. He knew exactly where to look at any given moment from having studied the footage, and was now looking back. He knew precisely which men to watch and where he would find them. And there they were.

Five members of Antifa, who were approaching the scene a few hundred feet behind Avid, saw the violence accelerate and watched Terence being dragged into the alley. They were on the other side of the street and could not push through the crowd in time to stop the attack, but they moved aggressively toward it, squeezing through the marchers, shoving some of them as they went.

Avid moved to one side for safety in anticipation of their approach. They pushed through the crowd shouting, "Move out of the way!" and raced to get to the alley as quickly as they could. Avid followed closely behind them, taking advantage of the path they'd formed in the crowd as they pushed their way through.

The white supremacists had pressed Terence against the wall of a building, and now looked over at the growing, staring crowd that had followed them and blocked the alley's entrance. They clearly saw the smart phones recording them as Terence's head fell forward, so they released him, then turned and ran in the other direction.

The Antifa marchers had now reached the scene, and shoved their way through the crowd and into the alley, pounding the ground and shouting as they chased the attackers to the street on the other side. Another of Avid's team members would be waiting to record the action when Antifa overtook the white supremacists and the two factions met up on the street at the far end of the alley. That aspect of the event was not Avid's concern.

Avid had now successfully slid into the alley, and was standing a few yards away from the victim. His assignment had begun.

Terence was mortally wounded. With the attackers no longer holding him against the wall, he slid down, barely conscious, and then fell to the ground where he lay, unmoving.

"Stand back!" a man shouted as he disconnected his emergency call to 9-1-1 and put the phone in his pocket. He had assumed the role of crowd control, and stood holding his arms out to keep everyone at a distance. "Keep it clear for the paramedics and police!" And then, "Is anyone a doctor?"

People continued to join the congregating crowd around the alley entrance to watch as Terence bled out his life, while his shaking and weeping girlfriend sat on the ground beside him and held his hand to her lips. A teenaged girl, also weeping, moved closer to squat beside her and hold her in a side hug.

A woman pushed through the tight, unmoving crowd at the alley entrance, and shouted that she was a pediatrician. She was not the best fit for the situation, but she was willing and available. She ran up, then crouched over Terence and did her best while he slipped away.

Avid remained detached and focused, not caught in the immediacy of the Terence Jackson event, even though he was witnessing it firsthand and was surrounded by people who were reacting in the moment.

In preparation for this assignment Avid had dutifully studied the statements that the victim's family and lawyer would make to local media within the next twelve hours. Their statements would be picked up by Reuters and published internationally, so the entire world would be aware of this murder by tomorrow. He knew those statements word for word, and knew the names of all the members of Terence's entire family. Before he arrived here he had memorized everything. He was tuned into their grief as part of his job, and had telepathically experienced it. He knew everything they felt so he could later describe it all as effectively as possible in his report. He had gone through extensive meditation exercises before this assignment to prevent those emotions from overwhelming him, so he was largely inured to the murder he was witnessing. The drama had no deep and lasting emotional impact for him because it occurred seven hundred and thirty-three years ago, and because he was trained to experience past events dispassionately.

He focused his mind on telepathically reading the people who surrounded him—that was his primary job—and was bombarded by their thoughts and emotions. He could not see the faces of about half of the people in the crowd because these people were wearing pandemic face masks. However, he could read their thoughts and comment on them in his report. To do this he focused on each person and shut out the thoughts and emotions of the others until he had uploaded each report and moved on to the next one, person by person.

Avid began with the people closest to the victim and moved outward from there. His first interview was with Terence's girlfriend. He gave the mental command, "Subject Data." In response, the holographic Alert screen displayed twelve inches from his face, and provided the woman's image and personal information. Avid briefly and unnecessarily reviewed this out of habit. He would not spend much time with her interview because the upcoming contemporary news reports were going to contain much more information than he could obtain from her now. Later in the day she would be coherent and eloquent about her experience, so this interview was just a quick snapshot of her initial reaction.

Subject: Irma Santana Morales. Born: San Juan, Puerto Rico, March 31, 1993. Died: May 1, 2043. Cause: Car accident. Occupation: Hairdresser, nail stylist. Married: October 1, 2015. Divorced: December 13, 2017. Spouse: Vincente Morales, born Puerto Rico November 18, 1989. Children: Cristina

Morales, born Washington D.C. May 14, 2016, Dante Jackson, born Washington D.C. April 17, 2019. Event consequences: PTSD. Depression.

He tuned into Irma, now standing shakily upright to make room for the doctor who was trying to stem Terence's bleeding with her scarf. She stood beside the teenaged girl, whose arms were wrapped around her waist and who was pressing close to her.

Avid stated in his report that Irma was suffering from shock. She hadn't processed anything yet and felt as if she were moving underwater in a surreal dream. He gave the mental command, "Save to file, today's local date."

The screen in front of him displayed a list of folder names. He identified and focused on, "Terence Jackson Witnesses." The folder name turned blue when his eyes connected to it. Avid mentally commanded, "Upload" and Irma's personal information uploaded to that folder, along with Avid's observations of her mental and emotional state. It would now be accessible to staff from the Education Project, who would review it and incorporate it into history courses for older children.

His next interview was with the teenaged girl.

"Subject Data," he silently commanded. His Alert Screen displayed her information.

Subject: Adella Santana. Born: Washington D.C., October 27, 2006. Died August 29, 2088. Cause: Cardiac arrest. Occupation: Registered nurse. Married: June 20, 2027. Spouse: Catalina Dixon, born March 2, 2001, died September 14, 2050. Cause: Breast cancer. Children: None.

Adella was nervously muttering expletives to herself as she looked down at Terence and then looked away, focusing primarily on her sister Irma, but frightened because she didn't know how to make it all better. Irma was unresponsive and her eyes were unfocused. Who should Adella call? What should she do? Should she lead Irma away? Should she wait for the ambulance?

"Irma!" she said urgently. She patted her cheek softly. "Come on, Irma." That was the most frightening aspect of this, aside from seeing Terence lying there on the ground in a pool of blood: not knowing what to do. Ordinarily she would have turned to Irma for guidance, but her sister had checked out, and Adella was left to deal with it herself. She pressed her cheek to Irma's and said, "It'll be okay. It'll be okay. It'll be okay." Irma responded with a slight nod and an empty look. Her teeth were chattering, and she was making a noise like a low hum. Adella patted her cheek again and then hugged her tightly.

Avid uploaded Adella's report, then scanned the rest of the crowd for his next subject. There he was! Avid smiled to himself, a little star struck, thoroughly enjoying the moment.

The small, slight-figured Black teenaged male in the backwards red Nationals baseball cap had wormed his way to the front of the crowd and was watching the scene in quiet panic. "This is me," Avid heard him think as he studied Terence on the ground. "This is how I die one day." And then Avid heard, "Is it always going to be this way?" And then, "Does anybody really care? Are we changing anything *at all*?"

The young man was just a few yards away from Terence and could see everything. He angrily, impulsively smashed his Black Lives Matter sign against the side of the building to his right, then emitted three guttural grunts with his face to the sky. He held his hands in fists at his side, and, then stopped to wipe snot from his nose and tears from his eyes with the sleeve of his jacket.

"God damn those fucking assholes!" he screamed.

"Subject data," Avid commanded.

The screen displayed: *Subject: Joseph D'Andre McKenna. Born: Washington, D.C. July 14, 2005. Died: March 13, 2097. Cause: Natural. Occupation: U.S. Senator, U.S. Ambassador to China, U.S. Secretary of State, U.S. Supreme Court Justice. Refer to the Joseph D'Andre McKenna historical file for extensive supplemental information.*

Avid now felt Joseph's hopelessness turn to rage, and transcribed his thoughts into the report. He would fight, the teenager decided in this galvanizing moment, furious and terrified. He would find a way to fight back. That thought generated a notation on Avid's Alert screen that read, "Event Consequences: Refer to the Joseph D'Andre McKenna historical file in its entirety." Avid filed the notation in the supplemental Terence Jackson Event Consequences folder.

Avid mentally uploaded his report to the Terence Jackson Witnesses folder, sending a duplicate copy to the Joseph D'Andre McKenna historical file.

The police arrived and began questioning the witnesses. Meanwhile, Avid reported on everyone within close proximity, uploading his observations one by one.

Two additional white supremacists and one man with sadistic sexual tendencies were enjoying the spectacle. They did not display any emotion as they watched, but Avid could telepathically sense their glee. He uploaded their files with his observations.

Seventeen of the people in the ever-growing crowd would die of COVID-19 at some point during the pandemic. Several had only weeks or months to live. Two of these were contracting the virus at this event, so Avid uploaded those files to Terence Jackson Event Consequences.

A group of teenaged girls of different races in matching soccer uniforms were clustered together, pressed close, in shock, linking arms and holding hands, watching wide-eyed. Three of these would become social activists after witnessing this event, and required uploads to both Event Consequences and their individual supplemental historical records folders. Also uploaded to Event Consequences folder was the PTSD diagnosis of one of the other girls. The rest would effectively push the event out of their minds and only refer back to it as a story they would tell from time to time. They required no further documentation.

Seven people were holding up smart phones and recording the event. One of these turned his camera to the crowd and recorded everyone's reactions, while three others were live streaming on Facebook. Avid felt from them all a sense of detachment because they were using the phones almost as emotional protection against the scene because the phone screens provided distance and made Terence and his pool of blood appear small. However, all had an inflexible sense of purpose equal to that of Joseph D'Andre McKenna. Each person felt as if he or she was making history as, in fact, each one was. The names of the people with the phones would eventually be obscured and then lost, but the video clips they recorded would become a part of classroom discussion for centuries. These were the same videos that Avid had studied in school.

Terence Jackson was dead. The paramedics had arrived just moments after the police, and were strapping his body onto a gurney, which they covered with a sheet and wheeled out of the alley, and then across the street to the waiting ambulance, while police held the crowd back.

Irma leaned heavily on Adella as the police continued to question them.

The pediatrician held her face in her hands for a moment, then slowly walked back to the march with her head down, tears streaming down her face. Her grief was personal, and she was berating herself, unfairly, for failing to save Terence. Avid added that observation of her to her report.

The videographers uploaded their recordings to YouTube, Facebook, TikTok, and Instagram, and then dispersed into the street. The event was over, but the march continued.

"Locate Terence Jackson videos, today's local date." The screen displayed a list of all the websites where the seven videographers had uploaded their footage.

Avid's eyes connected with the files. He gave the command to "upload the videos to the Educator database, today's common date."

The date he was referring to as "today's common date" was August 1, 2754. However, the files would later be copied to the database forty years earlier so that present and future Historian uploads would all be accessible from the outset of the Project. Avid chuckled to think that he was the one to upload the videos that he himself would study in school. He always enjoyed it when that happened.

Avid could now return to the control station.

He displayed his Alert screen and entered a pickup request with his coordinates. The control station's tracking system automatically scanned the area to determine a time and specific pickup point when and where there would be no nearby observers, and then sent instructions back to him. These indicated that he should arrive at Dumbarton Oaks Park after 16:37 hours, but before 16:51 hours when observers would suddenly arrive.

At 16:28 hours the Uber driver left Avid at the entrance to the park. Avid received Alert screen directions to the secluded area where his travel pod would be arriving in a few minutes. He had plenty of time, so he began walking slowly, breathing the fresh air and enjoying the scenery as he took a meandering, casual, unhurried stroll toward the pickup point. The instructions pointed him to a thicket, then told him to push through it and into a clearing, where he saw a small, unmanned travel pod hovering overhead, obscured from the walk path by trees. It scanned and identified him as he approached, and then landed in front of him. The door opened, and he boarded the aircraft. The travel pod rose, then silently sped upward and away at high speed. From the ground it looked like a black streak for perhaps half a second, and then it was gone.

Nobody saw it.

CHAPTER 2: THE HISTORIAN PROJECT

The Mitigators began building control stations in the year AD 2712, when Avid was eleven years old, partly in support of a massive effort by Educators to update their coursework and curriculum. Their intention was to replace the element of "history is written by the winners" with "history is a compilation of human experience." This shift in focus was the very beginning of the Historian Project.

The mid-Atlantic control station opened in about AD 900 to observe and study the indigenous North American tribes before the arrival of the Vikings, and to document the Viking settlements when the settlers finally came. When the Pilgrims and other European settlers arrived later, it would serve as a very busy station from which time travel staff could observe and record the locals. It was already in place to cover the rise of the United States, with Washington D.C. as the hub of the world for a time, only a few short minutes away by air. By the twenty-first century, it housed roughly the same number of inhabitants as the city of Miami, Florida.

The mid-Atlantic control station was very active during the twentieth and twenty-first centuries, particularly during periods of political upheaval within the United States. This was one of those periods. Large twenty-eighth century aircraft hid in the clouds to monitor and record satellite transmissions and action on the ground. They were not visible on the screens of air traffic controllers, who could not assign them clear airspace because they could not see them, so they simply dodged and evaded local aircraft, whose occupants spotted them and shared the sky with them every day, but who were still too afraid of mockery to report them as "UFOs".

On the ground, Historians attended pivotal historical events as live spectators, telepathically interviewing the main participants and the witnesses, and then submitting their reports to the twenty-eighth century Educator database so older schoolchildren could view the video footage, and then study and discuss the Historians' observations.

Hundreds or even thousands of Historians received assignments to record a myriad of internal high-level meetings among world leaders who met in Washington, D.C. and New York. The Historians who were assigned to these roles typically resided on-land and passed as "locals," working as interpreters or non-vital staff in the innermost offices of the government. Others monitored important publicly accessible events outside of government buildings and across the entire eastern half of the United States and Canada. When access to an event was impossible or too dangerous, scanner footage recorded it and someone from the Historian Project uploaded it to the Educator database.

Historians had telepathic access to government officials and could report on their true motivations and intent. They were privy to the secrets these leaders kept from the public, the threats they were under, and the closely-missed disasters the public never learned about. With access to this information, twenty-eighth century students had a far better grasp of the inner workings of historical world leadership than the locals could ever have had. In fact, many locals would have had been broken-hearted, had they known what twenty-eighth century students knew about their revered and beloved leaders.

In earlier time periods, before the Mid-Atlantic control station existed, time travel staff used "older" control stations in other parts of the world, and they traveled to North America from there, as necessary. While those were technically older because they were built earlier in history, they were all originally constructed at roughly the same time, from the perspective of Avid's era. Eventually there were dozens of densely populated control stations scattered all over the world.

The Mitigators built control stations in various time periods, positioning them where populations were about to increase, building more as earth's timeline progressed. They placed the first one on a stable underwater mountain range in the Pacific Ocean, far to the west of what was then the super continent of Pangea. This control station housed scientists and geologists who were documenting the earth's development and the movements of the continental plates, and who also recorded prehistory from the Middle Jurassic Era up to the earliest evolution of the human race, when the Historians first arrived to record human history.

The First Pacific control station also hosted and catered to a booming tourism industry. The Mitigators prohibited time travel tourism in eras that had hominids of any variety, only permitting unsupervised tourists to visit prehistoric eras where the climate was temperate, and dangerous predatory animals, such as dinosaurs, were not roaming the earth. To accommodate demand, the First Pacific control station housed the headquarters for the Hospitality Project, and along with a large number of inhabitants who worked for it.

Eventually the tectonic plates would drift apart, and the continent of South America would move west to meet the First Pacific control station, which would ultimately become convenient to the coast of Peru. After the completion of additional control stations in other parts of the world during later eras, the First Pacific control station began to focus primarily on events in the Southern Hemisphere, then eventually concentrated solely on South and Central American history from the eighth century up to modern times.

The next-earliest densely-manned control stations pre-dated the mid-Atlantic control station by tens of thousands of years, and were positioned to monitor Asia and the South Pacific, Europe, and Africa. Historians arrived to document the dominance and decline of various hominids as they evolved into homo sapiens, and tracked the migration of populations all over the globe, all the way up to the Bering Strait, across Europe and Asia, and down to the South Pacific, Australia and New Zealand. From these control stations Historians observed and recorded the social constructs and languages of the earliest humans, and the rise and fall of civilizations in the various areas of the world.

In the fifteenth century the Mitigators added a new control station off the coast of California, in time for Spain's exploration of the Pacific Islands and the Americas. This control station served all of North America west of the Mississippi until they added the Great Lakes control station, and then another in the Gulf of Mexico. They still kept going.

The construction and growth of control stations continued until the underwater complexes became sprawling cities that each contained hundreds of thousands of time travel support staff and Historians during particularly busy and eventful historical eras. This was one of those historical eras, so most control stations across the world were almost full to capacity.

After a control station's construction was complete, it maintained a permanent staff of maintenance technicians who repaired and updated the structures and kept everything in working order. These workers oversaw the hydropower from the ocean currents, monitored air quality, sewage, and water desalinization, repaired the travel pods, designed and furnished the living units and community spaces, and fixed the plumbing in the individual apartments.

Hydropower provided electricity, so power never shut down or ran out. Pipes pumped in fresh air from the ocean surface. Desalination pods provided fresh water. Sewage treatment buildings cleaned the waste, while Waste Control followed processes that left nothing impure in the oceans, and then eviscerated trash that meandered into their ocean space.

Each control station had one "forested" nature preserve building that grew full-sized trees, with soil and grass-covered flooring above the roots, and birds and squirrels, raccoons, deer, woodchucks, chipmunks, fireflies and honeybees milling or flying about to enable people to experience and enjoy a parklike environment.

The Culinary Project had fisherman who caught the seafood, and farmers who harvested edible sea plants outside the complex for the chefs in the main cafeteria and the luxury restaurants. Chickens and ducks wandered freely in their "natural" assigned space within the Farm building, and provided eggs. Dairy cows grazed in the midst of them, and provided milk and cheese. Multiple multi-storied hydroponics buildings had entire massive levels devoted to growing corn, potatoes, and rice, or grains like wheat, barley, and oats with a mill to grind them. Entire floors were devoted to vegetables and herbs. Other floors housed nut and fruit trees, berries and mushrooms, with bees that pollinated everything and supplied honey to the chefs and bakers.

Chefs fed the control station with the food the farmers delivered to the kitchens, while bakers baked with the grains they milled onsite, along with the chocolate and spices the kitchen support staff procured in bulk on-land. Except for the novel treats they brought in from on-land sources, the complex was almost entirely self-sufficient, and had been since AD 900.

The control station buildings that contained the living quarters were all cylindrical, more wide than tall, and had a common area in the center. Each building offered its occupants a large, free-but-basic cafeteria that could feed several hundred at a time, plus several luxury restaurants, indoor pools and saunas, exercise rooms, recreation rooms, a commissary, and rooms that offered holographic virtual reality experiences within any time or place that residents could select from a lengthy list. Residents had access to local television broadcasts and used twenty-first century computers to view contemporary websites on the Internet, but still had access to twenty-eighth century fare on their Alert screens.

The Sports Project maintained a building at each control station with sports arenas and sports training, and held sporting events with professional athletes who competed against athletes from other control stations and other centuries. Amateur sports enthusiasts who reported to other Projects could qualify for leagues at any level, which competed against one other locally.

The Arts Project building had theaters that presented films, live plays, dance performances and music concerts. Its Performance Arts and Music school contained studios to support students and practitioners of every type of musical, theater, filming or artistic expression. There was also a museum that displayed contributions from local talent. Amateur art, music or theater enthusiasts who reported to other Projects could participate in art classes, community theater productions and choir, or form their own bands.

There was an entertainment building with an amusement park, playgrounds, "outdoor" swimming holes with rope swings, bicycle paths, and dog parks.

There was an educational building where all the children went to school, and where adults could continue their education.

The hangars housed all of the larger aircraft that roamed the skies above North America, and which startled and alarmed the pilots of local commercial and military aircraft. These pilots were still keeping their thoughts to themselves.

The multi-storied main building in the complex was shaped like a wheel with spokes, and contained eleven specialty restaurants that served different cuisines, where people could splurge to enjoy meals that were superior to the free cafeteria fare and even the luxury restaurants in their own and other buildings. People who preferred to cook could purchase food at the commissary and prepare it in their apartment kitchens. They could even take scheduled cooking classes from the chefs.

Higher floors in the main building contained the restaurants and entertainment facilities, along with various other publicly accessible areas, while on the main floor there was a community center, a bank, the large main commissary, and a medical wing.

The Time Travel wing contained the time travel apparatus and the technicians who worked with it. The Historian Assimilation team worked out of the front of that wing and served the people who came and went as they traveled through time. They assigned local identities and biographies to Historians, provided them with sufficient identifying documentation and cash, obtained and distributed up-to-the-minute clothing in Wardrobe, and most importantly taught Historians and their on-land support staff how to behave in the society they were about to visit.

Control center inhabitants needed very little from the outside world, if the outside world did not have abundant resources at a particular time or place in history. People had comfortably lived this way for hundreds of years, since the very first ocean structures were built as a means of escaping climate change, long before construction began on the worldwide control centers. It was a very nice life, with very little sacrifice or deprivation for those who lived and worked there. The tradeoff was that some of the residents would never set foot on-land, or see the sun or open sky in their lifetimes.

Before the Historian Project, recorded history was merely propaganda that was written by the winners. It was incomplete and skewed by contemporary prejudices. It missed critical information due to widespread and extensive politically and personally-motivated cover-ups, and it relied heavily on unsupported hearsay from uninformed or biased sources. Huge knowledge gaps made much of it unreliable. It lacked commentary from the citizens who experienced history in real time, skimmed over their day-to-day experiences, lifestyles and emotions, and limited students in their efforts to fully understand and empathize with the people who endured events such as the eruption of Mount Vesuvius, the pillage of Genghis Kahn, or the annihilation of the Mesoamerican civilizations by the Spaniards.

History had always traditionally concentrated on war until the Mitigators shifted the focus of school curriculum at the very beginning of the Historian Project. Educators would now treat war, which history had always glorified, as a societal and leadership failure. School curriculum would still cover wars, but Educators would now deliver the content from the perspective of war victims, and as a means of identifying, dissecting, and studying the incompetence, poor judgment, and personal flaws of the leaders who engaged in war. That was the first, the most pivotal, and the most important change in educational focus.

There was no empathy in history classes or historical texts until the Historian Project. Religions tried to teach empathy, but sometimes succumbed to warlike behaviors in contrast with their scripture. Storytellers, novelists and films sometimes taught empathy, but more frequently focused on entertainment.

After the Final War, this oversight and educational gap emerged as a monumental crisis, and the Mitigators were committed to addressing it. There would be no more denial or detachment from sordid events, they decreed. Everyone must see history just exactly as it had transpired, with a clear, unflinching eye. There would be no more looking away. There would be no more rationalizing of poor behavior, or spinning it into a triumph worthy of celebration. There would be no more recitation in the classroom of the dates of wars and conquests.

History would now focus on individuals who, with the assistance of Historians, would each describe for twenty-eighth century schoolchildren the events, wars, upheavals and triumphs that they personally lived through. Students were now required to immerse themselves in the traumas of the past, and view history as the experience of real, specific individuals with names and lives, whom the Historians had identified and telepathically interviewed. Their various countries and various wars would now only serve as a backdrop. Educators presented this curriculum with an overview that described the events leading up to the moment of the interview, along with supplemental scanner footage of the events now taking place.

The Mitigators took the position that dramatic and traumatic events always require respect and appreciation for the people who experience them. In learning about the sacrifices and triumphs of people in the past, students must experience meditative introspection and clear-headed Educator-guided observational judgment of human behavior and its real consequences. There was no better way to teach children to be responsible and empathetic with their actions and their goals than to show them the real consequences of thirst for power, violence, personal aggrandizement, greed, and a lack of empathy prevalent in what was a brutal, dirty history of the Human Race. From now on, the people who actually experienced these events would personally describe them to the students through Historian transcriptions.

The Mitigators had an aspirational goal when they conceived of the Historian Project. They completely overhauled school curriculum in order to guide children to an empathetic adulthood...because empathetic people do not start mindless wars.

Empathy became the foundation of education. In the earliest school grades when children were small, Educators showed them holographic videos with numerous examples of charity, helpfulness, kindness and love. Children watched children sharing, and comforting other crying children. They saw children playing well with other children. They received effusive praise and applause from the Educators, staff and the other children, whenever they emulated those behaviors.

They were shown videos of sick or injured puppies, and their heartwarming transformations to healthy and playful because of someone's kind intervention. They saw animals that were natural enemies being friends and playing together, and were taught "no matter how different someone is from you, you can love that person."

Their days were filled with examples of sharing and loyalty, protection of the weak, and of generous encouragement, support, love and kindness toward everyone.

As the children grew, the Educators slipped in darker examples, with simple straightforward events that demonstrated clear "good" and "bad" behaviors in uncomplicated situations. Then, the curriculum of older children gradually included increasingly complicated and distressing trauma, still offset by heartwarming demonstrations of love and puppies. Children were always encouraged to feel what the participants had felt long ago in the darker examples, and to sympathize. They were taught to never, ever, ever engage in the "bad" behavior they witnessed in the events they studied.

When children reached their teens the messages grew darker still, and they had to finally watch and study the very worst of mankind.

Twenty-eighth century society did not have current news broadcasts with constant violent crimes, and constant streams of war footage and death counts. The people there and then, except for the very oldest, were not exposed to the shock of violence in their own time, and they did not accept it as an unavoidable part of the background noise. In order for students to fully understand the ramifications of violence, they had to vicariously experience it.

There were risks to doing this, so every student's exposure to historical trauma had to be measured, thoughtfully spaced apart, and offset at a five-to-one ratio by carefully administered positive lessons. To prepare students for lessons covering violent and disturbing historical events, Educators presented short "preview" clips to ease students into them gradually and acclimate them to the lessons before they could delve into them more deeply. Students meditated before class. They performed the required breathing exercises after class. Hugs were generously given to students as they processed what they watched, and sometimes an entire class was intertwined, holding onto each other in a group hug and crying, while the Educator and staff support spread wide hugs across the students on the fringes of the huddle. Psychological support was on site, accessible, and mandatory. Everyone would see history as it actually was, and everyone would receive support in coping with the impact history would now have on every individual from this point forward.

The objective of the Educators was to make historical events real to the students, to have them connect emotionally to the people who experienced the events, and to make them learn about the aftereffects of historically poor behavior so that society would never repeat that poor behavior again. People had not learned from history before, and so they had continually repeated it. The Historian Project would break that cycle, the Mitigators hoped.

Forty years earlier, a Mitigator at a global conference displayed historical footage and images of an ancient war and said, "History should not be dry; it should make us cry." It became a catch phrase in their society.

"What we propose is a deep dive into the thoughts, feelings and experiences of the people you see in these images, and in all the other images that will confront us in the upcoming years. We propose that we all respect—and honor—human hearts and experiences throughout history in all the events that we can record and show to you, and by extension the hearts and experiences of all the people whose images we can never see. We can study them, and we can learn."

The Project was successfully approved and launched. The effort began in earnest when Avid was twelve years old, when the control stations were now in place and being staffed with newly-trained support personnel. The Mitigators then interviewed and selected the first wave of Historians. By the time Avid was thirteen the very first of the new Historians had completed their studies and were dispatched into History. He dreamt of being one himself, and studied diligently in his effort to become one.

After the Project launched, the process of assigning, training, and deploying Historians became a worldwide-supported effort. Everyone wanted to be a Historian, in part because Historians and certain Historian Project control station support staff were permitted to travel into, and physically interact with, the past. People could pay to travel back in time to the various control stations as often as they liked, but they could never venture on-land because people create havoc with the continuum, and they trigger Anomalies without close supervision and intensive training. Those wealthy enough to afford the higher fares for on-land travel were limited to unpopulated locations in prehistoric times, or to blindingly expensive group tours led by qualified tour guides, who could interact with the locals on their behalf as they traveled within more recent eras. "Tourists" could never interact with anyone on-land at any price.

On-land tours were so expensive that people usually only experienced a few of them in a lifetime, if they were lucky enough to experience any at all. Consequently, promotion to "Historian" was a heartfelt dream for people who yearned to travel. They raced to take advanced courses in telepathy so they could qualify as Historians, studied the technical aspects of the job, practiced their meditation and breathing techniques, and sat for twelve-hour exams. Avid watched all this impatiently and waited for his turn.

The Mitigators narrowed down candidates based on intelligence, proven good judgment, and high placement on the empathy scale. Then they personally interviewed and selected each one.

Historians immediately rose in the social hierarchy, becoming quasi-celebrities. Admission to the program became more and more competitive as a result. Most people could not reasonably hope to be nominated to be a Mitigator or be appointed to the role of Educator, but "Historian" was within their grasp if they had the aptitude and worked hard enough.

In twenty-eighth century society, Mitigators were the top of the social hierarchy and acted together as world leaders. Educators were of the next highest social order, and Historians followed immediately behind them. Obtaining acceptance to a training class for Historians was a heady, giddy cause for celebration. Failure was crushing. Those who failed to qualify usually joined the Historian Project as control station support at some location in the past, applying for positions in maintenance, banking, housekeeping, restaurant staff, farming, finance, wardrobe, tourism and more. Many of those positions required them to go on-land to perform various tasks in support of the control center and the Historians. That was the primary lure to many of them, who all resettled in various control stations, scattered throughout time.

Most of the world's population lived in earlier eras, scattered everywhere, or lived in the ocean, which did not claim statehood. By the late twenty-seventh century geopolitical leadership was no longer feasible. The population was now divided into "Projects" instead of countries, with each Project focusing on a different aspect of day-to-day life and societal development. Each Project had its own separate team of Mitigators, who wrote the laws specific to that Project and led the people within it.

The Historian Mitigators drew up rules and laws for the Historian Project, covering the actions Historians could and could not take on-land, and the things they could and could not say to contemporary locals when they went back in time. They could not anticipate every outcome, and the project was still relatively new, so the Mitigators tweaked the rules as they observed the process in real time.

They would urgently find it necessary to implement a new rule today.

CHAPTER 3: THE McKENNA ANOMALY

SUNDAY, MARCH 14, 2021: TIME 17:16 HOURS

The door to the transitional chamber opened as the travel pod coasted through the water to the parking area beneath Avid's apartment building. The sound and vibration of the wildlife deterrent rang out as sea life scrambled to safety, rather than follow the travel pod through the door and get trapped within the chamber. Then the door closed behind it.

The pod slowly made its way through the low-ceilinged first chamber, where it was still submerged. The door to the second chamber opened, and the pod passed through it. The door closed behind it. The pod rose to the surface of the water within a high-ceilinged chamber, where it coasted to its docking station between two walkways that led into the building. Several hundred other pods were parked throughout the chamber waiting for, and available to, anyone for travel between the buildings, and for aboveground travel for those who had clearance to go on-land.

Avid disembarked onto the walkway, entered the building, and walked toward the apartment he was staying in for the duration of this assignment. As he reached his door, the Alert screen displayed pulsing red in front of his face. It simply said, "Anomaly."

The Criminal Justice Project addressed law enforcement, which had changed significantly throughout the centuries. That Project was particularly important to the Historian Project because Historians had the unique power to change history with a misspoken word or thoughtless action. Doing this and causing an Anomaly was a serious criminal act, even if it was unintentional.

Because they had the unique power to alter the continuum, Historians were more likely to experience imprisonment than any other group of people. The Mitigators could not prevent Historians from criminal infractions that caused Anomalies, but they, with the Criminal Justice Project, could implement deterrents that made Historians more cautious and less likely to commit them.

Historians were subject to the harshest laws and punishments of any of the Project teams. In that sense, the career was the riskiest of all of them, and was not suitable for people who spoke or acted thoughtlessly.

While the threat of an Anomaly was always in the back of Avid's mind, he took strict precautions to prevent himself from causing one, just as the Mitigators hoped all Historians would. To see the word "Anomaly" flashing on his Alert screen was terrifying.

Avid muttered "Whoa," and went into his apartment, where he nervously threw himself onto the couch. He pulled off his Nikes, kicked them under the coffee table and tried to compose himself, rubbing his temples and taking deep yoga breaths. He stared out the wide, tall windows onto a glorious panorama of artificially illuminated and teeming sea life, hoping it would calm him down. He wanted to give himself a minute before he faced the bad news. He had never before triggered an Anomaly. This was a Historian's highest crime and most chilling nightmare.

Outside his over-large windows the sea life was tranquilly beautiful, with fish swimming past and plant life calmly swaying in the currents. The surrounding ocean was essentially an enormous saltwater aquarium, with fish and plant life performing hypnotically for Avid's benefit, so he turned his eyes to the scene to brace himself before addressing the Anomaly.

A blue shark meandered past the window. Avid hoped this was not a bad omen.

"Proceed," Avid instructed the display screen. He nervously bit the cuticle of his thumb.

"Revised instructions," the screen read. "Conference."

The screen then displayed the live image of Vendi, who was one of the Mitigators' spokespeople. Avid had worked with her several times before.

"Hi, Avid," she said. "Change in plans. Here's what happened."

Avid froze. He held his breath and chewed the cuticle of his forefinger, trying to replay the event in his mind so he could pinpoint exactly where he had made the critical misstep.

"It's okay," Vendi assured him. "You aren't under any suspicion."

Avid hadn't realized how tense he was until he understood that he was not going to prison. He fell forward face first into his lap, and then shot back up with a grin. "Whew!" he shouted, clapping his hands.

Avid's upload of the Joseph D'Andre McKenna files had triggered an Anomaly, Vendi explained as Avid grinned and rubbed his feet. It indicated that something had occurred to change the already-recorded continuum of events between the time Avid uploaded the files and the time he returned home. New information indicated that Joseph would never become U.S. Ambassador to China, or anything else, because he would be lynched by a pair of white supremacists in eight weeks.

Avid went cold. What would world history be without Joseph D'Andre McKenna? It was beyond his imagination. Avid stopped grinning and let go of his right foot, which he had been massaging. His stomach rose in his throat. The earth was shaking.

"He's a critical save," Vendi said. "We can't let this pass. In fact, he's an urgent save. I've never seen the Mitigators this frantic before, if you want to know the truth, so we've already reassigned everything we'd scheduled you for, for the next eight weeks. You won't be reporting to your usual commanders for the duration of the effort. Also, you'll be working with the Heroes on this one, so I've scheduled them to meet with you in fifteen minutes. We're sending them to your place." She looked past his shoulder and scrutinized his apartment. "Straighten the place up."

At the word "Heroes", he peevishly moaned, "No-o-o-o" to himself, and then, *Damn it.* He neglected to erect mental thought barriers because it was only Vendi. He knew she felt the same way about them. Everyone did.

"I heard that," Vendi said with a wide grin, projecting a frowny-face emoji onto the screen. Then she grew serious.

Avid had no choice, she explained. He would have to work with the Heroes, and he would have to make the best of it. This was not negotiable.

If the Heroes were involved, this was going to be a miserable assignment, Avid knew. The mere prospect of losing Joseph D'Andre McKenna was already traumatic. Stirring in Heroes would make it miserable in every respect.

Being present for the murder of Terence Jackson was a difficult assignment, but some assignments were so difficult they were out of Avid's scope. For example, the first Historians required extensive mental health support when they returned from Dr. Megele's medical experiments in Auschwitz, the Nazi concentration camp. They could not accept new assignments until they were cleared for work again, which took time and significant effort because younger twenty-eighth century Historians had no exposure to any form of violence that was remotely comparable to the behavior they had just witnessed in the past. They were unprepared for the stomach-turning, heartbreaking, gut-wrenching cruelty they saw, and they responded poorly. Therapy and training helped them with some of it, but not with the worst of it. After the first assignments to particularly difficult eras and events like the Holocaust, some Historians could only take on happy "fluff" pieces for preschoolers about puppies and dancing cockatiels, and could handle nothing more taxing than that for the duration of their careers.

The Historian Project could not proceed if Historians experienced crippling psychic injuries on the job, so the Mitigators needed an immediate solution.

The team of Mitigators met with psychotherapists and social scientists, then ran their scenarios through the continuum projection program to identify the solution, which immediately became apparent, and which they immediately put into law. This was the very first of the tweakings and rule changes they made to the Historian Project to ensure its success.

For truly horrific human events most Historian, even the older fully-seasoned one, could not summon detachment no matter how studiously they prepared. So, from this point forward, the Historian Project could, by law, only deploy Historians with high psychopathy scores to the most difficult assignments.

Psychopaths can witness human tragedy firsthand without internalizing it or becoming damaged from it because they have severely weakened or suppressed emotions and no empathy, which their brain makeup prevents them from experiencing. This was an invaluable trait for people traveling throughout history to report on the worst of it. In addition, psychopaths were cool-headed and stable under the worst pressure, and could perform their tasks no matter what kind of danger, pressure or stress they experienced. They actually thrived on danger, pressure and stress, and typically enjoyed it. They were, in fact, very much like the action heroes you see in motion pictures, who might arguably also be said to lean toward, or be psychopathic. Consequently, they could participate as happy twenty-eighth century Rambos in dangerous, traumatic events, then carry on as if they'd just spent the day at the beach. For all this, they would earn the highest salary compensation, and enjoy the highest social status within the Historian community.

There were no longer any living psychopaths, since medical science had discovered the specific DNA strings that predisposed children to psychopathy. For hundreds of years the medical team had been adjusting their resulting brain structure differences to prevent and correct psychopathy because past leadership had naively or arrogantly presumed that psychopaths offered no benefit to society. Having now identified that benefit, and with no psychopaths conveniently at hand, current leaders had to reverse this thinking and manufacture (for lack of a better word) psychopaths from scratch. It would be over twenty years before any Heroes would be born, raised, trained, and ready for dispatch, so the Mitigators shifted to this new plan immediately, going back in time twenty-five years to run continuum projections so they could identify infants whose DNA indicated they were likely candidates, and who would not adversely impact the continuum if they were permitted to grow into psychopaths. Then they changed their approach to the brain modifications in these children, set up an educational path for them, and began immediately awarding perks to their families so they could get a jump on the pressing need for them twenty five years later.

After thoroughly educating themselves on psychopathy, Mitigators had no qualms or concerns about their behavior. There was no real threat to the public because there had always been more clinically verifiable psychopaths operating throughout history as industry CEOs, lawyers, salespersons, televangelists, politicians, computer hackers, government officials and robocall phone agents than there ever had been psychopaths who ended up as violent criminals or authoritarian leaders. Psychopaths clearly could function at a high level and benefit society without violence. This was particularly true in an era when time travel and scanner footage immediately located them at the site of a crime and implicated them if their behavior warranted it.

Their calculated self-interest would typically prevent psychopaths from doing something for which they would be immediately caught and imprisoned. That, and ample reward, would keep them behaving in a manner that benefited everyone. The Mitigators dubbed them "The Hero Class" and promoted them to the general public as an "Elite Special Force", which stroked their egos. Then the Mitigators saw to it that Heroes enjoyed the finest living conditions and the greatest perks, which suited their personal objectives perfectly. That was the upside.

The downside was obvious. Society was now going to be infiltrated by psychopaths who had little regard for the feelings of others, and who were deliberately subjected to very few social restraints. Educators would not discourage them from lying, embezzling, exploiting and cheating because those qualities were what made Heroes invaluable on-land when they assumed their character roles. They never tried to "retrain" them into being more pleasant to deal with, and never punished Heroes when they behaved in that manner toward the general public, primarily because punishment had no impact on their behavior. They just created new laws against specific behaviors as a warning, then quietly and generously compensated the public for the trouble they experienced whenever they had dealings with Heroes.

By Avid's time, the medical team conducted routine DNA screening tests, then contacted the parents to congratulate them for having a "Hero child", which brought with it immediate reward, high social status and joyous celebration within the family. Then they obtained parental consent to provide necessary treatment for the child's genetic tendency toward psychopathy.

The rewards and elevated social status softened the blow of the diagnosis and the confusion the parents felt about a condition they thought had been eradicated, so they were mostly amenable when medical personnel described their proposed adjustment of the child's brain connections. Parents reviewed the requisite legal documents they had to sign, to enable the medical team to proceed.

"We are managing the psychopathy," the medical team explained, but they specifically told parents they were not reversing it. If the parents requested a full reversal, which they had a right to do, they had to accept that the child would not qualify for the Hero program or any of the perks that came with it.

Parental consent came with the same top-level living conditions and endless perks for the entire family that the Heroes themselves earned throughout their careers. Consequently, parents almost invariably agreed to the suggested treatment to enable their children to become Heroes.

The medical team needed to place these children on the low end of the psychopathy spectrum so they were as close to "typical" as possible, but could still perform their jobs without suffering debilitating psychological aftereffects. As they grew, the children received recurring medical treatment to adjust the connections between their ventromedial prefrontal cortex, the part of the brain responsible for sentiments such as empathy and guilt, and the amygdala, which controls fear and anxiety, to place them precisely on the psychopathy spectrum where they needed to be.

In addition to consent, all parents had to sign non-disclosure agreements about their children's genetic tendencies and the reason for these medical efforts, with wording that prevented them from telling anyone *including their own children* that they were psychopaths. Parents all happily complied so the general public could continue to believe that psychopathy no longer existed, and to protect the child's reputation. This prevented any sort of stigma that might affect the public's perception of the deliberately elevated and glorified Heroes. The Mitigators, the medical team, and the parents were the only ones who knew.

Once the parents agreed to everything, the perks began pouring in. The Hero child and family immediately enjoyed improved living conditions, along with immediate wealth and high social status. They could now request the best tables in the most expensive restaurants and time travel to the most expensive times and places, to the envy of everyone else.

Educators separated Hero children from the other children. Specialized Educators and support staff led psychopath-only classrooms (called Hero Classrooms), where they intensely focused on their interactions with others, conditioned them with praise and reward to avoid any level of gratuitous violence, and tirelessly taught them rules and proper empathy-emulating behaviors before they permitted the children to begin training as Hero Historians. Parents attended classes of their own to learn how to parent their psychopathic children, and did this with ample resources and Educator support.

Hero children learned martial arts and artillery, studied war plans, and went through battle simulations and drills. They learned archery and swordsmanship, survival skills and hunting. They took classes in improvisation and method acting at The Arts Building, in addition to the typical Historian preparatory classes and the Hero-specific behavior classes. Later, as Historians, they arrived at their assignments fully-prepared.

Educators' primary focus was to train children, including psychopathic children, to behave in a manner that benefited society. A combination of rewards and the withholding of rewards, plus very clear behavioral expectations and the threat of being withdrawn from the program and losing their wealth if they did not comply, molded typical psychopathic children into adults whose behavior made them appear to be empathetic, even though they were not. Their complete lack of compassion usually came as a jolting surprise to anyone who was unprepared to deal with them.

The Mitigators arranged for scanner footage to trigger a notification to the Finance Project whenever someone experienced emotional or physical pain, financial loss, or any other kind of disappointment at the hands of a Hero. Then, after the footage was reviewed and validated (a short delay), someone from the bank that held the Hero's assets contacted the victim to arrange for compensation. One did not learn that this compensation was available until actually experiencing a Hero-induced loss of some kind.

People envied them and admired them, but generally did not like the Heroes very much. Fortunately, being roundly disliked by virtually everyone did not bother Heroes at all.

Avid was on the empath spectrum, which was the opposite end of the emotional scale from psychopaths. He was deeply attuned to the emotions and needs of the people around him, which made him an ideal candidate for the job of Historian, provided he prepared well for difficult assignments to reduce his potential trauma. In fact, most Historians were on the empath spectrum, as were most Educators. It was one of the qualities the Mitigators looked for when they selected candidates for either career.

Consequently, Avid could never meet Dr. Mengele. He could never travel on the trains that transported the European Jews to the gas chambers and ovens at Auschwitz or Treblinka. He could not go there anyway because his physical appearance would prevent him from blending in with any segment of German society during that era. That job assignment always went to someone from the Hero Class and the Caucasian Race Dynasty. The character role the Hero must assume determined whether the assignment went to a blue-eyed blonde, or to someone with a Mediterranean or Jewish appearance.

Vendi patiently waited for Avid to process the unwelcome news about his partners in the upcoming assignment.

Avid quickly put up his blocking defenses so Vendi couldn't hear him do the mental math about his past dealings with Heroes. He had had extensive therapy sessions from the time he had first encountered them in school. There was something about him that prompted them to antagonize him mercilessly, so therapists had trained him to be hard around Heroes, and to never give in to their demands or wheedling manipulations, insincere tears or dramatic threats. He could finally be tough after all these years—mostly—but it was still stressful to be around them.

Avid was thinking about all this with a curled lip. Then he suddenly remembered why he was having this conference. He became more focused.

"What's going to happen next?"

"We tracked it all backward on scanner footage. People showed up at the event who were never supposed to be there. The Mitigators ran the bulk of the projection snippets tomorrow and they came up with the emergency team next week. This is a week from Wednesday for me, by the way. I just popped back to let you know you're on the team, and to have you set up your meetings so you can get started right away. The most important thing is that you know immediately that you're not under any suspicion. There's going to be a lot of talk about you and this Anomaly in the next few days, so I wanted to prepare you."

What everyone knew thus far, Vendi continued, was that the two white supremacists Avid had interviewed in the crowd at the Terence Jackson event had taken issue with Joseph D'Andre McKenna's behavior at the scene of the murder. These men called themselves the Fairfax Freedom Fighters, which was a delusional, aspirational name for an organization with only two members. They had been planning a lynching in a rural pocket of Fairfax County, Virginia, and had been actively scouting for victims.

Heroes had already been assigned to their upcoming lynching event because it was going to be particularly gruesome, but the urgency of the original Hero role had just increased substantially because the subjects had decided to include Joseph among the group of young Black men they were planning to lynch. They had followed him home after the Terence Jackson event, taken note of his address, bookmarked it on their GPS apps, and were now making plans.

In the event of an Anomaly, an all-new snippet of history inserted itself into the existing continuum. Because it was new, no one could predict what the outcome would be, even though it took place in the past. The "new future" of the continuum could range from "no change" to "catastrophic", based on factors that were now in flux. Time travel projections presented the Mitigators with the most likely outcomes, and the percentage of likelihood for each. However, Mitigators could not predict which of these outcomes, if any, would actually occur.

The goal was to repair the breach and create an outcome that, ideally, was identical to the original one. They wanted the pre-Anomaly continuum to skip over that unwelcome post-Anomaly snippet of time, then progress seamlessly into the future, with the original continuum proceeding just as it had originally. Failing that, the future had to be as close to the original timeline as possible when the original continuum resumed, with changes that caused no major disruptions in the upcoming sequence of events.

The Mitigators had to devise dozens of potential scenarios, or "projection snippets," one by one, and insert all of the snippets into the program. Each snippet represented a different mix of players performing various different actions. The computer then ran a continuum projection, which gave the potential outcomes for each projection snippet, calculated a percentage of the likelihood of each outcome, and compared the outcomes to the original continuum. Mitigators were looking for a projection snippet with a potential outcome that matched the original continuum with a likelihood of, ideally, between eighty and ninety percent.

The Mitigators had to think of every potential snippet scenario themselves, seated in a closed conference room, where interruptions were forbidden and food was slipped through the door and left for them on the floor. The process required surgical precision to identify the correct approaches and the specific players involved so they could assemble the perfect emergency team and the perfect plan, and then hope for success.

Just as an Anomaly was a Historian's worst and most chilling nightmare, this manual effort was a Mitigator's worst and most chilling nightmare. It was so fraught with potential failure that they only took this approach when the situation was dire, as it was in this instance. In the past they had encountered situations where they could not come up with a successful solution, or else the participants had failed as they attempted to correct the Anomaly. These were instances that permanently changed the continuum and created an alternate history. The Mitigators were terrified that this might happen with the McKenna Anomaly. This one undersized adolescent male was supposed to play a critical role in both national and world history. Losing him now would be the historical equivalent of assassinating Abraham Lincoln before he freed the slaves. It was actually far worse than that, because Joseph's impact would be global.

Mitigators wrested full control of all aspects of the McKenna Anomaly, and made a public announcement that only Mitigators could perform even the most minor and mundane tasks associated with it. Even ordering lunch now became the job of a Mitigator, with Vendi contacting the appropriate parties to pass along their instructions or speak on their behalf.

Mitigators worked on various daily side tasks in four-hour rotations leaving the bulk of the Mitigators in a conference room, where they fed the program their projection snippets and studied the results. They had no time off except for once-daily six-hour rest breaks in staggered shifts.

Rotating Mitigators were already monitoring live scanner footage of all the players involved in the effort, and would intervene as necessary, or provide helpful information to the Historians if they hit a snag. Avid was therefore now under constant live surveillance by the Mitigators, who were not sleeping well. Vendi did not tell him he was being watched because the Mitigators advised her not to.

"Let him ease into the assignment," they had told her. He would figure out that they were watching him soon enough.

Vendi described the Anomaly repair effort to Avid. The two subjects were James Stoughton of the three-hundred-year-old Stoughton Tobacco Farms, Inc., and Max Richmond, son of the CEO of the Richmond-Steinbeck financial conglomerate. They were both age twenty-nine, residents of Fairfax County, and graduates of Ivy League colleges. Their social ranking and financial situation was unexpected for the type of mayhem they were planning, but Vendi theorized that they presumed they would get away with it because of their parents' money and influence. They probably viewed this as a naughty but legally escapable and forgivable joy ride. They had a history of alt-right political activities, which had thus far been buried and excused by their families and extended contacts, so they had become cocky. Until now, neither was considered dangerous.

In the original continuum their luck ran out and James Stoughton served life in prison without parole. Max Richmond died in prison of COVID-19 while awaiting trial.

They had now identified their team, so the Mitigators were studying different scenarios to determine what actions the Heroes could take to repair the continuum with minimal disruption, Vendi told Avid. Since the subjects originally had little personal impact on the continuum after the lynching, either in prison or dying while awaiting trial, killing them might be under consideration, if killing them would save Joseph.

If they were instructed to kill the two subjects before they'd completed their crime, the Heroes would then have to complete the lynching themselves to repair the continuum.

If they killed only Max before the lynching and left the other subject to complete the effort alone, the Heroes would have to ensure that the treatment of the victims was so ghastly that the murders warranted life in prison without parole for James.

If they killed James before the lynching, they simply had to kill the victims in a scenario that ensured prison time for Max. Once the Mitigators reviewed all the options and gave the go-ahead, the Heroes were free to do whatever they needed to do, to recreate the crime's original outcome. In the meantime, there was much to discuss.

Avid grimaced as Vendi spoke. This assignment was truly awful.

As for now, she continued, the Heroes had to study scanner footage of the original lynching event, and familiarize themselves with the actions the subjects originally took in order to ensure that the crime they potentially committed was equally horrific this time around. They could not do the job halfway and risk a shorter sentence for James, unless the Mitigators found that this trajectory had him dying in prison before he was released, or showed that he had no impact on the continuum after release. Snippet projections indicated this was too big of a risk.

Hearing all this, Avid was very grateful to not be a Hero. Still, he wanted out.

"You're being cleared for interaction with the locals. The Mitigators think that Max Richmond is persuadable. That's why we're going to attempt to redirect him so he reverts back to only lynching the original victims."

"Who's going to persuade him? Not me, right?" Avid felt a cold rush of anxiety. His eyes widened, and his heart raced.

Avid wasn't ready for this, Vendi knew. She inwardly winced, then gave him a perky smile. She displayed the image of a woman and her personal data: *"Helen Andersen, Psychologist. Date of birth: June 5, 1953, New York, NY. Married on June 30, 1976 to Barry Anderson, born August 12, 1949, died September 1, 2017, stroke. Son: William Barrett Anderson, born December 29, 1984, died February 15, 2017, suicide."* There was an additional link to Helen Anderson's community involvement and awards.

Avid glanced at it and did not notice that this person's bio information did not display her death date.

"This is Max's psychologist. She's treating him for a personality disorder, so he obviously has serious issues. They're working on his tendency to compulsively 'mirror' the behavior of other people. He's really susceptible to persuasion, which might be why he's involved with James Stoughton. It also might help us in pulling him back from lynching Joseph because you can make him do anything. He hasn't exactly confessed what they're up to, but he dropped some vague hints and Helen doesn't know how to decipher them. If you can give her insight into what he's telling her, the Mitigators think she can somehow persuade him that killing Joseph would be 'mirroring', and that to lynch him would be a setback in his treatment. Or something. Whatever. *Something.* We're not sure what, just yet. She'll probably figure out that part herself."

Avid cleared his throat miserably and grimaced. The gravity of the situation and his involvement in indirect, third-party persuasion tactics seemed insane and doomed to fail. Under normal circumstances he might have had an opportunity to decline to participate. But this came directly from the Mitigators, so it was a command, not an assignment.

Vendi tried to sound enthusiastic and positive, as if Avid would enjoy himself: "He's actually earnest and sincere about this treatment, believe it or not. That's what convinced the Mitigators to take this route. It's all we have, to back up the Heroes. If it doesn't work, the Heroes will cut the rope or something to save Joseph—they'll let us know what they've figured out—but that could backfire because the subjects have weapons. A lot of things can go wrong. They could potentially shoot everyone to death, including the Heroes, if they get riled up."

She needs to stop talking right now, Avid thought to himself, fully blocked so she could not hear what he was thinking.

When the Mitigators finally came to a decision, Vendi continued, they would instruct the Heroes on all acceptable courses of action. The Heroes would then assess the situation in the moment and choose from those options, then do whatever they needed to do. But…if Avid Burhan successfully persuaded Max Richmond's psychologist into talking him out of lynching Joseph, Vendi told him, the crime might take place just as it had in the original continuum, and the outcome might be identical to the original outcome.

She gave Avid another perky smile. Avid grimaced.

This was not Avid's strong suit. He had never ever done anything like this before and he was afraid he was going to fail at it, then lose his job, his comfortable lifestyle and his perks. He was so comfortable with his life. This would be so tricky. It was so critical. He felt so incompetent in the face of it. His life was *so* comfortable and he had plans. He didn't like this. He had never had to confront this kind of situation in his entire career. In fact, he had only ever had clearance to interact with the locals a few times before, and it was always more stressful than he liked. He never applied for those assignments anymore, despite the fact that they paid more.

"Are they sure they want *me* to be the one to take this on? I've never done anything like this. I'm not sure I can pull it off. They need to understand this. I really, really don't know what I'm doing here." He chewed the cuticle on his ring finger, then added, panicking, "Can't the Heroes just sling some sort of bullshit to talk these guys out of killing Joseph?"

"They're Heroes, so we're fully confident they'll sling whatever bullshit they must. It's what they do."

"Good to know. Nevertheless, isn't there someone who can do this better than I can? I swear I don't know how—*I really don't know how to do this*—and this is too important."

He felt his pulse race, and he could hear his heart beating in his ears. It was beating far too fast. He had never fainted before, or had a heart attack or stroke, and he wondered if he was about to do all of that at once.

"You're it, I'm afraid. Buckle up." Vendi grew thoughtful and she studied him. Avid's face was impassive but she telepathically caught his panic and self-doubt, and knew he wanted to pull himself into the fetal position and cry. "I'll buy you dinner in whatever place and time you like when this is over, okay? Anywhere and anywhen." She said it gently, consolingly. "I'm serious. This is a tough assignment from every angle, and I'm sorry. I'll make it up to you."

His heart rate had spiked at the words, "You're it," and was still racing.

He needed a hug right now. Sensing that Avid was emotionally paralyzed and about to experience a full-blown panic attack, Vendi sent him a long, warm telepathic heart hug. "You'll be great," she told him in his thoughts. Telepathic messages had far more impact than verbal ones, so she made hers persuasive and supportive. "We all know you'll be great, which is why they assigned this to you. And besides. You're just the backup. Nobody expects you to carry the full weight of the effort." She gave him a second long telepathic heart hug as a booster to the first. It had a visible effect in calming Avid down, and it made him feel stronger.

He regained his composure and looked up. "Fine," he said. "I'll do my best."

"It's a small ask, really, if you think about it, to talk with a psychologist. Just talk to her the way you talk to me or anyone else. You even have clearance to tell her you're a time traveler because she's legally and ethically bound to not repeat anything you say to anyone."

Considering this, Vendi added, "You'll probably have to tell her right away to get her to cooperate and to understand how serious this is."

"Wow." Avid pulled in a sharp breath. Vendi sensed the anxiety levels shooting even higher. "Hold on. Are you sure about this? Or are you setting me up for prison?"

Under no circumstances was a Historian ever—*ever*—permitted to admit to the locals he or she was a time traveler. Consequently, people on-land who said they were time travelers were almost always lying or insane. He'd never even heard of anyone doing it in his lifetime because the penalties were so severe. Or rather, he had heard stories about a few from many years back, who had ended up locked away in primitive insane asylums. The Mitigators always left them there as punishment for however long they deemed it necessary to make their point, a point that was duly noted by the perpetrators and everyone else, including Avid. When the institution finally released them or the Mitigators finally extracted them, they were relieved of their duties and sidelined from any sort of gainful employment for the term of their sentence, effectively preventing them from earning any perks until the punishment period expired.

It was "prison" but there were no cells and no bars. Criminal violators included Historians who admitted they were time travelers to the locals, Historians or other control station personnel with on-land access who triggered Anomalies, or others who broke various laws. They were moved into tiny windowless apartments, and as a penalty had to permanently forfeit some or all the perks they had in the bank. If they were permitted to keep any, those perks were frozen until the completion of their sentence.

Prisoners had only limited contact with anyone else, including dogs and other pets, and wore uniforms so everyone else could recognize and avoid them. They were completely shunned because anyone who spoke to or interacted with a prisoner suffered punishment. Prisoners were only permitted to speak to other people and receive heart hugs when they performed community service. However, they did not earn perks for their efforts, so their community service did not reward them as it normally would, except to give them human contact. Violators were very eager to serve the community in any capacity, without reward, just to have a human connection with anyone at all, or even to pet a dog or cat. Everyone who saw them was very eager to never be a prisoner. "Prison" was an extremely effective deterrent, and the person who triggered the McKenna Anomaly would be facing this punishment for a very, very long time.

"How do I tell someone with the power to institutionalize me that I'm a time traveler?"

"I know it's scary, but she's totally trustworthy. We vetted her, so you can tell her anything you want, except for the usual basic restrictions. There's a slight chance that she might think you're delusional and try to hospitalize you, but local laws prohibit her from doing that without your consent, so I wouldn't worry. We can extract you from the situation anyway, if something like that were to happen."

Vendi displayed a clearance document on Avid's Alert screen for him to review, with the unusual—in fact unheard of—addition of a clause that permitted discussion about time travel with one person, Helen Anderson, PhD. The clause stated specifically that it did not extend to any other parties. It seemed legitimate, so Avid reluctantly submitted his approval of the clause. His folded hands were shaking in his lap.

The "basic restrictions" Vendi had reminded Avid to adhere to prevented Historians from referring to any future events when they were on-land, even if they were not speaking directly to a local or thought they were alone. They also could not discuss politics or religion, or conversationally confess to a local what Jesus was "really like," for instance, and dish dirt on the water-into-wine situation or the healing of the lepers. They could not reveal what really happened to Amelia Earhart, or who really killed John F. Kennedy, or divulge the truth behind widely-known controversial twenty-first century mysteries that had not yet been definitively solved. Anything they said on-land had to be strictly appropriate for that date in history, and could only reference information that people of that time and place would already know, or could access through local writings or on the Internet, and confirm with a little effort.

Historians also could not interfere with anything that had occurred during the recorded past, lest they impact recorded history in any way and trigger an Anomaly. They could not warn people when they knew they were walking into danger, and they could never save them from it. All they could say was, "Goodbye," and they could only say that if they were cleared for local interaction. In fact, Historians could not speak to the locals at all, even in passing, unless they were cleared for interaction. Whenever they did, it was a frightening responsibility, so Historians typically did not speak much. Only the people with the highest career aspirations, and Heroes, applied for assignments that required sustained local interaction, weighing career advancement against the calculated risk of their own potential indiscretions. If a local attempted to start a conversation, most Historians, including Avid and anyone with clearance to interact, typically extricated themselves from the situation immediately and left without responding.

Heroes were almost always in situations where they had to interact, so they were almost always cleared for interaction. They were also required to adhere to the basic restrictions, with a few additional rules that addressed their enhanced risks and responsibilities. However, Heroes were highly unlikely to engage in what they largely considered a boring waste their time, chatting with the locals about ancient history. In addition, their propensity for lying made it unlikely they would ever tell anyone the truth about anything anyway.

Vendi smiled. "I'll need frequent updates from you. You'll be great."

Avid grunted because he had no words, and he shook his head.

"The Heroes will be in control," she assured him. "And their bullshit abounds. Rest easy about that. Signing off." The screen disappeared.

As Vendi had explained to Avid, the McKenna Anomaly occurred when the two white supremacists appeared in the alley, even though they were originally supposed to have kept walking to the National Mall. In the original continuum they'd overheard someone in the crowd talk about the fight, but he'd disappeared before the pair could ask him for directions to find it. The people walking near them were unaware of what was happening on the other side of the street, beyond the marching crowd, and couldn't direct them. However, this time the person they happened to approach for information and directions was the Historian who was covering that portion of the crowd, and who enabled them to appear at an event they had not attended in the original continuum.

"Back there." The Historian distractedly pointed to the alley behind them and across the street, and then returned to telepathically interviewing the surrounding marchers.

That communication constituted a serious crime. No form of direct communication was permissible between Historians and locals, unless a Historian had clearance to interact. This Historian did not. Furthermore, the Mitigators factored in the impact, whenever they assigned punishment, and the consequences of this misstep were incalculable. They were even considering a life sentence for the violator.

To address this violation and to prevent it from ever happening again, the Mitigators immediately instructed the Language Technician team to adjust the language settings for all non-authorized Historians, to prohibit them from speaking in the local language on-land in any year or location, even if it was a Historian's native language. Instead, Language Experts set their language implants to an extinct and archived language from an ancient indigenous North American tribe. That ancient language would now spew from their mouths whenever they spoke on-land. Mitigators could not prevent Historians from pointing fingers to give directions. They could only threaten. However, they *could* control speech security.

Avid hoped the violator wasn't one of his friends because in a situation like this one he might never be able to see or speak to that person again.

On-land assignments required significant preparation. The control station had a team of Wardrobe Experts, who specialized in wardrobe fashion and dressed the Historians in clothing specific to the time period and their character roles. Language Technicians adjusted the settings on the Historians' language implants so they spoke in the local dialect with local accents, and Style Experts styled their hair and, as appropriate, makeup or facial hair. Before Historians departed for their assignments, Social Assimilation Experts taught them appropriate behavior and cultural norms for both the location and the year, and created the Historians' Character Biographies, to which Historians would refer conversationally, as appropriate, whenever they interacted with the locals.

Assimilation tasks for regular Historians primarily involved assigning wardrobe and setting up local identities with government-issued ID cards, as well as the requisite cultural familiarity coaching. Everyone also received a smart phone with a local phone number, which they would use to communicate with locals, if necessary and if they had clearance, and to hold up to their ears to appear to be speaking on the phone as they conducted conversations on their Alert screens (in pre-cellphone eras Historians slipped into phone booths, or hid in a secluded spot so they could converse unseen). The Assimilation team also provided driver's licenses if necessary, and various other identity-confirming documentation, public records and social media accounts that would support the efforts of the Heroes in particular, and regular Historians on occasion. After the assignment ended, the Assimilation team went back and purged any of the public records that referred to the false identities.

An Assimilation Expert created biographies for the character roles the two Heroes would assume for the duration of the assignment, based on a brief he received from the Mitigator team. The brief described them as having wealthy parents, and it indicated past participation in a particularly raucous Ivy League fraternity, Beta

Gamma Delta, to which the subject Max Richmond had also belonged.

When assigning identities to Historians, this expert typically accessed the Name Registry Database, and then selected a first name from the more popular choices listed under the character's birth year, and a last name that matched their supposed nationality. However, he always used a different name selection method for Heroes. One could not fully customize the Name Registry Database just for Heroes, as the expert wished, so he switched to a twenty-first century laptop and launched a browser, which opened to Google. He typed keywords from the character's biography into the Search field (in this case "ivy league"), and then added the word "porn." He carefully considered the search results before making a decision.

Tying Heroes to porno movies was his ongoing secret pleasure.

One of the top results was the movie, "Boys on Call" about two Ivy League gigolos. A quick view and perusal of the movie revealed it to be perfect for this expert's purposes, so he assigned Azuka Hämäläinen the name "Chad Ford," and called Kirill Volkov "Dirk Van de Kamp" after the movie's starring characters. Then he created their social media accounts and printed out their identification documents.

Since their characters were "rich" the pair of Heroes shopped for vehicles with price stickers of more than $200,000. Dirk selected a roomy, high-end black Range Rover with tinted windows, in case it became necessary for him to transport dead bodies or hog-tied prisoners. Since Dirk had already addressed the practical aspects of car selection, Chad chose a red Tesla Roadster for looks.

An Assimilation Expert was now teaching them to drive in empty parking lots on-land. In addition, they were learning how to plug in the Roadster to charge it, and how to fill the tank of a Range Rover with gasoline. They would soon learn how to use the windshield wipers and the door locks. Neither was remotely successful at learning how to parallel park.

The Assimilation Expert had misgivings about their general performance behind the wheel and shared her concerns with the Mitigators. The Mitigators received the update and instructed the Human Resources team to assign a driver to each Hero. Those drivers also had to be Heroes because of the nature of the upcoming event, even though they would not actually be participating in the action, or interacting with the locals. They found two Heroes whose current assignment was just ending, and who were not scheduled for any pressing upcoming events. They were both on record as being experienced twentieth and twenty-first century automobile drivers, so the Time Travel Technicians dropped them off at the Mid-Atlantic control station on March 19, 2021 at 0600 hours.

These new drivers disembarked from the Time Travel portal in the main building wearing voluminous hoop-skirted garb from the American Civil War, and hauling their belongings behind them in large, over-packed, wheeled suitcases. Four residents of the control station assisted them by pulling or carrying the rest of their belongings for them. They went straight to their apartments, planning to visit the Assimilation wing afterward. The Heroes smiled ingratiatingly at the people who assisted them, but didn't think to thank them before they shut their doors.

And so Nectar and Janicyl moved into their Hero apartments and eagerly awaited their instructions to drive extremely upscale vehicles for two other Heroes for a few weeks. This was a very nice assignment, they agreed, particularly since their recent experience as Civil War field nurses had been extremely distasteful. All that blood and dysentery was disgusting. The smells. The cannon fire and the guns. The screaming and the sobs. The filthy, crusty bandages that they, Nectar and Janicyl, were tasked with changing. The maggoty gangrenous wounds. The limb amputations with no anesthesia. The stinking piss pots. All those dead bodies drawing flies.

Janicyl's debriefing report wherein she commented on the previous assignment at its conclusion began with the single word: "Ew." The remainder of the report listed her preferences for her next assignment and made no further mention of her experiences and observations in the American Civil War.

This new assignment met Janicyl's preferences very well indeed, was a well-earned respite, and was significantly more to her liking than the Battle of Shiloh and its aftermath. She was settling in happily.

Their arrival gave them three full days to familiarize themselves with Chad and Dirk and the vehicles, meet up with the Social Assimilation Experts, do a little personal research on the time period, and map out their sightseeing plans before they met up with the subjects on March 23, 2021.

Nectar and Janicyl coordinated with the Wardrobe Assimilation Experts to get their hair styled and makeup done later on the day of their arrival, and to prepare for their new assignment and its upcoming event. Before going to Wardrobe they had spent hours prowling the Internet for tips and ideas, scrolling through Instagram and YouTube for inspiration.

Janicyl was a very slender, dark-haired, green-eyed woman with preternaturally pale skin. She preferred a severe look, and instructed the stylist to cut and style her hair like the lead actress in the movie Amelie, circa 2001, with very short bangs and a straight blunt cut that came an inch below her ears. She liked smoky eyes, dark cherry red lips and bold metal jewelry in geometric shapes. She had an overall dominant and confrontational look that made you hesitate to encounter her in an alley.

Nectar was a petite blond with a sweet and engaging face, and a look of childlike innocence. She had large blue eyes and long, flowing, soft blond curls. She preferred her clothing to be long, flowing and soft, like her hair, with floral fabrics and lace. Her petite innocence would make your chest surge with earnest protectiveness that would prompt you to run into that alley to rescue her, only to have her turn around and cut you, then steal your wallet and call you an insulting name.

They did not like the shoes the Wardrobe Experts offered, so they applied for approval to obtain shoes and handbags on-land that were more to their liking. They insisted that they needed at least ten pairs of shoes each, as well as multiple handbags (Janicyl liked Hermes in this time period, and Nectar was delighted with Valentino Garavani). They demanded that the balance on their prepaid debit cards for this shopping adventure be increased to forty thousand dollars each, with no limit on daily or individual expenditures. Wardrobe experts would not mind, would they, if they also went shopping for clothes? When they examined the stack of blue jeans, Nikes, long-sleeved t-shirts, and workplace blouses, skirts, and dresses, they determined that Wardrobe clothing was not adequate for their needs. The money was a totally reasonable request, they insisted. They required nice clothing to bolster their failing morale. They also needed to get their nails done and were in dire need of a spa day after their sad experience in the American Civil War.

With an eye roll, a Historian Mitigator signed off on the request the Wardrobe Expert had escalated for approval, including the unapproved clothing choices, and then increased authorization for each woman's debit card balance to eighty thousand dollars. They would spend it all in less than three weeks, the Mitigator knew, but an insufficient balance would only result in them ceaselessly hounding staff until they got more. The Mitigator was familiar with them, knew exactly what to expect, and predicted they would come back complaining about their inadequate allowances more than once before the assignment concluded. In the meantime, a ridiculous allowance would buy everyone a few of weeks of peace and quiet. With the McKenna Anomaly to deal with they needed to be left alone, and not be harassed over handbags.

The cost of placating and appeasing Nectar and Janicyl was not a concern to the Mitigators. Another team that the Historian Project relied on heavily was the Finance Project, which focused on investment strategies to fund the control stations, and to supply legitimate local currency to personnel who ventured on-land. In more primitive times the Finance Project gave Historians shells and spices or gold, so they could barter with the locals. In later times they issued whatever currency the society on-land was using, and provided whatever material items were necessary to create the character's on-land lifestyle.

The Finance Project studied and followed the stock market and profitable business ventures. As the world economy grew, they invested in merchant ships, electricity, telephones, plastic, and railroads, then later purchased hundreds of thousands of shares of Apple stock at less than a dollar a share in nineteen eighty-two, jumped in to buy up Cryptocurrency in its early days, and "sold short" whenever it was profitable. They continually invested in soon-to-be lucrative companies during their infancy. They sold various securities immediately preceding market downturns, purchasing back the securities when they reached their rock bottom stock price and were about to rise again, turning seemingly endless cyclical profits. They knew exactly when to purchase puts and when to purchase calls. They knew exactly when to buy and when to sell, while carefully managing their activity to prevent themselves from artificially moving the stock market. With this parasitic piggybacking economic strategy, the Mitigators never faced a shortage of cash because there was never a shortage of you-can't-lose-if-you're-a-time-traveler investment opportunities that the Finance Project identified throughout history. The end result was that the Finance Project bank balance of cash and perks could generously support, reward, and incentivize the entire population of the continuum for thousands of years. Most importantly to the Historian Project, the Finance Project provided Historians with the money and the means to survive whenever they had to spend extensive periods of time on-land. It also occasionally went to support various Historians' need for expensive handbags.

The two Heroes were pleasantly surprised that their allowance and clothing requests had all been approved, particularly the approval that allowed them to select their own wardrobes. They had never been permitted to do that before. It made them feel emboldened by their critical importance to the project.

They spent all day Saturday, March 20, 2021, looking for upscale boutiques and shops where they could try on cute clothing and shoes, and spend money. When they finally found one that was open and willing to allow them in the door provided they wore pandemic face masks, they spent hours and thousands of dollars. Then they located a spa that was also open during the pandemic shutdown, where they could each receive a salt rub pedicure and manicure for only $400, along with complimentary wine or cucumber water, their choice (they chose wine), plus a scented neck and shoulder rub. They would return for a more thorough spa experience in a few days when they had more time.

An Assimilation Expert handed Chad an American flag decal to affix to the back of his car. Chad placed it on the bottom of the rear window, admiring how the red stripes and that dash of blue complemented his bright red Tesla. Flags and nationalism meant nothing to people in the twenty-eighth century, although Chad recognized it as having something to do with God and Country. He primarily felt the decal was an excellent design choice.

Dirk received a Confederate flag and placed it on his rear bumper. When he requested information about the flag, his Alert screen had to inform him that it represented the losing side of the American Civil War. That confused him. Why would he deliberately display a flag for the losers in a war? The Alert screen explained that the flag was a popular choice among white supremacists. That was fine because of this assignment, but it just didn't sit well with him, that the flag they'd given him suggested that he was a loser. Why had *he* gotten it, and not Chad, he wondered peevishly? It almost made him pout.

There were other details in the brief, which Chad and Dirk carefully studied and pondered while downing vodka and shooting darts.

It was a primitive game, darts, but they liked it. Dirk had ordered the set from Amazon.com and had just retrieved it from an Amazon locker on-land, then had Maintenance set it up on a flat wall in the main Community Center, where they now were. They relaxed there, newly named and calling each other "Chad" and "Dirk" to get accustomed to it, enjoying their vodka and their darts, reviewing the aforementioned brief between dart throws, and planning their upcoming assignment. They had been issued IDs and smart phones, and had debit cards with insane cash limits. They had actual paper cash in Gucci wallets and Burberry Chase London money clips. They had impressive vehicles and two luxury condos, one each, for entertaining the subjects.

They had visited Wardrobe and had procured their costumes, taking extra clothing and shoes with them to fill the condo closets in case they needed a change of clothing on-land, and to make the space appear to be lived in, should the subjects go snooping. The Finance Project had supplied their bathrooms with luxury shaving equipment, fluffy monogrammed towels and bathrobes, gold-plated nail clippers, expensive skin care products for men, and a basket of bath bombs next to each massive raised marble tub.

Their bathrooms had heated floors and voice-controlled heated and scented bidets, saunas and steam rooms, and $40,000 Spa Circolare Ceiling Mount Single-Function Flat Dream Light Chromatherapy Showerheads (Chad found the product online and requested it. Dirk decided that he needed one too, as he also felt that his character's shower experience should always involve an LED light show.).

Finally, the Translation Technicians adjusted their verbal translation setup so that when they spoke on-land their speech inflexions would sound like the upper classes in twenty-first century Fairfax, Virginia, with a hint of Ivy League.

Residents of the control stations spoke Hinduese. However, when Historians traveled on-land the language implant automatically shifted their speech to whatever language, accent, or colloquial inflections the language experts had programmed into their settings. Their accent might be Spanish, Chinese, or French, as the situation called for, just as soon as they set foot on-land and spoke, and they could do nothing to control it.

The translation implants automatically recognized their mental "speak" commands and translated their thoughts into the speech characteristics of their assigned characters. The implants also filtered out anything they did not specifically intend to say out loud. This filtering element took some training and practice, initially, but eventually became second nature to the Historians. The Heroes were particularly adept at communicating with the locals because they were almost always cleared for local interaction and used the implant almost constantly. People like Avid, who used it infrequently, found it slightly more difficult to sound "normal" to people on-land.

When anyone spoke to a time traveler on-land, the translation implant automatically identified the language of the speaker from the vast language database, no matter how obscure that language was, and enabled Historians to understand what the other person was saying. If they heard an unfamiliar word or term, they mentally requested the Alert screen, which defined the term and provided informational video footage with details so the Historian could respond appropriately. This was critical for any assignment, not only because of a Historian's initial unfamiliarity with a time and place, but because English had gone the way of Latin, and few people spoke it anymore at all, much less as a first language. English had been phased out by "Hinduese," a new language that was a mixture of Hindi, Latvian, and Chinese. This new language evolved because dominant world languages typically follow the language of whichever country dominates economically. China, the Baltics, and India had each taken its economic turn in the past seven centuries. With globalization, the languages simply merged, as did the races of the world.

The Heroes assigned to the upcoming event were going to assume the role of white supremacists, so they belonged to the Caucasian Race Dynasty. Their membership in a race dynasty gave them top status and top salary among the Heroes, and they liked this very much because it validated their own astute insight that they were superior to most people, including other Heroes.

Chad was a very tall, muscular, blue-eyed blond Finn whose biography for this assignment indicated he was a prominent wine connoisseur, and had once been a competitive chess player. Dirk was a smaller, thinner dark-haired Russian with beautiful, deceptively kind-looking dark and melting doe eyes, which were extremely effective with women who did not know him. His biography had him dabbling in The Arts, while being fully-supported in his artistic endeavors by his trust fund.

The two of them were now preparing to perform the role of wealthy, expensively-educated, subversive alt-right terrorists who seemed to have much in common with Max Richmond and James Stoughton, and their looks suited the role.

They both received instructions to meet with Avid Burhan in his apartment in one of the buildings adjacent to the main building they were now in. There conveniently was an air bridge between the main building and Avid's building that enabled them to easily stroll over there in just a few minutes, but they grabbed the bottle of Kirkland Vodka they had swiped from behind the bar in the Waterloo Restaurant, and headed to the travel pods to ride, rather than walk, to the building.

Avid heard the doorbell and braced himself. He internally accessed all the coaching he'd received in therapy to put up boundaries against them, then took a deep breath before opening the door to these assholes. For him, the moment was tense. Two smiling Heroes, one of whom was enticingly holding out a one-third-empty bottle of vodka, greeted him when he opened the door. Avid waved them in.

"I'm Avid Burhan," he said, responding to their open, friendly smiles with a guarded squint. "Nice to meet you. Come on in." He took the bottle of vodka from the dark-haired Hero because it was apparently what he was supposed to do. He didn't actually like vodka.

"I'm Chad." The blonde one touched prayer hands to his chin and bent over in a respectful Namaste bow. "We'll be working together for the next few weeks," he said as he returned to an upright position.

Avid stuck the bottle under his armpit and returned the bow.

"I'm Dirk. It's such a pleasure to meet you." Dirk smiled beatifically as if he had never in his life met anyone as worthy and charming as Avid. His Namaste bow went nearly to his knees. His smile was still beaming when he reestablished eye contact.

Avid knew better than to be disarmed, especially after noticing that Dirk appeared to never blink. That alone was disconcerting. He bowed his head and did a quick dash upward with prayer hands without adding any depth to the effort. It was more of a quick nod and a wave. "Have a seat. I'll get us some glasses."

The two Heroes wandered through Avid's living room, effusively admiring the Ikea bookshelves and Costco couch, touching every knickknack and decorative object, then commenting on its value and tastefulness.

Avid's apartment was furnished in a style that was consistent with the early twenty-first century era. That meant that much of the furniture was actually styled as "mid-century" from the nineteen-fifties, but updated to current tastes, and fortunately not pink or turquoise. It also did not include starburst analog wall clocks, standing ashtrays, or ceramic cartoon cats. Instead, the décor leaned more toward mauve or teal, with traditional mid-century black and white hexagonal tiles in the bathrooms, and with styling choices and tasteful staging items the Interior Design Team had observed on the HGTV show, *Fixer Upper*. They completely updated the decor for Historians every ten years or so, adhering to local style trends, and this apartment's furnishings were in Year Seven. Residents could replace the furnishings and personalize the space, if they desired, but Avid would never have thought to do that, because thought it was a ridiculous waste of perks. It was a modest display, a little worn, and far inferior to the furnishings of an actual Hero apartment, which would have been redecorated every two years. Consequently, the compliments were insincere, in Avid's opinion.

The two Heroes wandered to the windows where they lingered, watching a school of shiny, flashing fish meander past, with the rock formations on the base of the mountain range sprouting colorful plant life in the distance.

"So beautiful!" Dirk gasped in a low, reverent voice. "And so many windows! I need to paint this view!"

Chad was standing to the side, tapping the window to get the attention of a fish that was sucking the glass, searching for algae. The fish studied him for a moment, and then swam away.

Avid had always noticed that Heroes kept their thoughts entirely closed to any probing. They were always mentally blocked, so he could never get a telepathic sense of what they were thinking. Furthermore, he could never tap into their emotions at all. Those mental blockages were always airtight, and this meeting was no exception. Heroes controlled every interaction, forcing everyone they interacted with to take them entirely at face value.

One did not ever give a Hero the upper hand, he had learned from both experience and from extensive therapy. Avid was already blocked himself, but he raised and locked his mental and telepathic defenses even further in response.

And they always flattered and sucked up to you when they wanted something or were about to inflict grave damage, he thought. They were shameless suck-ups just before they stole your life out from under you and left you naked and alone at the side of a hypothetical desert road. He had shared the stories from school. Everyone shared the stories. It was alarming and worrisome to Avid that they were sucking up to him right now. It only added to his mounting stress.

"You paint?" He said that with a smile that did not reach his eyes. Dirk didn't paint. Avid would bet his life.

"I dabble in The Arts," Dirk replied, quoting his biography. If Avid had said "ochre pigment" Dirk would have had to consult his Alert screen because he was so unfamiliar with The Arts. The Assimilation Expert had suspected as much from Dirk's background check. His reasoning was: If a conversation turned to The Arts, Dirk would have to scramble to keep up. If he was asked to demonstrate his skills, his efforts would be embarrassing. The Assimilation Expert was smiling as he wrote the biography.

"Exquisite!" he sighed breathlessly, holding up a thumb as he had seen artists do in popular cultural depictions, analyzing the view.

"You must have had some impressive accomplishments, to live here," Chad commented with a wide and engaging toothy smile. "My sincerest admiration."

Avid interpreted that to mean that Chad had evaluated him and found him undeserving of the apartment, or much of anything else really, because it was public knowledge that he had fallen into this apartment by sheer luck. Chad was rubbing it in because he thought Avid was an idiot, he concluded.

Avid's apartment was technically above his status rank. This particular apartment should have gone to a Hero or an Educator, or that misguided someone who had cashed in a lifetime's worth of perks. However, Avid lived here because of fortuitous timing, as there were no available apartments suitable for his ranking when he checked into the control station at the beginning of his assignment. The Mitigators never permitted accommodation downgrades at the control stations (that would indicate disrespect and ingratitude for someone's service, and would adversely impact morale), but they did allow for upgrades whenever necessary, and Avid was the happy recipient of one of these. He had no doubt that Chad knew this.

It was already starting, only five minutes after they'd met, with weeks to go…

"Thank you," Avid answered, walking to the kitchen. "I'm honored that you like my humble home," he said with his back turned.

He pulled three Walmart shot glasses from one of the kitchen cabinets and returned to the living room where the Heroes had finally taken seats on the Costco couch they loved so very much. Avid placed the glasses and the bottle on the coffee table. The two Heroes immediately poured themselves shots, drank them, and poured second shots.

Avid poured himself a shot after Chad passed the bottle to him, put the bottle back onto the coffee table and settled into his armchair, facing them. He sipped to be polite, then set the shot glass down.

"Thoughts?" Avid asked them.

"What do you know about all this?" Chad countered.

The Heroes exchanged glances then looked at Avid expectantly.

Avid sighed, resigned to his role in this. "Joseph D'Andre McKenna is going to be lynched unless you stop it, and I'm supposed to back you up. We need to stop it, and I have to do what I can to help in case something goes wrong for you guys. Right now I have to get a psychologist to talk Max Richmond into dropping his plans to kill him. That's all I know."

"That's right," Chad said ingratiatingly with a quick glance toward Dirk. "You're here to back us up. We appreciate your help. Can't do it without you! You'll be great!" He smiled at Avid like a game show host.

"Save the little dude," Dirk remarked, lifting his shot glass in a solemn toast. "That is our sacred mission." He nodded in agreement with himself, his brow furrowed and his kindly eyes melting with altruistic concern for Joseph and The World. Then he threw his head back and poured the vodka down his throat.

"This changes our original assignment," Chad said. "Originally we were just going to record the lynching. Now we're going to work these guys from both ends, together, you and the two of us. You're going to work with the psychologist. We're going to work with the subjects. If we can't stop them from killing McKenna on our end, your psychologist might be able to do it on your end. If that doesn't work either, we need to explore other options. We're waiting for clearance on what we can do."

"That's all I know too," Avid said, shrugging. "Not much to go on." He remembered his conversation with Vendi, thought about the Heroes' role at the event, and shuddered. He picked up his shot glass and drank his vodka in one gulp.

Chad nodded. Dirk gazed at the scenery out the window with a contemplative, peaceful smile, posing innocently, much like Norman Bates during police interrogation after getting caught dressed as his mother in the movie, *Psycho*.

"We plan to 'accidentally' run into the subjects at a sports bar near Capitol Hill next week on Tuesday," Chad continued. "The twenty-third. Make friends with them. Invite them over for cocaine and porn, convince them to include us in their plans. If they don't, we'll need to force our way in somehow. We're still thinking about it, and we still need to find out from the Mitigators what our options are, like we said. Nothing is firm."

"Cocaine and porn?" Avid asked. *These guys*, he thought. Nothing about them had changed since school.

"Or a deep discussion about tobacco futures and financial derivatives. We'll play it by ear."

Avid scratched his chin. "I haven't gotten in touch with the psychologist yet, so I don't know when I'll have an update for you. I don't know how easy it will be to get in to see her, or when I even can. Vendi didn't tell me anything about that, and I'm kind of worried that I might be on my own." It was completely inconceivable that Vendi would abandon him, considering the gravity of the situation, but his thoughts had traveled in that direction anyway. He was experiencing anxiety over every aspect of this mission.

"Just tell the therapist you're going to kill yourself unless she sees you immediately," Chad suggested helpfully. Dirk nodded in firm agreement. "Tell her you're calling her from the roof of a building."

"That's a great idea, truly, but I think they make you call the emergency number instead," Avid said with an expression of seeming disappointment and apology that he had to reject such a splendid suggestion.

"Then cry. See if that works. That's what I'd do. Press on."

"Indeed I shall." He stood up in a way that indicated the visit was over. He was very proud of himself for having taken the dominant role in ending this discussion.

"I need to try and set something up with the psychologist right now, though, if that's okay with you guys. It's getting close to seventeen-hundred hours, and I need to get through to her before she leaves for the day."

The two men rose, grabbed what was left of the vodka, and smiled. "Wednesday next week it is, my good friend," Dirk said. "We'll send you an alert, and then we'll meet."

Avid smiled distractedly and led them to the door, then closed it behind them and immediately sent an alert to Vendi requesting a conference. It took a minute to reach her, and then Vendi appeared on the Alert screen.

"Hey," she said.

"What do I say to the psychologist to get in to see her immediately? I'm not sure how to approach this." Avid's voice was edgy and higher pitched than usual.

"It's all set. We already made an appointment for you tomorrow at ten hundred hours. We ended up having to go back a few months to do that for you because she books up in advance, but now you're good to go. I was going to send you an alert as soon as I finished what I was doing, but then it slipped my mind. I've been so busy with this Anomaly. It's crazy. Sorry!"

She pushed the belated alert out to Avid, who read the instructions, and nodded.

"Breathe," she told him. "Twenty minutes of deep breathing and you'll be fine."

"Okay."

"She's just starting to take in-person clients now because she's vaccinated, but she may ask you for Skype sessions after the first visit," Vendi continued. "Do you have your vaccination card? Two months ago when we talked to her the vaccines were still just rolling out and she said she was going to require proof of vaccination by March, or she'd only see you on Skype. And just to be safe, bring your mask. She'll tell you if she wants you to wear it."

Avid nodded. He had the card and had the mask.

"Sooo...how did it go with the Heroes?" She grinned.

Avid abruptly dismissed the screen and Vendi disappeared.

Vendi redisplayed the screen so Avid could see her pointing her finger at him and laughing. Then she closed the screen again.

CHAPTER 4: DR. HELEN ANDERSON

Dr. Helen Anderson opened the door to her office and looked down at Avid, who was sitting in the waiting room, playing Solitaire on his smart phone to calm his nerves.

"Avid?" He looked up and nodded. She smiled and waved him into her office, then followed him through the door and pointed to a chair, into which Avid anxiously seated himself. "You're vaccinated, correct? I think you mentioned it in your online form, but I'd just like to be sure."

Avid dug his wallet out of his pocket and pulled out the vaccination card the Assimilation team had given him.

Helen's glasses were hanging from her neck by a chain. She raised the glasses without actually putting them on, and glanced at the card.

"Moderna. Me too. Any side effects for you?"

Everyone wanted to know which vaccine everyone else had received; this was a typical conversation starter during these weeks as the vaccines rolled out, and people were approved to receive them based on their age, health status, and occupational exposure to the virus. Everyone wanted to know everyone else's side effects, both in person and on social media. Helen and Avid exchanged the obligatory description of theirs. Avid claimed he only had a sore arm (he, of course, was making that up). Helen admitted to fatigue for a day.

She was a tall, attractive, older blonde woman with loose medium length hair, a wide, easy smile, and circles under her eyes. She wore a brightly-colored flowy pair of silk pants with a complementary top, long silk jacket, and an objectively excessive amount of oversized chunky jewelry.

"Water? Coffee?"

"Water, please." A glass of anything would give Avid something to hold onto while he thought about how he was going to begin this conversation. He had been up for most of the previous night, going over all of his options in his head. By morning he still hadn't picked one.

While Helen fetched the water, Avid quickly requested her bio data from the Alert screen to remind himself of the information he'd skimmed over earlier. She was widowed after forty-one years and had lost her only son to suicide, he learned. All of this had only happened within the past four years.

He tuned into her telepathically. She was thinking about the grief support group she facilitated, and was reminding herself to buy snacks for the next meeting. She was unhappy with her car mechanic and was trying to think of anyone she knew who might possibly recommend another mechanic who was competent with BMWs. She was tired and depressed, running on fumes and wishing she could take a vacation...but she had no one to go with because she no longer had a family, so she kept working instead. This emptiness was also why she wouldn't retire. She was rapidly approaching burnout. She was almost always on the verge of tears. She never had a day off from grief and weariness anymore, and often wished she could simply die.

Avid *still* did not notice that her bio data was missing a date or cause of death and did not mention anything about her accomplishments beyond today's date. If he had noticed, he would have immediately realized that he would never be able to access any information about Helen Anderson's future because he was not permitted to see his own future. Blocked and missing information indicated that Helen was going to be a huge part of his life. That might have reassured him that he was not going to fail at this assignment and go to prison.

Instead, his nervous fears of failure were fully intact. He was nearly panicking.

She handed him a chilled bottle of water with a bright smile. "So happy to meet you!" She sat down in the chair across from him, in front of the desk rather than behind it, in order to appear approachable rather than imposing or distanced.

Avid marveled at how effortless her smile seemed, and how energetic she appeared to be, when he knew that she was exhausted and drained.

"I'm happy to meet you too," he said.

"What brings you in? The forms you filled out online didn't really describe the problems you're having."

Avid gulped and looked away. He looked down. He looked over. He looked back. He never had decided what to say, when he'd played this scenario over and over in his head all night.

"I'm here about Max Richmond," he finally blurted.

Helen gave him a startled look and leaned back in her chair. She studied him.

"Who are you with? Are you with the police? Did his mother send you here? He's my client. I can't discuss anything with you." She stood up and turned to walk toward the door. "I think I should see you out. I have nothing to say."

Thus, he had now learned from Helen's reaction that the option he'd chosen was not the correct one. He asked his Alert screen: *Can we rewind time and try them all until I hit one that works?*

His Alert screen immediately answered him with, "No." Avid would have to blunder his way through this with a bad start, which did not help his confidence. Perhaps he might get through this without making any other mistakes.

"No, I'm not with the police." He twisted the lid off his bottle of water and took a gulp. "It's okay. I'll just tell you why I need your help with Max Richmond. All right? I already know a lot so you can just listen." Was that placating enough?

No. It was not.

"Tell me what?" Helen tilted her head irritably. "What's all this about?"

"I already know what's going on with Max Richmond, so you don't have to violate any confidences. In fact, I can recite his therapy sessions back to you, what he said and what you said, word for word, if you want. I know everything you know, but I know a little more and I need your help. You don't need to say anything. You really won't be violating his confidence. Just please let me explain what's going on."

He could tell from reading Helen that he had picked yet another bad option. He blamed the Mitigators for not permitting him to start over. But it was done. Now what?

Avid had planned to issue a request to his Alert screen to display a transcription of one of their sessions. That would prove he was a legitimate time traveler. Even though he knew from Helen's thoughts that this was not likely to impress her—she wanted everything clarified upfront, no games—he made the mental request for their session last week. Then he changed his mind and asked the Alert screen to display a session where Max had given Helen hints about what he was planning. The screen displayed their session from January 14, 2021. He kept the screen open so he could refer to it when he needed it.

Helen's eyes widened with a flash of anger and her lips tightened. Then her eyes narrowed into a squint.

"Again, who are you?" She looked around her office. "Am I being bugged? Have you put bugs in here? Did you hack my laptop? Have you been watching me through my camera?" She was livid and on high alert. "Are you threatening me?"

Ah. In this time and place you can observe people by secretly bugging them, or by hacking into their computers and watching them through the camera. He had not thought about that, and was now getting thoroughly exasperated.

He *told* them he wasn't the right person for this assignment. Where was the Assimilation team? Honestly, how was he supposed to know about bugging offices without any sort of assimilation coaching for this meeting? Why hadn't anyone given him any coaching? He knew the Mitigators were busy with the Anomaly, but wasn't he, Avid, kind of important to the success of the mission? Wasn't he, Avid, the primary backup to the Heroes? He telepathically shot that thought to Vendi with a touch of betrayed resentment.

Vendi had nothing to say in response. *Fine*, Avid thought peevishly. He would take issue with her later. He also blamed Vendi personally for this debacle because she was his contact and the face of the assignment for him.

How was he going to dig himself out of this?

"I don't know how to say this."

"Say *what?*" she snapped. She was getting angrier and he knew she was considering a call to building security to have him removed. That would kill his mission, and he might be punished. He sank into despair for a moment, and then just said it because he had no other ideas on how to ease into the subject.

"I'm a time traveler." Avid said it bravely, stoically, proud of having uttered those words on-land to a local without fear of prison because he had signed a contract that gave him permission. He was a profile in courage right now, basking in a shining glow of his own self-effacing heroism.

He was surprised and a little insulted when Helen relaxed and smiled at him. Gone was the anger. Gone was the impulse to send him away. What calmed her down was her observation and conviction that Avid was psychotic and delusional. She was now in her own realm and no longer off-balance or afraid of him. She was in her wheelhouse. Crazy was her specialty.

"How do you know Max Richmond?" She asked this pleasantly, showing sincere interest. Then she reached over to her desk for a legal pad and a pen. She was poised to write. She was suddenly very intrigued by Avid.

"I don't know him. I never met him. But I actually *am* a time traveler."

"Why do you say you're a time traveler?"

Avid bristled. He had expected her to have a reaction like that to some degree, but he had not expected this to be *his* reaction.

"The fact that I'm a time traveler makes me say that I'm a time traveler," he responded tersely.

He caught himself. It would not help the situation if he aggravated her. There was nothing about this meeting that was within his control, and everything was spiraling.

"I can prove it to you." Could he really? What other self-defeating inferno was he about to unleash?

"I hope you can. I'm excited to meet a time traveler, if you are one. I have so many questions."

She might have been saying that to placate him, but she *did*, in fact, have so many questions. Avid picked up that she half-hoped he would prove himself to her because it would be the one bright spot in her otherwise anguished life. She loved science fiction. She loved Dr. Who. When she was a schoolgirl she had fantasized about being picked up by a UFO. Furthermore, whether it would be in fifty years or fifty thousand, scientists were one day going to figure out time travel, right? It was inevitable. And then…one of them might visit her time! A hopeful part of her accessed that little dream right now and wanted this to be real. Because what if it was? It would make her so happy! If not, well, this man was her job.

Avid asked his Alert screen to display something that would happen momentarily, live, and about which he could tell Helen in advance so she could see it for herself. He saw the response on the screen.

In seventeen minutes a man would enter a CVS pharmacy and begin shooting. Seeing the event on the Alert screen, Avid had no doubt that the Mitigators had arranged for him to be in Helen's office at this specific time so that he would be with her when the shooting occurred. Vendi's effort to "find an appointment with Helen" was an effort to find an appointment with Helen at this very specific date and time, when a local shooting would occur and Avid could use it to prove he was a time traveler. They clearly wanted Avid to make a dramatic impression on her. This kind of manipulation of events was how the Mitigators operated. They always crossed their T's and dotted their I's. He silently thanked them.

The Historian team that was covering twenty-first century gun violence and mass shootings had had some busy years, and he knew that someone from that team would be on assignment at the CVS pharmacy in the Woodland Park strip mall at this very moment.

"In about...it's about sixteen minutes from now, I guess...a gunman will enter the CVS pharmacy in the Woodland Park strip mall and begin shooting. One will die at the scene, and four others will be wounded. One of the wounded will die on the way to the hospital. The gunman will shoot and kill himself." He looked up. "CBS will air the story first. Go to their website right now."

Looking taken aback but curious, Helen got up and grabbed her laptop. She went to www.cbs.com, then clicked its Live Stream link. She nudged aside a table lamp and set the laptop on the end table between their two chairs so that both of them could see it.

The three morning hosts were discussing a local story about a high school that was trying to plan a no-contact virtual prom because of the pandemic. Then they shifted to the announcer for local sports.

"What if there really *is* a shooting, but you're involved somehow so you know about it in advance?"

He hadn't thought that part through either. He sighed. *Vendi*, he snapped telepathically. He figured she was aware of what was going on, so he needn't elaborate on the depth of her betrayal. He simply shot her telepathic sparks.

"Good question. Give me a second," Avid said. He mentally requested something that would happen on live TV right now, and which could not have been planned. The Alert screen told him that a host on CBS Late Morning was going to spill his coffee live on air three minutes before the shooting. That was very convenient. The Mitigators had sent him to CBS for the coffee spill so that Helen wouldn't even need to switch networks when it came time for the shooting. It was nice to know he had backup. He sent Vendi a tepid but still resentful apology. His final thought to her was, "*but still...*"

"Relax," she responded telepathically. "You're doing fine."

Was he though? This Anomaly and Avid's assignment had captured everyone's attention at the control station. There was talk. Avid and the Heroes who were assigned to the McKenna Anomaly were in the spotlight right now, and had earned everyone's recognition because of the Anomaly's severity. Everyone was watching and noticing Avid, which meant everyone would also notice when he messed everything up and went to prison. He was doomed to embarrass himself.

Avid had heard from multiple sources that the Mitigators were taking a hands-on approach with this situation, and were not even allowing trusted and experienced staff to take part in any decisions, or participate in any aspect of the effort, aside from Vendi's communication role with Avid. And Vendi might have had a Mitigator sending her telepathic instructions on what to say to him. Everyone but actual Mitigators had been completely shut out of the McKenna Anomaly recovery effort, he'd learned. Actual Mitigators were doing everything, down to the most mundane details, so an actual real live Mitigator had to have set all this up, Avid suddenly realized. Not Vendi.

He now suspected that he was being studied and evaluated from a live scanner stream at this moment by those actual live Mitigators. Typically Historians were tracked by scanner footage no one ever viewed, unless it was to assess a problem after the fact and determine fault and liability. Even the Mitigators had to go through the Criminal Justice Project to obtain a warrant, if they wanted to view historical footage of anyone. This was not that. This was far more serious. Live surveillance was a really rare action for the Mitigators to take, but it was likely they were doing that in this instance. Typically, alerts were automated, but in this case Avid now accepted absolutely and with severe anxiety that they were not. His Alerts were coming directly from a Mitigator...and Avid had stage fright.

It all sank in. He tried not to think about being observed on live feed by Mitigators because he might have a panic attack.

How had this Anomaly actually affected the continuum? What exactly had it triggered? No one would ever tell him, he knew. He would have to ponder it in his imagination for the rest of his life.

On the plus side, he could count on live, breakthrough Alerts to guide him when he got stuck, because the Mitigators would know what he should say or do. They could view scanner footage of the locals and gather important data he would need in "his" moment, then skip back and forth in time to deliver it to Avid after lengthy, painstaking research, without losing any time at all from his perspective.

"We're already on the CBS site, right?" He looked at his smart phone for the time. "In about ten minutes Evan Ewing is going to spill his coffee live on air. It's live, remember. It hasn't happened yet. Then they're going to cut away from that broadcast to tell us about the shooting."

Helen went back to her laptop's browser and clicked Full Screen on the CBS live feed display.

"So, what should we talk about for the next ten minutes?"

"Max Richmond."

"I can't discuss Max Richmond."

Avid shrugged. "I can, though, right?"

Helen nodded and shrugged, then studied him with narrowed eyes. She was back in "analysis" mode. Whatever Avid said or did was going to go through her filter of analysis and be subject to dissection. He was being dissected by everyone.

This was job stress.

But he thought again about the Mitigators being his backup, and how they had helped him thus far with the scheduling. It was almost as if he was doing this with them cheering him on, fully prepared to catch him if he fell. He decided to look at it that way. His heart rate went down a bit.

"He's sort of been telling you about his plans, but he's only been hinting and saying vague things to you, so you don't actually know what those plans are. We have to stop him."

"If you tell me something about Max Richmond, I can't confirm it one way or the other. You're wasting your time."

"You know that he's a member of the Fairfax Freedom Fighters, correct? They're a white supremacist group? You know he's a white supremacist?"

Helen did not know this. She said, "I can't tell you what I know or don't know about Max Richmond."

"You didn't know. It's okay. He didn't actually tell you. What he *did* tell you was that he was a staunch patriot. Remember your session on January fourteenth this year? It was right after the attack on the Capitol."

Avid was referring to the violent mob that attacked the Capitol in order to overturn the results of the recent presidential election.

"He was there for the attack and even made it inside the Capitol building with the rest of the mob. Did you know he was there? (Helen did not, Avid could read). And in your January fourteenth session he told you he was a 'staunch patriot.'"

Helen stared at Avid trying to analyze him, but she did not respond.

"He told you he wanted to be the one to trigger the change in this country...?" Avid studied Helen's face. "Do you remember? What he meant by that was he wanted things to go back to the way they used to be in this country, back to the 'real' America, when White men had the upper hand. He's calling what he plans to do 'the change' Do you remember that? It all ties in now, doesn't it?"

"Again, I cannot discuss Max Richmond with you or anyone else." Avid heard her going through that session in her head. She didn't know how she had missed his comment about triggering change as a staunch patriot, but now that Avid mentioned it, she remembered he'd said something like that. That comment should have put her on high alert. It was a red flag, and she missed it. Her mind must have been on something else because normally she would catch that kind of verbiage and address it immediately. For a moment she felt a sense of failure and helplessness.

"It's okay that you missed it. Don't be so hard on yourself. We're addressing it now," Avid told her.

She blinked at him in surprise.

"And you don't have to say anything. I'll do all the talking. You just listen." Avid checked his smart phone. "We have seven minutes before the station interrupts this talk show to report the CVS shooting at the shopping center. That means we have four minutes until Evan Ewing spills his coffee on live TV."

Avid paused.

"Max is planning to kill someone."

"Seriously? He's the CVS shooter?"

"No. He's planning to lynch several Black men in eight weeks. He's *not* being impulsive, but he might be mirroring someone, if I understand the term correctly. He's carefully planning this out with someone else we think is behind it all."

Helen leaned forward without speaking and stared at him. Avid could almost hear the wheels turning in her head. She was an extraordinarily fast and thorough thinker, going over the possibilities with both Max and Avid at lightning speed making it difficult for Avid to follow her thoughts. It was like watching one of those drug commercials they have on television in this time and place, where they scroll through a long list of possible side effects so quickly that you can't read them. Helen was a mental titan.

"We can't save those men. They were killed in the original timeline, so we can't interfere with those killings. But Max and his partner are now also planning to lynch a fifteen-year-old boy. This kid wasn't part of the original lynching, and we have to stop it."

"Original timeline? Original lynching? What are you talking about?"

"We had an Anomaly." What a mess he was making of this. "That means that someone from the future did something in your time that changed the course of history. We have to put history back to the way it was originally in the original timeline, before that person from the future screwed things up for everyone."

Helen blinked again and began to go through her spinning mental gymnastics. Then she gave up. This aspect of Avid's session was *not* in her wheelhouse. She just sat and listened.

He appealed to Helen's maternal instincts. "His voice hasn't even changed yet. He's small for his age and underweight. He looks to be about eleven years old, if I'm honest. I've *seen* him. Max is planning on lynching this boy. A Black boy. A *child*, really. A *boy*. Max is planning on killing someone who is still almost a child. He's going to *lynch* him."

Helen curled her lip. "I don't believe you."

"This particular young man is not supposed to die at the age of fifteen. He's supposed to grow up to be an extremely influential national leader who's going to change a number of things in his lifetime. His accomplishments will be staggering and far-reaching, and the Mitigators absolutely cannot allow Max Richmond to lynch him."

"Who are the Mitigators?"

"It's time. Turn up the volume on your computer and let's watch."

Helen turned up the volume just in time to see Evan Ewing twist around to speak to the weatherman, and then accidentally catch his sleeve on his coffee cup, which fell over and spilled. Hilarity ensued on the set as he quipped about the puddle of coffee, and the other hosts joked about his clumsiness. He made an exaggeratingly comical show of trying to wipe up the coffee with his hands.

"There you go," said Avid. "Coffee spill. This is live TV." Helen looked at him, and then looked back at the laptop screen.

"Breaking news." The screen cut away to a newscaster and a picture of the pharmacy. "We're interrupting this broadcast to bring you a breaking story. There's a shooting in progress at the CVS pharmacy in the Woodland Park strip mall." He named the intersection where the shopping center was. "At this moment the shooter is still active, so we're advising the public to avoid the area until further notice. Police are on the scene. We don't know the details yet but we'll keep you informed. Stay tuned."

Avid's Alert screen flashed a new alert, again from one of the real live Mitigators, and it directed him to Facebook. It provided the screen name for a person who was recording the shooting, and streaming it on Facebook Live.

"Go to Facebook," Avid ordered Helen. "Pull up the account of TimeTravel28cent and view the live stream of the shooting." He spelled the username for Helen who nervously typed it in. The handle told Avid that the person uploading the footage was the Historian who was covering the event. The Mitigators must have arranged this.

Helen displayed Facebook, hurriedly opened the TimeTravel28cent account and then clicked on the live stream, which displayed a gunman blasting bullets throughout a drugstore. The person recording the video appeared to be behind a counter at floor level. There were two people lying face down and injured within the frame of the recording.

"Oh my God," she breathed. "Oh my God."

"Four wounded, one dead at the scene, and the gunman kills himself. One of the wounded dies on the way to the hospital. Write that down please."

Helen wrote that down.

"You can confirm all that after our session because they won't report the full story for another hour or so."

Helen stared at him, appearing to be almost on the verge of tears. She tilted her head. She was feeling every emotion.

"What year are you from?" she finally asked softly, in a whisper. As sad and appalled as she was for the victims of this shooting, this was a dream come true for her. She felt lighthearted and uplifted for the first time in years. The little girl inside of her was jumping up and down.

Avid smiled. "Will you help me stop Max Richmond?"

"Yes, of course. Of course I'll help you. Yes." He could feel her eagerness and elation. He had brought her a gift that would distract her from grief and emotional exhaustion. She was powered by renewed energy, not exhausted at all anymore, and grinning widely.

"I'm from the year twenty-seven-fifty-four. Your help is going to be of historical significance. You need to know that. *Historical significance.* This is incredibly important." He lifted prayer hands and touched his chin. He bowed his head to her. "So we all sincerely thank you from the bottom of our hearts. All of us."

Helen clasped her hands under her chin and grinned as she returned Avid's bow. She bounced in her chair, a little bit.

Avid then explained his job to her, and described the Terence Jackson event and the Anomaly so she would understand how this situation came about. Helen listened, rapt, leaning forward with her hands still clasped. When her phone timer dinged to indicate that the fifty-minute session was over, she let out a loud, "Argh!" and shook her head in frustration.

"We need to discuss this some more. Can you come to my house later? After I get off work? I'll feed you dinner. Seven o'clock?"

Avid telepathically heard her wondering if she should ask her next door neighbor, Al, to check up on her this evening in case Avid was a violent nut cake, like the shooter.

"You can ask Al to check on you, but he can't come inside," Avid told her. "This is completely confidential. You can never, ever tell anyone what we talk about. Not ever." Avid sighed and shot her a skewed smile. "And I'm really not violent. I promise." He paused. "Is 'nut cake' a psychiatric term? I'm not familiar with it, but it seems kind of insulting."

"Damn," Helen said. "You're *scary.*" Then she burst out laughing and wrote her address on a Post-it note for Avid, who took the note and slipped it into his pocket.

"I'll see you at seven," he said, and left.

The travel pod dropped Avid off in an obscure location behind an abandoned office building. An Uber picked him up out front a few minutes later, and dropped him off on O Street in front of a beautiful Georgetown semi-detached row home, which had its porch light on for him. He could smell the food cooking from the street.

He rang the bell, and a woman answered. She was a small, thin, wiry lesbian with a nose ring and long teal-colored hair, with her head shaved on one side. She had tattoos going up her neck and onto her shaved scalp. She was wearing a chef's jacket and holding a wooden spoon. He introduced himself, and she then led him through the living room to an opened door in the back. The woman pointed her spoon to direct him into the office, where Helen was sitting at her computer.

Helen looked up and grinned. "Avid! Have a seat." She waved to a chair, and Avid dutifully sat down in it. "I hope you like Italian? Nelda is a fantastic cook, and she's doing Panzanella Caponata with panna cotta and berries for dessert. Fabulous. Trust me."

She shut down her computer and turned to him. "Wine? Or would you like something stronger?"

"Wine is fine. White, if you have it."

Helen rang a bell and Nelda appeared in doorway. "Could you please bring Avid a Chardonnay? Also, please bring a glass for me, and leave the bottle in an ice bucket. Muchas gracias, my darling." Nelda was not Hispanic.

Nelda smiled. "Dinner will be in about ten. Remember to wash your hands. COVID."

"Will do. And leave the dishes tonight, Nelda. You can go home right after you serve. We'll take care of the rest. Thank you so much," Helen said with a smile. Nelda went to get the wine and the glasses.

"We'll wait to talk until she leaves. In the meantime, let's just get to know each other."

"Sounds good."

"So, your story checks out. Four injured, two dead, and the gunman killed himself." Helen looked pleased.

"I know."

"How did you read my mind like you did?" Helen didn't waste time.

"Basically we're all genetically modified to be telepathic, and then they train us in school to be really good at it. If you become a Historian, like me, you have to take special advanced courses. We have to be exceptionally proficient at it to get this job." He was very proud of his skill level, and his job. "Not everyone can do it as well as

I can, just so you know. It's a learned skill like anything else, with a little boost to our DNA."

"I would have told you that you were a fake if you'd asked me yesterday. Mind reading. No such thing. Ha!"

"Why?" Avid was genuinely curious about why the people from the past were so frightened of anything that had to do with basic telepathic or psychic abilities. It made no sense. It was like being afraid of hearing, or tasting, or any of the other senses. It was like denying that red or green existed because *they* were colorblind.

"Well, because we're taught that there's no such thing. So we figure that anyone who says he can read minds is a liar. Or sort of a kook."

"If everyone is deaf and only one person can hear, all the deaf people are going to think the hearing person is lying or a kook. That's how we view it in my time."

"View what?"

"The certainty of people from your time that they should reject everything they haven't personally experienced with their basic physical senses. Anything beyond their own five senses either doesn't exist, or the people who *do* experience it or believe in it are crazy."

Helen was thoughtful about what Avid had just told her. She loved this conversation.

"They call it 'woo-woo'," she told him. "I called it woo-woo, too." She mouthed "woo-woo too" to herself and grinned. "The entire psychiatric community is on red alert when it comes to woo-woo. We're always looking for psychosis, and we figure that woo-woo is probably going to lead us there. It's a pervasive attitude in my line of work."

Avid rolled his eyes and laughed.

"Maybe I can teach you how to set up a mental block so I can't read you. They start teaching us to do that in preschool, but we'll need to find out if you're even equipped to do that without genetic intervention. You have to know how to maintain your privacy, but you won't need to block yourself much, except when I'm around."

"Can you teach me to read minds?"

"In eight weeks?" Avid sent a request to his Alert screen for information about mind reading. When it displayed, Avid read it to her.

"You can connect to people through their emotions, through the heart, but I can't train you to read their thoughts in eight weeks. You can only sense what they feel."

Helen looked a little disappointed for a moment.

"You probably already sense feelings at some level. We're going to work on honing your skills."

Avid could tell that Helen was already looking forward to that training.

The screen displayed more information. It was historical and it must be helpful if the Mitigators sent it to him, but it was not what he had hoped for or expected. It was scientific information Helen could research. It outlined the basics of telepathy on a mechanical or technological level.

"I've just received some data for you that you might find interesting. Right now, in your time, they've invented a device that can translate your brain waves and report on what you're thinking. You have devices that can read minds right now, today. Did you know that? They're not good yet because the technology is really new, but they will be."

"Data? You received data how? What data?"

"On my Alert Screen. Google 'device that reads minds' on your computer There's some information for you there that might explain it to you a little bit. They've just begun working on the technology for my Alert Screen in your time. Later on they add all the other technology, like the holographic images and all the rest, and the function that prevents anyone else from seeing my screen. They implant the device that controls it into our wrists. We all communicate with each other on it, and we use it to request information from the master database. It's kind of like your Internet, in a way, without a physical computer."

Helen was genuinely confused, but she turned her computer back on and did the Google search.

Avid wasn't used to interacting with the locals and had to remind himself that Helen wasn't familiar with things he took for granted. The Mitigators had redirected his conversation to explain the technical aspects of how he communicated and accessed information so Helen would be aware of what he was doing whenever he stared at the space in front of his face, or began to abruptly start talking to Vendi. And broke down telepathy into scientific advancements that would legitimize it for Helen. It made sense to him now.

He tried to explain it more clearly.

"In my time we all get implants that display holographic screens right about here." He waved at the area twelve inches from his face. "We control them mentally. So, if I want information, I focus on the area in front of my face and issue a mental command, like 'devices that read minds.' The screen launches and gives me the answer. Or, I can ask for the definition of a word, or display bio information about people. Everything comes from this really enormous database that holds all the information all the time travelers are gathering, from Pangea before the tectonic plates moved, to my time. It's an advanced version of what you're looking at in Google right now. Everything about everything is in that database, and we're not even done compiling it yet."

Helen was rapt.

"The implant reads my thoughts, accesses the information I ask for, and displays it on a screen that only I can see. We need it so we don't look stupid or inadvertently create problems when we're in times and places where we don't know the culture or the social cues very well. It even monitors the situation we're in and displays information when we need a prompt of some kind, like 'Bow to the waist with your hands straight at your side' or something. Like earlier today when I told you to look at Facebook. My screen automatically sent me that information without me asking."

No, my screen was on "Live Mitigator Surveillance," he thought to himself. Since then, they hadn't interrupted him with any other instructions, so he guessed he was doing pretty well on his own.

"The Alert screen uses a form of telepathy, only instead of *receiving* someone's thoughts and reading minds, you're *projecting* your thoughts by mentally sending commands to a device. Then the device picks them up from your brainwaves and responds to them. If you're really good at telepathy you can also project your thoughts into another person, and if the person is really good as well, that person can receive your thoughts without the device. The brain has natural receptors that control telepathy. Ours are just improved over yours."

"And you have proof of this in your time?" Helen asked.

Avid nodded and shrugged. It was like her asking him if they had proof of electricity.

"So this device actually emulates the brain. Everyone is already wired to project thoughts and receive someone else's thoughts, but the portion of the brain that controls telepathy shrank from disuse over the past twenty thousand years or so. It's still there, though. Some people actually have more developed brains, even in your time, and they can do it without genetic enhancement. You call them 'kooks.' "But in this instance I'm communicating directly with the device to access data from a database, or to communicate with other people as if we were on a Skype call. It's still telepathy. I'm just communicating with a wrist implant instead of a person."

Helen was amazed and happy, staring at him.

Avid held out his arm and ran a finger over a small bump on the inside of his wrist. "The Alert screen implant is right here." He let Helen touch it. Then he held out his other arm and pointed to a small bump on the other wrist. "This is my language implant so I can understand you and talk to you in your own language. They control it remotely from the control station. It operates on the same principle, reading my brainwaves, but then it translates my thoughts into speech in whichever language they program it for. That's what comes out of my mouth, whatever language they program for me. When I listen to someone speak in any language, the language implant translates their speech and then projects it into the language centers in my brain in a form that I can understand. We have no problem communicating with anyone at all. Literally."

Nelda appeared in the doorway and announced that dinner was served in the dining room. She again told them to wash their hands. "COVID," she reminded them. She then put on her coat and left, calling "Goodbye!" as she shut the door behind her.

Avid and Helen washed their hands. The food was delicious.

"Can you give me winning lottery numbers?" Helen chortled loudly over dessert and touched Avid's sleeve. "Let's go to the races! Woot!" She was on her third wine.

Then she looked at him steadily and said, "Your name is an adjective. Did you know that?"

Avid nodded, grinning. Usually he had to correct the pronunciation of people who thought his name was "Ah-*veed*."

"Is your middle name 'Lee'? Then you can be an adverb. Avid Lee. Avidly. Get it?" Helen thought she was very clever, and looked very proud for having observed this.

Avid burst out laughing.

Avid was finishing his second wine, reaching for his third, and was leaning on one elbow, having enormous fun with Helen. They had laughed throughout the entire dinner. On an impulse, knowing he could never do this on-land without the Mitigator approval he had received with Helen, he connected with her telepathically and sent her a heart hug. She didn't remind him of his mother, but she was a mother he wouldn't have minded having.

He had never sent a heart hug to a local before. Normally that was illegal.

Helen felt the heart hug and went silent. She looked at Avid, her eyes immediately brimming with tears, then clasped her hands together and pressed them to her chest. She looked down, trying not to cry. Alarmed by what he had just done, Avid jumped up and then hugged her from behind. She collapsed into heaving, wracking sobs, and he rocked her.

How separated and detached from each other the people are in this time and place, Avid thought to himself, holding her. How lonely it is for the people here. He was so glad he was only visiting and could leave. It was tragic for the people who had to stay in a place where even love was painful. That was all a heart hug was: love. And it had made Helen cry.

"We need to clean up the kitchen," Helen finally said, wiping her eyes and pulling away from Avid. "Will you help me?"

"So, what's the deal with the language implant?" Helen asked. She was rinsing off the dishes and putting them into the dishwasher, an appliance she had had to explain to Avid, who was still clearing off the table. "Do you not speak English?"

"No. Most of us speak a language called Hinduese that doesn't exist yet, in your time. But you can't tell, right? I sound like I was born here?"

Helen poured them each wine number three, and gave an embarrassed shrug. She took a sip. "If I'm being honest, and I have to be because you can read my mind, you sound a little…generic." He reminded her of Data from *Star Trek: Next Generation*.

Avid caught the reference and requested a sampling of videos of Data from *Star Trek*. He couldn't pinpoint the problem because he wasn't intimately familiar enough with English to recognize how his speech and Data's speech were different from a local's. He had always thought it was the accent that mattered, but she picked up that something was different because of the language implant's word choices, and his delivery.

"I only even notice this at all because I listen to people all day long and use their tones and inflections to kind of identify things about them. Voices, speech patterns and word choices tell you a whole lot, if you know how to decipher them. And yours kind of tripped off a red flag because it was just the *ti*-iniest bit stilted and forced. Tiny bit. Just a little bit." She squeezed her thumb and forefinger together and held them out for Avid to examine. "Like a robot, just a little bit."

Helen paused. "Drink," she ordered Avid. "Now that I know you're being translated, it makes perfect sense. The implant isn't putting a lot of personality into your words. You sound flat and dry, like you're reading from a book about finance or physics. Kind of like canned speech."

Avid frowned. He had never heard this about the translation implant. Presumably the situation would correct himself, after he had more practice, he hoped.

"The Language Project manages everything. They work with the Language Historians, who go back in time and create records of all the languages, upload them to the database, and then deliver them through the implants to make them accessible to people who go back to those times. They adjust the settings on the implant so we speak in that language."

"Language Project?"

"The Language Project focuses solely on language. They work to gather information about every language that ever existed, and they upload their findings into a huge language database. They also track accents from geographic areas and adjust word usage according to how the language evolves. For instance, in the nineteen eighties and nineties, all the languages in the world were updated with computer terminology. It was almost an overhaul, with all the new words entering the lexicon at once, changing virtually every single language that was in use at the time. That was one of the biggest language upgrades in history. During those years, the implant only permitted you to speak words that had made it into common speech on a given day. But every single day you had access to more of them. So updates are constant and ongoing. What comes out of our mouths is very specific to the time period, and the way we speak is specific to the place we either are in, or are supposed to be from."

"You work on a team then?"

"Everything is team-based in our time. We're all divided into Projects, and we work together with teams on specific assignments. We also work with other projects, whenever we need to. For instance, I'm in the Historian Project, but I also work with the Time Travel Project to move about in time, and the Education Project, which is where I send the reports that I upload to the database. Besides the Historian Project we have the Finance Project, the Scientific Advancements Project, the Medical Advancements Project, the Education Project, the Child Development project, the Psychological Support Project, The Arts Project, the Sports Project, the Legal Project, the Manufacturing Project, the Technology Project... I don't know how many of them there are. Dozens and dozens because everything falls under its own Project."

Helen had perked up with interest at Psychological Support Project. She was going to grill him on that one at some point.

"That's just a few of them. Every aspect of society has its own Project. Everyone reports to one of the Projects. That's what we all do. We train in one of the specialties, then we apply for a job in that Project and go to work. We're all affiliated with one of the projects. Everyone. Even people who don't work answer to the rules and laws of whatever Project they report to. Most of the rules are pretty similar, except for the ones that are specific to a job."

"So you're programmed for Washington, D.C. speech patterns right now? Can you speak in Hinduese so I can hear what it sounds like?"

"We speak Hinduese in our control stations because the implant is disabled there, but I'm set up for twenty-twenty-one English here, with Washington D.C. speech patterns. English is all that comes out of my mouth when I'm on-land. I can't switch back and forth because the implant doesn't allow me to speak Hinduese for you unless I get special approval."

Earlier in the day he had received an Alert, which updated the rules for speaking on-land without clearance.

"By the way, funny story. The Anomaly that happened around Max Richmond triggered a big change in language rules. The Mitigators set up a new rule where the language team can only set you up to speak this really ancient dialect from ten thousand years ago if you're on-land and don't have clearance to interact with the locals. They could just use Hinduese, except that the language evolved from contemporary languages and some locals might understand some of the words. Today, someone said something on-land in that ancient dialect, and it sounds so guttural and alien that the locals freaked out. One of them called 9-1-1 because she thought the Historian was having a stroke. So Historians are learning to keep their mouths shut, which is really all the Mitigators ask from them anyway."

"Who are the Mitigators? What do you mean when you're 'on-land'?"

"We live in the ocean, and you live on-land. We can travel back and forth, but we can't talk to you unless we have clearance to interact with the locals. If we don't, we speak gibberish whenever we leave the ocean and go on-land."

Helen was dumbstruck.

He grinned.

"Keep going. I want to know everything," Helen sighed happily. "Tell me everything."

Avid held up a finger. "Let me check with the Mitigator team to see how much else I can tell you." He was silent. When he had read the response on his Alert screen, he continued. "I can tell you anything you want to know, with a few exceptions. They'll tell me when we hit them. What do you want to know first?"

"How do you live in the ocean?" she asked.

He explained how they created the control station city complex. They began with the construction of the main building, which contained the time travel wing so they could transport people, construction materials, and other things from other times and places as they needed to. Until that was complete, the construction staff commuted from another control station and transported materials from there into temporary structures.

They used an advanced form of 3D printing to build each structure underwater with a durable building foam. When the outer structure was complete and sealed, they pushed wide hollow extrusion pipes up several meters above the ocean's surface, then pumped the water out, spewing it back into the ocean at its surface. Other pipes forced fresh air from the surface down into the structure to displace the water, until the structure was eventually dry.

When the building was complete they retracted the extrusion pipes that had removed the water, and kept them dormant down below, where they deployed automatically to pump water out in a flood emergency. They left the air pipes in place above the surface, and kept them continually operating to circulate fresh air, modulating the air's temperature as it entered the buildings. These air pipes closed automatically and retracted below the ocean surface during storms and high wave conditions, or whenever sea vessels approached.

The maintenance team fitted the three-inch thick curved and rounded windows on the internal side of the structure, sealed them, then cut the foam away from them on the outside of the structure to expose the view. When the building was complete and secure they installed all the necessary fittings, decorated and furnished everything, then filled the structure with people. They had control stations going back to Pangea, and during the current era and in the upcoming centuries they were virtually everywhere, in all the large bodies of water in the world, and held billions and billions of people over the full stretch of the continuum, far more than the earth could support if they all lived on-land at the same time.

"The Mitigators are constantly building more control stations and expanding existing ones. You would never go to a control station and not see some kind of new construction, no matter what year you were there."

"Who exactly are the Mitigators?"

"They're the world leaders. They're our world's equivalent of your Joe Biden, Vladimir Putin, Angela Merkel, Boris Johnson, Justin Trudeau, etc., and all the other leaders you have right now. We don't have presidents, kings or dictators anymore. We have Mitigators who work together like a board of directors for a company that doesn't have a CEO. No one can hold a solo leadership role anymore. They drew up a Constitution that makes it illegal for any one individual to hold that much power, even temporarily or by popular vote. They're nominated, then screened and selected by the other Mitigators, and they serve twenty year terms, so they aren't competing with each other for the top spot, and nobody is trying to conquer anyone else anymore. They don't spend time and money campaigning to keep their jobs, so they can focus on the work. We think that's an improvement."

Helen's mind was whirring.

"The Mitigators break out into smaller teams to lead the various Projects. I report to Historian Project Mitigators so I'm subject to their laws. People in other projects report to entirely different sets of Mitigators. In a way, you can think of our Projects as 'countries', but the leaders of these countries work together as a team to make sure all the countries are on the same page, and that we're all progressing satisfactorily as a civilization. Some overreaching laws affect all of the Projects, and these go up for popular vote among everyone all over the continuum, but for day-to-day operational things Mitigators just make the rules and we follow them, like they would in a company."

"You sound like a book about finance again, my poor darling." Helen poked his arm to let Avid know she was only teasing. "But this is truly fascinating."

"So what Mitigators do is solve the problems, figure out the best course of action in a global emergency, make the rules, dole out rewards and punishments, clean up all the messes, and act like the board of directors to make sure the Project runs smoothly. They remove obstacles so we can do our jobs and they provide the incentives for us to perform them."

"Like good managers," Helen inserted. "A good manager serves the workforce, not the other way around. This sounds like that."

Helen's mind was churning again, so Avid let go and let her progress through the spin cycle without trying to track her thoughts.

"That approach really works, even on a world scale, doesn't it?" She said that as a statement rather than a question.

"Yeah, I think so. People are mostly okay with the way things are. Nobody revolts against the leadership in my time. We haven't had any wars in a while because who are we going to declare war on? The Accounting and Mathematics Project when we don't like the numbers? The Sports Project when our team loses? Everybody has a place, and everyone needs everyone else equally. If we can sustain our current world order, we think we might make it to the end without any more wars."

"Hallelujah," Helen said. "We must look like knuckle-dragging Neanderthals to you," she added, laughing.

Avid laughed too, but he didn't find it as funny as Helen did.

Helen handed Avid a towel so he could hand dry the pots she had just scrubbed in the sink.

"Tell me more about living in the ocean."

Avid explained that it had begun as a reaction to climate change, when the population needed to find a place to live that was safe from fire, flooding, excessive heat, and violent storms. Real estate developers staked claims on the ocean floor near the coasts, and then began building and selling units there. That prompted the car manufacturers to design vehicles that could travel on-land and underwater. In the beginning, going home to the ocean floor was a clumsy effort that involved going down in sealed elevators, and then transferring to underwater shuttles that ran on rails. Eventually, about three hundred years ago, they came up with the technology to fly *and* travel underwater.

Later, when the Historian Project began, the Mitigators built control center complexes to house the people who lived and worked in all the historical time periods, so they could hide from the locals they were living alongside. They selected underwater locations that scanners indicated would never experience serious seismic disruption or accidental discovery by the locals.

"The Mitigators have a mission statement, which is, 'We Want Everyone to Thrive'." Avid laughed. "In Hinduese it's a catchy play on words and it rhymes. In English it just sounds kind of lame, but that's what the world aspires to in my time."

Helen's jaw dropped and she removed her hands from a soapy pot. She did a slow, soapy clap. "Bravo," she said. "Finally. The world makes sense. Well done, you."

"So they take care of all of our basic needs, like basic food and housing and clothing and medical care. Everyone has that. I mean, you shouldn't elevate yourself by making certain there are always starving or homeless people around to make you feel personally successful or superior. Am I right?"

"Someone told you that? It sounds quoted." She had a skewed smile. She "read" speech and speech patterns in her line of work, and just knew those weren't Avid's personal words. Avid was impressed. He had telepathy, but Helen could do this without any mental enhancements.

"Yeah. I asked someone why there were so many homeless people here, and why nobody took a minute to help them, and that's what they told me. You have to keep some people down in order to feel elevated yourself, they said. I see that in the racial assignments I get as well."

Helen raised and lowered her eyebrows, amused, but she did not disagree with Avid.

"That's just what they told me you all do here," Avid continued apologetically, seeing her expression. "But you can't do that when you live in the ocean. You can't open a window and push someone out and tell him to go swim with the fishes just because he doesn't have a job. Everyone needs the air inside of the control station, so everyone has a guaranteed place to live. If they're lazy or incompetent at their job, or whatever, it doesn't matter. They just get a simple life with no frills, no vacations, no fancy restaurant meals, no commissary spending sprees. Everyone has a place to live and food to eat. Maybe a not-so-nice place and really bland and basic food, but we don't have an endless bottom that people can fall through, like you do here. We think that it's the right thing to do."

"So what if people don't work?"

"Like I said, it doesn't matter. All the basic things are free. So we don't pay for basic food, clothing, shelter, childcare, medical care or education. Everyone needs those things, so everyone has those things. If someone has no ambition and doesn't perform well and doesn't care, they can live in really basic accommodations, which are just tiny rooms with no windows. It's a no-frill life, and you have no perks if you don't work. You eat and sleep, and you live in one room, but you can't buy anything or do anything that requires discretionary income. Some people are okay like that. There are always going to be people who don't need a lot and don't care about luxuries, and who also don't like to work, or aren't very good at working. We call them 'ascetics'. We don't think it's necessary to punish them for a lifestyle choice we don't happen to prefer ourselves. If we did, we wouldn't be showing empathy."

"So how do you get luxuries then?"

"They pay us our salary in perks, and we can earn more by doing other things, like community service. The more perks you get, the more you can improve your living conditions and your social status. We don't use money at all, except when we go on-land and buy things from the locals. We barter in 'perks' instead of money. And we have banks that hold our perks for us in accounts until we withdraw them."

"What's a perk?"

"Perks are a lot like your money, but they can be anything you want. They have different values, based on what you did to earn them, so you can get small perks or large ones. We have bank balances, just like you do, and we can spend our perks on different things, just like you do. But they supplement the basic necessities instead of going towards them, and we usually don't withdraw them as cash. We don't have to use them to buy food or pay rent, so we never have a negative cash flow, paying more for basic necessities than we earn. That would be like being an ascetic, except with a job. Or two jobs. Or three jobs. You have lots of people like that here. Sometimes those people in your time end up homeless because of a medical expense or a raise in rent, and they're the ones nobody takes a minute to help. So we like our system better than yours."

Helen looked thoughtful.

"Perks are always discretionary income. That's the primary difference between our monetary system and yours. We earn perks for high performance at our job, or for doing kind and generous things for people, or volunteering for community service. That sort of thing. The more we benefit society, which is our goal as a civilization, the higher the value of the perk. So people are always helping each other and volunteering in order to earn something they want. It pays to be nice in my time."

"Your civilization's goal is to benefit society?" Helen whistled through her teeth. "What a concept, huh? And it works?"

Avid looked at her. "Of course it works. Why wouldn't we all want that?"

Helen wasn't responsible for her society, but Avid still looked at her sternly.

"Why indeed," Helen pondered. "Fascinating."

"So we can cash in perks for anything we want, as long as we have enough perk value in the bank account. We can take time travel vacations to various places with cash to spend, or we get to eat in the fancier restaurants at the control station, or we can earn nicer furniture or apartments, or just get cash to splurge when we go on-land if we want. We have some eBay addicts at the complex who like to bid on auctions. Some of them pick up things when they time travel, rough them up a bit and then call them 'antiques' and resell them on eBay to supplement their perks. It's like a side job. Some people like online gambling or on-land casinos. They like to feel that rush. Some people like the clothing of the era they live in, and buy it. It just depends on what you want. It's just like it is in your time, except that everything you earn goes to whatever you like, instead of to bills and student loans. If you make any money on-land, you deposit it into your bank account and they convert it to perks. Or you can just spend it on-land or online."

Helen suddenly looked at the clock and sobered up. "I have work in the morning. I need to go to bed. We have to call it a night." She moved toward the door. "Are you okay to get home?"

Avid nodded and sent his travel pod pickup coordinates through his Alert screen, then received an address. He ordered an Uber on his phone and looked up.

"I know this is an imposition, but we have only eight weeks to prepare, so we have to spend as much time together as possible. Is that okay with you? Can I come back tomorrow?"

Helen threw up her hands. "Of course! Dinner at seven o'clock again? Let's plan on you coming over every night until it's over, okay? Except Wednesdays. I have a group on Wednesdays. But you can come by during the day on weekends, and we'll spend them together."

She smiled warmly. Avid knew he'd passed her tests.

"I truly had a wonderful time tonight. I'm so thrilled that I met you."

She was brimming with happiness over having something *really* important to do, new things to learn and think about, something to look forward to, and someone to spend time with. Avid was happy to see that she wasn't feeling at all depressed for the first time in four years. He could not detect any despondency or sadness at all.

Avid leaned toward her and gave her a hug. "Bon nuit, my darling," she murmured. "Good night. Now off you go!" She opened the door and nudged him out.

CHAPTER 5: APARTMENT SWAP

WEDNESDAY MARCH 17, 2021: 17:25 HOURS

Helen was busy with her grief support group this evening, so Avid was at home in the control station and relaxing with a game of chess on his Alert screen, when his doorbell rang. He got up and opened the door to find Chad standing there smiling, holding a bottle of wine and a bucket of Kentucky Fried Chicken, Original Recipe. Chad's wine was a chardonnay, thoughtfully selected to complement the poultry.

Avid looked up at Chad steadily, questioningly, without saying "Hello" or inviting him in. Finally, Chad broke the silence.

"I have a favor to ask," he said.

Avid was not surprised and waved Chad into his apartment. He sat down on the couch and motioned Chad to a teal-colored accent chair. He wasn't in the mood to entertain, but there he was, entertaining a Hero.

Chad placed the bucket of chicken on the coffee table, and then tilted the bottle of wine, resting it on his left forearm like a twentieth century French waiter, so Avid could assess its quality and vintage. It was a bottle of Trader Joe's Charles Shaw wine, 2020, a vintage that had easily aged for several months.

"They call this 'Two Buck Chuck,'" he said. "You have to try it. It's so much better than generic quick wine, and it's really cheap." He looked at Avid, relaxing on the couch. "Do you have a corkscrew?"

Avid stood up and walked to the kitchen where he opened a drawer and poked around for a corkscrew. He returned and handed the corkscrew to Chad.

"And wine glasses," Chad prompted.

Avid obediently walked back to grab two wine glasses then returned to the living room. He placed the objects on the coffee table, then sat back on the couch and let Chad open the bottle and pour the wine.

"And plates," Chad continued. "Are you hungry?"

Actually, Avid *was* hungry and the chicken smelled good. He had been a vegetarian for most of his life, but had gotten pulled in by the flavor of meat, somehow, during his various excursions to destinations where meat was the sole or primary diet. He had never tried KFC, but he'd seen the signs alongside the road and his curiosity overcame his distrust.

He stood up and fetched some plates, and cleverly grabbed a roll of paper towels before he returned, guessing correctly that Chad would have waited for him to sit down before requesting that Avid get up and fetch paper towels.

Chad, meanwhile, was unpacking a paper bag that held small tubs of mashed potatoes and gravy, coleslaw, and green beans. He unwrapped the biscuits and placed them on a paper towel. He poured the Two Buck Chuck into the wine glasses and took a sip with a satisfied sigh. He swept his hand over the feast and encouraged Avid to join him.

Avid sipped the wine and thought it was identical to quick wine, but that was fine. He would not have requested this wine and vintage himself, as he had his own favorites. However, wine was wine. You never noticed it after the second glass if you were drinking to get drunk. Avid was not certain if he was drinking to get drunk right now, but a second glass might take the edge off of this visit, so he gulped to quickly make his way through the first glass.

He still had said nothing.

Chad handed him a plastic spork.

Avid accepted the spork and examined it closely, turning it around in his hands. He took another gulp of wine. He held up the spork and looked up at Chad blankly. The spork made no sense.

Chad handed him a container of mashed potatoes and gravy, and said, "Eat." When Avid continued to look at him questioningly, Chad pointed to the spork and said, "With that thing."

"Ah," Avid answered, and pealed the lid off the container. He sampled a bite with the spork. The food was strange, but not bad. It appeared to contain ample quantities of salt. The spork appeared to work, to a degree, so he took a second bite and then raised his wine glass to his lips. By now the wine was, frankly, not too bad.

"Do you like white meat or dark meat?" Chad asked.

"It doesn't matter. It's all the same color brown," he said, observing the fried chicken. He had never tasted chicken until he was twenty-nine years old, had never ordered chicken from a restaurant or discussed chicken with anyone in his life, and when he was served chicken during his various stints throughout history its color hadn't come up in conversation. He had seen dark-colored chickens and white chickens, but had no idea what color chickens these were before they had been deep-fried and had taken up residence in a bucket. Therefore, he was noncommittal.

Chad handed Avid a leg. Avid took a bite, raised his eyebrows and chewed thoughtfully.

"Mmm," he said.

"Good, right?"

"They put too much salt on everything here. But yeah, it's really good." He ate the meat down to the bone, which he discarded on his plate. He then tipped the bucket over to select another piece. He tried a different shape this time, a fat triangle. It was a thigh. That was good too, so next he chose a smaller piece, a wing, and liked that as well. The only piece he hadn't tried was that big shapeless thing, so he picked up a breast and took a big bite. All good, he thought, as he chewed. He had no preference, and still did not understand why Chad had asked him about light and dark chicken.

"Don't forget your vegetables," Chad said encouragingly, pushing containers of coleslaw and green beans toward Avid. He poured wine into Avid's glass, and watched him grow increasingly sated from the food and mellow from the wine. He had created his own pile of chicken bones and plastic side dish containers on his plate, but was drinking his wine more slowly than Avid.

"I like these things," Avid said, biting into a biscuit. "What are they?"

"Some kind of bread, I think."

"Mmm," he said chewing. He drank a large mouthful of wine to wash it down, then placed his glass back on the coffee table. Chad added more wine to the glass as soon as Avid's hand moved away from it. The bottle was now empty.

"Quick wine?" Avid offered. He was now feeling a touch convivial, and didn't even mind having Chad there anymore. He had not forgotten about the favor Chad would ask of him, but was feeling a bit more generous and gracious than he had before the Two Buck Chuck.

The quick drink generator was a ubiquitous kitchen gadget that turned water into other organic liquids, including various types of wine, beer, fruit juices, alcoholic beverages, coffee and tea. It offered a large number of variations of each. Nobody outside of the Technology Project understood how it worked, but everybody had one, and every control station Commissary carried them in stock. It rearranged the water molecules so the resulting drinks tasted exactly like the originals.

The device warranted extensive usage when one was short on palatable things to drink, or living in a place and time where there was no ready access to palatable drinks. Historians could carry them in their pockets and pull them out anywhere, so they always had whatever they wanted to drink, provided they had a water source. They could even adjust the setting to simply have it disinfect the water, if they were uncertain about the water quality when they were on-land.

Chad nodded, so Avid went to the kitchen where he filled a pitcher of water from the tap. He fished the cigar-shaped quick drink generator from the drawer and brought both into the living room. "Any preferences?"

Chad shook his head, so Avid connected to the device from his Alert screen, selected the generic white wine and dipped the gadget into the pitcher of water, where it began to whir. The water took on a pale yellow cast, and when the gadget stopped whirring Avid withdrew it and set it on the coffee table.

You could request any vintage from a quick wine generator, but the generic version was the equivalent of a house wine. It was the selection you made when you had just become old enough to drink and didn't know what to request, just wanted to get drunk, or were already drunk and just wanted to top it off.

"Help yourself," Avid said. "I asked for generic. Let's compare. Better? Or worse?"

Chad poured wine into his glass, swished it around, then sniffed it and raised the glass to his lips.

"I think my wine is better," Chad said. They both took a sip.

"They're both the same," Avid said.

"No-oo! That can't *be*..." Chad tilted his head in surprise, consulted his Alert screen, and then laughed and read the text to Avid. Apparently the quick wine generator used the molecular structure of classic Two Buck Chuck whenever anyone requested generic wine.

That was good to know, Avid thought. He could use that as small talk during awkward conversations.

Chad still hadn't divulged what the favor was that he was going to ask of Avid, and at this point Avid no longer cared much.

"I have a favor to ask," Chad finally said. Avid nodded genially. "Can we please swap apartments?" He smiled hopefully.

"Why?"

"A woman," Chad replied, shrugging. "She's in this building. And also because another woman I would like to get away from as soon as possible is in my current building. I would be very grateful."

Avid thought for a moment, then answered, "No."

Chad was prepared for this. "You'd still be in a Hero apartment. In fact, mine is the same size as this one. It even has a hot tub."

"I have a hot tub here. I think I'll stay." The wine had made Avid brave.

Chad had a list of persuasive tactics and thus far had only used: a) charm, b) cheap wine, and c) fast food fried chicken. He was prepared to travel the distance to "f)".

"I'll give you a perk."

Avid's head shot up. "What kind of a perk?" Heroes had the very best perks of anyone, and he had always wanted to share in those experiences.

"Five-star resort in Hawaii for one week. Ocean view." Chad's face showed no emotion, and once again he was blocking any telepathic probing, but Avid had a sense that he could push this further with him. He had looked at Hawaii more than once when he cashed in273 his perks at the bank, but he had never been able to save enough. A five-star resort with an ocean view would always be beyond his reach.

"Okay. I want two weeks in that same ocean view resort, except that I also want a dinner cruise, a helicopter ride over a volcano and a parasailing ride—no two."

Chad looked thoughtful, and then sighed and said, "Fine." He pulled up his alert screen, accessed his bank account, gave the bank the list of items he wanted to withdraw, and then sent a contract to Avid. It popped up on Avid's Alert display.

Avid read through the list of perks Chad agreed to transfer to him. It appeared to be complete. He accepted the offer, signed the contract for the apartment switch and the Amendment that transferred Chad's perks over to him. He then issued his own alert to Building Maintenance to move him into Chad's apartment. Chad issued the same alert to his Building Maintenance team, in reverse.

He didn't really care that much about switching apartments. In fact, Avid felt as if he had cleverly conned Chad by making him give Avid all those extra perks. He actually liked the idea of having to walk eight hundred meters to the main building. He needed the exercise and he enjoyed the panoramic undersea view in the walk bridges. He was going to Hawaii. All in all, Avid was feeling pretty smug.

CHAPTER 6: NO PERKS FOR YOU

"What do you mean, the perks aren't valid?" Avid had been awake half the night, planning his vacation to Hawaii. By the time he had made it to the bank in the morning, his entire existence revolved around a parasailing excursion over the Pacific Ocean. No, two.

"Your first clue should have been that you didn't receive the contract from the Legal Project. He gave it to you directly, person to person, and he added a clause. Move down to the bottom right of the text." The bank representative sent an image of the contract to Avid's Alert screen, with the clause highlighted in yellow.

Avid ran his eyes down the right side of the document display until he reached the bottom.

"This agreement must be countersigned by Ajay Singh," Avid read out loud. "So, we just get Ajay Singh to sign it."

"Ajay Singh is dead. He's been dead for a while." The bank teller had a patient look about him, as if he was used to explaining simple things to people who were slow to understand. "Also, we don't accept retroactive signatures, if you wanted to go back in time and ask him to sign this contract when he was still alive. That's illegal…um…in case you were going to suggest that."

"So we get Chad to remove the clause."

"Okay," the bank representative said, still patient. "You do that. Then come back."

Avid got the distinct sense that the representative, who was telepathically blocked, was laughing at him.

"Is that all?" Avid was angry at Chad, but also angry at this man who was not being particularly helpful.

"I'm just wondering. Have you ever had any transactions with Heroes before?"

"No."

"I see," he said, nodding sagely. "No, that's all. Thank you."

Avid stared at the man, whose face had no expression, then turned and left.

CHAPTER 7: TOUR OF CHAD'S APARTMENT

FRIDAY MARCH 19, 2021: 13:32 HOURS

Avid had taken a travel pod to Chad's apartment, not only to inspect it for his upcoming move into it, but to confront him about their contract to transfer the agreed-upon perks to Avid. The visit was prearranged the previous evening, and Chad had confirmed this morning.

When Chad answered the door he was naked, and a woman behind him was throwing on a dress. She said hello to Avid, then paddled out the door barefoot and into a Historian apartment down the hall. This was apparently the woman Chad wanted Avid's apartment to escape from.

"Come in! Can I get you something to drink? Have you eaten?" Chad led him into the living room and offered him a seat. "I've been looking forward to this so much! You finally get to see my apartment—I mean your apartment."

"Weren't you expecting me?" Avid asked, looking pointedly at Chad's penis.

Chad laughed and went into the bedroom to put on some clothing. He seemed to be in a very jolly mood. Avid had no doubt that he was.

Avid momentarily wondered if the woman knew Chad was about to disappear from her life.

"Sit in this chair over here. It's more comfortable," Chad said as he came out of the bedroom. He walked over to a chair that had been transported to the mid-Atlantic control station in twenty-twenty-one from a furniture maker seven hundred years from now. The chairs had been on sale, and Chad could not resist. Plus he had the perks to pay for shipping.

The chair was heaven. Avid missed home sometimes because of things like this chair. He sank into it and closed his eyes.

"So what would you like to drink?"

Avid opened his eyes and asked for a glass of water. Chad went into the kitchen to get one. Avid closed his eyes again, then reluctantly opened them and jerked straight up, half-dozing, when Chad returned. If he leaned back into the chair again he would be unconscious in minutes.

"So, do you like the apartment?"

Avid turned his head right and left and shrugged. He got up and took a tour of the place, moving from room to room, noting the piles of clothing, empty liquor bottles, fast food containers and trash, and a bathroom that appeared to not have been cleaned in weeks or months.

"Don't you get room service?" Avid called back to Chad. "I thought everyone got room service."

"People are too nosy. Robots are too noisy and they break things." It was the "people are too nosy" statement that rang more true. Chad wanted no Maintenance Project cleaning staff poking through his things, even robots.

"Are you going to clean this place up before I move in?"

"You don't like it?" Chad asked with dismay that seemed genuine. He seemed a little distraught and embarrassed over having disappointed Avid.

Avid didn't answer. He returned to the living room and checked his water glass to see if it looked as if it had been washed. He noticed a ring of something dark in the bottom edges of the glass and put it back down.

The bank teller had explained to Avid that the portion of the agreement that covered the apartment trade was separate from the Amendment that contained the additional perks (the trip to Hawaii). The apartment trade was outlined on a standard downloadable contract that was valid unless someone tried to change the verbiage. When that happened, it required the Legal Project's blessings, and they had to be the ones to deliver it. Chad had not changed anything in the apartment trade contract, so it was valid. The problem was with the Amendment, which was also a standard downloadable contract that required the Legal Project for any changes. Chad had added the clause that required the deceased Ajay Singh's signature to make the Amendment valid, but had not run it past the Legal Project, where someone would have routinely checked to confirm Ajay Singh's current viability, or lack thereof.

So, the apartment trade agreement was binding, and the two men had to switch apartments. However, the Amendment was invalid so Avid would not receive his trip to Hawaii until Chad agreed to remove the clause and present Avid with an original and unchanged downloadable Amendment form.

Avid had just learned all of this from the bank representative, and immediately took it up with Chad.

"The bank won't honor the Amendment. Could you please redo it? It can't have that clause at the end that requires a cosigner."

Chad widened his eyes in lip-quivering dismay. He was being very genuine again.

"I'm so sorry!" he said to Avid. "I didn't have the perks in my bank account. I blew them all at Carnavale in Brazil, 1979 last month. So I asked my friend Ajay to lend me some of his until I could pay him back at the end of the month. He told me yes, but he has to co-sign in order for the bank to pull the perks from his account and put them into mine. Simple. Just contact him and get him to sign it. I've done this before. The Legal Project lets it go through if the co-signer signs."

"Ajay is dead."

"No he isn't! I just saw him last month in Mexico, 1910 before I came here!"

"You apparently saw a younger version of him. He was probably assigned there years ago, but you just saw him there last month when your visits intersected." Avid gave Chad a headshake. "You do know how this works, right? He's legally dead. If you'd done this correctly through the Legal Project they would have told you that."

Avid's indignant tone of exasperated affront came from his having just learned all this himself.

A time traveler could not enter into a valid contract while dead. In fact, all parties to any contract had to be alive at the time of signing. All contract dates were based on the common date in the twenty-eighth century when the Legal Project recorded the signatures, regardless of the continuum time period during which the contract was signed.

The same was true with death dates. The Legal Project used the twenty-eighth century common date to record a death, regardless of the historical year the person was living in at the time of death. If you visited a time and place where the soon-to-be-deceased had been prior to dying and you encountered that person there, that still-alive "deceased" person might be willing to enter into a contract with you, but legally could not if the legal signature date occurred after the twenty-eighth century death date.

This law prevented exploitation of the soon-to-be deceased by the people who outlived them, and it protected the rights of their heirs. The Mitigators had had compelling reasons to draw up this law which was, interestingly, inspired by Heroes.

"I asked the wrong version of Ajay..." Chad slapped his forehead. "Gah! I'm such a dumb ass." He looked at Avid confused. "But how do you ask someone if he's dead? How would he even know?"

"The Legal Project tells you."

Chad had no response, and no reaction.

Furthermore, Avid had a counter argument. He had just requested an image of Ajay Singh on his Alert screen.

"Say you are a dumb ass and don't know how to obtain a legal contract. Let's think about the facts. How was a member of the Indian Dynasty ever sent to Mexico? Ajay didn't look Mexican."

"He was doing support in the control station, monitoring the situation on the scanner and sending instructions."

That was a slick answer. Avid wouldn't be likely to know if Heroes from Race Dynasties were sent to locations that were inappropriate for them. Avid didn't know anything about Hero assignments, so he couldn't say it was a lie. If it was, it was well-played.

He also didn't know if Mexico, 1910 was Chad's previous assignment before he arrived here last month. It was also unlikely that a Caucasian Dynasty Hero would be dispatched to Mexico, but realistically there might have been some Caucasians who participated in the Mexican Revolution because the United States was right across the border. He just didn't know for certain. It seemed suspicious to Avid, but not enough to entirely discount Chad's claim. Finally, he didn't know if Chad was really broke or not.

Was Chad a dumb ass? Or had he deliberately cheated Avid out of the promised perks?

"Can you wait until Tuesday? It's just a few days. Then I get paid and I can rewrite the Amendment."

"Tuesday. Then I report you." Avid was stern. Pressure might be the only way he could squeeze those perks out of Chad.

"I promise. Tuesday." Chad smiled charmingly. "I promise," he repeated reassuringly. "Really."

"Fine," Avid said, and got up to leave. "What day do we make the apartment switch?"

"Monday," Chad replied.

The score was: Chad 1, Avid 0.

Avid later conducted some research just to make certain he could not obtain a signature, and found that Ajay Singh had primarily focused on assignments in ancient India, and took only a few vacation side trips to the twentieth century. Mexico, 1910 was not in his travel history (neither was it in Chad's travel history). Ajay died on a common date in the twenty-eighth century seven years ago. Ajay was definitely dead for Avid's purposes, and Chad was most definitely a liar.

The score was: Chad for the win.

CHAPTER 8: DATE OF DEATH LAW

After returning home and conducting his research on Ajay, Avid also researched the Historian Date of Death law, completely misunderstand it, and thus concluded that the Amendment was still valid without Ajay's signature.

He went to the Bank and presented his discovery and his conclusions to the same bank representative to whom he had spoken earlier.

"The Amendment you signed is strictly for transferring perks from one person's account to another. It's a standard boilerplate contract, and it's valid unless one of the parties makes any changes to the wording, which means Legal needs to be involved, which they were not. In addition, it requires a counter signature from someone who is deceased and cannot sign. We have two issues here. That addition of a countersignature makes the Amendment invalid for starters. Read the disclaimer."

He sent the contract to Avid's Alert screen with the wording highlighted in yellow.

"Since one of the parties is deceased, the entire Amendment is even *more* void than it was with just the added clause. The contract is voider than void. *Really* void."

Avid was crestfallen.

"And after all this time, anything Ajay had in his account would have been disbursed to his heirs, so there wouldn't be anything left in there anyway."

Avid looked at him, sadly hopeless.

"Didn't Chad agree to a new contract when you asked him?" He asked this with a straight face.

Avid, again, got the distinct impression that the bank agent was inwardly laughing at him.

"He said he's broke, but he gets paid on Tuesday. He'll transfer the perks to me then."

"Ah!" the bank representative said brightly. "Then all is most certainly well with you. Congratulations!" He smiled a winning smile. "I'll see you back here on Tuesday when you come to cash in."

Avid left uncomfortably certain that the bank representative was mocking him.

"See you Tuesday!" the man called after him with a wide smile, waving. "Have a nice day!"

CHAPTER 9: PRESCHOOL LEVEL TELEPATHY

"The problem is that they've been using genetic manipulation for hundreds of years to enhance the part of the brain that controls telepathy," Avid told Helen. "Your brain doesn't have those genetic enhancements, so I'm trying to figure out where to begin and what direction to take. They told me you can't learn to read minds, remember? That doesn't leave me a lot to work with."

They were sitting on Helen's couch about to commence with her first telepathy lesson.

From what Avid had learned in school, innate telepathic ability was present and in use among early hominids, but it had been mostly dormant since the arrival of spoken language in homo sapiens. The segment of the brain that controlled telepathy could be activated and nurtured in virtually everyone. However, the resulting telepathic functionality was usually very weak without genetic enhancement. You might be able to pick up extreme messages, such as that a loved one was in trouble or hurt, but you would not be able to read the actual words floating through someone's mind, or would only catch fragments. There were some here who had skills that were better than that, but they were rare. Avid doubted anyone in the twenty-first century had been born capable of achieving his skill level. It had taken him hard work and long years. Too much personal effort and genetic intervention had gone into it for it to randomly occur in nature, he thought.

Avid was frowning. Helen could learn something, he knew, or he wouldn't have been sent to teach her. But what she could learn would only involve emotions, not thoughts. That's what they'd told him. They didn't have "emotion" classes where he came from, they had telepathy classes. Consequently he could not recreate any lessons for her, and he had no idea how to construct a lesson plan with nothing to refer to.

But there obviously must be another segment in the brain that enabled people to connect to one another on an emotional level. Avid guessed that honing in on, and activating the segment of the brain that controlled emotional connections might involve the same kind of effort he'd made when he was learning Advanced Telepathy.

In Avid's time, the brain was mapped out, so they had a clear idea of which segments of the brain controlled which various functions. They'd used a twenty-eighth century version of biofeedback in his Advanced Telepathy courses to teach students to mentally locate, identify, activate, and improve the function of the various brain sections that controlled or supported telepathy. It made sense that he should begin with biofeedback. Maybe the Mitigators could provide some guidance on that, he thought. Perhaps they could arrange for him to meet with an Educator who taught Advanced Telepathy to discuss what Avid needed to do.

The Mitigator-on-duty telepathically heard Avid, who was deliberately unblocked to invite their input while he mulled over his options, and immediately sent an appointment to his Alert screen. Tomorrow he would travel to the twenty-eighth century to meet with an Educator who would give him a crash course in biofeedback, from an instructor's perspective. He could receive that training for as long as took him to become proficient. Then he would return here, the same day he left. He would lose no twenty-first century time, but would have the near-professional ability to guide Helen with biofeedback in just a day or two, from her perspective. He relaxed. They had a plan!

Helen gave him an exaggeratedly wheedling look.

"Can I please learn how to *sort* of read minds, just a *little* bit? Is there any way *at all?*" If they handed her a list of superpowers, such as flying, being invisible or reading minds, and had told her she could only pick one, she would choose "reading minds" one hundred percent of the time. This was a once in a lifetime opportunity for her.

"I'm working on it." Avid said to Helen. He had an appointment for tomorrow and a plan, but what could he do right now?

An Alert displayed a scanner clip of a preschool classroom full of tiny children, all of them about three years old.

"Thank you!" Avid said out loud. The image flickered off and then on again to acknowledge his thanks.

Helen knew by now that Avid was talking to the Mitigator-on-duty and was looking at something on his screen. She picked up a nail file and worked on a nail to keep herself occupied while Avid watched the clip.

In the clip, an Educator stood in front of about ten children sitting in a half-circle on the floor and raised her hand. "How many of us love Mommy?" She asked.

All the children raised their hands as high as they could reach.

"Very good! We all love our mommies. And how do we feel when we love Mommy? Does it feel good?"

The children all bobbed their heads up and down.

The Educator pointed to a little boy. "If you close your eyes and think about Mommy, does she feel a certain way to you? Is there anything about the way she feels to you that is just Mommy and nobody else?"

The little boy closed his eyes and thought about Mommy while the other children watched. He nodded his head.

"The way she feels is different from the way Daddy feels to you, or Grandma or Grandpa, isn't it? She feels like Mommy and nobody else."

The little boy nodded.

She pointed to a little girl.

"You have two mommies, but they feel different from each other, don't they? Mommy feels different from Mama, doesn't she? So, it isn't being your mother that makes your Mommy feel the way she does to you. She feels the way she does because she is a person. Every person feels a special way to other people, even you."

The little girl grinned and twisted around to see if everyone noticed how the teacher was talking just to her.

"Other people know you from the special way you feel to them when they think about you, and it's different from what they feel when they think about any other person in the world! It's you! That's what they feel. You!"

The Educator looked around the room.

"I want you to all think about Mommy. This is just practice. We're going to practice giving Mommy a big heart hug. When we learn how, we're going to surprise her, aren't we?"

The children all nodded.

"Will your heart hug make her happy or sad?"

"Happy!" all the children cried out.

One little boy yelled "So happy!" and rolled on his back giggling.

"So happy!" Several other children yelled in response, also giggling, also rolling on their backs.

"Why will it make her happy?" She pointed to a little girl.

"Because it feels good."

"It feels good! It feels like love, doesn't it? Do you know why? Because it is love! And love feels good!"

She walked behind the children and lightly ran her fingers over all the little heads in turn. Then she returned to the front of the class.

"We've all had heart hugs, haven't we?" The children all nodded. "Sometimes *I* give you heart hugs. I gave heart hugs to some of you today. Did any of you ever notice?"

Several children raised their hands. She turned to a child who hadn't raised his hand. "What if I were to give you a heart hug right now? Would you like that?"

The child nodded.

"Okay, get ready for your heart hug!" She focused on the little boy and telepathically pushed her love into him. He squirmed and giggled.

"Did you feel that?"

He nodded, grinning.

"Me too! Me too!" The teacher went around the room and gave each child a heart hug. Afterward they all stood up and scrambled over to her laughing, and threw their arms around her neck, pressing their cheeks against whatever part of her they could reach. She was draped in little children. She wrapped her arms around children for a minute, as far as she could stretch. Then she asked them all to sit still on the floor again.

"Think about how a heart hug feels to you. Mommy gives you heart hugs, doesn't she? That's how she tells you she loves you. Anyone can give anyone a heart hug, though, and you can give a heart hug to anyone you want, but first we need to learn how to give Mommy a heart hug. She gets the very first one, okay?"

"Then Daddy?" A little girl asked.

"Yes. Then Daddy. Then anyone you want, even me!"

She pointed to a little boy. "When is a good time to give a heart hug to someone?"

"When they're sad," he said.

"That's right! Anyone else?"

"When they're scared!"

"When they're hurt!"

"You're all right! We give heart hugs to people when they're sad or scared or hurt. We also give heart hugs when they're happy, so they know that we're happy that they're happy! We can even give heart hugs to people who are lonely so they know they aren't really alone."

She walked around the room again while the children's eyes followed her.

"We can even do it with strangers too, if we feel sad for them. That's harder, so we'll learn that last, but it's very important. It makes them happy for a minute, doesn't it? You can make sad people happy even though you don't even know them, just by giving them a heart hug! You'll do a lot of that, once you learn how, won't you? That's right. We'll all do that every day for someone who's sad."

There was more to the scanner clip, but Avid had seen enough. He had watched the Educator, refreshed his memory on what he had learned from her and how, and knew what to do now. He closed the image.

The higher Helen was on the empath spectrum, the more easily she would be able to learn to do this, so that was still a variable he had to address, but he had hope. The Mitigators had assigned Helen to the Anomaly recovery effort. She had to have the capacity, at the very least, to learn to send heart hugs. Otherwise, they would have either chosen somebody else or simply guided Avid to take a different approach. He had no idea where Helen placed on the empathy scale, but she was the person the Mitigators had given him to work with, and he trusted them.

"Okay, I'm ready," he told Helen. She was very eager, and looked up with a smile.

"I feel a little stupid for not thinking of this immediately. It was just so long ago, I guess. We're going to start with heart hugs. They're really basic. They're the first thing they teach us in school."

"What's a heart hug?" She asked. Then her expression grew solemn. "That's what you did the other night, wasn't it?"

Avid knew that she had been deeply impacted by it—in a good way—but she wasn't ready to talk about it.

Avid nodded. "A heart hug directly connects you to someone else on an emotional level. It's basic maintenance in my time, like food and water. If you don't connect enough on an emotional level with anyone you can get angry, anxious, depressed, violent in some cases, physically ill, or you can die prematurely. It's a primal need. In fact, nobody in my time would ever have allowed you to go on this way for as long as you have, any more than they would have let you starve." He sounded indignant. "Any one of us would have stepped in to prop you up at any time, if we saw that you needed it. I'm so sorry."

Helen was reacting with shame and embarrassment for having been needy. It was not Avid's intention to make her feel ashamed, and it saddened him.

She was like a desert, Avid thought. That's what happens to most people here, isn't it? That's what happens when you haven't connected with anyone for so long that even love hurts. He didn't like this time and place. It was one of the worst he'd seen for human connection.

Helen sighed and looked down at her nails.

Avid had pondered that situation for the entire time he had been here. In earlier times, even in the most brutal, barbaric times, there was community support and connection. But here, people had to carry so much alone without any help or backup. Families split apart and lived in different houses, different towns, different countries. Neighbors never spoke, and didn't even know each other's names. People primarily kept track of one another on Internet social media sites, where people anonymously trolled one other cruelly and mercilessly, or on their phones (even as they were sitting across from other people, whom they ignored), and they had little or no personal face-to-face interaction. This wasn't even entirely due to the pandemic lockdown. It was systemic to the culture, and only getting worse.

Religions were supposed to fill the void, but some demanded that you think a certain way or be a certain thing, like heterosexual for instance, or they rejected and ejected you. In fact, the trend in this era was to leave religion altogether and be "unaffiliated," so growing masses of people were losing that fellowship, and had nothing to replace it.

It was all so disgraceful, that so many of the people here were walking wounded who committed crimes, committed suicide, got ill, were hurtful toward others, or died prematurely without any intervention at all. This society even begrudged some people food, shelter, and medical treatment. But there was nothing he could do about it. He couldn't even give a homeless person a heart hug because it could impact the continuum. Of all the things he'd seen, that was the one thing that haunted him the most.

"What's a gutter ball?" Avid was reading from his screen. "The Mitigator-on-duty is saying that there are too many gutter balls in this time and place, and that your society just lets them fall to the wayside, and it isn't right."

Mitigators did not normally engage in small talk in situations like this, nor did they inject their commentary into interactions they were only supposed to observe. They normally employed Vendi, or someone on her team, to conduct personal conversations. Otherwise, they sent anonymous, distant, emotionally-detached instructions for everything else, and only did that when absolutely necessary. This Mitigator must be personally distressed to have said this directly to Avid on his Alert screen. He apparently wasn't the only one reacting to this time and place.

Helen looked at the ceiling. Avid knew that the gutter ball reference had meaning for her, and that she was holding back tears.

"You can't fix the gutter balls with the tools they gave you," Avid said. "You can't fix them when you're a gutter ball yourself. You want to give up sometimes." He was reading Helen's mind, and those were her thoughts.

Helen looked at him sharply.

"But you keep trying." Avid said to her gently. "I love that you do that, Helen." His Alert screen flashed. It was another message from the Mitigator-on-duty. Avid read the message.

"The Mitigators want you to know that they've been monitoring you too, this whole time." Avid gave Helen a sheepish grimace. "Sorry about that. But they think that you're magic with your grief support group—that's the word they used, 'magic'—and they all want to tell you how much they really appreciate you."

Helen's face changed.

"Chinatsu is the Mitigator who just sent you that heart hug."

Helen laughed with tears in her eyes. "Love you, Chinatsu!" she shouted. "So I just got a heart hug from the historical equivalent of Joe Biden, right?"

"Yeah."

"Can we pretend it's the historical equivalent of Justin Trudeau?"

Avid laughed. Helen wiped her eyes and was herself again.

"So, let's get started, okay?" Avid adjusted himself in his seat to face her.

"What were you watching on your screen just now?"

"They pulled a scanner clip of my first day of school when I was three years old, and they played it for me. They teach you about heart hugs on your first day, and they work with you until you can do them without help. The Mitigators were just reminding me to begin at the beginning. I'll explain everything to you, and then we'll start working with biofeedback until you're ready to fly on your own. You should pick it up pretty quickly, I'm thinking."

Helen sat with rapt expectation.

"So let's begin at the beginning," Avid said.

Helen nodded.

"Do you remember when your son and your husband first died, and you felt them around you?" Avid didn't know that she had specifically experienced this, but he knew that everyone else did.

Helen looked alarmed. She'd never told anyone about that.

"That was really them. When people die, they surround their loved ones with their energy and embrace them. It happens with almost everyone. Don't look so surprised. It's more common than dirt. That's an expression, right? "

Helen didn't answer.

"And you knew it was them because there's a part of your brain that recognized their energy." He interrupted himself. "Do you know what a barcode is? I don't know what that means, but it's on my screen. Thank you! It's says everyone has an individual barcode, and when you sense a person's energy your brain reads that barcode, the same way it recognizes a smell and then ties that smell to a memory. Whenever you feel that specific sensation, you associate it with a specific person the same way a smell brings back a memory. You know exactly how they felt to you, so you know exactly who that person is, without guessing. You just *know*, like you knew it was your husband and your son. It's a kind of telepathy, but it's so basic to your emotions, and so universal, that you don't usually need to learn how to use it. You already have it. Everyone does, I think."

Helen's eyes were wide.

"Our consciousness is energy, and physics teaches us that energy can't be destroyed, it can only change forms, so the person you're sensing can be alive or dead. You can sense their energy either way. But I want you to just focus on how to deliberately tune into it. Think how it felt when you felt your family. You'll feel something like that now, but different because you're going to tune into my barcode, not theirs. We're going to have you start with me. Poke around in your head until you sense something that you know is me."

Helen looked at him a little warily.

"If you were to close your eyes and think of me, do you sense something that's only me and nobody else?"

Helen closed her eyes. After a few moments, she nodded.

"Okay. Now keep focusing on that. Don't let go of it. Wait until I tell you to stop."

He let her sit there for two or three minutes and monitored how well she was tuning in to him. It came and went, but it was actually a pretty good first effort. Her empathy ranking must be above average, he thought, because he was essentially a stranger to her, but she still pulled it off.

"Now let go."

Helen opened her eyes.

"This connection happens a lot when you fall in love with someone. That's the best example I can give you. You just want to crawl inside of that person, so you poke around with your heart until you feel them on that level. Remember how it felt with your husband."

"You don't have to be in love to do this, though, right?"

"You don't even have to be in like. It can be a total stranger. It's just an action, like opening a door. But if you think about being in love, it brings you closer to understanding what I'm trying to teach you to recognize."

Helen looked thoughtful and determined.

"After you connect, you focus on feeling love for the person. It can be completely impersonal love. Or call it empathy. We all have the capacity to love and connect to every other energy, so you can do this with anyone. Then you rev up that energy connection that you're feeling, and you push that love in their direction, toward *their* energy. They feel it. It's nice, and it helps them."

Helen's wheels were spinning. Her first thought was of her clients . She was anxious to get to the point where she could do this to anyone at all, even someone she didn't know well, or at all.

"Is this part of psychotherapy where you come from?" she asked.

"Yeah. It goes a little further than that, but yeah. Emotional connection is the foundation of psychotherapy, in fact." Avid was pleased that he actually had some experience with this. "I took a few psychology courses in school, so I can kind of explain the process to you."

"How is that different from psychotherapy here? Other than heart hugs, I mean. How does it work?"

Avid didn't know how to approach the subject delicately. Psychotherapy was in its very early infancy in this time and place, and it really wasn't as effective as it needed to be, no matter how skilled or well-meaning a therapist was. Only about seventy-five percent of people in therapy showed any improvement, while the rest of the patients remained gutter balls. That percentage would be completely unacceptable in his world.

Here, people received treatment that involved talking about emotions while the therapist retained a detached distance and dissected their psyche and gave instructions on how to think or behave, or it relied on drugs to numb you or adjust your brain chemistry. It worked to some degree, but wasn't one hundred percent effective one hundred percent of the time, and patients had to deal with the side effects of drugs. It was too inexact and experimental. He didn't want to insult Helen by disparaging her life's work, but it all made him sad.

On the other hand, her own thoughts had been "can't do this with the tools they gave me," so she was aware of its limitations.

In Avid's time, Educators had also used the biofeedback technique to teach student psychotherapists how to control their access to the Portal, so they could channel their therapy readings from the Collective Consciousness. He had had a few lessons, so he wasn't completely unprepared and could even do it himself, to a limited degree. Could he possibly learn enough from his upcoming training to show Helen how to do this? Was she capable of learning any level of twenty-eighth century psychotherapy?

"I'll show you. Give me your hands." Avid held his hands out, and Helen placed her hands in his. "Don't say anything. I do all the talking until I tell you."

Avid energized the telepathic part of his brain that dealt with emotion and locked eyes with Helen, but his eyes were slightly unfocused. Yet they were "seeing" at the same time, Helen noticed. They bore straight into her but it wasn't frightening, and she didn't feel exposed. It felt as if someone had shown up with water when she was dying of thirst. She stared back, hypnotized.

He began his probe, which did not involve mindreading at all. He could not hear her thoughts because he was channeling her emotions. At the root of it, his world's psychotherapy was primal and visceral, not intellectual. He gently probed her to locate the sore spots. He knew they were there, and he knew what they were because he knew Helen, but a trained therapist could do this without knowing anything about a person. Avid had just enough training so that this type of probe was giving him all the additional information about Helen that he needed to help her.

Anyone hearing a "therapy conversation" would never be able to follow it, and it only made complete sense to the patient. Sometimes even the therapist didn't understand, but the patient always did. As Avid spoke out loud, he also used telepathy to send the words straight into Helen so she couldn't dismiss them or misunderstand them. This boosted his words and give them more power. He was speaking to her both verbally and mentally. Then he tapped into the Collective Consciousness through the portion of his brain that had access to it, and began to channel the words in the same way artists and musicians channel their creative inspiration. It all came from the same Source. When the compulsion to speak overcame him, he began. The words came *through* him, not *from* him.

"It wasn't your fault, and it wasn't your failing," Avid said. "It had nothing to do with you." He was probing the painful spot that involved her son's suicide." He gently applied salve to that wound, deliberately aiming love directly toward her pain. "The problem is that there's a distance between a child and a parent. A parent can't bridge that gap. There are always things your children can't tell you, and things you can't do to help and protect them, even if you spend your life helping and protecting everyone else, and even if you've saved other people from the same threats that your children are facing.

"Children always pull back and hide a part of themselves from their parents to protect their parents and themselves. Shame, sometimes. Shame most of the time. It doesn't matter how desperate the situation is because a parent can't ever access that gap. It's a chasm that separates the two of you from where you still meet, to where the child is after pulling away. This was a situation where he had to find someone else who could reach into that gap and help him, and he happened to not ever find that person. That was the tragedy, not what you did or didn't do. We need to mourn the fact that he was lost and no one ever found him in that gap you couldn't access. It was never your failure."

Helen's eyes widened. Avid had never seen her look so completely vulnerable.

"And you didn't fail your husband. You didn't kill him. You certainly didn't kill him with anything you failed to do to save your son. Whether or not he died of grief or shock—and we don't know, do we?—it wasn't you. It might have been in the cards for him to die when he did all along, even if your son had lived. If not, blame that gap and its consequences, not yourself." Avid applied salve to that wound, focusing on her husband a little longer."

Helen interrupted. "I feel my husband right now."

"He agrees," Avid said. "Listen to him. Let it go."

He continued to telepathically apply love to the wounds. Helen continued to stare at him with vulnerable, helpless eyes.

"What happened to you was preparation, not punishment. You apparently have some really important work to do that you could only do after experiencing that level of grief. The Universe doles things out with purpose. Always remember that.

The words had stopped coming, so the session was complete. Avid was now speaking as himself.

"A Mitigator told you that they all admire the way you manage your grief support group. Remember? How effective would you really be if you hadn't had your experiences? And you got a compliment from a *Mitigator*. I know you have no idea what that means, but in my world you'd have bragging rights for the rest of your life. You need to feel so proud of the way you're helping people. Really. You need to feel so proud."

Avid let go of her hands. Helen's hands remained mid-air as if she wasn't prepared to let him go yet. Her eyes were almost pleading, and they were brimming with tears. It had been the most profound experience of her life, and she felt lighter now.

"Holy shit," she breathed. "How in the hell did you do that?"

"Are you okay?"

"Holy shit. Wow. Oh my God."

"Really, are you okay?"

"I'm wonderful." She leaned over to hug him. "Thank you, my dear friend. Thank you. Thank you. Thank you." She released Avid and leaned back into the couch. "I have to learn how to do that. I have so many questions."

"Sure. We can go over it."

"I didn't say a word. I never said anything. It was all you."

"That's how it works."

"But I never told you any of those things that you knew."

"I knew about your husband and son. They told me in your bio."

"But you didn't know how I felt about it."

"When you probe someone, it's right there. I feel what you feel, and that's what I felt, so that's why I said whatever I said. It's not magic. It's brain wiring and practice, with a little bit of assistance from the Universe. You can learn it too. I *think* you can. I'm pretty sure you can. We'll see."

She looked into the distance. "Wow. Psychotherapy comes a long way, doesn't it?"

"It has its own Project in my time. People devote their lives to fine-tuning it, and real psychotherapists are much more skilled than I was just now."

Avid heard her wondering if she could ever meet a psychotherapist from his time and have a discussion. And a session. She would love to do this again.

"The Mitigators require this for everyone so we don't become gutter balls." Avid said. Whatever *that* was. He still didn't know. He made a quick Alert screen request for a definition of gutter ball. "We all get periodically fine-tuned with booster sessions because it's mandatory. But we don't need many sessions to get through actual problems. Sometimes people only need just one."

Helen turned her head toward Avid. "I can totally see that. Wow."

"I was talking to you telepathically at the same time I was talking verbally. Did you notice? That would be how we do it. You might not be able to learn to speak telepathically because I don't think I can teach you that. You'll just connect emotionally and push love into the person while you describe what you sense from them. That's really basic, but it works in a pinch."

"Stereo. You were speaking in stereo. Very cool." Helen threw her head back and laughed, excited.

"We'll practice it every day. We'll use biofeedback so you can learn where the brain sections are and activate them at will, and then practice your aim. Okay? But enough for now. I'll order an Uber and let you settle in for the night."

Avid returned to the control station, where he then gathered some personal belongings before traveling to the twenty-eighth century Main Headquarters control station. He spent the next four weeks in training, learning how to teach Helen to give heart hugs and therapy so she could possibly conduct her own twenty-eighth century psychotherapy sessions on Max.

When his training was complete, he returned to Helen's the day after he had left, and then began to teach her.

CHAPTER 10: NECTAR DRIVES A CAR

Nectar and Janicyl had met with Chad and Dirk in the morning for introductions, and they were all about to explore Washington, D.C., 2021. Nectar had been assigned to Dirk as his driver, so she was going to drive the Range Rover, which was large enough for all of them to travel together.

The last vehicle she had driven was a 1962 Nash Rambler convertible stick shift, with controls that included an AM radio, a cigarette lighter and ashtray, and a knob you turned right and left to control the heat.

The Range Rover presented her with some challenges. Even getting into the locked car with keyless entry had left her stumped for several moments as she tried to figure out how to insert the key fob into the door. The fob had buttons, so she pressed them. This made the car beep once, then beep twice. Finally she pressed the button that triggered a shrieking alarm that startled her and made everyone jump.

Her Alert screen came to the rescue. The first order of business was to press the alarm button again to stop the noise. She did that. The second order of business was to press the button that unlocked the door, and then open it. She did that too.

They all climbed into the car, Janicyl and Dirk in the back, with Chad sitting next to Nectar in the front. Their Alert Screens displayed, instructing them to fasten their seatbelts, with a video demonstrating how. They all complied.

Next Nectar was confronted with the steering column and the dashboard, neither of which had a place for her to insert that key fob. She pushed the buttons again, avoiding the one that screeched, because one of them had worked before. However, they did not work this time. She was stumped until her Alert screen automatically displayed a video of how to turn on the car and use the controls, and how to shift it into gear and back it out of its parking spot. Nectar had to turn her Alert screen on "audio" in order to receive instructions without having to read them as she gingerly backed the car out of Dirk's condo parking spot, then crawled through the garage and slowly turned right to ease out onto the road. She proceeded at a brisk fifteen miles an hour, determined to drive straight until infinity so she would never have to navigate any turns, because they were far too complicated in this traffic.

She wasn't afraid, exactly. She was primarily trying to avoid wrecking the car and appearing to be incompetent. Life was not worth living unless your associates feared and respected you.

The graphic-heavy control panel distracted, confused, and annoyed her. She ignored it for now and followed her Alert screen instructions. So far so good. Growing in confidence, she pressed down on the gas pedal until her speed reached twenty-five miles per hour. Gradually she worked her way up to forty miles per hour. She might even make a turn, just to try it out, she thought.

Meanwhile, the three other Heroes created distractions with their animated conversation, and as a result Nectar had several near misses.

She finally pulled over and hit the brakes.

"Shut up all of you, or get out," she said ominously. Her words held power for a small, curly-haired blonde person dressed in a long, floral Stella McCartney maxi-dress hiked up to her knees so it didn't interfere with the gas pedal, which she was able to reach only after she had pulled the seat all the way forward with help from her Alert screen. Everyone took note and shut up. Nectar pulled away and continued to drive in somber silence, gripping the wheel with both hands, bracing for the left turn she saw coming up on her dashboard GPS screen, which was creating even more confusing challenges.

The Language Team had adjusted their language settings so that all four Heroes could communicate in both English and Hinduese. This way they could freely communicate with each other in Hinduese without the subjects understanding what they were saying. Hinduese was going to be safe in their limited assignment circle and was preferable in this situation because it didn't have the shock value of the language Historians were now forced to speak on-land to make them keep their mouths shut. The Mitigators made this exception just for the Heroes in this assignment because of that 9-1-1 call by that well-meaning bystander.

They had intended to enjoy a very expensive dinner at a restaurant, to discuss the upcoming plans to meet with the subjects on Tuesday. Then they planned to enjoy a night at the clubs. However, once the Heroes received Nectar's permission to speak, they each consulted Yelp on their smart phones and conveyed to each other that most of the restaurants were only offering carryout, while most of the clubs were closed because of the COVID shutdown. So they placed an order for carryout at the restaurant that appeared to be the priciest, picked it up, then visited a liquor store and purchased copious amounts of liquor. They then went to Dirk's on-land apartment, where they enjoyed their luxury carryout meal, and drank to excess.

Nectar had already played with the scented bidet (she loved antiques) and was excited about the forty thousand dollar antique light-show shower fixture after Dirk gave the ladies a tour, so she accepted Dirk's offer that she experience it herself. While she was showering amid the light show, Dirk decided to experience it with her, so the two of them were doing that. Chad and Janicyl sat in the living room smoking weed and drinking, and playing Grand Theft Auto on Dirk's ninety-eight-inch television screen. Shouts and whoops came from both rooms.

A short time later, Dirk returned in a towel to watch Chad and Janicyl blow up shop clerks and bomb civilians from airplanes, without mentioning Nectar who was drying her hair and getting dressed in his luxurious bathroom. When she returned to the living room she barked at Dirk to put on some clothes and stay the hell away from her. Then she sat with her back turned to him and watched something on her Alert screen.

At about twenty-one-hundred hours Chad remembered that he had to switch apartments in the morning, so he ordered pickup coordinates for the women and himself to return to the control station. Dirk remained behind, but would regret that later when everyone else reported back to him about the party. The three Heroes traveled home together in a travel pod with eleven full boxes containing the bottles of liquor and wine they had purchased earlier.

Upon arriving at the control station, they all went to Chad's apartment, wheeling the boxes of liquor on a momentarily unattended push-truck they found near the entrance to the building's commissary. They left it in the hallway outside Chad's apartment instead of returning it. The individual who was using it came back to find it mysteriously gone, and searched for it fruitlessly.

The three of them had some more to drink, and passed a smoking bong amongst themselves while Chad thought about what he needed to do, to prepare for his move in the morning. The marijuana was eroding his motivation to prepare, but the liquor demanded action, so he invited forty-three other Heroes to join them.

They all came, and some brought friends.

At some point the party got out of control. It perhaps began with the couch fire, which erupted when someone dropped a lit joint between the cushions. As the smoke billowed higher, the sprinkler system doused everyone and soaked the carpet. The water stopped when the fire was out, but everyone was wet now. Some of the people felt chilly and had begun taking off their wet shirts to get warmer. At this point, Chad pumped the music up. Everyone found naked musicality to be very festive, so the other attendees began to strip, and some of them stripped naked. There was now a pile of wet clothing in the corner of the living room. After Chad raised the volume even higher, the attendees began to dance maniacally with drinks and joints in hand.

Inspired by the sprinkler system, Janicyl found a bottle of champagne in Chad's kitchen and shook it, then popped the cork and aimed it at the partygoers. What a good idea, the others thought, and raided Chad's stash of champagne to spray the walls and each other.

Having used up the champagne but still feeling inspired, they broke into Chad's supply of red wine and poured it on each other, the walls, and the carpet. When that ran out, they created quick wine, and used that.

Feeling nostalgic for the couch fire, and wanting to see the sprinkler system go off again, one Hero set fire to the drapes, thus prompting the sprinkler system to reenact its earlier life-saving efforts. The cold shower began again. The attendees laughed and danced with more fervor. The carpet was nearly liquid. But fortunately the fire was out again.

Chad concluded that you could hardly see the heavy smoke stains on three walls in the living room, or the fingers of smoke that spread into the hallway and the bedrooms. Avid would never notice. If he did, the apartment wasn't Chad's problem anymore.

And so the party continued until nearly dawn, at which point Chad sent everyone away and grabbed a quick hour-long nap in the driest bedroom before preparing for his move. When he awoke, he packed his clothing and his personal belongings. His liquor was gone now and the empty bottles were scattered throughout the apartment, so his load was light.

Next, he reminded the maintenance team that he needed Avid's old apartment to be redecorated with all new furniture suitable for a Hero, instead of moving any of the furniture from here, except for his twenty-eighth century chair, which he was keeping, and wanted moved, as per his earlier move request. He was assured that they would make the change tomorrow.

He added, finally, that he wanted his twenty-eighth century chair cleaned before they moved it to his new apartment. Then he left.

CHAPTER 11: THE MORNING AFTER

Chad was not in the complex, or anywhere to be found. He had completely disappeared after leaving his apartment for Avid to clean up, so Avid could not confront him about the perks Chad owed him. There was too much on Avid's mind right now anyway.

He had reported the issue, and was waiting for the maintenance team to prepare his temporary apartment, where he would stay until they had cleaned and refurnished this one. He had brought his personal belongings, but found it necessary to leave them with a friend because there was nowhere dry to set everything down.

He looked around his new apartment in despair. He found a merely-damp corner in one of the extra bedrooms, curled into the fetal position, and stared at the splattered wall. The place smelled like sour wine, smoke and wet carpet, with the lingering essence of cannabis. All of Chad's original garbage and dirty dishes remained where they had been when Avid had first visited, except that the fast food containers were now disintegrating into the wet carpet, while more recently-used red plastic Solo cups seemed to be abandoned on every flat surface. There were empty liquor bottles everywhere. The hall bathroom was even more disgusting than it had been earlier, as someone at last evening's party had vomited in the bathtub without cleaning it up.

There, inexplicably, was a pile of wet clothing on the living room floor. It did not appear to be Chad's because the sizes varied and the clothing styles applied to persons of both genders. Avid correctly deduced that a number of wet people had stripped out of their clothing and then pranced home naked.

He had closed his eyes and pressed his temples, and was pondering his pointless life when his Alert screen flashed green. It read, "Happy Tuesday! You're going to Hawaii! Come back to the bank for your perks!"

This managed to bring some hope and solace to Avid, who immediately pulled himself into an upright seated position. Then he stood up and jogged through the hallways of the building to the travel pod garage with his wet shoes squeaking each time they hit the ground. He climbed into a pod and instructed it to take him to the main building, where he jogged, still squeaking, from the garage to the bank.

His bank representative was waiting for him, grinning. Several other people were gathered around him, smiling broadly, all looking at Avid as if it were his birthday.

Avid waited for someone to say something because he was thoroughly confused. A woman called out, "Aloha!!" Everyone laughed. Were they laughing at him? It was hard to tell.

His smiling bank representative led him to a seat, then said, "You can't tell anyone what I'm about to tell you. Not anyone."

Avid nodded.

He sent a contract to Avid's Alert screen and folded his hands on his desk.

"This is a non-disclosure agreement. Once you sign it I can tell you what's going on, and you can get your perks."

Avid reviewed the contract, and his eyes widened as he read through it. "Are you serious?" he asked.

"Completely serious."

After Avid signed, the bank representative reiterated what Avid had just read in the contract. The Mitigators had decreed automatic built-in compensation for anyone who ever experienced any negative dealings with Heroes. If anyone felt abused, cheated, or unfairly treated by a Hero, that person was to report to the bank, which would check the scanner footage to verify that person's story, and then provide compensation amounting to a twenty percent upcharge from the standard compensation for typical social mishaps and victimhood. Whenever any Hero did something bad to Avid, one hundred and twenty percent of the standard perk reimbursement awaited him.

"We were notified about the situation with your new apartment, which is what prompted us to reach out to you. Prior to that, we were awaiting confirmation about the situation with the contract Chad had you sign, but couldn't say anything until it was approved. My sincerest condolences. You get one perk for each of those things, plus an extra perk because the Mitigators are feeling generous today.

Also, your first transaction with a Hero gets you double the perks on top of the three we just gave you, for a total of six. So now you can go through the Wish Book and pick something nice for yourself."

"You asshole," Avid said to the representative. The man had tormented him for days, strictly for his own amusement, when he absolutely knew he'd give Avid those perks. It was a good-natured jibe, though. The moment was celebratory.

"Sorry," he answered smiling. "We all live for this moment. This…" He gestured around himself at the bank. "…is a career from which dreams are made." He sighed happily over his exceptionally fortunate lot in life, and then genially poked Avid in the arm. "We like to milk it a little for our own benefit, but it's also educational for you to stew in it. Never conduct any business dealings with a Hero. Or conduct business with Heroes every day, all day long, at your own discretion. Up to you. Now you know."

The bank would actually deduct Avid's perks from the Hero's bank account, the representative continued, so Chad would be punished, in a way. However, he would never realize he was being punished because he would never miss the perks.

Punishment ultimately didn't matter, though, because it never seemed to deter a Hero. The Mitigators knew this. They were just strategically moving assets from one ledger column to another to keep everybody happy.

"Hardly any of them keep track of their account balance. They earn so many perks that they never know what they have in their accounts. They only care that they have enough to do whatever it is that they want to do, and they always have at least that much. But if they don't have enough for you for any reason, we cover it for you and then recoup it from them later on." He added that if Avid were to occasionally run into Heroes who kept jealous track of their perks, the bank would pay Avid from a slush fund, rather than tip them off to the fact that they were involuntarily compensating their victims. The bank's reasoning was that if the Heroes discovered anything about this, they would switch tactics to something that might be worse. Primarily it was more fun for everyone this way. Plus, regular people got to live the Hero Dream simply by being their willing scapegoats and victims. Everybody won.

"So Chad isn't broke." Avid said that as a statement.

"Chad will never be broke. He can't use his perks fast enough to even make a dent in his bank balance, and the perks just keep coming. He's a very wealthy person. Heroes usually are."

"And they let him get away with this?" Avid was indignant.

The bank representative shrugged.

"The Mitigators draw the line at murder and violence and that sort of thing. Other than that, Heroes can do whatever they want to do most of the time, and the Mitigators don't do anything to stop them. I don't know why, they just don't. What they do, however, is compensate the victims for their trouble. And that is the best part of my job."

He pointed Avid to the holographic kiosk that displayed the Wish Book. The other people in the background clapped for Avid as he stood up and walked over to it.

Avid thought about it as he flipped through the holographic images and videos of various time and places, and realized that this could work to his advantage. He would have to ponder it.

"Which plane to Hawaii has the best First Class cabin?" Avid asked, looking up.

The bank representative consulted his Alert screen and replied, "The DC-10 in the nineteen-nineties. Big plane, lots of room. Security is lax by today's standards because it's before the World Trade Center attacks when everything changed on September 11th. Plus, in the nineteen-nineties the airlines serve full meals during your flights, even in Economy, and they still have legroom and somewhat comfortable seating. Luggage is free, there." He added, "You absolutely do not want to fly in current local time. You can stand in line for hours in your stocking feet, waiting for someone dig through your carryon bags and scan you before they let you put your shoes back on and board the plane. If they don't like your stuff for some reason, they confiscate it. And now people are getting violent on planes because they don't want to wear face masks the way they're supposed to, or else they're getting tetchy because the seats are so cramped these days. And probably also because they're hungry. So they punch flight attendants, who have to tie them down with duct tape to subdue them. You can watch the videos on YouTube."

"I hate this place," Avid said conversationally. "But it's a living."

"It's a jungle up there for the locals. And *then*, when you get to where you're going, most things are still closed because of COVID restrictions. The nineties are much nicer. I highly recommend that time period, just in general."

"Sold. I would like to fly from here to Hawaii on a DC-10 in First Class in the nineteen nineties. I want a window seat on every connection. I'll let you pick a good year for me."

"We can send you straight to the Mid-Pacific control center and then put you on a travel pod to Hawaii, you know. It's much faster. You really don't have to fly there."

"I really love to fly, so I really want a very long flight in First Class on whatever plane has the best First Class cabin, and I want a window." Avid grinned. "It has to be First Class on the best plane, and it has to be a window seat. Please? That's what I want."

The bank representative entered Avid's preference into his Alert screen form, which then displayed it on the Wish Book so Avid could request it.

Avid arranged the vacation of his dreams, beginning with that first class seat on a DC-10 in the nineteen-nineties. He requested two thousand dollars spending money in nineteen-nineties currency. The bank representative gave him five thousand dollars instead, and told him to keep going.

When he was finished, Avid had a three-week stay in a five-star all-inclusive resort with an ocean view, unlimited helicopter rides, unlimited parasailing excursions, and three separate tour cruises throughout the islands. He turned up his nose at scuba diving and snorkeling. He didn't know why they even offered that, or who would choose it.

When Avid asked if there were any other Hawaiian activities that involved flying, the bank representative mentioned sky diving. Avid signed up for two of those.

"I'll throw in a luau."

"Thank you." He had no idea how he could possibly spend five thousand dollars when everything he wanted was already included. Maybe he'd hire a private plane? Make a side trip to Fiji? He would give it some thought.

Avid was giddy with excitement. He had never had enough perks for a vacation remotely like this, and was trying to mentally slow his heart rate so he didn't pass out.

"Might I recommend something for your next perk?"

"Sure."

"Would you be interested in going to the Albuquerque Balloon Festival?" He sent images to Avid's Alert screen. Avid looked them over with a slack jaw and shining eyes. His heart began racing again. He bounced a little. "It's less expensive, so I can put you down for three of those."

"Yes!" Avid cried. "Can I ride in a balloon?"

"We'll make the arrangements."

For his third perk Avid vacillated between the Woodstock Festival, 1969 and The Beatles in the Cavern Club, Liverpool England, 1961. He finally opted for Woodstock because it lasted longer and had Jimi Hendrix and Janis Joplin, whom he had heard about from other Historians. Furthermore, it was a Love Fest where everyone in the crowd was on psychedelic drugs, so he figured his non-Caucasian appearance wouldn't bother people much, as it might in Liverpool.

"Three more perks to go," the bank representative said. Avid requested the Beatles after all, thinking that perhaps he might possibly blend in acceptably to some degree, then asked to have the remaining perks banked for future use to give him more time to think about what he'd like to do.

"And there's more." The bank representative reached under his desk and retrieved several objects that Avid recognized as his own. "Dirk stole these from your apartment. Here you go."

Avid accepted the items, which the bank representative had thoughtfully placed into a shopping bag with handles.

"Chad also took a few of your things, but he opted out of room service, which is why we don't have them yet. You might find them in the apartment when you return. I believe he left in a hurry."

"Thank you," said Avid, and happily rose to leave, giving a very earnest Namaste bow.

CHAPTER 12: QUESTIONABLE FASHION

Having eschewed the knowledge and wisdom of the Assimilation Experts regarding their clothing, Nectar and Janicyl referenced their own tastes, which they had developed over a variety of centuries and most recently on the Internet. They modified their personal styles in deference to the year twenty-twenty-one based solely on their own research on YouTube and social media, without having a clear understanding of what styles were current in any specific year, and in particular, this one. In some instances their choices were arguably almost timely, but more often, they did not quite hit the mark.

However, the most important rule of clothing is that it must make you feel good to wear it. They felt good, and they were pretty enough to read as "sexy" regardless of how they chose to style themselves. The feedback they received from men confirmed to them the astuteness of their choices. They didn't notice or care that they received the side eye from most women.

Janicyl was dressed up for their first meeting with the subjects, sporting her Amelie, 2001 hairstyle. She had borrowed her overall look from the Britney Spears "Baby One More Time" video, 1998, with a very short pleated school uniform skirt, complementary jacket, and a tailored white shirt that she tied just below her breasts to expose her midriff. She wore fingerless black lace gloves reminiscent of Madonna, 1985, with four-inch heeled platform ankle boots, black tights and a black chauffeur hat tilted slightly askew. Her look invited comparisons to High School Dominatrix Barbie.

She arrived at Chad's apartment early, and watched him while he tried various ways of artfully wrapping long scarves around his neck in the mirror to appear dashing, wealthy, and post-collegiate. He periodically turned to her for input, to which Janicyl responded with a bored look and a shrug. She finally told him he looked like a tool, and should ditch the scarf altogether, and so he did.

Somehow the act of artfully wearing a scarf had made Janicyl lose respect for him. Chad didn't notice, and if he had he wouldn't have cared.

Nectar was wearing a Christian Siriano gown, suitable for evening, with large hoop earrings. She preferred a "romantic" look and had a fondness for long skirts and dresses. She wore them whenever she liked, regardless of the time of day or type of event. This dress would again interfere with her ability to shift from gas to brake, so she would still need to hike it up to her knees while driving. That was a small price to pay for Fashion. She wore her hair swept back into a loose bun, with tendrils framing her sweet and angelic face. She looked like a very expensive early twentieth century Gibson Girl, or somebody's bridesmaid.

She reported to Dirk's apartment, where he answered the door and slowly looked her up and down. When he leaned toward her to kiss her hello, she pushed him away with an exasperated grunt and took a seat in the living room, choosing a chair that did not permit Dirk to sit next to her. She glared at him with her arms belligerently crossed over her chest.

Dirk was unperturbed but slightly annoyed. He had thought they had a moment together in the shower the other night, before Nectar had screamed at him to leave her alone with the light show. He didn't like it when women flip-flopped like that, disrobing in his bathroom and then screaming at him to leave, especially when he had extended his hospitality in order to allow her to enjoy all these impressive amenities. She owed him.

In response to her belligerent arms, he made a sharp comment about her obvious sexual frigidity, but it evoked no shame from Nectar, as it should have. Furthermore, she was insultingly unmoved by his virility. That cut deeply. He wished he could find an opportunity to seduce her with his astonishing Disco dance moves, and show her how misguided she was to reject him.

Dirk's last assignment had been in the United States in the nineteen-seventies, when many men translated "free love" from the sixties to mean that inviting a woman to dinner and paying for her meal was the equivalent of paying in advance for her sexual services. The woman was expected to willingly oblige, because the aforementioned Free Love entitled men to enjoy sex on demand, particularly when they had already paid for it at the restaurant. If she declined, the man's obvious course of action was to accuse the woman of being a "prick tease," no matter how primly she had behaved. If she continued to decline, she warranted the disgraceful label of "frigid." If she refused to even defend herself from the accusation of frigidity by taking off her clothes to prove otherwise, it was a man's personal responsibility to demonstrate his affront at her insulting behavior and, sometimes, to simply rape her in order to extract compensation for his generosity. Dirk had come to embrace these principles himself, except that he had to personally draw the line at rape because the Mitigators required him to obtain advance approval for any sexual activity. That was a shame.

Dirk felt a deep yearning for that assignment. Had he any normal emotions he might have felt sentimentality and homesickness.

Dirk had assimilated a little too deeply into that era, and had spent ten years reinforcing thoughts and behaviors that his schooling and training had specifically tried to curtail. Heroes were given leeway for behavior that was typical for the era they were assigned to, but it had apparently gone undetected at the time that he had become noticeably entrenched in the culture, and that his character role was no longer an act. After he was reassigned to another decade his thoughts and ideas had not reverted back to the thoughts and ideas, and most importantly, behavior, he had been trained for, as they should have.

Dirk and the other Historians, including the Heroes, had not been raised and conditioned by their Educations to treat women in this manner. Disrespect or abuse toward people because of their gender, or anything else they could not help or control, was a punishable offense. Punishable gender-related offenses were not just limited to rape. Everything related to touching another human required consent. Verbal abuse and verbal disrespect were also punishable. Somehow this slipped Dirk's mind.

So Dirk knew better, but systemic misogyny and sexual predation were deeply-engrained in the culture of United States, 1970s, and were particularly prevalent in the drug-fueled urban club and disco scene Dirk loved so much. His emulation of that behavior was not really punishable in large city nightclubs of that era, provided Dirk obtained advance clearance of his local sexual partners from the Mitigators, and obtained advance verbal consent from those partners to avoid causing them trauma and triggering an Anomaly. "No" did not mean "Yes," for Dirk, in other words. He had actually adhered to this.

He had only left that era behind a few weeks earlier, after spending the entire decade following a bevy of serial killers who included John Wayne Gacy, Ted Bundy and Son of Sam, to name a few, along with some of the earlier efforts of Jeffrey Dahmer. He considered that time and place to be "home" and was not adjusting well to leaving it all behind. ("It was the golden age of serial killers," he liked to say. "I almost got there in time for Charles Manson too, but alas.") Dirk was still mentally and philosophically sipping Harvey Wallbangers while emitting seductive whiffs of English Leather or Canoe cologne. In his thoughts he was still carefully trimming and waxing his thick handlebar mustache, which the Assimilation Experts had shaved from his face only moments after he walked through their door. Unwillingly refashioned for the twenty-first century, he ran his fingers over his upper lip where the moustache once was, like an amputee reaching for his phantom limb. He kept his skintight polyester bell bottom slacks, his fitted, shiny, wide-collared polyester shirts, his eight-track and cassette music tapes and players, and his heavy gold chains in the box where he kept his most valuable keepsakes. He sorely missed the obliging "anything goes" ambience of Studio 54 and other nightclubs, where he had learned to be an exceptional Disco dancer, to the overwhelming delight of every woman who was privileged to watch him.

He remained living in that era in his mind, and was already planning to travel back there for his next vacation adventure by having the bank arrange for him to be an extra on the movie set of *Saturday Night Fever*, the most iconic film of all time, in his opinion, with John Travolta being history's most iconic dancer. He first had to regrow his hair and moustache for that trip when this assignment was over, but in the meantime there was Nectar.

Dirk's abrupt appearance in the living room wearing just a towel the other night had not been because he was clean from showering. At the Battle of Shiloh, there was an enormous number of flies in the battlefield and in the tents. In that time and place, Nectar had learned the skill of killing flies on hard surfaces by swatting them with a wet rag, and had done this to Dirk's genitals with a dripping washcloth. The trick, she explained to Janicyl during the Civil War, was to hold the rag diagonally with both hands from two opposing corners and stretch it taut. Lift your hands over your head like this, she demonstrated, reach backward a bit, then let go with your left hand and snap down hard with your right. It was amazing how accurately it hit the target, and how effectively it made flies flop dead on their backs. Janicyl had thanked her for the tip.

Dirk's whoops had not been from pleasure, and so he had left in a hurry.

Nectar would not let down her guard henceforth, but she felt no need to report him because she knew the Mitigator team was closely monitoring all of their movements for this assignment. She also knew that they did not tolerate sexual harassment, so she felt supported. Her restraint was rewarded in less than ten minutes when Dirk cornered her in the hallway as she was returning from the bathroom. He leaned over for a kiss, and then stepped away with a surprised and pained expression on his face.

The Mitigators had remotely programmed his Alert Screen implant to jolt him with a burst of electric current whenever his thoughts turned to predatory behavior toward women. This approach was like a dog's shock collar, except for men. It eventually trained men to behave properly, and the tactic was particularly useful with cocky teenagers. In the beginning, the current was mild and located in the vicinity of the wrist, where the implant was. The level of the current increased with each violation. Repeated failure to heed the warnings of the shock could result in a higher voltage in a more sensitive area. The Mitigators were confident from past experience that it would not escalate that far, but they were ready.

Dirk walked away from Nectar confused over what had just happened to him, but he would try again later, and would try again after that with the same result. He would make the same attempts with other women, and would suffer the same effects. By the end of the week he would cease trying with anyone, to everyone's relief.

Their departure time was pre-arranged, so the ladies took the wheels of their respective vehicles, requested the location of parking for the sports bar from their GPS apps, and then turned on their engines. Dirk made himself comfortable in the back seat of his Range Rover. Chad found the back seat in his Tesla Roadster to be insufficient for his height, so he climbed up front beside Janicyl, pleased that her jaunty chauffeur cap clarified their relationship to anyone watching. He liked having a driver.

The sports bar where the subjects were to arrive was only open at fifty percent capacity, due to the pandemic. James and Max would be arriving this evening at 21:18 hours, so the Heroes had planned to get there earlier to ensure they got into the bar before it hit capacity.

They had made this plan prior to the addition of two drivers, so Nectar's concern was that the four of them might have locked out the subjects by filling too many available slots at the bar, thereby creating a new Anomaly or impacting their ability to correct the current one. Everyone on the team was now very averse to Anomalies.

Chad requested a scanner report, which indicated that there would be room for James and Max until 22:11 hours, so they relaxed and settled in to observe the crowd. Had there been a problem with capacity they would have had to eject two or more people from the club by spiking their drinks with nausea drops to make them sick for an hour or so. Then those unfortunate people could return later when the nausea and vomiting subsided, provided there was room for them. The Heroes had the nausea drops handy, as always, but that effort proved not to be necessary.

The Assimilation Experts had advised the team against wearing masks to the assignment because of the political leanings of the subjects. Those political leanings apparently made James and Max believe that the pandemic was a hoax perpetrated by the opposing political party, so masks would immediately trigger their distrust. They noticed that only a few people in the bar were wearing them, and these were employees.

Historians in general were never permitted to drink or take any substances that might impair their judgment while they were on assignment. Heroes were especially forbidden to imbibe because they usually had to interact with the locals in general, and their subjects in particular, and because that interaction always required quick thinking and sometimes challenging improvisation, or fast, reflexive action. Consequently, the men ordered non-alcoholic beers in glasses, and the ladies ordered virgin cocktails.

Chad and Dirk soon noticed the dartboard, and abandoned the ladies at the table for a loud and lively game of darts with two other patrons.

The ladies reminisced about the Battle of Shiloh for a minute or two while they awaited the arrival of the subjects. Then they planned their spa day. At that point, the two women ran out of things to discuss with each other, so they sighed, rested their elbows on the table and leaned their chins on their fists. Nectar silently looked around the bar with bored and empty expression, and eventually buried herself in her phone. Janicyl perused the men in the vicinity and locked eyes with the ones she found attractive.

Several of Janicyl's men approached the ladies to buy them drinks and socialize, but Nectar's steady, deadly look gave them pause. When she snapped at them in sharply-worded Hinduese, they quickly edged away.

"Stop it," Nectar hissed at Janicyl. "We're working and you don't have clearance to interact with them anyway."

A disappointed Janicyl pushed out her lower lip and slouched.

At 21:18 hours the two subjects walked into the bar. All of the Heroes had been checking their phones for the time, so they were all aware of the entrance, and they all became alert. They were all watching the door when James and Max walked in.

The ladies turned away and resumed talking to each other, watching from the corners of their eyes. The men continued the dart game to its conclusion, and then begged off another game. They wandered to the bar and casually stood near Max and James, who were ordering their first drinks.

Chad made the first move.

"Max? Max Richmond? How are you?" He leaned over with his hand outstretched, and Max took it, confused. "I can't believe I'm running into you after all this time. It's been years since college."

The mention of college gave Max a steadier footing in this exchange. He smiled genially and said, "I'm sorry...?"

"Chad Ford! From the fraternity!" His Alert screen displayed personal information and video snippets that he could describe to Max. "I can't believe I'm running into someone who was at that Halloween party during sophomore year, because I was just telling a friend of mine about it. What a weird coincidence, isn't it? What was that girl's name? The one who fell into the punch bowl? Do you remember that party? You came dressed in a toga? Oh my god. And Cal Preston was dressed as an ape. Passed out under the stairs. What a dick. Do you remember him? Majored in synchronized baton twirling or some shit. Total loser." He paused and grimaced. "I'm sorry. I hope he isn't a friend of yours...?"

Completely charmed because Chad was so charming, Max laughed and punched Chad in the shoulder. "I haven't thought of Cal in years. What happened to him, I wonder?"

"We shall find out," Chad said, pulling out his phone. "Cal Preston," he said to Siri with an impish glance at Max.

Siri displayed a list of links.

"Wall Street. That asshole. Would you have guessed that?" Chad said. "He's making a fortune apparently."

Max laughed. "His father has an investment firm. Cal could have majored in anything and eventually gotten richer. In fact, I'm pretty certain that he flunked out in junior year and never graduated. Nothing would ever have made any difference."

Chad laughed appreciatively.

He leaned over and paid for the subjects' drinks. They thanked him. "I didn't introduce Dirk," he said apologetically. "Dirk, this is Max Richmond, an old friend of mine from college. Max, this is Dirk Van de Kamp. Our parents are friends, and we grew up together."

"Van de Kamp. Fish sticks? Is that your family?"

Dirk's blank expression prompted an Alert screen image of a package of frozen fish sticks.

"You can call me 'Sushi'," he quipped. "Just kidding. That's not my family."

The two of them bonded over fish products, while James held out his hand to Chad. "James Stoughton."

"Happy to meet you! I'm Chad Ford."

"Ford, as in cars? Any relation?"

Chad pretended to be embarrassed, and admitted that yes, he was a member of the Ford Motor dynasty.

"Here's something for you," he said to James conspiratorially. "I never learned to drive."

Max heard the admission, and he and James both laughed. It was so... vieux riche (old money)...to not know how to drive when your fortune was built on the automotive industry.

"Janicyl is my driver."

He pointed to Janicyl, still sitting at the table in her jaunty chauffer hat. He waved to her. She adjusted her piercing green eyes to full effect and gazed at Max and James, alluringly seductive, but a little bit scary. She gave a small wave in return.

Dirk, somewhat redundantly and unnecessarily, also waved to the ladies, who curled their lips in response. He then invited James and Max to join them. The four men moved toward the table. Chad pulled up two extra stools for the subjects.

"Our drivers don't speak English. They're both from Kazakhstan." Chad had recently watched "Borat Subsequent Moviefilm" on Amazon Prime Videos, where he'd learned about the supposedly muddy, impoverished and backward country of Kazakhstan. It would work as the ladies' homeland. "My father has a manufacturing plant there—cheap labor—so Dirk and I went there for a few years as interns. We even learned the language. Then the ladies asked if we could sponsor them for American citizenship. So we said yes. They needed jobs, so we hired them." He shrugged. "So, now here we all are."

"This is my driver, Nectar," Dirk said offhandedly. He could see the two men were greatly impressed by their drivers. "Check out her tits. That's why I picked this one for the job." He laughed conspiratorily, not noticing Janicyl's steely stare at being dismissed as the less attractive of the two women. "I can say that because she doesn't understand a word of English."

The men all laughed and laughed.

Dirk sent an appreciative look toward Nectar, who stared back coolly and levelly. Then she looked adoringly at Max.

"Did you go to school with these two?" Dirk asked James, laughing, gesturing toward Max and Chad. "What a shit show that must have been, am I right? I've heard all the stories."

"No, I went to Princeton. But yeah, I would agree to that, from the stories I've heard. I actually was in the ROTC program so I never joined a fraternity."

"Yale, here," Dirk answered. "We had our own shit show there." He laughed.

"Do you remember that girl's name?" Chad resumed that thread of conversation with Max. "I've been trying to think of it for days now."

"Jessica! Did you know Jessica?" Max was warming to the conversation. He remembered the party. He remembered the girl who lost her balance and fell backward into the punch bowl. He remembered his toga costume. (He didn't have a lot of imagination; he'd stolen the idea from the movie *Animal House*.) He didn't remember Chad at all, but why would he? He really only noticed the women when he was in college, and furthermore he was usually drunk or high. He suspected nothing.

"I thought she was hot, but no. I didn't know her. I wanted to, though."

Chad turned to James with intense interest. "ROTC, eh? Do they teach you anything about guns?"

James nodded.

"Very cool."

"Why do you ask?" James was testing Chad.

"I collect them. I just wondered if you did too."

James nodded, then began to describe his gun collection in detail. Chad responded by reciting a list of various guns and their meaningful attributes, one by one as they displayed on his Alert screen. His enthusiasm for that lengthy list was infectious and convincing. The two men bonded as compatriots in that moment, or so it seemed to James.

"I'd like a gun," Dirk said thoughtfully in a voice that sounded a little drunk. He ran his finger around the rim of his non-alcoholic beer and pretended to suppress a belch. "I could use a gun, I think," he said. "I think I might buy one. Maybe I'll buy a few. I think we'll all need guns with this illegitimate administration taking over and destroying America."

Chad gave Dirk a sharp look and made a point of kicking his leg in an obvious way so that James and Max could see him do it. He wanted the subjects to think that Chad and Dirk were hiding terrorist secrets and intentions, as Max and James were.

"Sorry," Dirk said. "Let's not get political tonight." He slapped his thighs and stood up. "I'm just going to get another beer. Does anyone want anything?" He repeated the question in Hinduese for the ladies.

Nectar looked at Dirk with surprised gratitude at the offer and replied, "Check out her tits? Go fuck yourself sideways, you fucked-up asshole." She wrinkled her nose and smiled, nodding.

Dirk smiled back at her. "Got it," he said in English. "Calm down," he said to her in Hinduese, looking offended. "I'm an actor playing a role. My character is from this time and place. This is exactly how the men view the women here. It is therefore completely appropriate for men to say things like that about women behind their backs."

"Play a different character," she replied, smiling. "Or I will destroy your life. Do you understand me?"

Dirk nodded and said in English, "This little lady wants an umbrella in her drink. I have no idea if they serve umbrella drinks here. We shall see." He went straight to the bar without looking back at Nectar.

Nectar was not impressed by Dirk's show of wounded affront. She was also disappointed in the Mitigators, who apparently did not believe that Dirk's insults were worthy of a painful shock, because Dirk was not wincing in pain right now. So, Dirk was right, and this kind of behavior was typical of some of the men in this time and place. The two subjects were clearly of that type because Dirk's crude comments had landed with them just the way they were supposed to.

Revenge must be hers alone.

It would require some thought and planning.

Janicyl was waiting impatiently for all the attention to shift to her. When it appeared that it would not shift without her intervention, she turned and smiled at James, who was sitting next to her, then lowered her eyes shyly. It was interesting that she was able to emulate "shy." One would never have guessed.

James perked up and moved an inch or so closer to Janicyl, shifting on his stool to somewhat face her. She smiled at him and James smiled at her. He was at a loss as to how to communicate with her, so he decided he would keep plying her with drinks until she was either compliant or unconscious.

Dirk returned and placed the two faux cocktails in front of the ladies. "No umbrellas, I'm afraid," he sighed regretfully. Then, to Max and James he added, "They both get virgin cocktails this evening because they have to drive."

James looked crestfallen as Dirk returned to the bar to collect the rest of the drinks, including seconds for Max and James. It was fortunate that the subjects were not drinking beer, so there was no risk of accidentally switching non-alcoholic beers for the real deal. Everything about this evening was moving smoothly.

"Maybe after this we can go to my place and get the ladies liquored up for you." Dirk emitted a short, but virile and manly "ha-ha-ha" laugh.

Janicyl sent him a telepathic: *Fuck you.*

Nectar's telepathic message followed: *I warned you. I'm coming for you.*

Dirk laughed. "I'm only kidding about liquoring them up. They're actually saving themselves for marriage, so liquor wouldn't do anyone any good, unfortunately."

"But one can always try," James said, raising his glass with a wink. Again, the men all laughed and laughed, while the ladies exchanged furtive death glances before looking down.

James tried to process whatever it was that Dirk had just said about plying the ladies with liquor, versus them saving themselves for marriage, and was trying to guess whether or not he stood a chance with either of them this evening. Which of Dirk's statements was the actual joke? He did not know, but he was interested in finding out because fifty percent of Dirk's statements leaned favorably in his direction. Those were decent odds for a Tuesday night.

"So, what do you think? Come by my place? They can leave both cars in my garage and take a cab home, so they won't have to worry about driving. Ergo, they can drink."

Chad and Dirk both looked encouragingly at James, who pretended to be hesitant. He finally sighed and acquiesced just exactly as if he hadn't hoped that either Chad or Dirk would make that kind of an offer.

The ladies sipped through their straws, still looking down.

"I'm in," he said to Max. "How about you?"

Max appeared to be thinking it over, and seemed to be inclined to take a pass. All of the Heroes heard him leaning toward bed and masturbation.

Nectar fixed her eyes on Max and gave him a tentative smile. She turned to Dirk and instructed him to tell Max that she wanted to know if he was married.

"Nectar would like to know if you're married," he said to Max.

"No," Max replied, flattered. "I happen to be very single at the moment." He returned Nectar's smile. Then he turned to Chad and Dirk. "I'm in too," he said. "Do you live far?"

As it happened, they did not.

The subjects had taken an Uber to the bar so they could drink as much as they liked, so Dirk offered them a ride in his Range Rover. Max and James followed the group to the parking lot, where they both showed a high level of appreciation for the Tesla. Chad agreed to let James ride with Janicyl so he could experience both the car and its driver. James was visibly excited as he climbed into the vehicle, and he slapped the dashboard happily before settling back into his seat.

Max pointed to the Confederate flag on the Range Rover and gave Dirk a thumbs-up. Dirk smiled, and let Max sit in front beside Nectar, then slid beside Chad in the back.

After they all arrived, Max and James made themselves suitably comfortable in Dirk's luxurious condo, and were enjoying the carefully composed and masterfully-directed ambience. A fire was crackling in the huge carved marble fireplace. The music was soft and soothing. The lighting was warm and low. The ladies were beautiful and spoke no words. The unwitting subjects were happy and completely taken in by the illusion.

Dirk served three-hundred-dollar-a-bottle wine to James and Max, which he prominently displayed in a sterling silver ice bucket on the coffee table with several other bottles of wine. Then he offered the Heroes a non-alcoholic version from a bottle with a different label, which he had whipped up in the kitchen with the quick drink generator.

At some point Dirk resumed his discussion about needing guns because the opposing political party was destroying America. Chad let him explore the topic without giving him a leg kick. James and Max were both receptive to Dirk's message, and eventually offered some restrained insights of their own.

Dirk confessed that he was tired of white supremacists being called out as if they were bigots when really it was Antifa all along, and he wished there was something he could do to fight back in order to save America.

Max and James exchanged glances, but remained silent.

One more bottle should do it, Chad said to Dirk telepathically, and reached for the corkscrew.

Eventually the word "lynching" came up in conversation in connection with someone's bitter joke about race relations and the state of America. Once they'd crossed that line it was not difficult to get the now very drunk Max and James to confess to their plans, and it was not difficult to get them to agree to include Dirk and Chad in them.

Janicyl rewarded James by sitting next to him and edging closer to him on the couch. When James moved his arm behind her on the back of the couch, she leaned into it and sighed. James was very pleased with his new friends, overall.

The gentlemen all exchanged contact information and agreed to meet again at Dirk's condo in a few days to discuss the logistics of brutally killing multiple people.

The Heroes' effort was moving forward splendidly.

Having settled all that, Chad sorrowfully confessed that he had to get back home because he was still hungover from the previous night, which was completely true, and because the additional drinks he had consumed tonight had exhausted him. Dirk stood up to walk him to the door, and Janicyl slid off the couch and away from James.

Nectar yawned and reached for her three thousand dollar handbag, then stood.

Max and James understood from the signals that the party was over.

Nectar pulled out her smart phone to arrange a ride with Uber. She and all the Heroes, except Dirk, would ride together. The Tesla could wait until tomorrow, Chad said, because Janicyl had had too much to drink.

All told, it was a productive evening, except from the perspective of Max and James, who both went home alone.

CHAPTER 13: EBAY AUCTION

Nelda answered the door and gave Avid a quick hug. Then she returned to the kitchen.

"What's for dinner?" Avid called after her.

"You're going to France!" she called back. She grabbed a bottle of chilled French wine and poured it into some glasses. Then she quickly ran over to Avid with his glass.

"I love you so much," Avid told Nelda when she handed him his wine. She kissed his cheek and laughed. Then she went back to preparing the appetizers.

"Where's Helen?"

"She's on eBay trying to win an auction. It's over in a few minutes. She likes to swoop in at the last minute and conquer. She'll be out soon," Nelda assured him. "Watch TV while you wait, if you want."

Avid tuned into the last few minutes of the Nightly News and watched ancient history unfold. He still sometimes felt disoriented when he tuned into local broadcasts, but found them fascinating.

Helen whooped and hollered from her office. "I won!" she screamed. "I won!" She came running out to hug Nelda first, and then Avid.

"What did you win?" Avid asked.

"Art deco jewelry," Helen answered, elated. "Diamonds and aquamarine. White gold. An entire set with necklace, earrings and bracelet. I'm swooning! Oh. My. God!" She sat down next to Avid and gave him a hug. "I won. I won. I won." She clapped her hands and reached for the glass of wine that Nelda had left her on the coffee table.

She turned to Avid. "So how was your day? Did you move into your new apartment?"

Avid had almost begged off from tonight's meeting with Helen after seeing what he had to contend with at home. Then he decided to come after all, because he couldn't stand to be there. He told her the apartment needed straightening up. He didn't tell her all the background information about the agreement, about the apartment trade, about the perks, about Chad, about Dirk, about anything, really.

He couldn't tell her now, with Nelda so close by, so he told her he would get her up to speed when they were doing dishes. But he would like to see the jewelry she had just purchased.

Helen pulled out her phone and swiped to her recent auction win. She handed her phone to Avid, who issued all the appropriate compliments, but who also had his Alert screen capture a quick image of the jewelry and the listing. He stored it in his personal file, and handed back her phone.

French accordion music began playing over the sound system when Nelda left the kitchen with the first course. The music continued throughout the meal, while Helen and Avid shifted into the same banter and laughter they had begun on the first day they met, only now it was peppered with private jokes.

During their now-nightly kitchen cleanup, Avid told Helen about his day. He described the Heroes, who they were and what they did, described the frustration everyone had in dealing with them, described his experiences with Chad and Dirk, described the apartment swap and his trashed apartment, described the fake Amendment to the contract, and described the remarkable perks he had earned for suffering at their hands.

"So I'm now waiting for Maintenance to prepare a temporary apartment until they can hose down and fumigate the one I'm supposed to live in now."

"Stay here. Move in until they straighten everything out. It's no problem, and I have plenty of room." Helen tugged his sleeve and led him up the stairs to a guest room that was remarkably cozy and beautiful. "Do you like it?" she asked.

Avid loved it.

"Stay as long as you need to. Stay tonight."

Avid nearly wept with gratitude over the fact that he would not have to go back to the control station. He hugged her.

Helen was fascinated with the Heroes and wanted to learn more. Avid shared stories he had heard over the years, and Helen responded to them with spin thoughts that he could not telepathically catch.

"So apparently the Mitigators know they're assholes because they automatically approve hundred-and-twenty-percent perk compensation for anything a Hero does to anyone. And they apparently don't monitor the bank when it reimburses you, because the guy was hurling perks at me that went way beyond that hundred-and-twenty-percent. Double or triple. That's why I got so many great perks. The bank was *not* stingy, and the Mitigators didn't intervene even though I *know* they were watching us. But they never punish Heroes. That's what kills me. They let them steamroll over everyone. They even make you sign a non-disclosure because they don't want the Heroes to find out they aren't getting away with it." He added, "I wish you could meet them. They're kind of strange. This one Hero, Dirk, doesn't even blink. It's creepy."

Avid caught Helen thinking the word "psychopaths" at a moment when her mental whirling slowed. For whatever reason, that made him feel confused and defensive because Chad and Dirk weren't violent criminals, and they weren't the despotic autocrats he'd learned about in History class. Psychopaths didn't even exist anymore, because the medical team corrected psychopathy in any children who were developing in that direction. In his time they most associated the word "psychopath" with historical criminals and various world and business leaders who hadn't led properly throughout history.

The Heroes were simply raging assholes.

"They are not psychopaths, Helen. That's crazy."

"It is. I know that. I can't diagnose them without meeting them, and they have to go through a series of tests," she said. *They're totally psychopaths*, she thought.

"Oh come on. Are you serious?"

Avid's Alert screen flashed, and a non-disclosure agreement displayed. Avid read through it with his mouth open.

"Holy shit, Helen." Helen's favorite expletive had rubbed off on him. "You're right! The Mitigators just asked me to sign a contract stating I can never tell anyone that the Heroes are all psychopaths."

Helen clapped her hands and burst out laughing. "It's so perfect," she said. "It's pretty brilliant, actually. Kudos to the Mitigators once again."

Helen explained to Avid why it made perfect sense to give the most harrowing jobs to psychopaths. It also made perfect sense to give them free rein within limits, because it boosted their egos, which needed to be continually stroked.

"They're probably considerably worse than they would be if they were scattered throughout society here, in my time. Lumping them all together to reinforce each other's proclivities, and then giving them sketchy boundaries *has* to make them insufferable. But they do have limits, I would guess," she said. "Am I right?"

Avid thought of the various laws in place, and realized the Heroes did have limits. Then he thought back to his school years and slumped in defeat.

"They've been tormenting me since school. Not lately as much, because we don't usually work on the same assignments. This is the first time I've ever had to work with them, but I still have all of the many, many scars."

"I'll bet you do," Helen said fondly.

Avid looked at her. "What's that supposed to mean?"

"You're more of an empath."

"How do you know that? I never told you." He realized the question was dumb as soon as it left his mouth.

Helen gave him a look and rolled her eyes. "It's my job to spot you guys."

"So?"

"Psychopaths are like sharks, and they can smell the blood of empaths. Once they identify you as someone who is 'sympathetic' to other people, so to speak, they suck you dry. So do narcissists and sociopaths. You're a sitting duck for any of them, if they think you're useful. It's nothing personal. It's just their nature. You know, like the sharks. You can't blame them really. They're just being who they are, looking for easy prey. Which you are."

"Great. I feel better now."

"But consider that the Mitigators made it right with you, did they not?"

Avid nodded.

"And Heroes take on assignments you could never do yourself, am I right?"

"True."

"And *why* couldn't you do those assignments?"

"I'd probably have a breakdown. Or I'd get into my own head and fail in a crisis."

"Exactly. The Heroes are keeping you from having a mental breakdown because they do all the worst jobs. And think about it. Those jobs don't impact them at all, do they? Isn't that what you said? They show up after some unthinkable, terrible tragedy as if they just got back from a day at the beach. That's because psychopaths can experience the fight or flight response, but they have no emotional reaction to a crisis. The Mitigators assign them the jobs that would give anyone else Post-Traumatic Stress Disorder. PTSD. It's perfect."

She thought some more. "The Heroes are just having a little fun with you. It's actually pretty benign, when you consider that you come out on top with the perks, afterward. I'd milk it, if I were you."

"What does that mean?"

"Encourage them to screw you over. Don't get angry. Pretend you believe them when they say they're sorry or tell you that the situation was out of their control. If you do that, they'll think you're a sucker and mess with you even more. The more they mess with you, the more perks you earn."

Avid thought for a minute. "I could get rich off of them." He liked her advice.

"And furthermore, it should lower your blood pressure to recognize that they can't help being what they are, and that it isn't personal, like I said before. Let them play right into your hand, and don't get upset about any of it. The Mitigators always have your back and everyone else's, from what I've seen, so you have nothing to lose."

Avid's Alert screen flashed again. The Mitigator-on-duty had just sent him a thumbs-up emoji, Avid told Helen.

Helen shouted, "Love you, Mitigators!"

The Alert screen responded with a big red heart.

CHAPTER 14: MEETING CANCELED

WEDNESDAY, MARCH 24, 2021: 10:01 HOURS

Avid was expecting to meet with Chad and Dirk sometime today, but had just received an Alert that said the two Heroes had successfully settled everything with the subjects, and that everything was going exactly according to plan. There was no reason to meet for now. They would schedule something with Avid if the situation changed, or if they needed his help as backup.

That was fine with Avid. He still needed time to recover from the apartment exchange, and didn't want to see Chad right now. Or ever.

He was also moving into Helen's house today, so a meeting would be inconvenient. The assignment was all working out from his perspective as well.

CHAPTER 15: AVID MOVES TO HELEN'S

Avid appeared at Helen's door with cardboard boxes of his clothing and possessions. He didn't bring much because he didn't really intend to stay long. Furthermore, he would be traveling back and forth to the control station, and would have ample opportunity to grab things that he needed whenever that need arose.

Nelda answered the door, with Helen standing behind her. Helen was on her way out to meet with her grief support group, so she gave Avid a quick hug and dashed away. Nelda led Avid up the stairs to the guest room, carrying his suitcase while Avid carried two boxes, sniffing, trying to identify the aroma he smelled.

"You aren't cooking tonight, are you? Aren't you off tonight?"

"I cooked her an early dinner and was just about to eat myself and clean up. I saved you some," she said, and walked downstairs to the kitchen. Avid followed her.

Nelda scooped some chili into a bowl, then pointed Avid to an array of things to dollop on top of it: sour cream, chopped green onions, chopped tomatoes, grated cheese, jalapeno slices. She pried a wedge of cornbread from a cast iron skillet, put it on a plate and offered Avid the choice of butter, regular honey, and honey infused with jalapenos. She then placed a tossed salad on the plate and handed him a bottle of Ranch dressing. She would usually have made her own dressing, but it was Wednesday.

Nelda prepared a bowl and a plate for herself, and placed them on the table across from Avid. "You don't mind if I join you, do you? Mary's working a double shift again at the hospital because of COVID, and I have nothing to go home to." She shrugged. "I can't complain though. It's so much worse for her than it is for me."

Avid was thoroughly pleased to have her company for dinner, and grinned welcomingly with a full mouth, nodding his head. He watched her pour the ranch dressing on her salad, not knowing until then what it was for, and then followed suit. He took a bite of chili, and the jalapenos kicked in. His eyes widened and he looked helpless.

"Too hot?" Nelda asked. "Eat a spoonful of that sour cream to tone it down."

Avid obeyed, then gulped from his glass of water.

"I've never had these before." He was mentally adjusting his pain receptors to dull them so he could enjoy the meal. Then he decided to halt the dulling process before it was complete so he could have the full experience of chili with jalapenos. He actually enjoyed that little kick, he discovered, once it was more manageable. Eventually he would learn to love jalapenos full force.

"I wondered if you were like my brother when you threw that many onto your chili," she answered, smiling. "I have a brother who can eat jalapenos raw by the fistful, but you have to work up to it. You also have to be a little bit nuts to eat jalapenos raw by the fistful. He is."

"It's really good," Avid said, nodding enthusiastically. It was. He was now completely focused on the cornbread, which he found to be divine. He reached for another wedge from the plate of cornbread Nelda had placed on the table, and smeared it with butter and honey. "This is incredible," he breathed between bites.

"If you're hungry later, grab it from the fridge and put it in the microwave for thirty seconds. Or have it for breakfast," Nelda said. "I'll leave the honey out for you until you find your way around the kitchen."

"Thanks."

"No, thank you." Nelda looked serious. "I've been wanting to thank you for a while."

"Why?"

"Helen. This is the first time since her husband and son died that she's been herself again. She said you were some kind of freaky New Age therapist and that whatever it is that you did, it worked."

"It was nothing."

"It was everything, and I am really grateful to you for it." Nelda teared up. "I love Helen like my own mother. I love her more than my own mother. My mother is a bitch who disowned me when I came out." She caught her breath in a sob and tried to wave the tears away with her hand. "Helen saved my life. Literally. I was planning to commit suicide when I got out of prison."

Avid did not know this, or anything else about the relationship between Nelda and Helen. What he had primarily gotten from Nelda had been her choice of ingredients as she prepared the food, the steps to prepare it, and the time each item took to cook. When she was finished her thoughts moved to going home. Now that he was probing her, he felt waves of pain and gratitude, and saw more evidence that Helen was on this earth be a Helper.

Nelda told the story of how she was imprisoned for selling methamphetamine, and had lost most of her teeth from using it, so she now had to wear dentures. She was part of a group therapy session that Helen was conducting in the prison. Helen looked past everything and saw Nelda behind the tattoos and the teeth and the fearful, hurt anger. She was gentle and kind, and when Nelda was paroled Helen offered her a job as her personal chef based solely on Nelda's word that she had gone through culinary school and had worked in restaurants before getting strung out on drugs. She hired Nelda without ever tasting her food.

At first Nelda had cooked for the family. It was tough because she was earnestly trying to stay clean, and Helen's son was a drug user who would sometimes try to share drugs with Nelda when he visited. He was in and out of rehab, Nelda said. Clean for a month, and then using again. Nelda tried to avoid him whenever he was around, but he saw in her a kindred spirit and followed her around, trying to nudge her into furtively using with him out in the backyard. It scared her that one day she might accept something from him in a weak moment, and be back on the streets.

"But, thank God, I never did. Never. It would have been a betrayal after everything Helen did for me."

Avid was now getting more seriously pulled into this time and place. He was now emotionally connected to two people. He stopped himself from giving Nelda a heart hug after the way it had affected Helen, because he didn't want to have to explain what it was to her, which would mean explaining who he really was. He just listened.

"You can't fix someone else's addictions," Nelda said. "Helen felt like she should have been able to do that for her son because, honestly, she had kind of done that for me by giving me something to live for. That's all I personally needed, but beyond that you just can't. He had to do it himself. Finally, he just gave up and deliberately overdosed to end it all. He left a note telling Helen and Barry not to blame themselves, but they did. Then Barry died, and Helen became this half-dead creature. It broke my heart. I could never, ever leave her, not even for twice the money, because I have to always be here to make sure she's okay. Then you showed up with your New Age therapy and you hung out with her, and it's like a light switched on. I have my Helen back." Nelda burst into embarrassed tears.

Avid got up and hugged her from behind, the way he had with Helen once. He rocked her while she sobbed. Avid did not have permission to interfere with Nelda. Even hugging her was a risk at an Anomaly, but the Mitigators weren't interrupting to stop him. Apparently nothing about this evening would change the continuum.

"We'll take care of her together," Avid said. "We'll be a team." Avid could literally check in on both of them for the entire rest of his life and theirs, going back in time to do it, helping Nelda and Mary for as long as he needed to. He had the sudden realization that these women were now his family.

Nelda wiped her eyes and Avid stepped away, then sat down in his chair again, reaching for another wedge of cornbread and honey.

"We've already gotten everything put into place through Helen's lawyer," Nelda continued. "Whenever the time comes, Mary and I are going to move in and be her caretakers. Helen will never, ever go to a nursing home as long as we're alive to take care of her. She hired someone to oversee the whole arrangement. I don't know law, so I don't know exactly what the agreement is, but if anything happens to Mary and me, there are people who will step in, so everything will be okay no matter what happens."

Avid nodded. Everything Nelda told him checked out with what he was seeing in her thoughts when he probed her. He could tell from something in the back of her mind that she was Helen's sole heir, but Nelda didn't think about that as having any major significance. If Helen wanted to leave her anything, it was a link back to Helen, and it gave Nelda something to remember her by. That was all that mattered to her. Nelda was a Helper too.

If Avid had to be stuck in this time and place, these were the two people he was happy to be stuck with. It almost made sense for him to be here. He was almost grateful to be here just to know these two incredible women.

CHAPTER 16: ABORTION PROBLEM

Avid and Helen were sitting on her couch with glasses of wine, watching Rachel Maddow on MSNBC. When the show was over, Helen turned to Avid and said, "You never have any opinions on what's going on here."

Avid shrugged. He had figured it was best to keep his thoughts to himself because he was pretty certain his opinions wouldn't sit well.

"To me it's ancient history. That's all."

Helen poked him in the arm. "Come on. You have to have an opinion about *something*. Tell me."

Avid turned to her and gave another shrug, then shook his head.

"What we just watched. Say something about what we just watched. Abortion, for instance. You saw the story." She leaned over and grabbed his arm, then shook it with mock aggressiveness. "Say something about abortion. What do they do about abortion in your time?"

Avid attempted to appear noncommittal about the story they had just seen where the U.S. Supreme Court seemed primed to make abortion illegal.

"We don't need abortion all that much in my time. It's legal, but it isn't an issue. Most of the women who have abortions are carrying non-viable infants or their lives are at risk. Aside from that, most babies are wanted."

Helen cocked her head. Apparently we finally figure out the solution to abortion, she thought. Fabulous!

"How did you do it?"

Avid turned to her with a curled lip and sighed. This time and place was so exasperating. They couldn't see the obvious.

He had been here since last year, too long, and couldn't let just let go of this society's foibles and shortcomings the way he usually could when he went to a place and time for an assignment, and then left without staying long or forming ties. He needed to schedule an appointment with a therapist. He needed to extend his morning meditations by another hour, and he needed to do his breathing exercises twice a day, instead of once. Otherwise he would be consumed by anger and impotent affront. It was beginning to percolate, and that was unacceptable because anger and affront would not save Joseph D'Andre McKenna.

"You people all like to wear your right shoe on the left foot," he finally said, cranky and accusing.

Helen her threw back head and laughed. "How so?" But her interest was piqued. She shook Avid's arm again because he had turned back to the TV, looking taciturn. "What do you mean?"

He turned to her.

"You punish women for something they didn't do and you give the actual criminals a pass."

"Criminals?"

"The men who impregnate them without their consent," he answered. "The illegal impregnators."

"True enough. It's always been that way. Minds are difficult to change when we're used to seeing things a certain way." Helen was intrigued by his word choice. "You call them criminals?"

Avid suddenly decided to share his opinions.

"In my time, consent for sex and consent for pregnancy are totally separate things, with separate laws. Impregnating a woman is legally treated as an assault, unless the man obtains her signed contractual consent prior to conception. If she didn't willingly sign the pregnancy contract and she gets pregnant, she can file charges and the man gets a prison sentence." He paused. "She doesn't *have* to file charges, but she can. They give her time to consider it. *That's* how we solved the abortion crisis. It wasn't all that hard to figure it out. Honestly. Not that hard."

He looked at Helen and tapped his forehead as if to imply that her people were all idiots.

"*Really*. Wow."

"Nine months of prison. From the first day to the last you can't drink alcohol or eat any of the foods they recommend that pregnant women avoid. For the second and third month they administer a drug that makes you nauseated, so you can't ever hold food down before noon, plus sometimes randomly later in the day, at their whim. At the third month they strap and lock a weighted pregnancy simulator around your waist. They increase the weight of it every two weeks until you're carrying about sixty pounds at the end of your sentence. You can't even take it off to sleep or shower, and it has an embedded device that randomly kicks you in the stomach, particularly at night. The kicking gets harder and more frequent, the further you are into your prison sentence. You don't really sleep much, I've heard."

Helen was grinning broadly, leaning into the conversation. *Nice*, she thought, trying unsuccessfully to suppress her smile. She pressed her lips together and frowned to force the grin away.

"You can't interact with anyone when you're in prison. Nobody is allowed to talk to you, and you can't talk to them. They move you to a small one-room apartment with no windows, and they socially isolate you from everyone, except when you're doing community service. You can only talk to other people when you're doing community service."

"What's community service like in your time?" Helen asked.

"It's varies. For illegal impregnation it's mandatory, every day, and they usually make them chase after children in the playground without many opportunities to sit down. That's to trigger back pain, and to make them appreciate what pregnant women have to deal with when they already have children."

"Interesting," Helen murmured happily.

Avid's read on Helen was that she was thoroughly enjoying this conversation, even though she didn't comment much. She was pressing her lips together to keep them shut and unsmiling, but her eyes were dancing.

"By the fifth month in prison, when they've been nauseated for a couple of months and the Medical team induces hemorrhoids, the men mostly all understand what they had actually done to another person. They also begin to apply pressure to the bladder so you always have to urinate. Usually the men suddenly feel empathy, which is the entire point of their punishment. And they opt to undergo sterilization." As an aside, he added, "You always freeze your sperm first so you can still have children. In fact, it's pretty lucrative for Race Dynasty men, because they get a big perk for donating sperm. That's how they get all the Dynasty children that non-Dynasty people request."

Helen nodded, fascinated.

"The ones who don't feel empathy decide to be sterilized so they don't have to go through this punishment again. Suddenly life isn't all about protecting their sperm count, because they can still have children. That is the *point*. They can still have children. They have no reason to take the risk of another prison sentence."

Helen sighed wistfully.

"After the seventh month the simulated pregnancy weight is about forty-five pounds, and the kicking gets harder and happens more frequently. That's when they let them have a desk job."

"Do they put them through any labor pain at the end of the nine months?" She asked this dispassionately. However, Avid heard her thinking, *Please yes, oh please yes.*

"They do. On the last day of their sentence the medical staff induces abdominal spasms for twelve hours that increase in intensity and frequency toward the end. They're really painful. Then they give them a big pain surge in their groin. After that, they're free to go back to their lives again."

"Wow," Helen said. "Do they inject them with hormones for nine months? Give them water retention with elephant ankles? Because that would be educational for them, I think."

Avid didn't know.

"Do they actually have repeat offenders?" Helen asked.

"Not that I know of. The longest holdout I ever heard of was someone who lasted until they induced hemorrhoids at month five. That's when he asked for sterilization. I've never really heard of anyone going the entire nine months without getting sterilized."

"And it works?"

"What do you think?"

Helen laughed.

"Abortions went down to nearly zero. Problem solved."

"Nicely done," Helen said.

"Yes it was. Because we put the right shoe on the right foot."

"You really think of the women as victims there?"

"Did they impregnate themselves against their own will?"

Helen shrugged and shook her head..

"What other things can you do to negatively disrupt or ruin someone else's life, physical health, mental health and financial security, and have it not be a crime? Some women even die. I can't believe you don't see them as victims yourself. Even if you ultimately decide you're happy to have the child, you still encounter those risks."

"It's a paradigm shift I'm happy to make," Helen assured him. "I can easily think of women as victims and the men as criminals..." She thought of some of the things her female clients had experienced, and sighed. In her time men were still in charge for the most part, and they would never agree to something that benefited society in general, and women in particular, if they had to make a personal sacrifice or suffer the inconvenience of managing their own fertility and its aftereffects. It was simpler to shift the blame and responsibility to women, and they got away with doing that.

"So, after their sentence, they have to report for mandatory community service for four hours a day for the next eighteen years, helping watch over toddlers and preschoolers. Every day. No days off. If they have to miss a day, the Mitigators tack it to the end of their sentence. And if they don't perform the job satisfactorily and enthusiastically, the Mitigators make them take child rearing classes and early education classes, then extend their sentence and increase their daily hours. The Mitigators take child development very seriously, so you can't mess up with it. They don't stand for it."

Helen stared at Avid with no expression, then abruptly burst out laughing. She had tears streaming down her face and was bent over, holding her stomach. She began choking and coughing, then moved past that to laugh some more. She took a breath. She looked at Avid through tears, and then burst into a whole new barrage of laughter.

"Don't have a stroke," Avid cautioned her. That set Helen off again.

She caught her breath.

"If you tried that here, the men would all say that the punishment is too extreme and inhumane, especially the eighteen years of community service with children. They'd *scream*. But they have no problem with anything that happens to women." she said with twisted smile. "And the Mitigators came up with this?"

Avid nodded.

"Oh my God," she said. She loved the Mitigators more and more every day. She wiped her eyes. "You know, I'm not surprised that men opt out of fertility at only the third month, and I'm guessing it isn't because they feel any empathy toward women."

Her last remark had tinges of bitterness and anger. She had spent most of her life being angry about the things women had to endure, because she'd spent most of her life trying to piece women back together, and she was tired.

Avid picked up on this.

"The men in my time actually *do* feel empathy for women. We're taught to. It's ingrained in us. When we don't understand it on our own, we have laws that force us to. The whole time those men were in prison, they had therapy that reinforced it. They came out of it different."

Helen had doubts, and Avid heard them.

"Really, they did. But regardless of why, the punishment acts as a deterrent and the deterrent works because I haven't heard of anyone committing the crime in years."

"I'll just bet they haven't," Helen chortled.

"When they first passed the law, there were men who didn't want to be sterilized. It's always a choice, so they opted out." Avid rolled his eyes. "It's a painless procedure and it's reversible. It's a lot like your vasectomies today. It's not a big deal. You can reverse it as soon as you get consent from a woman, and if you never reverse it they still have your frozen sperm for in vitro pregnancy, so it isn't as if you can never have children. Who knows? Maybe you'll decide you want a Dynasty Child instead, right? Lots and lots of people go that route because of the perks and the status. Otherwise, most men never reverse it because we don't want to pay that kind of price for an accident. It makes no sense to not opt in."

"Some men think that having a vasectomy emasculates them," Helen offered.

"You get drunk, and the next thing you know you're bracing yourself for nine months of hemorrhoids and stomach kicking, then twelve hours of labor pains and a huge kick in the groin.

"That's fair, though," Helen said. "Women already do that here."

"I should think that *that* would be emasculating to men. So it mystifies me when men opt out."

He stood up and waddled a few steps with his hands cupped around an imaginary pregnant belly. "Manly," he said dryly, looking at her sideways.

Helen had a mouthful of wine in that moment and spewed it all over Avid. She hopped up to grab a towel and then patted him dry-ish.

"So that didn't last long," he continued, sitting down again. "Other men heard the stories and stopped balking at sterilization. Now it's a rite of passage, like a Bar Mitzvah (his Alert screen had just provided that reference). You *choose* to have it taken care of as soon as you have viable sperm to freeze, even if you're gay, because you get a really enormous perk for doing it. Then everyone throws you a party."

"Very clever." Helen's mind whirred for a moment. "And that's how you effectively ended abortion." She went back to her mental whirring, considering all the factors and the end result. The Mitigators nailed it, she concluded.

"Right. But *you* all act as if abortion is going to stop if you make it illegal and close abortion clinics. You're vicious, with the signs and the protests and the shouting at the clinics, and all the laws you pass, and the sanctimonious judgments, and forcing children to have the babies they conceived out of incest. How has that approach worked for you so far? It's as if you aren't quite bright, you know?"

He rolled his eyes and tapped his forehead again. "Nobody ever sees *the men* as the problem, only the women. Right shoe, left foot."

Helen nodded in thoughtful agreement. "It completely upends your life forever, if you keep the baby, and not always in a good way. Or it can cause long term emotional distress if you give it up for adoption."

Add to that, financial disaster and determining whether or not you can afford to work, considering the cost of daycare, Helen thought to herself. Leaving school. Getting attacked for needing food stamps and Medicaid to care for that child by the same people who didn't want you to have an abortion. Not being able to provide the best for your children. The list goes on and on.

Avid heard her, and was miserable and resentful that he even had to be in the proximity of this kind of abuse. In this time and place they leave those people to deal with it alone, without help or support, and frequently with judgment and condemnation. He was indignant.

The same was true with gun violence. Despite worldwide evidence to the contrary, they believed that more guns and lax laws meant less gun violence…so people kept dying. The Gun Violence team was constantly showing up to mass shootings. It hadn't been hard at all for the Mitigators to find a day and time when they could make an appointment with Helen and have one occurring live during the office visit. This society was insane.

He felt himself spiraling. His wine hadn't taken the edge off of his futile anger. This time. This place. It was all more than he could handle. He thought about the things he saw on the streets, and on the news, and at his assignments. He began to shake with fury. He drained his wine and poured another.

This isn't real for me. These people are all dead, he silently repeated to himself. *This isn't real for me. These people are all dead.*

But Helen wasn't dead. She was right here, and he had gotten extremely fond of her. She was his family now. She was his very favorite aunt. This time and place had moments of light, like Helen. He couldn't completely condemn and reject a time and place where Helen was. Where Nelda was.

Therapy. Meditation. Breathing exercises. He needed them now. He would schedule therapy tomorrow and meditate before bed tonight.

They picked the wrong Historian for this assignment, he thought hopelessly. I am not equipped for this. I cannot ever take another assignment that requires this kind of emotionally draining effort. He wondered if it was time to sign up for assignments involving puppies and dancing cockatiels.

He slumped in his seat on the couch and glared at his wine glass.

"What is it, honey?" Helen asked gently. She took his hand and massaged it.

"I can't stand it," he whispered. Then louder, he said, "I go out in public and there's absolutely nothing I can do to fix anything. They assign me these events that are *truly disgraceful,* and the people are violent and full of hate, and I can't stop any of it. I see death and anger and hostility and it's all so stupid. *It's all so stupid.*"

"I know," Helen said, still rubbing his hand.

"And then I see news shows that report on things I can't see personally, things that are just as bad as, or worse than the things I see with my own eyes, and I want to do something about the things I see, but I can't. Like homeless people. I see homeless people and I want to *scream* because I can't even give them a heart hug."

Helen reached up and squeezed his shoulder, and massaged it.

"We're taught from our first day of school to take care of other people, whether we know them or not. If we see someone suffering it just takes a second to give them a boost. It's free. It takes no effort. The Mitigators have clinical proof that heart hugs save lives and stop crime, and that the people we help usually pay it forward, and that every single one of us in our chain of influence is happier. Just from one heart hug to someone who needs one. Just from that little bit of basic human connection."

He added, "Not one of us would walk past a homeless person without doing something to help. Not one of us. Not even the Heroes, and I'm pretty sure they would walk past their own mothers."

He fiercely turned to Helen in frustration, with angry eyes.

"I can't even give a hurting person a heart hug here when I pass them on the street. Just doing that one small thing might uplift them enough to change the continuum, so I can't. Just walking past them without doing anything to help goes against every single thing I was ever taught, and I have to do that every single day. Every day I have to turn my back on people who are suffering. Every single day."

He was angry and distraught, and he was close to shutting down. "I *hate* it here," he muttered.

Suddenly he felt something...

Helen had successfully tuned into his frequency and was sending him a small, tentative, uneven but earnest heart hug. It was her very first, and she wasn't entirely proficient, but it was clearly a heart hug and it had successfully reached him.

He turned to her in amazement. She had done this in less than a week. The biofeedback was working, Avid noted happily.

"You did that," he said. "You *did* that!" he shouted.

"I did it!" Helen screamed. "I did it!" She got up and began to dance the Boogaloo, and then the Twist. She was referencing the nineteen-sixties, Avid noted happily. He had been there. So had she.

She was moving into the Watusi when he got up and hugged her. He twirled her around. She was giddy, laughing.

"Think of what this can do for my patients!" She shouted. "I'm a rock star!"

CHAPTER 17: GAME NIGHT

Helen, Avid, Nelda and Mary were all gathered around the dining room table, setting up a game of Yahtzee.

"It has to be a game that uses dice," Helen explained to Nelda and Mary. "Because Avid cheats at cards."

Nelda had prepared popcorn and served tortilla chips with salsa, and had handed a bottle of craft beer to each of them. She put retro rock and roll on the sound system. They all prepared to slaughter their opponents.

They had plans to do this every Saturday night, playing all the board games Helen had kept in her closet since her son was young. They had not been opened or used in over twenty years.

Avid had never played board games before, and was delighted. Saturday would now become his favorite night.

CHAPTER 18: PANTS

The Heroes and the subjects had returned to Dirk's apartment to discuss the upcoming lynching event, but were taking time off from that discussion to play everyone's favorite, Grand Theft Auto.

Nectar suddenly rose and addressed Dirk and Chad in Hinduese.

"I think I'm having stomach issues right now," she said. "It feels like it's going to be bad. I'm going to go to your en suite, Dirk. It's further away from here than the hall bathroom so the smell shouldn't reach the subjects. Tell everyone to steer clear, okay? This is going to take a while."

Dirk and Chad both looked unabashedly disgusted, and had no urge to experience the scent of Nectar's effluents. They wouldn't dare go back there.

Dirk had recently mentioned that he had moved everything here from his apartment at the control station because this condo gave him ready access to the local bars, those that were open, anyway. So that meant he had brought all of his clothes, and Nectar knew that they were all right here, right now.

Nectar went into Dirk's bedroom closet with a small pair of scissors and carefully cut out three teeth close to the bottom of the zipper on every pair of Dirk's pants. He would not be able to zip up his pants so he would now have to face the world with an open fly.

Nice tits indeed. Her threats of vengeance were now coalescing into plans, and she was only just beginning.

Afterward, she returned to the living room holding her stomach and looking as if it were going to happen again.

The other Heroes edged away from her with revulsion, and focused on the 98 inch TV screen where the Grand Theft Auto world was exploding.

CHAPTER 19: THANK YOU, CHAD

Avid was with Chad and Dirk and the other two Heroes in the main building's community hall. Avid had described his progress with Helen, and the Heroes had updated Avid on their progress with the subjects. The meeting was simply an update and did not require any further discussion.

This was the first time that Avid had seen Chad in person since the incident with the apartment swap. Chad did not appear to think that anything untoward had happened between them, and he displayed no guilt, remorse or shame.

Now that he had a plan Avid took a moment to tell Chad that he loved the apartment. He thanked Chad for swapping. He didn't mention the perks.

"Good doing business with you," Avid said to Chad. "You left a bit of a mess, but I got them to clean it up, so now everything is perfect and I really like being in that building."

"My pleasure," Chad replied with charming and gracious aplomb.

Avid turned to leave, while the Heroes all watched him go, thoughtful but expressionless.

CHAPTER 20: SEX TOYS

Avid's Alert screen flashed with a "knock" from Janicyl. And so it begins, Avid thought to himself smugly as he answered the call.

Janicyl re-introduced herself and reminded Avid that they had met at the Heroes meeting the other day.

Avid assured her that he could never forget a woman as beautiful as Janicyl.

Janicyl accepted this clear and obvious assessment of herself with a satisfied, "Thank you," and went straight to the point. She needed help. Would Avid be available to help her?

"By all means! I would be thrilled to help!" he told her.

"I'm tied up," Janicyl said apologetically, "and I desperately need someone to pick up some things for me. Could you please do that for me, and bring them to Dirk's apartment? I'll pay you back as soon as you get here."

"No problem," Avid assured her.

"Thanks much," Janicyl told him.

Avid's Alert screen displayed a list of items with a holographic image of each. He blinked. He was going to an adult store to buy sex toys and porn DVDs for Janicyl and presumably Dirk.

His Uber driver was willing to wait outside the adult store regardless, but Avid handed her a one hundred dollar tip for her trouble and thanked her. Then he went inside and looked around himself in wonder. So seedy! So fascinating! It was delightful, in a way. He'd never seen anything like it. He wished he had more time to explore.

He went straight to the counter and told the clerk he had a long list of items he needed to purchase immediately. Would the clerk help?

He would indeed. Avid grabbed the items in a nearly full shopping bag, including four porn DVDs that were originally filmed in the nineteen seventies. He pulled out his debit card and had them ring up the purchases, which totaled about twelve hundred dollars.

Then he hopped back into his Uber and went to Dirk's apartment. His Uber driver was willing to wait for him again while he went inside to drop everything off after he slipped her another hundred dollar bill.

Dirk, naked, invited him in and took the shopping bag from Avid.

"Janicyl is going to pay me. Here's the receipt."

Dirk glanced at the receipt and said, "Janicyl's tied up in there. She can't come out and pay you just now."

"Can *you* pay me then?"

Dirk gestured at his naked self and shook his head. "Bad timing," he explained.

Avid heard the headboard bang against the wall as Janicyl twisted in her ropes and handcuffs to adjust her position on the bed. She called from the bedroom.

"Thanks, Avid! Can I pay you on Monday? I'll meet you at the community center at noon. We'll have lunch. Okay?"

"Sounds great!" Avid pocketed the receipt, said his goodbyes, and left.

CHAPTER 21: PANTS AGAIN

"I'm Dirk Van de Kamp's driver, and he asked me to pick up the pants you fitted him for the other day. They had a problem with the zippers, I think. Are they ready?"

The Wardrobe Expert checked his Alert screen and nodded. "I believe so. I'll be right back."

"Thank you."

Nectar absently watched the wardrobe staff measuring and fitting Historians for their excursions on-land, or custom tailoring their clothing on antique sewing machines. She still didn't like their clothing options, but had safely averted their poor taste herself so they no longer had any impact on her happiness.

"Here you go." The Wardrobe Expert placed a pile of pants on the counter, and thanked Nectar as she grabbed them and left.

She retreated to her apartment, where she opened the Amazon package she had just retrieved from an on-land Amazon locker. It contained a seam ripper, which she tore out of its packaging and placed on the coffee table.

She lifted the first pair and studied the seams, deciding on the seam at the seat of the pants. Then she used the seam ripper to carefully cut the seam's thread every inch or so from the waistband to the crotch. She folded the pants, smoothing out any wrinkles, and placed them at the side of the coffee table. Then she reached for the next pair, and then the next, and then the next.

CHAPTER 22: STILL MORE PANTS

SUNDAY, APRIL 4, 2021: 14:03 HOURS

"I'm Dirk Van de Kamp's driver, and he asked me to pick up the pants you fitted him for the other day. So I picked them up and then found out he's moved out of his apartment here, and is living on-land. I have to be here for the next several days and we won't have a chance to meet up until Friday, so I can't deliver them. Could I please leave them with you? Could you please tell him they're ready and he needs to come and get them?"

The Wardrobe expert slid the pile of pants off the counter, placed them in a storage cubby for items awaiting pickup, and told Nectar he would be happy to oblige.

CHAPTER 23: JANICYL NO SHOWS

Avid dutifully waited for forty five minutes after he was to have met Janicyl for lunch. This was the lunch where she was supposed to have paid him back the money he'd spent on her sex toys. He decided that forty-five minutes was sufficient, then walked over to the bank and up to his usual bank representative.

"I have been egregiously misused by a Hero," Avid told the man.

"Indeed," the man answered. "I'm so sorry. May I ask what you've had to endure?"

Avid described the incident with the sex toys and the money he'd spent to procure them. He produced the receipt.

The bank representative consulted the scanner footage and concurred with Avid that he had been sorely mistreated.

"My cash out-of-pocket is twelve hundred dollars. Can you add anything extra to compensate me for my shame and humiliation?" He was testing the waters. He had a suspicion about the bank representative.

"I can."

"Thank you. Also, I tipped my Uber driver five hundred dollars because I knew that Janicyl would have wanted me to. She's very generous. Could you please compensate me for that as well?"

"Indeed I shall."

It was just as Avid had suspected. He decided to press this as far as he could until someone stopped him, or he ran out of ideas.

"Thank you. But I have to tell you that Janicyl and I were supposed to meet for lunch. That's where she was going to reimburse me. I was going to suggest to Janicyl that she and I have lunch at the Windsor House on the top floor, and I'm feeling victimized because of my disappointment when she failed to appear. Might I please have compensation for the perk value of the meal I was anticipating?"

"As you command," the bank representative replied. "Do you have anything specific in mind that you would like to request as compensation for your sad misfortune? A wingsuit skydiving flight over a canyon near the Himalayas, perhaps?" He sent Avid a holographic video of someone hurling himself into the depths of a canyon, riding the wind in a special "flying squirrel" wingsuit with nothing but that suit to support him.

"Yes, please. I'll take that."

"Head to the Wish Book and put in your request."

"Thank you." Then Avid paused. "May I ask you a personal question?"

"That depends," the bank representative answered.

"Did the Heroes make your life miserable in school?" Could that be why he loved his job so much?

The bank representative looked away guardedly, and said, "Why do you ask?"

"Me too," Avid said, and bent over in a Namaste bow. Then he went to the Wish Book and ordered his Himalayan wingsuit excursion.

CHAPTER 24: DIRK 'S RESERVATION

The Heroes were having their weekly meeting in the control station Community Center. Dirk was telling Chad that he had met a woman on-land, and was taking her out to dinner. He named the trendy Michelin star restaurant they were going to go to, and told Chad that it had just finally opened up to half capacity. When the restaurant had made the announcement that it was reopening for indoor dining, the reservations had filled up so quickly that they were booked months in advance after only two days.

Dirk knew the restaurant manager from having played darts with him at the sports bar. He had offered him $200.00 to find him a table for two any evening before May 14th. The restaurant manager had demurred, so Dirk increased his offer to $500.00. The restaurant manager had accepted, and Dirk was proudly telling Chad he had a reservation tomorrow evening.

When Dirk mentioned the date and time of the reservation, Nectar perked up. She slipped away under the pretext of needing a bathroom, and sent an Alert screen message to a friend of hers who had clearance to interact. When the friend answered, Nectar gave him Dirk's name, the name of the restaurant, and the date and time of the reservation. Then she instructed her friend to call the restaurant and introduce himself as "Dirk Ford," then cancel it.

The friend complied.

CHAPTER 25: NECTAR'S ESSENTIALS

Nectar left Dirk's apartment and went back to the control station because he no longer needed her to drive him to his dinner date this evening. Consequently, she had the night off. On her way to her apartment she stopped off in the main building and went to the commissary to pick up some more non-toxic nausea drops from the pharmacist in case she needed them again. Heroes always kept some on hand in case they were caught in a tricky situation and needed to escape. She had just run out.

While she was there, she purchased a "gag quick drink generator," which creates drinks that all taste like soap. Then she went home.

CHAPTER 26: DIRK'S AILMENT

THURSDAY, APRIL 8, 2021: 19:11 HOURS

Avid's Alert screen issued a knock from Dirk. Avid answered, and gave him a friendly wave and a Hello. He was now always happy to hear from a Hero.

Dirk didn't know what to do and needed help, he told Avid. He was supposed to meet this woman for dinner, but he was running late. He'd spent five hundred dollars on a bribe to get the table, and someone had to show up for the reservation or he'd lose it even if he was just a few minutes late. Would Avid please show up as a placeholder, give them Dirk's name, and grab the table so they didn't lose it? He'd texted his date, and told her to go in if he didn't show up right away, but he couldn't risk her showing up late and losing the table, or getting impatient and leaving. Could Avid please sit with her just until Dirk arrived? He didn't want her running off before he got there.

"I would love to. Do I get to join you for dinner and sample the food?" Avid chuckled "ha-ha-ha" like a co-conspirator. This was very fun.

"Absolutely not. Her name is Amelia, and she's going to meet me in front of the restaurant at twenty-hundred hours. Any later than that and I think she'll be inside." Dirk sent Avid an image of a lovely brown-haired woman with a nice smile.

Avid explained the situation to Helen and Nelda, and then dressed nicely because he was going to be entering an upscale restaurant. He ate a few bites from the plate Nelda had already prepared for him, to be polite, then ordered an Uber so he would arrive at twenty-hundred hours.

It was not quite twenty-hundred hours, so Amelia was still outside looking for Dirk when Avid climbed out of the vehicle. She was dressed for an evening out at an expensive restaurant, but looked comfortable in her clothing as if she was used to upscale living. Dirk was fishing in the "wealthy woman pool" for dates, apparently.

Avid approached her and introduced himself, explaining the situation with Dirk.

"He'll be here in a little bit, he's just running late. He asked me to grab the table for him so he wouldn't lose the reservation, and to keep you company until he gets here. He didn't want you to be sitting alone." Avid made that last part up. Dirk had said nothing at all about the comfort of his date, and in truth would never have considered it.

Amelia smiled and thanked him. They both walked into the restaurant, with Avid holding the door for her because his Alert screen had just told him to do that. This was his first venture into a local restaurant with a local woman in this century and he hadn't really known what was expected of him.

The Hostess greeted them with a condescending smile, and checked the reservations for "Dirk Ford."

"I'm sorry, sir. There is no reservation." She had a French accent.

"Are you sure?"

"Quite sure, Monsieur." She amped up her condescension just a notch.

Avid pulled out his smart phone and called Dirk, who didn't answer. He then sent him a text message.

"What should we do?" Avid asked Amelia. "I don't want to stand outside and wait for him. Do you know of any other restaurants? I'm new in town and don't have any idea which ones are good. Then I'll text him to tell him where to meet us."

Amelia thought about it for a moment and then suggested another pricey restaurant in the area. It was close enough for them to walk to it.

Avid found the phone number on Yelp and called the restaurant to see if they had any seating available. Unbelievably they did, so Avid gave them his name and told them he would be there momentarily. He and Amelia walked the half block to the restaurant, chatting amiably about the weather. When they arrived, they were greeted and seated. Avid texted Dirk to tell him where they were. Then they ordered drinks while they waited for Dirk to join them.

When Dirk still hadn't responded to his text message or the voicemail Avid had left for him, Avid excused himself and went to the Men's room, where he held his smart phone to his ear so he would look as if he were speaking on the phone. He then tried to reach Dirk on his Alert screen. Dirk answered looking ill. Avid could see he was kneeling in front of a toilet.

"I don't think I can come," Dirk said. "Tell Amelia I'll need to reschedule. I keep heaving."

"What's going on?"

"Food poisoning, I think. But no, that can't be right because I haven't eaten anything. I'm not dying or anything, but it's bad enough so that I can't leave the bathroom."

"What did you eat?"

"Nothing all day. I started feeling sick after I had a drink tonight while I was getting ready. Maybe vodka doesn't sit well on an empty stomach, I don't know. Or maybe I'm coming down with something." He paused to ask, "Aren't we supposed to be immune to all known diseases in this time frame? I'm going to get checked out with Medical." He shook his head, exasperated. "It came on all of a sudden. Nectar came over to drive me to the restaurant, we had drinks, and the next thing I knew I was face first in the toilet. It's been about an hour and I'm starting to feel better, but I don't want to take any chances."

"Is she sick too?"

"No, she's fine. It's just as well, though. I picked up some pants from Wardrobe, and had to return them all for repairs. When I tried on a pair and sat down, the seat tore. Every pair was the same way, so I wouldn't have anything good enough to wear out to dinner anyway. I don't know what's wrong with Wardrobe, by the way. They stuck me with bad zippers on that entire batch of clothes I picked up from them for the on-land apartment, and after I sent them in for repairs, they came back like this. I might have to report them."

Avid returned to the table and explained the situation to Amelia. Dirk wasn't coming because of some kind of food poisoning. Then he asked if she would mind spending the evening with him instead. It would be Dirk's treat. She didn't mind at all.

Since Dirk was paying, so to speak, Avid ordered several appetizers and several courses, plus a very expensive bottle of wine. Then he ordered a second bottle of wine. He encouraged Amelia to select the most expensive entre on the menu, then sighed happily as the server came with plate after plate of exquisite, very expensive food. They had no room for dessert, but Avid insisted on ordering it anyway.

He was satisfied when the bill exceeded eight hundred dollars. With a five hundred dollar tip, the total would be well over one thousand dollars. The "twenty percent upcharge" he would receive at the bank for being victimized by a Hero would be well worth his effort, which was a nice bonus for an evening he had thoroughly enjoyed. Even though Dirk had not deliberately made him a victim, Avid thought that the bank representative might compensate him for his time and the money he spent tonight. It was just a hunch.

It had been a delightful evening for both of them. The conversation flowed, they both enjoyed each other's company, and dinner was fabulous. Avid and Amelia sipped their after-dinner coffee with sated contentment.

Avid walked Amelia to her car, told her Dirk would be calling her soon, and waved to her as she drove away. Amelia went home with a far better impression of Dirk than she would have had if she had actually spent the evening with him. Avid would ask the bank to view that as "community service" and reimburse him for it.

Avid gave the Uber driver his now-standard five hundred dollar tip and then went up Helen's front steps, unlocked the door, climbed the staircase, and crawled into bed.

CHAPTER 27: FLIGHT LESSONS

FRIDAY, APRIL 9, 2021: 13:01 HOURS

"How many flight lessons will this get me?" Avid was cashing in on his dinner the previous evening. As he had expected, the bank representative reimbursed him for everything, including community service.

"Private plane or commercial pilot?"

"Private plane, I think."

"We can get you three stages of private pilot training totaling one hundred forty four hours with additional ground training and weather training."

"Excellent!"

"Very good. It has been my pleasure, and I expect to see you very soon. For now, I invite you to request your flight lessons from the Wish Book. You know what to do."

"Thank you."

CHAPTER 28: HELEN FEELS PAIN

SATURDAY, APRIL 10, 2021: 16:15 HOURS

Helen had been shifting uncomfortably in her seat as she practiced mentally connecting to Avid. Avid had sensed this immediately when he first met her, that she was experiencing pain, but it was getting more noticeable. She knew she had arthritis, but it was getting worse in her hips and was beginning to impact her walk. She had also been concerned about her eyesight and suspected she had cataracts. She was irritated that it all might slow her down, so she just kept pushing through and taking Aleve and CBD gummies to dull the pain, muttering sometimes, but not complaining. Avid could tune into her though, and saw that her problems with pain were increasing.

Avid sent a message to the Mitigator-on-duty without Helen's knowledge to ask if they were willing to send a twenty-eighth century doctor to treat her. No one he knew of had ever made a request like this, so he was doubtful that they would permit it. However, he got the approval, and was immediately given an appointment time the next day, Sunday. The doctor would be arriving at fourteen hundred hours, and Avid should advise Helen about the appointment so she could mentally prepare.

He told Helen, who was thrilled, less because she was going to receive treatment than because she wanted to see exactly what twenty-eighth century medicine looked like.

CHAPTER 29: HELEN'S DOCTOR

SUNDAY, APRIL 11, 2021: 12:47 HOURS

The future of medicine was one of the things Helen had the most questions about, right after the future of psychotherapy. She was as giddy as if she were planning a trip to Europe, waiting impatiently for "her" doctor, Gabai Dang, to arrive.

"Will the doctor beam down right into my house? How does it work? How will he get here?"

"They land at the control station, then they take a travel pod to somewhere on-land, and then they get an Uber." He had no idea what Helen was referring to when she said "beam."

"No seriously."

"I'm serious. That's how we get around. Did I not ever tell you that? We take Uber and public transportation after we get dropped off on-land." His Alert screen displayed Captain Kirk saying, "Beam me up", then showed him transmitting in a shimmery glow from a planet to a spaceship. The alert included an update on the progress of that effort by the Technology Project so he could tell her that they were working on making that kind of transmission more widely useful.

"We call your beaming 'extraction' and we only use it in an emergency. If someone is injured or in a really dangerous situation, the time travel team can pull them out. Right now, though, they can only use it to pull someone out of a time period in the past and back to the twenty-eighth century. If we're on-land and traveling from place to place within the same time period, we take Uber or the bus."

Doctors were frequently dispatched into the past to treat time travelers, or to recommend extraction if their condition was critical or the danger level was severe, as in a war zone. Doctors traveled to the injured Historians, applied palliative treatment, and then arranged for them to transmit directly to the twenty-eighth century without stopping at the local control station's time travel facility. When they arrived back home the Historians received more thorough medical care. Heroes in particular were highly subject to injury because of their job difficulty level, and extraction for them was frequent.

Doctors all had language implants in addition to their Medical implants because they automatically received local interaction clearance for every assignment. There would be no problem with communication.

But doctors didn't usually travel back in time to make house calls to locals complaining of arthritic joints. This was a new development.

When the doorbell rang, Helen leapt up and ran to answer it. Waiting for her on the other side was a youngish, slight woman of mixed Asian, Hispanic, and West Indian ancestry wearing blue jeans and a sweater, with a denim backpack slung over one shoulder. She was holding a box of gourmet cupcakes.

"Dr. Dang?" Helen held out her hand. "I'm so pleased to meet you."

Helen shook Dr. Dang's hand enthusiastically and smiled widely. Dr. Dang permitted Helen to shake her hand without squeezing back because she wasn't certain of the protocol and was too excited and distracted to notice the Alert that was coaching her. She looked past Helen with awe, taking in her home and its furnishings. Then she peered up at Helen with a confused look on her face as Helen pumped her hand up and down. She had never shaken hands with anyone before and was processing it.

"I've never had an assignment quite like this," she said when the interesting handshake ended. "It's really exciting for me!" She handed the box of cupcakes to Helen and told her they were a gift from the Mitigators, while looking around herself with obvious interest in everything she saw. It was as if she were drinking it in so she wouldn't forget.

"It's exciting for me too! Please come in!" She led Dr. Dang to the living room and invited her take a seat. Then she went to the kitchen where she arranged the cupcakes on a plate, brought them into the living room with paper napkins, and set them on the coffee table. She grabbed one, then motioned to Dr. Dang to take one as well. They spent a few seconds chewing and making noises of pleasure.

Dr. Dang turned her head back and forth as she looked around the house. "This is the first time I've ever been inside a local's house. I don't typically have permission to travel on-land, and I've never been to twenty-first century America either, so this is an adventure, and all very fun for me!"

Helen insisted on giving Dr. Dang a tour of the house, upstairs and down, with a quick walk through the backyard. Dr. Dang smiled in awe the entire time, touching things and asking Helen what she used them for. Helen demonstrated how to turn on a table lamp and how to use an electric razor. "This is a paper shredder." "This is the garbage disposal, and this is what it does." "This is the garage where I keep my car, and this is how you open the garage door. Sit in the car for a minute, if you want."

Dr. Dang marveled at the antiquities and was fascinated with the television, then was completely enamored by the appliances in the kitchen. "I've seen these in images!" she cried, turning the gas stove burners on and off and giggling, turning to Helen so she could share her amazement.

Dr. Dang was particularly thrilled by Helen's backyard. She kept peering up at the sky with a reverent look on her face. Suddenly, her jaw dropped when a plane flew far overhead, and she intensely followed its course until it disappeared.

"Amazing," she breathed. "Have you ever been up in one of those?" she asked Helen.

Helen nodded off-handedly. Of course she had flown, she thought, amused.

Dr. Dang's expression turned to awe and admiration.

"Did you love it? I don't know of anyone who wouldn't give a fortune to fly in a plane just once. I'd love to fly in one of them one day and look down at the clouds. I've seen images. Did you love that when you flew? Seeing clouds?" Helen nodded, smiling. Dr. Dang added, "There isn't much of a view from a travel pod. It's all a blur."

Helen had been amused by Avid's obsession with the perks he had traded in for helicopter rides, balloon rides, sky diving, parasailing, and flight lessons. She had thought it was a personal quirk of his, but looking at Dr. Dang's expression it seemed to be a deeper cultural yearning, to escape the ocean in order to fly in the air.

Dr. Dang was still looking up, searching the sky for another plane. When she saw one, she grew visibly excited. She was completely focused on it as it crossed the sky.

There was something touching about her excitement, Helen thought. It made her feel a little more grateful for the things she had, not knowing precisely what she had that Dr. Dang did not.

Outdoor settings were exotic to people in the twenty-eighth century, and were normally only a holographic experience for them, unless they traveled to the nature preserves or visited prehistoric times. Dr. Dang suddenly squealed with pleasure when a bird flew down and landed a few yards in front of her, then clapped her hands with delight when a squirrel scurried up a tree. They did not have live animals in the holograms.

Helen hadn't noticed either animal at all until Dr. Dang said something.

"Did you see that? It went right up that tree!" Dr. Dang cried, pointing. "What do you call that adorable animal with the fluffy tail?"

"You don't have squirrels?"

"Squirrels? Lovely! We probably do, but they'd be housed in the nature preserves. I'm so busy I never get around to visiting. But after seeing all this…" She waved her hand around the tiny yard, "I have to make a point of doing that soon! I love this!"

Then she squatted to study an ant hill, watching the ants with amazement. She gingerly put her finger down to gently push one aside so she could see what it would do. Then she did it to another ant, looking up at Helen and laughing. She reminded Helen of her son when he was exploring the yard as a three-year-old, which made her feel a rush of aching, protective affection for her. Something was really off, but she couldn't quite pinpoint what it was. She wondered if Avid could explain it to her, or if he would even notice the doctor's strangeness, since he came from the same world.

Dr. Dang turned her face back up at the sky and studied the clouds for a minute or two, then stood with that look of happy peaceful reverence on her face. She closed her eyes and took several deep breaths, smiling.

Helen found the doctor to be charming but oddly disquieting. There was something deeply, unnervingly sad and poignant about her childlike delight with the backyard that Helen couldn't identify. It was like watching someone who had experienced extreme deprivation taking her first step into a large, fully-stocked grocery store. She was like someone who was colorblind wearing glasses that permitted her to see colors for the first time. It made Helen quiet and thoughtful, almost to the point of tears. For some reason she wanted to give Dr. Dang a hug, but didn't dare. She wanted to keep her here with the birds and the squirrels and the ants and the planes, and not let her go back home.

Avid walked up and joined them. The doctor turned to him. "And you're Avid," she said. "I've been hearing a lot about you. Tough assignment they gave you, eh? Backing up the Heroes? But I hear you're doing a great job."

Avid thanked her and the two of them gave each other Namaste bows. They all turned and went into the house.

"We have cupcakes, Avid. Help yourself. They're on the coffee table." To Dr. Dang she asked, "Can I get you something to drink?" Helen was eager to please this poor woman.

Dr. Dang asked for a beverage Helen didn't recognize because it hadn't been invented yet. Avid nodded knowingly and went to the kitchen where he pulled out his quick drink generator and whipped one up for her. He made two more for Helen and himself, and brought the three mugs into the living room on a tray.

Helen tasted hers. "What is this? It's good!" It was a kind of tea, similar to chai but with different spices and a hint of dark chocolate and mint. Then she looked at Avid, bewildered. "How did you make this? Do I even have these ingredients?"

Avid explained what the quick drink generator was, and promised to give her a demonstration later. He had never shown it to her before because the subject had never come up in conversation, and Avid had never thought to use it because the kitchen already contained everything he might want or need. Helen was, once again, delighted at having one more thing to discover.

"Let's talk a little about what you're feeling," Dr. Dang told Helen. "Hips, correct? Eyes? We'll focus on them specifically in a little bit, but I first want to give you a full-body exam and a youth booster."

Helen looked at Avid with a skewed and questioning smile. She mouthed the words "youth booster" then made an expression of open-mouthed surprise.

"With the youth booster you won't age anymore. This is how old you'll look for the rest of your life," Avid told Helen. He had had no idea they would ever be willing to let her have one. He would have thought it would impact the continuum, but was thrilled for Helen that the Mitigators were willing to take that chance on her behalf. He had become increasingly aware of their fondness for Helen, and this was one more example of what they were willing to do for her.

"Have you had one?" Helen looked at him and studied his face. "How old are you, Avid?"

"I'm fifty-three. I have two grown children and a granddaughter."

Helen stared. "You don't look a day over thirty."

"That's usually about how old we are when we get the youth booster. But I was actually thirty-four at the time, so that's how old I should look to you, thirty-four."

"You have a granddaughter?"

"I do. She's four years old."

"And your wife?"

"Amicably divorced. I'm single."

"Girlfriend?"

"I'm close friends with a woman in eleventh century, Scotland, so it's a long-distance relationship."

"No kidding," said Helen.

"She's working as a Nordic priestess and landed there in a longboat with the Vikings. She's staying in one of their settlements right now. Her assignment will be up in two years. After that, we'll see."

Helen stared at him with a bemused expression and raised her eyebrows in muted astonishment.

"So there's no talk of marriage yet, if you were about to ask me."

"How long have you known her?"

"We met in Baltimore, 2046 a few years ago, and now I visit her whenever I get the chance. She *would* come to this time period to visit me, but I'm staying with you, and the McKenna Anomaly is my primary focus, so it isn't really convenient. I have to go back to then, which I've only been able to do a few times, or else she'll join me on vacation when I cash in my Hero perks."

Helen sat in stunned silence. Nothing about Avid was anything like she had imagined. They had talked about his world and his time, but they had never discussed anything personal. She should have asked more questions.

The doctor had begun mentally probing Helen while she and Avid were talking. She didn't touch her at all, but Helen could sense it. The full body exam the doctor promised was primarily a series of mental instructions to her medical implant, which then did something that Helen could feel. Dr. Dang tested the various internal organs, joints, bones and chemical balances throughout Helen's body, and noted any abnormalities. Then she mentally applied some kind of vibration to areas of concern. Helen felt her hips twitch intensely, then felt some pressure around her heart, and then she felt it in her eyes.

"The doctor has a medical implant," Avid explained. "She's looking at a screen like mine to see what's going on with your body, and then she activates the implant to treat you with sound waves and whatever else the implant does. I have no idea how it works aside from what I just told you. I think it's an advancement on the ultrasound therapy you have here. I'm not sure."

Helen looked at the doctor for more information, but the doctor didn't explain her process because she was focused on the task at hand. She just kept moving from one body part to the next, and the vibration followed her. Helen's joints all began to tingle. Her hands began to ache and shudder while Helen watched the joints in her fingers go from swollen with arthritis to normal as the cartilage regenerated. She flexed her fingers. Her hands were perfect. Her hips weren't in pain.

"Can you read this?" The doctor held up a book she found on the coffee table.

"Yes! It's all clear again! Wow!"

The doctor looked up. "You've just had a complete tune up. I found a couple areas of concern that were planning to cause you problems in the future, but I took care of them for you, so you should be fine. Just be sure to drink plenty of water for the rest of the day. You need to flush away the toxins I loosened up in your joints. I'm serious. Lots and lots of water. Do you have any questions?"

"I'll never look a day older?"

"That's right."

"Wow. What about my prescription medications? Should I keep taking them?"

"No, I corrected your arteries and your blood pressure, and your heart functionality is normal again. You can throw your medicine away if you want."

"You've just healed the crippled and given sight to the blind!" Helen laughed and hugged her.

Avid suddenly received an alert telling him to handle her questions carefully so that he didn't break any laws. This was troubling and he began to feel uneasy and fretful. What was Helen going to ask? What specifically had triggered the alert? But Helen didn't have any questions right now. She was talking to Dr. Dang.

"Do you have any training in psychotherapy?" Helen asked.

"A little. What do you want to know?" she replied.

"Everything."

Dr. Dang laughed and probed Helen's mind a little so she knew what kind of knowledge she already had, and what she was looking for. The doctor explained how they corrected the physical causes of mental conditions that were brain-related. She specifically referenced the psychopaths and the modifications they performed on their brains to make them as close to normal as they could be, while still retaining all the important qualities of psychopathy that enabled them to do their jobs. They had found ways to adjust brain chemistry without drugs. They could repair brain damage. Then, after they'd addressed all the physical abnormalities, they focused solely on the patient's emotions.

"Psychological pain is a mostly emotional experience, as you know. It isn't an intellectual exercise for us, the way it is in your time. The patient doesn't talk through problems because we only have to probe in order to know what they're experiencing. We can still verbally redirect someone into choosing better paths and taking healthier actions, the way you do with your patients, but it helps if we quell some of the pain first, and teach them how to avoid it, endure it, or minimize it themselves. The first thing we do is make them feel supported, safe, and loved before they even begin that kind of work. Then they have that same support throughout the entire process. I'm told you already experienced a short session. How do you feel about it?"

"Amazing!" Helen said. "I want to learn how to do it myself."

"Your abilities are always going to be a little limited, but there are some things you can do. Avid is helping you learn them. You'll be a stellar therapist when he's done with you. Your patients are very lucky." She smiled and touched Helen's arm.

Helen looked humbled and a little embarrassed by the praise. Avid couldn't read her thoughts except to hear her client list in rapid passing, and the approach she hoped to take with each patient. She was very excited.

Dr. Dang, having completed her exam of Helen as well as her tea, rose to leave. Helen hugged her at the door when the doctor's Uber arrived, then watched her hop down the stairs and into the vehicle, on her way to her travel pod pickup point and back to the twenty-eighth century.

"I can't tell you how wonderful I feel right now," Helen told Avid. She held her hand out at shoulder height, then attempted to kick it. She was successful.

"Oh my God!" she cried. "That was my bad hip!" She bent down and touched her toes. She got down on the floor, then lifted herself up again without any difficulty. "I have the body of a forty-year-old!" she crowed. "Hallelujah! And absolutely nothing hurts! Nothing!"

Helen ran up and down the stairs. "Hallelujah!" she shouted. She lifted heavy objects. She opened a jar of pickles. She tried to think of what else she could do without difficulty, then decided to surprise herself with it later. She sat back down, grinning.

"Could I please see your drink generator? Would you show me how it works?"

Avid went into the kitchen and held a pitcher under the faucet, filling it with water. He brought it back to the living room with glasses. He pulled the drink generator from his jacket pocket and handed it to Helen to examine.

"I control it from my Alert screen. It connects to the device, like your Bluetooth, and then I select a beverage, and command the device to make that specific beverage from the water. It makes the water hot for tea and coffee, unless you expressly request cold. Then, it chills it. It can even create ice cubes." He explained how it was necessary in times and places that didn't have clean water or drinks that were palatable to twenty-eighth century tastes. "You don't want to drink Viking ale, for instance. Flat, sour, awful—I am here to tell you no, emphatically, to not drink it. Ugh. So, we make our own."

"What specifically can you make?"

"Hundreds of things, I think. I'm not sure how many. Do you want a Starbucks coffee with soy milk and whipped cream? It can do that."

"No," Helen answered. "I want to see you make wine." There was something intense about the way she said that.

"Any preference?"

Helen thought about it, and then named a very expensive wine and vintage that she and her husband had splurged on for their fortieth wedding anniversary. Avid entered the request into his Alert screen, then watched the drink generator connect. He placed the device into the pitcher while Helen studied everything with completely focused concentration as it whirred and the water changed color. Avid poured her a glass. Helen stared at him while she raised the glass to her lips. She sipped.

"Oh my God," she said. "Holy shit."

"Good?"

"Perfect. Wow. How does it work?"

"It rearranges the molecules of the water to match the molecular structure of the drink you want. On a molecular level it's the same as the real drink."

"So you can turn water into wine?" Helen asked. "And you can make food with this thing?"

Avid's Alert screen flashed a warning to him again. He was thoroughly confused over why that might be. He couldn't read Helen's spinning thoughts, so they were not giving him any clues either.

"We need a different device for food, but yes. That device is an organic version of 3D printing, but it also rearranges the molecules so they're exact matches to the food you request. You have 3D bioprinting now, right? In your time they're experimenting with it to create human tissue and organs with organic materials. Later in your century they also learn how to use that technology to create edible food. Rearranging the molecules comes a couple hundred years later."

"And your psychologists can probe someone and dispel demons?"

"Demons? I don't know what you're talking about. What do you mean?"

"People have traditionally thought that brain dysfunction and brain damage were caused by demons that make people behave as if they're possessed. Newsflash. They're not."

"Yes, I guess so. What does that have to do with—"

"Do you have any sort of flotation device that lets you walk on water?"

"Of course. We live in the ocean. We can do lots of things with water."

Helen stared at him.

"Could your food generator make loaves and fishes? Was Jesus a time traveler with a medical implant and a food generator, and a drink generator that turned water into wine?"

"*What!!?*" Avid's Alert screen was flashing red. He was irritated, aiming that question at both the Mitigator and Helen. He was completely bewildered.

"Did the Mitigators extract him from the tomb after the crucifixion?"

"What tomb?"

"Was Jesus a time traveler?" she repeated.

Avid had never studied Jesus. He knew very little about him except from indirect exposure to Christians during his various assignments.

Avid had no idea. It was possible, he thought, that "Jesus" was the character role of a time traveler. It seemed possible that he might have been serving up Two Buck Chuck to the crowds back in Biblical times and scooting across the water in his hover boots, but that wasn't something that he'd ever heard anyone discuss. And the laws against a time traveler being anyone's messiah were pretty harsh, so it was unlikely.

His Alert screen flashed, "Tell her no. Jesus was not a time traveler."

"The Mitigator says no," Avid said to Helen. "Jesus wasn't a time traveler."

"I see," Helen said. Then she laughed.

"It wouldn't be possible because there's a law against it. They would have stepped in to stop it."

"Law against what?"

"Against preaching to the locals about anything that can be interpreted as a 'religion.' You can create an Anomaly or an alternate history and it can send you to prison."

"There hasn't been a Second Coming. *Right? Hmmm?* Maybe that's why. Is that what happened? Prison?"

The Mitigators weren't flashing the warning anymore, but they *were* forcefully commanding Avid in a huge pulsing font on his Alert screen to immediately change the subject, while emphasizing these commands telepathically. This was the first instance where a Mitigator had communicated with him telepathically, so they were very serious. Avid and Helen were apparently approaching the boundaries of what the Mitigators would good-naturedly tolerate.

"No more speculation about Jesus. The Mitigators want us to stop," Avid said.

"Fine," said Helen. She shrugged, but her thoughts still kept churning.

"He couldn't be a time traveler because the Mitigators put new laws into place after that mess with the Sky People in Central America and Mexico," he said. Then he told her the story of one of the early "mistakes" that had required Mitigator tweaking. The Sky People were time travelers, whom the early Mesoamerican tribes revered as gods when they showed up in their travel pods and interacted with the locals. "Google them," Avid told her. "And no, they weren't aliens from outer space. That's just a myth."

When they first sent Historians to Mesoamerica, Avid continued, the Mitigators were not familiar with the "Sky People" because Sky People never existed before the time travelers arrived. The continuum Avid and Helen were living in right now was actually an alternative history that was created at that specific historical juncture. Scientists theorized that the original continuum still existed apart from this one in some other universe, but they weren't certain what happened to it. They were still looking into everything, comparing the "pre" Historian Project continuum to the "'post" Historian Project continuum, trying to figure out how scientific laws controlled alternative histories. It had only been twenty-six years since the Sky People Anomaly had become apparent to the Mitigators, so they hadn't gotten very far in their research yet. In the meantime, no one could return to the original continuum. As a result, the world Avid and Helen inhabited now had Sky People in its history, whereas the original continuum did not.

Around that time the Mitigators changed the laws so that regular tourists were primarily limited to prehistoric times with no interaction with any variety of hominid. They created laws to forbid Historians, or anyone else, from interacting with the locals henceforth unless they had received extensive training, had clearance to interact, and were closely monitored. They made every effort to cloak any air pod travel in populated areas. They began aggressively addressing Anomalies. They made religion an off-limits topic for discussion and made laws against religious preaching, or even casual conversations the locals could interpret as religious preaching. Off-limit topics included the twenty-eighth century's understanding of the afterlife, the meaning of life, and the factual or non-factual nature of local religions.

They also recognized the need for Race Dynasties to make personal interaction less necessary in highly populated areas, the Historians themselves less godlike, noteworthy, and saga-worthy, and physical attack less likely in the more primitive locations.

Avid explained all this to Helen, whose thoughts were churning and inscrutable.

"I see," Helen repeated, raising her eyebrows. She could believe whatever she liked, so she decided to believe that Jesus was a time traveler, like Dr. Who, and it didn't matter what the Mitigators said.

CHAPTER 30: PERSONAL QUESTIONS

"I have never asked you enough personal questions, not really," Helen said to Avid over dinner. "I've only just gotten started. For instance, what kind of a name is 'Avid'? I've been wondering this whole time."

Avid poured himself a wine, and held the bottle over Helen's glass. She gave him the go-ahead to pour. He did.

"My parents work for the Space Exploration Project, and the mission they were working on when they met was a series of space flights that were all called 'Avid,' just like the Apollo mission in your time had all those space flights called 'Apollo'. They're exploring black holes in my time, and using wormholes to travel out of this galaxy. That's what my parents do for a living. They're essentially 'rocket scientists', in your vernacular."

"Wow." Helen was suitably impressed.

"The specific spacecraft they worked on together was the 'Avid Voyager." I was their oldest, so my name is Avid. My brother's name is Voyager. If they'd had any other children the next one's name would have been 'Seeker' because Avid Seeker was the next mission after Avid Voyager. Then they might have had other children named Traveler and Sojourner, but they didn't."

"You have a brother? Is he also a Historian?"

"He's a musician, and he has a dual role working for the Historian Project and The Arts Project, like my dual role is working for the Historian Project and the Education Project. He's cataloging ancient music for The Arts Project and also sending the information to the Historian Project. The Arts Project people only very rarely have assignments on-land, and it's usually to observe, not interact. But by working for both projects he still gets to immerse himself in the music division of The Arts project, which he loves, but he also gets the personal interaction with ancient musicians, which he also loves. So he's learning the lute right now in fourteenth century Spain and recording the music they played on it. The earliest surviving piece of sheet music for the lute dates to the fifteenth century, so he's very excited to see what they did earlier."

"I thought your appearance kept you away from those centuries. How is your brother able to go there?"

"I'm a standard bio child, but he's in the Caucasian Dynasty so he can go to Spain. But he wouldn't be able to go on-land to study African music or Inca music, for instance. My parents went for a Dynasty Child with him when they saw how excited I was to be a Historian. They thought they'd give Voyager the same opportunity, if he wanted it, so they opted for him to have Dynasty status to boost his chances. If he didn't want that, he could have a more lucrative career than usual as a doctor, or someone else who has to travel on-land. Being in a Dynasty means you earn more and have more on-land opportunities than bio children. He could always pick something else to do, they figured, but this way he'd have more choices. Competition is tough. It turns out he was interested in it after all and he qualified, so he's grateful."

"You mentioned that your parents are still working?"

"Sure. They're only in their eighties. They won't retire for another thirty years or so.'

"You people live how long?"

"Average lifespan is about one hundred twenty with a high end of about one hundred and fifty years. My parents don't look any older than I do, and the youth booster slows down physical breakdown, so they aren't technically physically old, from your standpoint."

"And they live in the twenty eighth century?"

"That's right."

"And your granddaughter is there too?"

"She's with my daughter at the Asia Pacific control station during the Han Dynasty in about 100 B.C. Both of my daughters and my ex-wife are Historians. They're all in the Asian Dynasty, and they all work from the Asia Pacific control station. I go there a couple of times a week to visit, and schedule it so that I can come back immediately after I leave so it doesn't look to you as if I went anywhere.

Helen did not know that Avid had been traveling back and forth in time during his entire visit with her. There was so much about him that she didn't know.

"I have a question about the twenty-eighth century," Helen asked. "Why was Dr. Dang so excited to see my backyard? She acted as if she'd never seen a squirrel before. What happened to squirrels in your time?"

Avid's Alert screen flashed red, warning him to be careful with his answers. Avid thought about it with the Alert still flashing.

"We live underwater," he tentatively began, "So that's what she's used to." The Alert stopped flashing. "And the medical team is really busy, and they hardly ever have a chance to go on-land, unless they're in a Race Dynasty. That's all. She just doesn't get out much."

Helen had to accept his answer because she knew she wasn't going to get another one. However, she didn't think that answer was entirely complete.

"You're almost as good as my granddaughter is at heart hugs now," Avid said, changing the subject. "And she has a genetic advantage. You picked them up really fast."

Helen took the bait and allowed Avid to pivot the topic of conversation away from squirrels.

"I'm going to try one on Max tomorrow and tell you what happens. I'm feeling a little trepidation, but I'm really excited."

"You have good instincts, so no matter what he does I'm confident you'll know how to react."

Helen nodded with pursed lips and concerned eyes. *This is scary*, she thought.

"We still have a month," Avid reassured her. I'm looking for results that are cumulative, so you'll have four more opportunities to reinforce the message with him. "I'm thinking we'll move to the Vulcan Mind Meld tomorrow night, and see how you do."

Helen had begun referring to the process Avid had used when he conducted his impromptu therapy session as the "Vulcan Mind Meld" from *Star Trek*, and she'd been asking him to show her how to do it.

"So, tomorrow you try the heart hug during your session and tell me how it goes," he said. "Then we'll work on the Mind Meld after dinner."

CHAPTER 31: MAX GETS A HEART HUG

Max was sitting in the chair looking sullen and defiant. He always approached his sessions that way, then grew slightly more cooperative and opened up to Helen later in the hour. Helen greeted him warmly, and offered him coffee. He accepted.

Helen was aware of what was going on with the lynching, and kept looking for signs that Max was going to confess. He began to ramble in a way that was angry, unhappy, and frightened. He wasn't really telling her anything, though.

Helen listened. Then she tried to tune into him, the way she had done with Avid several times. It took her a minute, but it wasn't really difficult. She pushed one of her heart hugs toward him as an experiment, and watched to see if it had hit its target.

He froze and looked up at her. His eyes were confused and pleading.

So that's how I looked to Avid, Helen thought to herself. Was Max going to cry too?

Yes. Max gulped and grabbed the arms of his chair, and twisted around so Helen couldn't see him. That didn't stop it. He choked and sobbed.

This was unacceptable. Men did not cry like this, particularly in front of women. He stared at her silently, defiantly, clutching the arms of his chair until his knuckles were white, and he said nothing. Then he looked down at his lap and sat there rigid and unmoving.

"I'm here for you," Helen said gently. "It's all right. Tell me why it hurts." She leaned over and rubbed the back of his hand.

Max curled himself into a contorted twist in his chair, turning his face away from her, and then collapsed into sobs.

CHAPTER 32: HELEN'S DEBRIEFING

Helen had been waiting impatiently for Nelda to leave because she couldn't contain herself. As soon as the door closed behind Nelda, Helen grabbed Avid by the arm and squeezed.

"It worked. I did it."

Avid had already read her and knew that, but he pretended it was a surprise.

"With Max?"

Helen nodded excitedly.

"Tell me what happened." He paused. "You know I can read your mind, right? I'll know everything he said anyway, and I promise you that you won't be violating his privacy because I won't tell anyone. You can tell me everything he said."

Helen looked uncomfortable at the prospect of sharing. She had only planned to describe how Max reacted to the heart hug. But he was right. He probably already knew everything.

She sighed.

"He's very closed off, so after two years I still didn't know that his mother was verbally and physically abusive, or that his father sexually assaulted him from the time he was four years old until he was eleven. I only knew that he was estranged from his father, and that he had issues of some kind with his mother. I figured it must be something like that because of his diagnosis, but I've been waiting this whole time for him to tell me. And he finally did after I gave him that heart hug."

"Did he seem better afterward?"

"He did, like a weight had been lifted. We set up a plan to address the real issues, instead of skirting around them with me guessing what had happened to him. He's been dodging my questions for two years. I sometimes wondered why he even bothered to come see me. Maybe he's been trying to work up the nerve this whole time, poor kid. I feel so sorry for him. He's always struck me as a really, really tragic figure. I always thought that, but now my heart is really breaking for him."

Avid nodded in solemn respect for Max, then shifted gears and grinned happily. "I cannot believe how good you got at this, as fast as you did."

"Vulcan mind meld then?" She smiled coyly.

"Fine. We'll give it a shot when we're done cleaning up."

About thirty minutes later, the two of them were sitting on the couch.

"I'm not sure you can do this without the genetic modifications." The Educator who instructed Avid wasn't sure either, because no one had ever attempted to teach an unenhanced local before. Avid would find out and report to him. "It's an emotional connection though, not telepathy, so maybe you can. We'll see. I just want you to know that I won't be disappointed if you can't. I just hope that *you're* not disappointed."

"I'm fine, whatever happens. Primarily I'm curious. I want you to tell me what you do, and what you experience while it's happening. We'll see how close I get to that."

"That's a healthy attitude," Avid said. "So we're just going to pretend. This isn't real. I'll walk you through it, and you don't expect anything. You just pretend along with me, okay?"

Helen nodded enthusiastically.

"I want you to focus on the middle of your forehead right now. Pretend you have a searchlight right there in the middle." He touched her forehead an inch or two above her nose."

Helen began focusing.

"It's called the 'third eye.' You can google it if you want more information. I'm not going to go into it now."

Helen nodded.

"Imagine that there's a stream of energy that's shining out of that spot on your forehead. It doesn't have to feel very strong. You're focusing a light, in a way. It isn't a power force. It's just a flashlight. You're aiming that beam of light on me. Aim for my third eye. Imagine that the light is beaming out of your forehead and into my forehead, right here." He tapped his forehead. "Now sink into a kind of meditative state. You aren't thinking, you're floating. You're meditating while you focus that light into me. Floating. Meditating."

Helen's eyes grew unfocused.

"Floating. Floating. Touch my third eye with the light from your third eye while you float."

Helen focused. Avid followed her effort, and was surprised and impressed because he could feel the probe.

With her eyes still unfocused, Helen sighed. "I don't know why I'm going to say this," she said. "It's like a compulsion."

Avid sat up straight, flabbergasted.

"I just have to say this, okay? I could be totally wrong."

Avid nodded, excited.

"Honey, your parents don't need you to be a rocket scientist. You're so hard on yourself, and you think you aren't making them proud, so you've talked yourself into all kinds of self-doubt and insecurities you really shouldn't have. They knew it wasn't your path the first time you failed a math test. They're so proud of you and your brother. They're so proud. And remember, your brother isn't a rocket scientist either. He's just following his path, like you are. You see how proud they are of him, right? And that's what your parents want for you. You both are so skilled at things they'll never be able to do, and they know and appreciate this. Please stop shortchanging yourself. Please stop being so afraid of failing—that fear is choking you. It's so entrenched you won't even let your therapists reach you there, so you're paralyzing yourself. Please stop second guessing yourself and apologizing for being the very wonderful person you are, and never ever again worry about being less than your parents want, because they want you just the way you are."

Avid stared at her.

Helen blinked. "I'm so sorry, Avid. I feel like I overstepped." She looked embarrassed and startled. "I don't know why I said those things. I mean, you've never confided in me. I shouldn't have overstepped. I'm so sorry. I need some wine." She stood up and went to the kitchen, then came back with two wine glasses and an open bottle of wine. She poured and handed a glass to Avid.

"You're high on the empath spectrum, aren't you?" Avid asked, impressed.

Helen sighed disgustedly. "Yes. Damn it. How did you know? It's always been the bane of my existence. I have no idea how I've been able to do my job for as long as I have because it's grueling to connect to everyone else's pain day after day. Ugh. So how did you know?"

"Because you did it the first time you tried. You either have to be on the empath spectrum or high on the creativity scale to do that. That's how you access the Collective Consciousness. Remember when we went over the biofeedback? We worked on a portion of your brain—let's call it a 'radio receiver'—that can access the Portal to channel...hmmm...let's call it 'inspiration'. That's how artists, writers and musicians create. It all comes *through* them, not *from* them, except for the effort they put in to place their own stamp on things. Their technical abilities are their own, which is why not every creative person is a genius even though they all get inspiration from the same source. Some people can connect but don't have the technical skill to execute. Think of someone who can write brilliant music but can't play any instrument well enough to perform. Other people are technical geniuses but they can't connect, so they aren't creative. Think of someone who's really skilled at art forgery, but can't do anything original.

"So anyway, that's what I was teaching you to access. People high on the empath spectrum and creatives are the two types of people who have the easiest access, while everyone else kind of struggles, or they can't connect at all." He laughed. "We're an elite crowd."

"I did it?"

"That's all you do. The words just come. It's weird, isn't it? I don't know where those words come from, but do I know that compulsion to say things that I have no business knowing. I've always thought it must be strange to be a real therapist."

Helen nodded, confused and shocked. "I really did it? That was it?"

"As just a warning that you should never inject your own thoughts and your own ego when you speak to the patient, especially negative thoughts. Just let the words flow. The words will always be the right ones, if you do it the right way."

Helen looked stunned. "I did it. And it *was* weird. It was I weird."

"You can practice on me again, as much as you like. Okay? And then when you're doing it, I want you to try to give me a heart hug at the same time. It might be tough and it might take practice and some more biofeedback exercises, but I want you to try to do both at once. And then next time we're going to try and focus that heart hug on specific things you feel from me. If something seems particularly painful to you when you're poking around, focus the heart hug energy onto that pain. Got it?"

"This is really powerful stuff."

"It's powerful stuff. I agree."

"I did it."

"You did it. And you have a week to practice before Max's next session."

"We'll practice every day."

"Every day. You'll be perfect. You're so great, Helen."

"I rock," Helen agreed. "I totally rock the house down. I'm a goddess, don't you think? "

"Totally. You're totally a goddess. Cheers." Avid held out his glass, and Helen grabbed hers and lifted it. They clinked glasses in a toast.

CHAPTER 33: HELEN'S PACKAGING

"So what's religion like in your time?" Helen wasn't religious, but she was curious.

The topic of religion was off limits to locals, so Avid held up one finger and consulted with his Alert screen to see if he could answer the question. He was amazed to receive the go-head.

"We have a church we can go to." Avid had just finished scrubbing the last pot after dinner. Helen was loading the dishwasher. "Every control station main building has a church wing."

"What religion are you?" She was sipping her tea, happy, leaning against the counter and taking a short break.

He had learned his way around the kitchen and the house, and was fully at home now. After drying that pot and putting it away, he made them both some tea and handed a mug to Helen.

"There's only one church, but I don't know what religion it is."

"What do you call your religion? Did you figure out which is the One True Religion in your time?"

"We just call it 'Church.' I'm not sure it matters whether or not it's the final final final iteration of the Truth, actually. At least, I don't know of anyone who thinks it matters because everyone realizes that religion is still always evolving. Let me ask." He didn't expect a response.

"So…? What is your *specific* religion like?"

He mentally asked if he could respond. The screen displayed, "Yes."

He gathered his thoughts. He was not expecting this, and wasn't certain how far he could go. Then he tentatively proceeded, slowly, waiting for his Alert screen to flash if he ventured out of bounds. Once again, he marveled at the leniency the Mitigators always demonstrated with Helen. He correctly guessed that this was one of the few ways they could compensate her for her assistance with the McKenna Anomaly disaster, since they couldn't reward her with perks. Instead, they were satisfying her curiosity, which in her mind was probably a far greater reward than any material compensation. They knew she would never tell anyone.

"The one true religion in our time is Love with a capital L. That's all it is. Love was always the basis for *all* the world's religions, so anything above and beyond it is just packaging. Like you. You're an atheist, but I see you being loving all the time. You're religious by twenty-eighth century standards, just stripped of all the mandatory beliefs—all the packaging—you see here with organized religions."

"You think I'm religious?" Helen asked incredulously.

Avid nodded. The Mitigators still weren't stopping him.

"In my time we call loving atheists like you, 'Religious No Packaging'." He added air quotes. "We categorize people based on their religious adherence, not on *which* religion they practice. That's because there's ultimately only one religion, and *that* religion is Love. That's all you get, where I come from. We dropped all the packaging."

"It's like the John Lennon song, 'Imagine,' isn't it?"

Avid made a mental note to listen to "Imagine" later. He continued. "It'll take the world a couple hundred more years to figure it out and recognize that we need to adhere to Love on a larger scale, but by my time we have. That's what the heart hugs are for. We're raised to act out love every day to everyone, whether we know them or not. It's how we practice our religion."

"So do you people all run around being piously loving, never getting into arguments, everyone being all Kumbaya with everybody else?"

Avid's eyes twinkled and his mouth twitched.

"Um, *no-oo*...," he said. "We do not." He pulled the left side of his mouth down in a grimace of good natured embarrassment, then laughed. "Knowing and doing are two separate things. We've begun to try a whole lot harder in the past forty years, though, and we're moving in the right direction. In fact, that's why they created the Historian Project, to drive the point home. Since *that* all started we even give heart hugs to the people we hate when they need them, because the education system drills it into us. That's an improvement over what you people do here with *your* hatred, am I right?"

"What a strange turn of events. Wow. Do you believe in anything besides love?"

"The Mitigators are pretty keen on everyone understanding compassion and ethics on a deeper level, so in my time those two things are critical. The Legal Project Mitigators even run time travel projections on tricky hypothetical ethics questions to examine the impact of all possible outcomes before drafting laws. It's serious business."

He paused, then continued, "Our religion doesn't tell us what to think. We're taught to question everything, and Church encourages discussions where different people reach different conclusions and approach it as an intellectual exercise. We aren't supposed to just accept things at face value and then attack or even kill other people to defend our beliefs or impose them on somebody else. We're only supposed to hash it all out and view everything through a lens of love and compassion. Then the Mitigators run their ethics projections for clearer guidance, and scientists explore the arguments to see if they can prove anything one way or another about the afterlife and whatever else we wonder about, or question. Scientists are a really important component of our church, by the way. They field our questions and theories, study them, and report back. They give a lot of the church sermons."

Helen gave him a quizzical stare.

"We leave it to the scientists to figure it out because it doesn't matter what you believe. If believing made things true the world would still be flat," Avid said in response to her look. "We need proof."

"Honey, some people *still* believe the world is flat. You might need to change your axiom for the crowd around here."

Avid looked at her with a pained expression. "I hate it here, Helen," he said to her seriously. "I really do."

She laughed.

"So, in your time you leave religion to the scientists? Not the pastors and the priests?"

Avid nodded then continued.

"We do, but we aren't atheists. Whatever it is that created heaven and earth is what put the rules and laws into place that govern them. Those are the Sciences, so we view science as the 'word of God'. Everyone has science in common, and it works exactly the same way for everyone, whether you believe in it or not. There aren't a thousand variations. It never changes because of what your beliefs are. I mean, sometimes we learn new things and our understanding of science changes, but the essential underlying rules and laws never change, and you can't change them by believing something else. We draw parallels in our lives to the laws of the sciences. The more you study them, the more perfect they are, and the more insight they give you into the Creator, and life in general."

"And death?"

"You look at physics. One of its rules is that energy can't be destroyed, it can only change forms. You call it a 'soul' but we call it 'life force energy' because we believe that an external energy source powers every living thing. That's what I've been teaching you to tap into with telepathy and heart hugs. Our lasting consciousness is energy that cycles into our bodies when we're born, and it cycles out when we die. Your body is inanimate unless it has an energy source, so when your energy leaves your body, your body dies. Our essential selves are eternal because energy can't be destroyed, so when we die our energy just goes somewhere else. "

"I've always thought that when you die you're just dead." She switched on the dishwasher. Then she began wiping down the counters and the stove.

Avid sipped his tea, leaned back against a counter, and moved aside when she reached him with her dishrag.

"That's probably the only after-death option that science definitely won't let you have, so you'll have to pick something else to believe. And it won't matter what you pick because believing doesn't change what's true. 'Truth' is what it is, whatever *that* is, and it's still true whether you personally believe in it or not."

"So if I don't actually die when I die, do I go to heaven or hell?"

"Let me check." He asked his Alert screen to refresh his memory on the concept of heaven and hell.

"They aren't mathematically feasible," he told her. "Another rule of physics is 'every action creates an equal and opposite reaction.' You can't possibly do enough good things or bad things to warrant an eternity of either punishment or reward. Nothing you do in one short lifetime could ever add up to eternity, so that's out. Physics says you can only get back exactly what you give."

"Karma."

"That's right."

"So…reincarnation?"

"Right. The properties of energy apply here again. If you can successfully perform a scientific experiment on energy once, you can perform it again an infinite number of times. If the same conditions are present you'll always get the same result. If your life force energy can enter a physical body once, it can do it again an infinite number of times." He leaned in closer. His eyes were twinkling. "Electricity doesn't die when you turn off a lamp. It just goes on to power something else. So do we."

"Wow. I don't like that. I don't want to come back."

"The Universe doesn't ask for our permission." Avid said, grinning. "I'd recommend that you just pick something else to believe. Then let me know if that changes anything. I'll report your findings to our scientists."

Helen ignored Avid's cheeky jab at her, and looked thoughtful.

"So, what about 'God?' Do you really believe that there is a God?" she asked. "I don't. Never have." She rinsed out the rag and placed it on the edge of the sink to dry.

"You can use the Law of Probability to calculate the odds of there being a God. And, again, it doesn't matter what you believe because you won't change what's true. That's why people in my time keep guessing and debating, and our scientists keep probing. It isn't blasphemy in my time, or—'woo-woo', did you call it?—to poke around and look for real evidence and actual signs of God or lifeform energy activity in other dimensions. It's science and common sense."

With cleanup complete, Avid gestured to the couch in the living room. Helen grabbed her mug and followed him.

"There are fifty-two playing cards in a deck, right?" Avid was getting this reference from his Alert screen.

"Right."

"How likely are you to shuffle them so that they're all in the exact order they were in when you first bought the deck? All the suits are sorted just the way they were when you opened the deck, in the exact ascending order, one after another. Can you do that?"

"No. I'd have to sort them by hand."

"And there are only fifty-two playing cards. So now tell me how many rules and laws apply to physics."

"Millions. I don't know. Billions? Lots."

"And they're all in perfect order with no mistakes, except in the minds of people who don't know physics or don't understand it. Did that happen by accident? What are the odds that the Universe shuffled itself and its millions and billions of laws into perfect order by accident during the Big Bang?"

"Incalculable."

"Pretty unlikely. So that leaves us with intent. The odds are that physics rules and laws were all intentionally put into place because they could not have spontaneously created themselves by accident without there being mistakes or total chaos."

He read from his screen. "'Fifty-two Pick Up'. What's that?"

Helen laughed. "It's a pretend card game we used to play to torment the little kids. You ask them if they want to play Fifty Two Pickup. When they say yes, you yell, "Fifty-two pick up!" Then you throw all the cards in the air and make them pick them all up. Fifty-two cards, pick them all up. Get it? 'Fifty-two Pick Up.' It only works one time on each kid—"

"You were an awful child, Helen."

"—so after that, you always have to find a new kid."

Helen raised her eyebrow challengingly.

"Who said I was a child when I did that?" She winked.

Avid rolled his eyes and snorted. "But the game represents what, chaos?"

"Yeah, I guess."

"So you should view that small child you so cruelly victimized as 'intelligent intervention.'"

Helen laughed again.

"The Universe after the Big Bang without intervention and intent would be chaos, just like the cards on the floor. So, now add together all of the sciences, and all of their millions and billions of rules and laws, then calculate the odds that all of them are perfect, which all of them are, by the way. They're all sorted and all in order. Our scientists will attest. Figure out the odds that they *all* got that way by accident without any mistakes. Slim odds, right? That only leaves 'intent.' This suggests that some kind of overreaching force created everything and put the rules in place. Otherwise, there would be chaos."

"Hmm."

"And again, it doesn't matter what conclusion you reach. Believe it or don't believe it. You won't change anything because everything is what it is. Our understanding of a God and the afterlife might change over time, depending on what scientists learn, but in my time we're open to studying it and adjusting our beliefs as new information rolls in."

"They're studying God and the afterlife?"

"Of course. We're curious and we want to know. Don't you?"

"Well, what have you learned?"

"We've decided from the Law of Probability that there really *is* a God of some sort, or something that intelligently intervened to put everything into place. We've decided from the laws of physics that there really *is* an afterlife. These things aren't even up for debate anymore in my time. We only debate the details of where that intelligent intervention might come from, and what the afterlife looks like and where it takes place, such as what other possible dimensions or what other possible universes our life form energies might go to after we die, and before we come back here again. As for life in this dimension, they've developed a way to measure life form energy so they can tell precisely when it enters or leaves a biological host, such as a person or an animal, or even a plant or a one-celled amoeba. Everything alive has an energy source, and the device tracks whether it is, or is not present. You could use that here, with all the people you have on life support."

Helen nodded. That would be useful.

"So, if you believe in a God, do you guys ever pray?"

"I guess you could call it prayer. We communicate telepathically, and that's all prayer is: telepathic communication. If nobody intercepts it telepathically, scientists think it all goes into a cosmic brain dump or a living database where it gets sorted. Or something."

"I'm trying not to imagine that brain dump as some sort of churning cesspool," Helen said. "But that's just me and my job."

"This is all theory, and they haven't proven anything yet. In my time, I'd just tell you to go to church and not sleep through the sermons."

"If *only*. I'd love that."

"But in your time people can't telepathically connect with other people, so they send a telepathic help signal to the Universe and hope God answers it with some sort of supernatural intervention, or a miracle. That's what prayer is, a telepathic message in a bottle, where you're communicating with your mind to someone unseen, just like I can. I don't know where the communication goes, or who receives it, but it *does* go somewhere, apparently, and it *is* received by...someone. Or something. Who or what, I don't know. So, prayer is just another form of telepathy floating around in the Collective Consciousness, if I recall that sermon correctly—"

"A repository that contains everyone's desperate pleas for their high school football team to win. Can't wait to tap into *that*, right?"

"Stop it, Helen. It's not like that." Avid thought for a moment. "Actually, I have no idea what it's like." He shrugged.

She grinned.

Avid continued. "Then the Universe dispatches someone who can help. Sometimes dispatched people actually *do* help, but mostly they don't, at least not in your time, so it isn't foolproof and it doesn't always work. For instance, maybe someone finds a wallet on the ground filled with lots of money. The owner of the wallet prayed to get it back because he was on his way to pay the rent with that money, and now he'll be out on the street or something. Then some guy was dispatched to return it to the person who lost it, but he decides to keep the money and throw the wallet in a dumpster instead. That's what usually happens in your time. Whenever a person returns the wallet with all the money, it makes the news because it's so unexpected. Typically, your people all just sabotage each other's prayers whenever they're sent to help. They're self-serving, opportunistic, and kind of mean-spirited sometimes."

Helen couldn't really argue any of his points, so she breezed past them. "What do you mean, dispatched?"

"Scientists have a theory that the Universe intervenes from some other dimension to dispatch living people to answer prayers, or even just to help you in certain situations, whether you've prayed or not. One theory is that it, whatever 'it' is, selects certain people for certain tasks, then nudges them to go to a place or be in a situation where someone needs their help. Most people aren't aware they're being nudged and they usually think it was their idea to be there, but it's not. They're 'sent by God' so to speak, to find that abandoned baby or save that family from a house fire. So they have no idea why they took that route today, or had that compulsion to be where they are. Once they show up, they have total free will to either do what they were sent to do, or not."

Avid thought of something.

"When I was interviewing Joseph D'Andre McKenna, his entire career and contributions showed up as 'Event Consequences.' That means that the event was the catalyst for his entire career, and all of his contributions. When I was a kid, that one aspect of my interview triggered all kinds of interest and speculation when the Educators received it at the beginning of the project, so they turned it over to the scientists."

He told Helen as an aside: "When I studied the footage in school, I had no idea I was going to be the one to conduct that interview, so I was really excited to find out I'd gotten the assignment. He's a major historical figure, and we all had to study him. In fact, he's the reason I applied for this assignment because I wanted to actually see him in person. It was *so* cool."

Helen looked slightly taken aback. Time apparently operated a little more fluidly than she had expected.

"What will he do that makes him so important?"

"I can't tell you. It's in your future."

Helen sniffed.

"The Terence Jackson murder was the reason for his career, and his career changed the world, so Educators taught us that he was probably dispatched to be there that day. *We* all presume he was dispatched, anyway. One of our church sermons focused on the event, and speculated on the way they think the Universe operates in cases like this. They guess that Joseph was specifically dispatched because he had the capacity to address certain problems with his intelligence, motivation, drive, and heart. And then he stepped up. He had the choice *not* to, but he stepped up the way you always hope people will, but they rarely do. I don't know whether he showed up to the murder because of someone's prayer or if it was all part of some universal plan. We can't know things like that—yet. But in retrospect, it all seems to be part of the design."

Helen pondered.

"Anyway, scientists are pretty sure that prayer really works on some level, but they aren't sure how, yet," Avid continued. "People in your time expect God's supernatural intervention to answer *every* prayer with miracles. They think it's all out of their hands because God is going to just fix everything for them, which is incorrect and a huge mistake. And they think all help comes directly from God, which it might, but not in the way they expect. Right now scientists think the 'God' that services your prayers is primarily a dispatcher, maybe a huge cosmic mind-reading device like my Alert screen implant. Maybe it's connected to a computer that sorts through humanity, looking for a match, and then plants a suggestion when it finds the right person, or gives a nudge. Maybe we get the nudges from the energies on the other side. Maybe that's how you spend your afterlife, nudging people to do the right thing. Who knows? They're still debating theories and setting up research environments to test them. What they think—and you can see it yourself if you look—is that the tangible help is mostly all right here. Whether or not you receive it depends on the people who were dispatched."

"So does praying for somebody else ever help them?"

"It can, and in my time it does because people are telepathic and can literally hear cries for help. If we can't personally help, for whatever reason, we can call out for someone else who possibly can. Otherwise, prayer is a way to just send your support when it's all out of your hands, like when someone is ill or lost a loved one. Your prayer telepathically sends your love to uplift them. It can be the next best thing to a heart hug.

"But here you have lots of people who cheat when they pray for other people. I think lots of them were actually dispatched to help and decided not to because praying for someone who needs them is easier, and it lets them still feel good about themselves, and look good to other people, without them actually making a sacrifice or putting in any effort. It's human nature. But if everyone prays instead of actually helping, the result is still tragedy.

"In our church they teach us that most of the tragedy you see in the world is the result of people who were dispatched to help, but decided not to. For example, let's say that you pray and a dispatched person shows up. That person decides that you and your problems are too much trouble and walks away, or keeps the money and dumps the wallet, or else prays for you instead of actually helping. Your prayer is technically answered, but you ultimately don't receive any actual, tangible help. Tragedy. Multiply that by all of the people in the world, and that's what's happening everywhere, all of the time, every day. It doesn't mean there is no 'God'. It just means that people don't step up when 'God', or whatever, dispatches them to help. Blame yourselves and each other for the state of the world."

That's what we *do*, Avid thought to himself.

"So you believe that when we pray we're asking each other for help, not a 'God' per se?"

"Sometimes help really does come from the other side with no living person in sight, like when someone takes a step to the left for no reason, and then doesn't get crushed by a falling piano. They think we really might have some backup out there." Avid waved his hands in a general gesture to symbolically include The Universe. "But that never lets us off the hook because that doesn't really happen much. We still have to take personal responsibility for each other."

Helen stared at him silently.

"Our understanding is that 'God' is *not* a powerful male entity who sits on a throne and judges and smites us. It's *everything*. It's just the energy that comprises *us* plus everything else, combined. We call it 'universal connectedness.' Or we just call it 'The Universe.' We view the *entire Universe* as 'God'..." Avid used air quotes. "But we could be totally wrong about everything, which is why we still have debates about it in church. When they figure it all out, we'll know better what it is, how it works, and what to call it. But the important thing is that we believe that we're all connected, so we're all equally responsible for each other and everything else, including the earth and everything on it. Love is really just valuing, supporting, and helping our connections, and not harming them. Getting back to your original question, *that* is our religion."

Whether we've actually practiced it one hundred percent of the time, or not, Avid thought. He sighed.

"So, if we see someone who needs help, we presume we've been dispatched. In your time you think a quick prayer will fix things or just let you off the hook, whereas we think it's a good idea to actually step in to help that person. In my time helping is second nature. In your time dispatched people stop to help so infrequently that it makes the Evening News, and I'm really not adjusting well to that."

CHAPTER 34: JOYRIDE, NO BOYS

TUESDAY, APRIL 20, 2021: TIME 12:57 HOURS

Chad never used his condo on-land, and he never used his Tesla. The team primarily piled into the Range Rover and traveled everywhere together, with the now-proficient Nectar at the wheel. They always convened at Dirk's apartment because he actually lived there.

"Let's go for a joyride," Nectar suggested to Janicyl via Alert Screen. "Just grab the Tesla and go."

Janicyl liked that idea very much and she had the key fob, so the two of them requested an Uber, met up in the Community Center then zipped by travel pod to their drop off location on-land. They took the Uber to Chad's condo building where Janicyl used the door remote she kept with her to get into the garage. They entered the vehicle without anyone's permission and simply left with Janicyl driving. She was adept at driving the car because she'd had several twenty-first century assignments, so she took off smoothly down the road with no hesitation.

She didn't help Nectar learn how to operate the Range Rover in the beginning, because watching her struggle was too entertaining.

Nectar had rolled down her window and was letting the wind blow her hair, with her face toward the sun, as Janicyl smoothly maneuvered the car through traffic. Men in other cars saw the Tesla first, and the ladies second, and tried to get their attention with waves and smiles. Nectar just closed her eyes and smiled to herself and ignored them, and she breathed, experiencing a rare moment of total freedom. Janicyl hummed along with the music on the sound system and waved back at all the men, grinning.

CHAPTER 35: THE VULCAN MIND MELD

Max looked up at Helen with an open, trusting expression as Helen leaned over to hand him his coffee. She smiled at him as she took a seat.

"How are you feeling today?" Helen asked.

"I'm good!" Max almost smiled back. He very rarely smiled. "I feel good."

"How was your week? Anything you want to talk about?"

"Nothing in particular," Max said. Helen didn't feel discouraged. This was his usual opening to every session.

"I was hoping to try a different approach today, if you're onboard with it," Helen said. "I went to a conference and learned a new technique. I'm looking for a guinea pig."

Max looked at her suspiciously, thought about it, and then shrugged and nodded.

"Really? I was hoping you'd say yes! Thank you!" Helen smiled and shifted in her seat to get comfortable. "They call it the Vulcan Mind Meld. Have you ever heard of that?"

Max laughed and nodded. "That's hilarious!" he said. "Yeah, let's do it!"

Helen, who had been practicing on Avid all week, prepared herself and then assumed the position. She held out her hands. Max almost involuntarily offered his hands to her, and she loosely held them.

"Just relax," she said. "You don't have to do anything." She tuned into him and activated her third eye, then focused. She looked at him, seeing and unseeing at the same time, and she probed.

Pain, she sensed. Terrible emotional pain and emotional isolation. His father. Terrible pain. Awful. She worked on her heart hug, and aimed it toward the pain. Max's eyes widened in surprise, but he didn't cry. Then the words came.

"Sometimes people are just evil and wrong. Sometimes you just happen to get in their way, and they hurt you. Honey, it was never you. You were never a bad boy. You were in the way of something evil and wrong, and it hurt you. You were never a bad boy. You just got in the way because you were there, and the evil was there. You just got in its way."

Max's jaw was slack as he stared at Helen with his eyes welling with tears.

"Sometimes you can hurt, and then you want to hurt someone else so you can know in your heart that there are other people hurting the same way you are. I know that. But you don't really hate those people that you want to hurt, do you? You just want someone to know how you feel."

Max stared at her, and gave an imperceptible nod.

"You don't really want them to hurt, honey, do you? You don't really want people to feel pain. You just want someone to *know*. You want someone to know how much it hurt you, and to try to make yourself feel better."

Mesmerized, Max nodded.

"You're a good boy, Max. No matter what they told you, and no matter what anyone did to you, you're a good boy and it isn't your shame. It was never your shame. You just got in the way by being there. That's all. You were there, so it happened to you. It would have happened to any other child who was there, but in this case it was you. You were there. I'm so sorry you were there, and I'm so sorry they made you feel ashamed. But it wasn't you. You're a good boy. You just got in the way. It wasn't your fault."

Max nodded again.

"And you don't want to hurt people, do you?"

Max shook his head.

"Because you're a good boy. You want to help people who hurt, not hurt them more, don't you? You know what it feels like to hurt, and you want to stop other people from feeling that way, isn't that right, honey?"

Max nodded.

"You're such a good boy. I'm so proud of you." Helen aimed another heart hug at Max. He shuddered. The words weren't coming anymore, so she focused her eyes again, and she released Max's hands.

Max sat there with his hands still extended, as if he didn't want the connection to end. His face screwed up for a moment as if he were about to burst into tears, and then he composed himself and smiled. It was a real smile. Helen had never received a smile from Max before.

CHAPTER 36: SESSION FAILURE

Helen was somber when she reported today's session to Avid. The session had seriously shaken her.

"The words that came out were for a little boy," she told Avid. I was talking to someone who was about five years old, not to a grown man." She shook her head with bewilderment. "I thought I was doing so well, until that happened. What went wrong?"

"It's this place. I hate it here," Avid replied matter-of-factly.

Helen curled her lip. "Really? Thank you for that."

Avid rolled his eyes at her, and then he sighed.

"You would never, ever see this in my time. Nobody has ever done a thing for this man since he was a child. He's been carrying this around with him for his whole life, getting sicker and angrier because of it, getting ready to commit murder because of it, and nobody really addressed it until you did, today. It's barbaric. I'm sure he's had contemporary therapy his entire life, talking about what happened to him, or maybe not talking about it, but nobody ever directly connected to his emotions because your therapists are trained to stay at a really safe distance. But this is what happens when things fester. What you did was just exactly right. The words knew how to reach him, and you just said them out loud. You did everything exactly right."

Helen nodded, relieved.

"You have to remember that the words aren't yours. You're channeling them, which is why you can't ever insert your own thoughts or opinions into the session. Whatever you channel is the correct thing to say to this particular person in this specific moment."

"I know you explained it all, but I still don't understand, I guess. I'm still getting my bearings with it. This all still feels really strange to me. I feel like I should be more in control, so it's hard."

"I don't know how to explain how it works. The Psychological Support Project is monitoring and observing The Arts Project for clues because they're the other ones who can channel input from the Source. Creative people have always done it. And they're trying to find practical applications for it in other areas. They actually didn't apply the process to psychotherapy until about three hundred years ago. They've been testing it with medical diagnosis as well, though they haven't made it a part of mainstream medical treatment yet. For now, doctors still need the implants to diagnose. They expect to not need them after they figure out how to channel things instead. So, even if it's hard, you just have to trust it and roll with it."

Helen's mind spun.

"If you've ever been around creative people," Avid continued, "you might hear them refer to the 'Portal'. Or, they'll say they're 'drawing inspiration.' Or they just call it their 'muse'. Or they're in the "creative zone." I've heard my brother mention it when he's writing music. Empaths and creatives seem to have enhanced access to the 'Portal to The Universe', which is one of the things we're still calling it until the scientists give it a formal name. They're also trying to figure out why some people can access it and others can't. Most likely it's just how well-developed the radio receiver is in your brain. They're hoping they might find a way to strengthen and enhance it in everyone.

"So, when artists or musicians connect to that Portal, they go into a kind of meditative state where they pull their creative inspiration from something outside of themselves. It flows into them, and they filter it through their own intellect, skill and experience to create the art or the music, or whatever. But the source of it isn't entirely them. They're pulling ideas and inspiration from outside of themselves through that 'Portal', like accessing a dream in waking life. Composers receive entire melodies. Writers get pre-written passages that just pop into their heads, complete. Artists get shapes and colors. Dancers see the dance and know the movements. That's where the words came from: a sort of waking dream while you were in a meditative state. That's what you did."

Helen stared at him. "That's so bizarre," she whispered. "This happens a lot? Really? You never hear anyone talk about it."

Avid's Alert screen displayed.

"You hear about it all the time. Really. All the time. Here's one. Paul McCartney from the Beatles channeled the song "Yesterday" in a dream. You can access the Portal in your dreams too. Here's another. There's a documentary we can watch about a group called the BeeGees. Have you heard of them?"

Helen nodded.

"We'll watch that BeeGees documentary I just mentioned. Apparently someone named Chris Martin describes it for you. Do you know who that is?"

Helen shook her head.

"The Alert screen says he's a musician. Cold Play? Is that the name of a band? We'll see what he says about it when we watch."

He paused and shrugged while Helen stared at him and thought: Woo-woo. Avid heard and sighed at her loudly.

"It's all perfectly normal. Your reaction goes back to being afraid of anything that goes beyond your five senses. You've been conditioned to steer clear of things like this, which is kind of disingenuous because you've just experienced it yourself, so you should personally know better than to question it."

Helen looked a little chastened.

"In my time, scientists study it. Now that you know you can do it, you'll just flow with it and it'll feel natural to you. But what it sounds like is that Max needs help going back all the way to his early childhood. That's why you said what you said. So how did he react?"

"He smiled at me. He'd never really smiled at me before. It was surreal."

"See? You reached him, and it worked. I'll be interested to know what he's like at your next session, and what you have to say to him."

"Me too."

CHAPTER 37: EBAY DELIVERY

The package was sitting on the coffee table, waiting for Helen to return home from work to open it. Avid had been sitting on the couch looking at it, excitedly holding the gift he intended to give to Helen to complement the items he knew were in that package. He wanted to thank her for her hospitality and her assistance, and he knew this would excite her like nothing else could.

When Helen walked through the door, he looked up at her grinning.

"It came!"

Helen let out a shriek and ran to the package, tearing it open. She withdrew the gorgeous pieces of Art Deco jewelry that she had ordered on eBay, ran to a mirror, and began putting them on.

"Oh my God. So beautiful. I'm swooning. Oh my God."

She studied and caressed each piece, and studied it again, and held out her wrist to admire her bracelet, and touched the pendant and the earrings as she posed for herself in the mirror. She turned her head left and right, lifted her chin and sighed happily.

"We have to go out for dinner so I can wear these. I'll talk to Nelda in a minute so we can plan things."

Avid nodded and held out what appeared to be a kind of a booklet.

Helen looked at it quizzically, and asked, "What's that, honey?"

"Look at it." Avid gave it to her and could barely contain himself as he watched her.

Helen took the booklet and opened it, bewildered. It was a series of pictures of women who all appeared to be wearing her jewelry. The earliest picture was of a man creating the jewelry in a workshop. The next picture was of a man purchasing the items from a jeweler's storefront.

Helen turned the page and the man was handing the jewelry to a beautiful young woman whose clothing suggested the year was in the early nineteen twenties. The next page was the same woman wearing it as she posed for her wedding photo.

"What is all this?"

"I had them use scanner footage to compile and print out a history of your jewelry. These are all images of the actual people who owned it, starting with the jeweler who made it."

Helen was stunned, and hungrily flipped through each of the pages with an open mouth. Impatient, she flipped to the back of the booklet and found a picture of the man who had sold it to her. She flipped back to the beginning. Page after page advanced the years and displayed the woman wearing it to various events as she grew older. Helen turned to another image of her, now middle aged in the nineteen fifties. She was giving it to a woman who appeared to be her daughter. Then the daughter appeared in her wedding photo wearing the jewelry. The pictures showed the daughter wearing it occasionally after her wedding, but not often, perhaps because it was now out of style. In the nineteen eighties the daughter, now older, was handing it off to a woman who appeared to be *her* daughter, and who also wore it for her wedding. That daughter passed it on to another daughter in the early two thousands, who also wore it for her wedding. But then that picture was followed by images of a home robbery, a pawn shop, an antique auction, and ultimately the collector who sold it on Ebay.

Helen grew silent, softly fingering the edges of the pages.

"What do you think?"

She looked up with tears in her eyes. "I can't keep this. It's not mine. I have to give it all back."

Avid hadn't looked closely at all of the pictures, wasn't aware of the jewelry's history, and was feeling guilty for making Helen sad and for being the reason she was going to lose something that had made her so happy.

"I'm so sorry. I didn't look through all of the pictures before I gave it to you. I really didn't mean to do this to you. I'm so sorry, Helen. Really I am."

"Did you get the names of these people, the ones in the pictures?"

"I can do that."

"I need to contact the woman who lost this jewelry and give it back to her. My heart is totally broken, but I have to do this."

"I completely understand," he said, leaning over and giving her a quick hug.

Avid consulted his Alert screen and received the name and contact information for the woman who was robbed. He also received the Mitigator's permission to return the jewelry, pleased that returning it was not going to adversely impact the continuum. He then asked them to provide some plausible explanation for how Helen found out it was stolen so she would know what to say when she returned it to the woman. He also needed to know what Helen should say about how she knew who to return it to.

The Mitigators provided him with a local Seattle news article dated May 30, 2019 detailing the theft of the jewelry, and its history. They gave him a back story of what Helen was researching when she stumbled on the article on the Internet and how she located the owner on Facebook. No one would ever guess the truth.

He wrote the contact information down, told Helen what to say when she contacted the woman, and then texted a link to the woman's Facebook page from his phone to hers.

"She won't mind if I wear it to dinner just one time, right?" she asked, sighing with resignation.

"She won't mind," Avid assured her.

"We'll still go to the best restaurant in town, okay?"

"And you'll look gorgeous."

"I will, won't I?" Helen threw back her head and laughed.

CHAPTER 38: EATING OUT IN JEWELRY

Helen and Avid were enjoying a spectacular five-course meal at the very expensive, well-below-capacity restaurant of her choice. Helen was wearing her Art Deco jewelry and thoroughly enjoying it as much as she was enjoying the food, even though hardly anyone was in the restaurant because of the ongoing pandemic restrictions, and virtually nobody except for their masked server could see her wearing it.

She had received a reply to her Facebook message earlier in the day. The woman who had previously owned the jewelry was beside herself with gratitude, and mentioned in her message that she was crying, she was so happy. Helen had asked for her permission to wear the jewelry just once before she returned it, and the woman replied with an enthusiastic *Yes*, along with an offer of one thousand dollars to compensate her for what she'd spent on the jewelry, telling her to keep the rest as a reward.

Helen refused the money and when the woman insisted, Helen asked her to please donate it to a suicide prevention organization in Seattle, and to then send confirmation that the organization had received it. She would send the jewelry to the woman by registered mail in the morning, she assured her. She took a picture of herself wearing it, sent the image to the woman, and then thanked her for letting her borrow it from her.

The woman had responded with a big "Thank you" gif that exploded with animated hearts.

"That's a wonderful thing that you're doing, Helen. You've made her so happy."

"I was dispatched to return it to her," Helen said simply. "What else could I do with *you* looking right at me?" She made a face at him, and he laughed.

CHAPTER 39: SIDE EFFECTS OF DIURETICS

The subjects were due at twenty-hundred hours, as was usual for a Monday. The Heroes were in Dirk's living room, amusing themselves with games on their Alert screens or fiddling with their smart phones.

"Would anyone like anything to drink?" Nectar asked from the kitchen.

"Tea for me please," Dirk said.

"Tea all around, I think," Chad added. Janicyl nodded.

Nectar prepared the tea with the quick drink generator and gave Chad and Janicyl their mugs. Then she went back into the kitchen and dropped a diuretic into Dirk's tea. The next time he needed to urinate, Dirk would stand and watch his inexplicably blue-colored urine stream into the toilet. She stirred the tea until the diuretic had completely dissolved, tasted just a sip to see if it would pass undetected, and frowned.

"Dirk, do you want milk and sugar?"

"That sounds good. Yes please."

She doctored up his tea with milk and sugar. The next sip told Nectar that this iteration of tea with diuretics would definitely pass. She gave the mug to Dirk and then settled back into her chair to enjoy her own tea.

While she was thinking of it, she asked her Alert screen to provide a list of the specific things one should never flush down a toilet. She made a mental checklist of the items, prioritizing things that Dirk already owned, then opened her phone calendar and set up a schedule with reminder alerts.

CHAPTER 43: AVID EXPLAINS THE SCANNER

"What is this 'scanner' you're always talking about," Helen asked Avid. "I mean, I get what it does, but I'm trying to imagine how it works."

Avid requested a description from his Alert screen that Helen would understand. His screen displayed an image of a Google Street View car, which had a large three-hundred-and-sixty-degree camera affixed to its roof.

"Do you know what Google Street View is?" Avid asked, reading from his Alert screen. Helen nodded. "The scanner is like the cars they use to take three-hundred-and-sixty-degree pictures of all the streets in the world. It's telling me they do that with ambient radio waves." Avid didn't know what ambient radio waves were. He was just reading aloud.

"It says it has something to do with the ambient radio wave cameras your scientists are experimenting with now, but in my time we don't need the cameras, and we can also capture sound. I don't know how it works. Go to Google and search for 'ambient radio wave cameras' and see what you find. They've improved on it for seven hundred years so the information you find will be really preliminary. Whatever they do is beyond my scope, so I couldn't even understand enough to explain it to you. I just know that they input coordinates in our time, then the scanner records everything within those coordinates and lets you view the footage from any angle."

Helen was Googling "ambient radio wave cameras" on her phone while Avid spoke. When she found it, she listened and read at the same time.

"The area can be as small as a closet or as big as a city. Then you can input a search for 'living things,' for instance, and it highlights anything emitting a biological heat source on the image or the video. You can narrow it down to type of living thing if you're looking for a person or a lost pet, or whatever. You can set the parameters on the search feature however you need to, even drilling down to a specific person. You can also view the person or thing within a timeframe so you can move forward, or backtrack footage to a crime, for instance. And you can identify objects that don't belong in that time and place and display the locations where somebody left them. I think it's a vibrational measurement of the object? Again, no idea, but there is something different about things that originate in the twenty-eighth century versus earlier in history, and the scanner can detect it."

Helen had finished reading the article and looked up while Avid continued.

"Off-topic. We're supposed to leave all twenty-eighth century items in the control station, and never take them on-land, or else be extremely careful when we do. There's a scanner feature that alerts the Time Travel team, which looks out for things like that. If I leave my drink generator behind, I'll get a notification to come back and pick it up, and then I'll have to pay a fine for leaving it, just so you know."

"I couldn't use it anyway without your implant."

"Right. So it comes with me." He paused. "Funny story. They put that law into effect after twentieth century scientists found a modern screw embedded in a three-hundred-million-year-old rock formation. Your scientists have theories that it's a fossilized sea creature that's shaped like a screw and could have gotten there naturally, or else they blame it on aliens from outer space, but actually it was one of ours. So the Mitigators put down the law forever afterward. We can't leave any trash behind."

"Google?"

"Yeah, search for '300 million year old screw.' But let's say we're looking for a criminal. You enter the coordinates of the scene of the crime, and then enter a range of dates, and the scanner acts like security footage. You can see exactly who did what on scanner images or scanner video. If there's any question of intent, a Historian who's working in that time period gets assigned to the exact date and time of the crime, then watches the scanner footage and telepathically reads the criminal from a distance. It only works if you're viewing people live at the moment of the crime because you can't get a telepathic read on someone from security footage after the fact. Once we know the intent of the person committing the crime, we can eliminate charges against anyone who did something by accident.

Except for carelessness. They'll get punished for that if it applies, even if the event was unintentional."

"Nicely done!"

"We like it. Except that there isn't any aspect of our lives that isn't archived and just waiting for someone to pull it up and view it. You get used to that, though. In your time people are getting acclimated to living their lives in a fishbowl, like the TV show 'Big Brother.' After a while they forget about the cameras and the live Internet streams, and they just live their stupid fake TV lives with millions of people always watching. That's kind of how we live. In our case, though, you need a warrant to view the footage."

Helen nodded.

"You all live that way too, if you only knew."

"Yikes!"

"Especially if you're historically famous. Some famous people, Hitler, for instance, have their entire lives studied and scrutinized from the first trimester of the pregnancy. Even their parents get the full study long before they're born. If you're in any way associated with anyone who becomes historically famous, you're a star too."

"Huh."

"Knowing that doesn't change your life though. You've been living under Mitigator scrutiny for weeks without suffering, right? No stage fright?"

"True."

"You get used to it."

CHAPTER 42: NECTAR'S EMERGENCY

THURSDAY, APRIL 29, 2021: 09:54 HOURS

"Avid, could you puh-le-ease do me a small favor?" Nectar was on Avid's alert screen looking frightened and distraught, twirling one of her curls like a worried little girl. She batted her eyelashes and pouted prettily.

"I would be thrilled," Avid told her sincerely.

"I've had an emergency, and I have to take care of it right now." Nectar looked distressed as if her emergency promised, or had already delivered, tragedy. She was a tragic, helpless figure on Avid's Alert screen. She was a helpless, tragic figure, experiencing so much helplessness amid such tragedy. "I placed an order for some couture—"

Avid requested a definition for "couture" so he could follow the conversation, then nodded sympathetically at Nectar's sad plight.

"—and I can't pick it up. I need it by fifteen-hundred hours. Could you please help me?" Nectar's expression looked like a kitten's, open and trusting. Only Avid could save her. Only Avid could make her purr.

"I would be happy to," Avid told her.

Nectar sent Avid instructions on where to pick up her clothing, and Avid signed off with a wide smile.

He arrived at House of Couture and walked through the door with a bounce in his step. He was assisted by a woman who smiled at him ingratiatingly, then went to fetch Nectar's custom order. She hung the garments on a rack beside the cash register, covered them snugly with a plastic bag she tied in a knot at the bottom, then asked that Avid pay the balance due of seventeen thousand dollars.

"A seventeen with three zeroes? Seventeen *thousand*?"

"That is correct." The sales person raised her eyebrows at the question, smiled tersely, and gave Avid a disdainful look. "Seventeen thousand dollars is the very reasonable price of her custom couture." She held out the itemized sales slip with a limp hand for Avid to inspect, securing it between her index and middle finger, looking away as if Avid were beneath her station for having expressed surprise at the cost.

"Of course it is! I'm just doing some mental calculations and wanted to verify the correct amount," Avid said to her brightly, hoping Nectar would call on him again soon. He gave her his debit card.

The woman ran the card, smiled at Avid more warmly this time, and handed him the garments. Avid smiled warmly in return, then left the shop and connected to Nectar on his Alert screen. He did this strictly for his own amusement because he already knew what the resolution would be. It was a very fine day.

"Nectar?"

Nectar nodded and smiled as he held out the garments for her to see, holding up his smart phone as if he were speaking to someone on Facetime, aiming his camera at the clothing. None of the people on the street saw anything amiss about him.

"I have your clothes. Could you please have seventeen thousand dollars waiting for me when I get there?"

"Of course!" Nectar said.

"I'll be over as soon as I can," he assured her, then scheduled travel pod pickup, and ordered an Uber.

When Avid arrived back at the control station, Nectar answered her door, disheveled and distraught. She was sobbing. She grabbed the clothing from Avid's hand, wailing, "Emergency!" then closed the door in Avid's face without paying him.

Avid went straight to the bank, which he had planned on doing anyway.

CHAPTER 40: VULCAN MIND MELD AGAIN

Max was sitting in the chair looking alert and engaged, and ready for his session. Helen smiled at him, handed him his usual mug of black coffee, and took a seat. He smiled back.

"How are you today?"

"Good!" he answered. "Real good."

"What did you think of the Vulcan Mind Meld?" she asked.

"It was really strange," Max answered. "But I want to try it again, if that's okay."

"Excellent! I'd never tried it on anyone before you. You were my first. I'm glad you like that approach because I need the practice."

"Bring it on," Max said, chuckling.

This was new, Helen thought. This is not the Max she'd been seeing for two years. She held out her hands, and Max, with no hesitation, placed his hands in hers with a tiny smile playing at the corners of his mouth.

Helen's eyes unfocused, and she probed. The words came, just like before, but this time it was different. She found confusion. A magnet pulling him off the edge of a cliff. Betrayal. False friend. Misplaced trust. Indoctrination. Meek acceptance. Fear.

She aimed a heart hug at the fear. Max received it with a sigh and a twitch that suggested a smile.

"Sometimes we can't resolve issues with the people in our lives," Helen said, "and it haunts us. It can even cripple us. If we can't face those people directly, we call in surrogates. We find people who are just like those people we can't face for whatever reason, and we attach ourselves to them, hoping we can finally make things right. But sometimes we really can't.

"We have to break the cycle. We have to bury the person who hurt us, and not try to earn his acceptance from the surrogate. If the original person is evil, so is the surrogate. You won't find healing from evil. You won't find acceptance from evil. You won't find knowledge from evil. You have to break away and look for something entirely different that will actually give you that acceptance you need but never got from him."

Max had a frightened expression this time.

"The acceptance you're looking for is tainted. It's harmful. It harms you. You have to turn away from the person and break away from him in your thoughts. Neutralize him in your thoughts. Remove his fangs in your thoughts, and the harm he caused, and distance yourself from him. He is nothing to you now. Then you have to reject his surrogate and find your own path, not follow his, because if you follow the surrogate's path you're going to get sucked down a hole that contains pain and loss. It contains evil.

"Let your father go. Don't ever try to replace him with someone else because the acceptance isn't coming, not from him or his surrogate. Don't try to emulate the surrogate. Don't let him influence your thoughts and opinions. Don't let him make you do things you know you shouldn't do, and don't want to do. Put up barriers when he tries to influence you, and stand strong. You're a good man with bad friends. Pull away."

Max was stunned and silent, thoughtful, anxious. He twisted in his seat.

Helen released his hands, and Max nervously placed them in his lap.

"Do you want to talk?" Helen asked.

Max shook his head, and sat for a minute in silence, looking at his hands. Then he excused himself and left the room with twenty minutes left on his session. Helen didn't stop him.

Later in the day he called to cancel his session for the following week.

CHAPTER 41: MAX CANCELS

"What now?" Helen was distraught. "We only had two sessions left, and he canceled the next one. He might not even show up for the last one. What do we do?"

Avid thought about it. This was concerning. It was extremely worrisome to him. He was chewing his cuticles. Failure failure failure.

"We have to trust the words," he said. "That's all we can do." He was reassuring himself as much as Helen.

"It's his friend. What's his name?"

"James."

"His friend is a replacement for his father. He's still looking for his father's love and approval, and James is just like his father. James is apparently a real piece of work, evil as hell, and he's behind everything. Max is just following along to earn his father's approval in his mind, and he's never going to get it." She shook her head. "It's so frustrating. And now I messed everything up."

"You did not mess anything up," Avid reassured them both. "You said the words that came through, that's all. Blame The Universe. We have to blame The Universe. We only did what we could do. We did the best we could. It will be fine. It will."

"We never even got to explore his mother. Ye gods. What a mess those parents made with that poor kid."

CHAPTER 44: THE JEWELRY'S OWNER

FRIDAY, MAY 1, 2021: 19:55 HOURS

Helen was checking her email when she opened a message from the woman who owned the art deco jewelry. In the email message was a link to a local news story, a link to a video with a local newscaster telling her story, and a link to a GoFundMe page. The woman wrote Helen a long missive, thanking her, telling her again how grateful everyone in her family was, and expressing her sympathy for the loss of Helen's son and husband.

She had done some sleuthing to find information about Helen before she called local news outlets to tell them about how she'd gotten her heirloom jewelry back. She suggested that Helen forward the links to local news in Washington, D.C. to see if they could keep the momentum to get more money for suicide prevention.

Helen clicked the video link first, and saw the newscaster reading the news while an image of Helen's selfie in the fancy restaurant displayed behind him. The newscaster told the story of how Helen purchased it on eBay, how she tried to find information about the jewelry online to learn when and where it was made and what company made it, and whether or not she could find a ring to match the set. Then she stumbled on a news story about how a set of jewelry identical to the set she just purchased had been stolen. The owner's name was in the article, so Helen located her on Facebook and sent her a message. She returned the jewelry the next day, refusing a reward or reimbursement for the purchase, asking only that the woman donate her reward money to a suicide prevention center in Seattle.

"In looking for information about this good Samaritan, Kelly Romano discovered that Helen Anderson's son had committed suicide. This explained her instructions that Kelly donate the money to a suicide prevention center. Kelly opted to donate the money to the Trevor Project, which provides suicide prevention services to LGBTQ youth, because Kelly's own son is gay and had lost a gay friend to suicide last year. Then she set up a GoFundMe account to try and obtain more funding in Helen Anderson's name."

The image behind him displayed the GoFundMe page, which had an astonishing donation balance.

"Her GoFundMe account has already received over eighteen thousand dollars since only yesterday, surpassing its goal. Donations keep coming in, and we hope that our viewers will take the time to donate a few dollars and save some lives. And now we turn you over to Bill Cooper for sports."

Helen craned her neck toward the living room where Avid was watching television.

"Avid!" she screamed. "Come here!"

Avid ran into Helen's office, where she was frantically pointing to her computer screen. "Avid! Look!"

Avid watched the news story, which Helen replayed from the beginning.

"Amazing, isn't it?" she said. "I think I might have really been dispatched to return that jewelry to her. Look at what happened."

"The Golden Rule is always a good one to follow," he answered grinning. "We still use it in my time."

"That's good to know." Helen said. "She told me to forward her message to local news here. I really think I'm going to. I'm about to be famous!"

She pulled up Google, searched for all the local stations, and forwarded the email to each one in turn, with a lead-in message explaining what had happened, in hopes that one of them would broadcast the story. Later it would broadcast on three live newscasts and seven news websites, and the GoFundMe campaign would be a complete success.

CHAPTER 45: MAX NO SHOWS

MONDAY, MAY 3, 2021: 20:15 HOURS

The Heroes were sitting with James, waiting for Max to arrive. James heard his phone ding, and reached for it in his pocket.

He read the text. "Max can't make it tonight," he said. "Let's just go to the bar."

CHAPTER 46: A THREAT TO UNDERWEAR

Nectar told Dirk and Chad in Hinduese that she didn't want to leave for the sports bar with the subjects just yet because she was feeling a little nauseated. The men were discussing the logistics of the lynching, as they did every Monday and Tuesday evening, and they appeared to be about ready to wrap up that discussion and head out much sooner than she had anticipated.

Max was there, to everyone's relief. He didn't say much or give anyone any eye contact, but he was there.

She suddenly looked prepared to vomit. "I feel sick," Nectar said, and dashed toward the toilet in Dirk's en suite.

But she did not go to the toilet. Instead, she went to Dirk's dresser, where she found his underwear drawer, and she opened it up.

Just then Dirk burst through the door with concerned eyes, looking around to see if Nectar had already vomited on any of his belongings in the room that he slept in, or if he had time to head her off before she did.

He stopped.

"What are you doing in my dresser?" He asked. "Get out of there."

Nectar looked at him, slightly irritated that she'd finally been caught and had no Plan B. Damn Dirk for being so unbelievably dumb and oblivious that she'd gotten lazy and sloppy.

"What's that in your hand?"

"Nothing." Nectar quickly hid the hand that was holding nothing behind her.

"Let me see."

"No! Let me go! Ugh!"

Dirk grabbed the can of itching powder from Nectar's grasp and stared at it.

"You were going to put this in my underwear? Why?"

"You know why," she hissed.

Dirk was bewildered. He honestly did not know why.

"I honestly do not know why," he said. He did not often speak the truth, but there it was: Truth. "I don't remember ever doing anything to you."

Nectar's jaw dropped. She focused her death stare on Dirk.

"The comments about my 'nice tits' and the jokes to the subjects about getting us drunk so we'd have sex with them? *You don't remember?*"

Dirk shrugged dismissively. Nectar reacted.

"You don't set women up to be raped, especially when they don't have clearance to interact and can't be messing around with the locals anyway. That's a high crime, and in this case *you'd* be accountable, not us."

She took a few deep, threatening breaths.

"You never disrespect a woman. It's illegal. You were breaking the law." She paused for another long hard breath. "And what do you mean, you don't remember? How do you forget that you committed a crime?"

Dirk didn't remember saying those things, although they admittedly sounded like things he might have said. He still didn't think they were all that insulting. They certainly couldn't be criminal, even though he knew on some level that they were, but he'd forgotten that too. Still, she should have taken the one about the tits as a compliment, right? And it was also a compliment when he repeatedly tried to force himself on her, even when she pushed him away. She should be flattered that he found her so attractive. And yet here she was, punishing him for something she should actually be thanking him for.

He raised the can of itching powder and said, "Have you been doing this sort of thing to me since that night? That would explain a lot." The more he thought about it, the more he realized Nectar must have been behind most of what had gone wrong in his life during this assignment.

"What *are* you, a *psychopath?*" he snapped.

Nectar looked down at five-foot-eleven-inch Dirk from her height of five feet and one-half inches, and raised her eyebrows.

"I am a woman, you sad little man." She leaned into him with a steely stare. "You do not denigrate me, or assault me, or serve me up on a platter to other men and then laugh about it. You do not conveniently forget you did those things to me because, for whatever reason—and you can explain it all to me—you don't seem to view me as being worthy enough to even register on your radar of poor behavior. You don't even *remember* doing all that to me."

"I just forgot," Dirk said in his own defense. Nectar visibly reacted with an expression and body language that indicated she thoroughly detested him. How could their relationship have gone so wrong, he wondered?

"Because I'm insignificant?"

Dirk rolled his eyes and blew air through his lips in disdain.

"You're always hysterical and overreacting. Calm down. I just forgot." Wrong answer.

Nectar's face rearranged her death stare to exude patronizing haughtiness, in addition to fury and contempt.

"When an employee with a penis is distracted by it to the degree that it overpowers their focus while they are performing their job, it results in a division of priorities that is detrimental to job performance, and thus endangers the employee's professional objectives and the success of the group. This distraction can express itself in several solitary forms. However, whenever employees impose their sexual preoccupation onto coworkers in a predatory manner, it disrupts and creates distress for others on the team. This creates morale problems and a decrease in work volume and quality throughout the work group, undermining the successful completion of the required tasks, and the ultimate achievement of the team's and the Project's goals."

Nectar had displayed one of the rules that governed sexual harassment in the workplace on her Alert screen and was reading it to Dirk, who was responding with a curled lip.

"When this occurs," she continued, "offending employee will experience the Shock Collar until they are no longer a threat." She paused momentarily to glare at Dirk. "Alert screen access to porn will be blocked during working hours, and access to other tools for viewing porn will be denied. The Mitigators will then reassign the employee to jobs that do not provide the opportunity for sexual distraction, and where they will henceforth only work with the gender to which they are not physically attracted. If they are bisexual or pansexual and show overpowering and distracting predatory compulsions toward coworkers of any gender, they must work independently, remotely, and in isolation. In this way the employees and co-workers can regain focus on their jobs and improve their performance. The Mitigators will replace the offending employee in their original role with someone who does not have a penis, or someone who has demonstrated zero distractions, reduced job performance, or work group disruption while having a penis in the workplace. Punishment for violators will be determined on a case-by-case basis."

Nectar had now finished reading the rule to Dirk.

"I decided to give you some repercussions myself until the Mitigators can enforce this rule on you at the end of this assignment."

Dirk rolled his eyes. "Lesbian," he spat. That was a go-to accusation that men used on unwilling women in the nineteen-seventies to persuade them to have sex, and/or to eliminate any suggestion that the man himself might not be attractive. It held equal weight with "frigid."

Suddenly Nectar's five feet and one half inch grew by several inches while Dirk shrank.

"If I *am* a lesbian, the consequences will be significantly worse for you because your comment denotes disrespect for me because of something over which I have no control. That's illegal. So, if I *am* a lesbian, you just gave me another serious charge to file against you." She gave him her dazzling smile. "In the meantime, I'll let you wonder whether or not I'm a lesbian while you anticipate your punishment."

Dirk was trying to think of a retort that would stick. "Frigid" had previously failed him, and he was short on ideas. In the meantime, Nectar continued.

"The Mitigators didn't stop you because they can't do anything to you right now or risk killing this mission. They'll find you after this is over. In the meantime, the law states that you must show me respect, both as a woman and as a possible lesbian. So that is what you will do. Do you understand?"

He looked at her with no expression. He still didn't see any problem, rule or no rule, law or no law, and was irritated that Nectar was so sensitive. His job performance was sublime, with or without his harmless flirtations. Ask anyone. The Mitigators would never punish him because he was too valuable to the Historian Project in general, and this mission in particular.

"Do you understand me?" She paused for his reaction, which turned out to be passive disinterest.

"I did *not* break any laws." He sniffed indignantly.

He bitterly missed the nineteen seventies when women were so much more reasonable. When he first showed up in nineteen-seventy, women couldn't even apply for credit cards without their husbands' signatures, and they appreciated not having to worry about money. They appreciated staying at home and not having to work, or having the easiest jobs set aside just for them so they didn't have to think too hard and get confused. Let's go back to that, he thought, looking at Nectar. That decade was the best of all possible worlds, he had decided. He wasn't used to this anymore. It was like being back in school.

She gave an exaggerated sigh.

"The Mitigators are going to go after you anyway, but I'm filing separate charges to increase the punishment you're going to get for all this. You'll get punishment for what they've observed you doing, plus punishment for my charges, plus what I'll demand as personal compensation. It gives me great pleasure to do this."

There was another inadvisable eye roll from Dirk.

"How did I break the law?" He sniffed derisively this time, instead of indignantly. He had a repertoire of expressive sniffs.

"You were involved in a conspiracy to assault me with people you knew were extremely dangerous, and even that wasn't enough for you. You then had to insult me by not even *remembering* that you did this to me, and I do not take kindly to insult. Also, general disrespect. That's the other law you broke."

"Conspiracy to assault you?" He did another "pfft" through his lips. However, he stopped himself from telling her to calm down this time.

"When you told the men you were going to 'liquor us up' you were conspiring with them to rape us. You were promising to get two women drunk for the benefit of two very dangerous men, dangling us in front of them and offering us up for sexual favors. That's a crime. I was just going to let it pass because you're a moron and filing charges is a pain..." Nectar's approach had also been boundlessly more amusing to her than the required paperwork. "...but I'm definitely coming after you now."

That rang a bell for some reason, Nectar saying: "coming after you..."

Ah! There it was, Dirk realized.

"No, it was a joke. I backtracked when you got angry, remember?"

It was all coming back to him now.

"They'll send a Historian back to do a telepathic read on the subjects and see if they interpreted it as a joke. As I recall—I was there, remember?—as I recall from *my* telepathic read on those guys, which any other Historian will corroborate, the subjects didn't think it was funny, and they were hoping to rape both of us, particularly James. James in particular wanted to get Janicyl so drunk that she'd pass out so he could do whatever he wanted to her. And he picked her to rape primarily because she was sitting closest to him. If he couldn't do it to her, he would have done it to me. I don't appreciate the risk you exposed me to."

"I can't be responsible for how people interpret the things I joke about."

"You can stop them, though, *can't you?*" She said "can't you" through her lower teeth. "You were there. You decided that we and our safety are so insignificant that you didn't even need to commit your actions and the subjects' intentions to memory, much less stop them from raping us. You deliberately jeopardized the team on the most high profile mission I've ever heard of, much less participated in, and you don't even remember doing it."

She did a "pttt" of her own, then continued.

"Fortunately, Janicyl and I haven't had any problems with them since we began keeping our distance and stopped paying any attention to them. No thanks to you. You should have stepped up and protected us."

Dirk laughed out loud at the thought of "protecting" the very formidable Nectar. She did not take that well.

"You aren't suited for this job," she snapped. "In your next assignment you'll no doubt be trapped in a sea of men. Let's hope they all find you attractive."

Nectar had no doubt the Mitigators would do that, just for starters. He should have been grateful for her taking an approach that had minimal impact, she thought. He should have thanked her for the overflowing toilets and soapy wine.

"Look, I'm sorry," Dirk said. Why did she keep talking? She was so irritating, he thought to himself. "Just calm down," he said to her again.

"Too late for apologies," Nectar replied, bristling dangerously at his order for her to calm down. "Criminal Justice is going to conduct a scanner review of you after I file charges. They'll see you forcing yourself on me, and probably other women. They're going to freeze your perks and put you on administrative leave back home—or prison, we'll wait and see."

She wrinkled her nose and smiled.

"No Saturday Night Fever for you, asshole."

That last comment hit its target with spectacular, stunning precision. Nectar suddenly had Dirk's full attention and respect.

"No, please," Dirk begged helplessly. He *must* be an extra on the set of *Saturday Night Fever*. He *must*. He simply *must* dance in that movie for all posterity, and to impress the women he had yet to meet. The bank had finally confirmed his reservation back to the filming of the movie and had arranged for him to be on the set as an extra, but for some reason he had to wait for approval to go, and approval kept not coming. He had thought it was because of the mission he was working on, but had noticed the other Heroes taking side trips and vacations. Only Dirk was in this holding pattern, waiting. It was not until this very moment that he finally began to understand that he might be in some sort of real trouble.

"The Mitigators have been watching you on live scanner feed this whole time, dumb ass. They even had to give you the shock collar, which should have tipped you off to the fact that they're evaluating your competence right now, and that you're in trouble. I've never even seen them use the shock collar on any man past adolescence before."

She glared at him.

"What are you, *stupid?*"

Dirk looked at her and considered that thoughtfully. Yes, he apparently *was* stupid, he concurred, stunned.

Dirk suddenly grimaced and grunted in pain. The Mitigator-on-duty had decided that Dirk required an electrical jolt right now, for no particular reason. He now absolutely understood on a deeper level that he might not ever be able to fix this.

Seeing the pain on Dirk's face, Nectar turned and calmly went back into the living room. Later, she cheerfully drove everyone to the bar.

From that point forward Dirk treated Nectar humbly, contritely, and with the utmost respect. He was hoping that he could charm her and persuade her to reconsider. She was thoroughly unmoved, and filed the charges against him anyway.

Nectar's charges prompted a new law that limited the period of time that Historians and Heroes could remain on assignment, anywhere, to prevent complete and thorough time period/geographic location assimilation and rejection of their upbringing, which Dirk had demonstrated.

In addition to other punishments, the Mitigators would restrict him from any further travel back to the nineteen-seventies. He could never go home again.

CHAPTER 47: "THE END OF THE WORLD"

"So I've been thinking," Helen said. "With time travel and the control centers, there is no end of the world. Ever."

Avid looked at her quizzically.

"Hear me out." She gathered her thoughts. "Say we have some sort of disaster that causes the end of the world. All we have to do is take everyone and send them back in time, right? The world blows up but the people are still alive and safe somewhere in history, living their lives. So society makes its way back to the end of the world again, and they send people back in time again. Infinity. It's a constant loop, and the world never ends because it's still operating at some point in time, forever."

"Interesting concept." It was interesting, Avid thought. "Well here's reassurance. The Mitigators can travel into the future. They're the only ones who can, so they will know, or do know, when the end of the world is. They haven't sounded the alarm yet. We still have a world in the twenty-eighth century, and the Mitigators are apparently confident that things are going to continue because we're all still carrying on."

"But one day they'll do it like I said, right?"

"Probably. It's something to think about."

"I just bet I'm right." She sipped her tea thoughtfully. "That's how I'd handle the end of the world, anyway."

CHAPTER 48: MAX NO SHOWS AGAIN

Max was a no-show for his therapy session. Helen paced back and forth, frightened, concerned and sorry. It was the last possible chance she would have had to get through to him, and now it was lost. Now she would need to fret for days because the lynching was on Friday, and this was only Tuesday.

And she knew that Avid would be fretting. The two of them would be total wrecks until the mission was over. Avid actually had his freedom at stake—Helen's failure could send him to prison. She couldn't possibly live with herself. This was torture.

There was nothing left that she could possibly do. She wanted to cry.

CHAPTER 49: THE LAST SUPPER

Avid handed the bank representative the receipts.

"The five of us went to dinner to celebrate the end of our mission," he explained. "We ordered everything, and had probably six bottles of two hundred dollar wine. It was like a Roman orgy of food in an extremely expensive restaurant."

The bank representative nodded sympathetically. "I'm so sorry," he said.

"The price of the average entrée was over one hundred dollars, and even the appetizers cost about seventy five dollars each. Chad ordered two. Everyone got dessert. Chad ordered two. Then, on top of the wine, we all ordered specialty cocktails."

"Go on. I know you're strong. You can tell me," the bank representative said encouragingly.

Avid wiped a finger under his eye and emitted a deep sigh with a slow head shake.

"We ordered everything, as I said. Then, as we were finishing dessert, I left the table to go to the restroom. When I came back, everyone had left me there, and the server was waiting for me with the check. The tab came to over two thousand dollars, as you can see." Avid gestured toward the receipt.

"Closer to three thousand," the bank representative said, studying the total. "Such a tragedy. I am so sorry."

"And of course a five hundred dollar tip was insufficient for the exemplary service we received, so I felt compelled to leave a two thousand dollar tip."

"Indeed. As would anyone."

Avid nodded solemnly.

"And of course you need compensation for experiencing their cruel betrayal, no doubt?"

"I do." Avid then sighed and looked down. "The Heroes had never once included me in anything before." He looked back up at the bank representative, sadly. "I thought they finally wanted to be my friend."

"Pain and suffering." The bank representative shook his head, aghast. "I'll add that in."

"Thank you."

"What do you have in mind for your compensation?"

Avid perked up. "Downhill skiing. At least two weeks in a chalet for the first trip. Austria might be nice, but I'll consider anything appropriate. Let's include ski lessons and a fashionable ski wardrobe with top of the line equipment, plus a generous cash allowance and a first class flight to wherever it is—let's go back to the nineteen-nineties and the DC-10, if you don't mind. I loved that plane. Also, I'd like a window seat. I'll let you know later about the other trips after I give it some thought."

"Of course. I have a number of options for you to examine. Let's step over here to the Wish Book."

"Thank you."

CHAPTER 50: SIX FLAGS

FRIDAY, MAY 14, 2021: 08:47 HOURS

Nectar and Janicyl took the Tesla out for one final joy ride, and went to Six Flags America for a few hours on the rollercoasters before they slipped back into character and returned to Dirk's apartment.

Nectar did not wear a long dress today, but could still have shown up at a cocktail party and fit in without comment in her dazzling dinner outfit with diamond accessories. Janicyl wore a black sports bra under a very expensive oversized silver lame bomber jacket, with slouchy, baggy designer cargo pants rolled up above her ankles, and her hair in stumpy pigtails. She had been online, studying North America, 2021 street fashion for the last few weeks and watching Project Runway, and was making an effort. They both wore low heels after consulting with Janicyl's Alert screen, to Nectar's disappointment.

They arrived at the park's opening, and made every effort to see and experience everything they could before they had to leave at three p.m. They focused on the thrill rides, ignoring anything that didn't have a warning for people who were pregnant or had heart conditions. They ate the Dippin' Dots and the funnel cakes, tried the hotdogs with everything and a side of nachos, and then split a Philly cheesesteak. When they were fed and had ridden everything twice, they returned to Dirk's apartment to prepare for the event.

Janicyl parked the Tesla beside the Range Rover in the garage. When Dirk let her in, she placed the key fob on the kitchen island per instructions from the Finance Project. Finance would come afterward to retrieve both cars and all the apartment furnishings, which they would repurpose for other assignments, or resell.

Chad had cleared out his own virtually-unused apartment. He left the clothing because he wouldn't need it anymore, but took some toiletries from the bathroom, and anything that originated in the twenty-eighth century. He was now at Dirk's, where he settled in and watched Dirk pack his belongings into liquor boxes. Chad's own two boxes were in the gathering pile of Dirk's belongings.

Nectar had the car running and was waiting outside of the garage entrance door for the other Heroes to gather up and carry Chad and Dirk's belongings down to the car. She would take them to the travel pod pickup location so Dirk and Chad could transport everything back. The two men would unload it all at the control station, then quickly return for their meetup with the subjects at the sports bar at eighteen hundred hours. Nectar and Janicyl would be waiting for them, snacking on buffalo wings and fries, and sipping virgin cocktails.

CHAPTER 51: FIND MAX

Chad and Dirk ran into James outside of the sports bar as they were all about to enter it. James couldn't reach Max, he said. Should they go to his place and see what was going on?

Chad and Dirk had a quick telepathic discussion about Max's behavior before Chad shrugged and said to James, "He's probably just in the shower. Let's grab the ladies and go get him."

The telepathic conversation resumed. *Which plan do you want to follow?* Dirk asked. Chad displayed his Alert screen and asked for Max's exact location so they could avoid wasting any time. *He's at home,* Chad told Dirk. Both Chad and Dirk exchanged looks, then went in to fetch Nectar and Janicyl so they could head to Max's house immediately.

CHAPTER 52: MAX PROVES USELESS

FRIDAY, MAY 14, 2021: 18:01 HOURS

Max answered the door looking disheveled and sleepy because he had taken anti-depressants and anti-anxiety medication with two shots of Tequila. The doorbell, and then the pounding on the door, roused him from a short nap on his couch.

Chad and Dirk had left James in the car. They both telepathically heard Max prepare to tell them that he was ill and couldn't join them this evening, so Chad grabbed one arm and Dirk grabbed the other. Dirk thought to close the front door before they dragged Max down the steps and shoved him into the backseat of the Range Rover next to Dirk. Chad was in the front seat with Nectar, and turned slightly so he could keep an eye on Max.

Janicyl, sitting in the far back of the vehicle beside James, kept a close watch from behind, just in case.

Nectar followed her GPS to the parking lot where James had left his van, dropped him off, and then kept driving toward the homeless shelter with James following behind. Max sat slumped over, staring at his phone. When they approached a red light, the Heroes all heard Max planning to open the car door and jump out at the light. Nectar quietly set the child locks so that Max couldn't open the door, and then slowed to a stop.

Max surreptitiously tried the door handle as the car waited for the green light, then fell back in his seat, defeated.

During the preceding few months the subjects had prowled Washington, D.C. looking for potential opportunities and potential victims. If the men they chose were homeless they probably wouldn't be missed, so Max and James felt their chances of getting away with the crime increased. They settled on one particular homeless shelter, and studied the flow of traffic in and out of it for weeks, looking for nearby secluded or hidden places where the homeless might go to do drugs, or deal drugs, or just have a private moment to enjoy a cigarette.

Max and James thought they might offer work and a hundred dollars each to the men they planned to abduct. The company van would make the offer seem plausible. They focused on the men who seemed the most desperate so it would be easier to lure them. They identified several, and in the original continuum had found four of these in the alley, smoking, at 20:02 hours.

James had a utility van with no windows. He pulled away from the Range Rover and parked the van in the vicinity of the homeless shelter with the company name painted on each side and the rear, in full view of anyone. Nectar circled back around and pulled up behind the van.

CHAPTER 53: MISSION COMPLETE

It was going on right now, in this exact moment. Four Black men were being lynched in a field in rural Virginia with the Heroes at the helm and, hopefully, in control. Joseph D'Andre McKenna may or may not be the fifth victim, depending on how well the Heroes performed. After weeks of work and effort and worry, it was terrifying to think that Avid might have failed the Heroes and their mission.

Avid and Helen sat together on the couch without saying much as they silently obsessed over the situation, what each of them had done up until this moment, and how it was all transpiring. Would the Heroes pull it off? Were they saving the world? Had Avid done enough to assist them? Was Helen's therapy enough? This was job stress.

Avid was visibly unsettled and nervous. Helen watched him sympathetically but warily, remaining silent because she knew better than to offer him platitudes. She had her own internal demons that she was trying to fend off. Failure. Failure for both of them. This went beyond words, and she knew there was nothing she could say. She reached over and patted his hand and sighed while they both watched a show on her television, unseeing and unaware of what was being broadcast for their entertainment.

They reached for their coffee. Avid kept chewing his cuticles. They sat like statues, staring ahead, stiff and waiting.

And waiting.

At 23:43 hours the Alert screen displayed a flashing green message: "Mission Successful." The color green almost didn't register with Avid. In his frequent nightmares the screen was always flashing red, underscoring his own failed attempt in the effort and sending him to prison. But it was green. It still said "Mission Successful" after he blinked. He studied the link to the report that contained a more detailed description of what had transpired, and a brief outline of where the integrity of the continuum stood, now that the mission was complete. He was afraid to open the link just yet.

"Mission Successful," he said to Helen. "It's done. They did it. I helped them, and you helped me, so we all did it."

Helen's head shot around and she grabbed his shoulder to shake it. "They did it? They did it?"

"They did it!" `

Helen hugged him tightly and kissed his cheek so hard it left a bruise. Avid was giddy.

"What happened? What does it say?"

"I'll read it now." Avid's eyes fixed themselves on the link. Pausing, he caressed the link with his eyes, then gave the command to open it. As it opened he shut his eyes tight. Then he opened them again and looked. A detailed description of tonight's events displayed. Avid read it silently, growing more and more confused, and then stunned.

Helen watched him with impatient excitement until he turned to her with a look of astonishment and wonder.

"What does it say?" she asked.

"It's the official report. It says I wasn't the backup for the Heroes. It says that they were the backup for the two of us. It says that you and I did this, not the Heroes. We saved the continuum. You and I. We did it, not the Heroes. It was us."

"What?" Now Helen was stunned.

Avid returned to the report, which stated that the hundreds of continuum projections the Mitigators had run at the beginning of the mission had determined that pairing Avid with Helen resulted in a projected 98.7% success rate in putting the continuum back in order. No other pairing of various Historians with various people close to Max or James gave a projection above 53%. No other scenario or combination of players had even been under consideration, once the Avid/Helen pairing displayed.

"I'm afraid you're it," Vendi had told him. He'd had no idea the degree to which she meant that.

The Heroes were there to ensure that the final 1.3% of risk was managed properly, and they had successfully done that. This was not to diminish their efforts, but their success was largely due to the fact that Max had lost interest in lynching Joseph or anyone else after experiencing Helen's heart hug and Vulcan Mind Meld therapy. Helen's therapy had reached him in a way that nothing else could have because Avid had patiently taught her how to reach him, and she had willingly learned.

Just two therapy sessions had been enough.

There was a caveat with that projection, which is why the Mitigators had been so closely involved, watching them, listening to every word of their conversations. When the Mitigators ran the projection and entered a variable that made Avid aware of how critical his role was, the probability of success dropped to 24.5%. Therefore it was essential that everyone hide the vital importance of Avid's role from him until the mission was complete. Everyone who was aware of the mission and the possible dire consequences was ordered to reassure Avid that the Heroes were the critical players in the mission, and that Avid was just their backup. If he were to have found out that everything depended on him, the mission would quite likely have failed.

The Mitigators had been chewing their own cuticles, preparing themselves to leap in and lie to him about his participation in the project if he showed even the smallest indication of understanding his real role. They had an entire plan in place to manage his anxiety and self-doubt, and a therapist on standby. All of the Mitigators had roleplayed and practiced their plan in case they needed to use it. But they fortunately did not.

That explained why everyone who was familiar with the mission had kept commenting to Avid that he was "only the backup." He had thought it was odd and a just little insulting, if you think about it, that everyone always pointedly told him that he was just an "also-ran" in the mission. Everyone had pointedly said that to him throughout the entire effort. When Avid thought back, he realized that all of those people had been blocked at the time they'd said it. The fact that absolutely nobody involved in the mission would permit him to read them should have raised his suspicions, but it didn't.

"We need to work more on your confidence and self-esteem," Helen said to him fondly, ruffling his hair. "Does it tell you what happened at the lynching? I don't want the details, please, just an overview."

"Right." Avid skimmed the report and paraphrased it all for Helen.

Chad and Dirk knew which four men had died in the original continuum. When the Heroes arrived at the homeless shelter they needed to make certain that their group only snatched those specific men. To ensure that no mistakes were made, they asked Max and James to wait for them behind the van as lookouts, and keep the rope and duct tape ready to hold the men down when the Heroes returned with them.

The Heroes wandered into the alley where the four men were sharing a cigarette as they had in the original continuum, just where James and Max first found them. Chad offered a lit joint to them, then charmingly joked and laughed with them for a little while.

"We have to pick up a shipment from the train, and we don't have anyone to help. Would any of you be interested in working for a couple of hours? We'll pay you a hundred dollars each." He pointed to the van with the logo and company name on it as proof that the business was legitimate.

"A hundred dollars?" one of the men had asked. The other men leaned forward with interest.

Dirk said yes, and led them to the van. Just like that, the four men willingly walked to their doom. Chad followed behind everyone to make certain none of the victims wandered away.

They opened the back door to the van. Dirk climbed in first. The men followed, and were greeted by Max and James, who were pointing guns. The Heroes grabbed and shoved the victims into the back of the van, hogtied them, stuffed their mouths with rags and duct taped them shut while James cocked his gun and glared. Max listlessly aimed his gun at the men without showing much enthusiasm, frequently looking away. When the men were satisfactorily roped and tied, James climbed into the driver's seat and programmed his GPS to take them to James D'Andre McKenna's address.

But Max said no.

"We need to get away right now," Max insisted. "We'll get that little prick next time." In reality, he no longer had the stomach for it, after his sessions with Helen. In fact, he no longer had the stomach for any of this. He was going through the motions because he did not know what else to do, or how to get out of it. It didn't register with James that something was odd about the way the Heroes had assumed control of the lynching, and it didn't register that Max was no longer really participating. The energy and enthusiasm of the Heroes drew his attention away from Max.

Chad and Dirk agreed with Max. No time. No need. He was a little punk. Who cared? Just a kid. Not even worth the trouble. Too much to worry about as it was. Let's get the hell out of here before anyone saw them. Now. Drive now. Go.

Without waiting for James to object, the Heroes hopped out of the van, pulled Max after them and slammed the van door shut. Then they climbed into the Range Rover, where Nectar put the vehicle into Drive, and drove.

A half-hidden witness none of them saw took note of the company name on the van, just as she had in the original continuum. She took down the license plate number of the Range Rover, then called the police and reported the kidnapping of four men from the shelter, providing all the information she had, including a description of the kidnappers. The police would never track the owner of the Range Rover, who had paid cash for the vehicle and appeared not to exist. However, they would ultimately, and very easily, locate the van.

"Pull out of here like lightning," Chad told Nectar in Hinduese as she started the car. "Get out in front of James."

Grumbling but overruled, James followed the Range Rover, which screeched out of there so quickly that it overtook the van and kicked up dust from the side of the concrete road. The Heroes wanted to ensure that James was following them and would not lead the way to Joseph's house, in case he planned to buck their dissension and regain control. But James himself agreed that it wasn't worth it, and pulled away from the curb to drive to the field in Fairfax, not even thinking about making the side trip to Joseph's house, considering the way things had turned out. This was just as the Heroes had hoped and planned.

In the van, the four men were face down on the floor, shaking, letting out muffled screams. One of them wet himself. Two of them were weeping. They had their hands tied to their ankles behind them, so they rolled and bumped on the floor of the van every time they hit a pothole or took a sharp turn. James just drove on, not paying attention to the sounds of distress in the back.

In the Range Rover it became clear to the Heroes that Max was not going to cooperate anymore. He asked Nectar to stop and let him out, saying he was done. She had already locked the passenger door again so he could not get out. He fell back in his seat, slumping, staring out the window.

Chad coldly told Max to stop being such an asshole.

Nectar kept driving.

Max continued sullenly staring out of the window, hunched over throughout the entire drive to Fairfax.

They didn't need Max. The Heroes had studied the wounds and the abuse Max had performed on the men in the original continuum, and were prepared to replicate every injury, just exactly as Max had inflicted it. James would do the rest.

The event was gruesome, just as it was supposed to be. It was gruesome enough to earn James life in prison without parole, which was everyone's goal. Chad and Dirk allowed Max to stand at the sidelines and look away because it didn't matter whether or not he participated. James would implicate him as a co-conspirator, so even though he had not done anything beyond the planning stages, he would be imprisoned and would die while awaiting trial, just as he had in the original timeline. His failure to kill did not affect the continuum at all.

Avid read that line to himself but did not tell Helen, that Max was going to die in a few weeks, because it would happen in Helen's future, so she couldn't know.

The ladies had waited in the vehicle as the lynching occurred, and played no role in the event. When the mission was successful, they drove back to Dirk's apartment where Nectar left the Range Rover for pickup by someone from the Finance Project, and placed the key fob on the kitchen island, as Janicyl had already done with the fob from the Tesla. Then they all immediately returned to the control station. Since both Heroes had cleared out their personal items earlier in the day, they never needed to return again.

The Heroes could never again go on-land in this time and place because James and Max had once taken pictures of them with their phones, which would soon be confiscated. Chad and Dirk would be wanted men from this point forward.

Nectar and Janicyl would be wanted for questioning. The police were searching for an interpreter who spoke whatever the language was in Kazakhstan so they would be prepared when and if they located them.

Within less than four hours the police tracked the utility vehicle to one of the Stoughton tobacco farms and turned their attention to James as a person of interest, confiscated his phone, accessed its history and followed the GPS route he had taken to the field, where they discovered the bodies.

Chad's report mentioned how sloppy their planning had been, considering how many weeks they had spent planning. The Heroes could not offer ideas or suggestions during their meetings, so they just listened and watched, and encouraged them to take whatever ill-conceived approach they came up with, marveling at the degree to which Max and James had set themselves up to be caught from the very beginning.

James used his own company's vehicle and carried his own phone, instead of abandoning an untraceable van. He didn't use a throwaway device for the GPS, so his route tracking history was intact on his personal smart phone. So was his child porn. Furthermore, James had stopped at a nearby station that had security footage of him getting out of the vehicle to fill it up with gas. That was the mistake that caught him because it was clearly him on the footage, not another employee. It all led the police to the Stoughton tobacco farm, where several employees identified James as the figure in the grainy gas station security footage, resulting in James's arrest.

Furthermore, the men hadn't even thought to park the van in a less open location, or have one of them stand watch for witnesses. Instead, they posed with their guns in the back of the windowless van, out of which they could not see.

"Unbelievable," Chad wrote with disdain. The Heroes were not concerned about protecting themselves, and they could not interfere with the continuum by evading any witnesses, which was how the two men were caught in the original continuum. They were just doing their job and didn't care who saw them. But the subjects...wow.

James and Max had to have been on the outside of the van in the original continuum to lure the men into the van, Chad continued in his report. He guessed when they did have the chance to spot witnesses the first time, they never bothered to look around, because the same person had reported them during both versions of the event. They both just probably felt that punishment didn't happen to people of their wealth and social class, and because of that, they were lazy. Or maybe they were idiots, like he'd said before. The eye roll in Chad's report was palpable.

The Finance Project resold the Range Rover and the Tesla as "low mileage vintage vehicles in pristine condition" forty years in the future, making a tidy profit. They also scanned Chad and Dirk's condo buildings for a sufficient span of time during which they could move about undetected, then deactivated the security cameras and cleared everything out. They sold both of the condos, all the furnishings, and the $40,000 light show showerheads. Proceeds from the sale went to the investment account of an untraceable, but scrupulously tax-paying corporation with P.O. Box for an address.

James threw his legal team into motion. They were looking for a plea deal, so they advised James to plead guilty and then implicate Max, even though he did not participate.

He also implicated Chad and Dirk, who would be on the FBI's Most Wanted List for many years, evading capture. The FBI would never find them or any trace of them under the names and addresses that James provided. Both apartments were empty when the police went to investigate, and the building managers could not provide any security footage, traceable names, or forwarding addresses. Again, the Heroes had paid in cash. Then they left without notice.

Nectar and Janicyl kept the clothes, the shoes, and the handbags, and would leave with four large wheeled suitcases each, instead of three. Janicyl had sold a number of her acquisitions on eBay before packing.

Three of the Heroes had already received their new assignments and would all be leaving for other times and other places in the morning. Dirk, however, would be going home to face the Mitigators. None of them would think to say goodbye to Avid, who was relieved to be rid of them. They also would not think to say goodbye to each other.

Joseph D'Andre McKenna, who had been in his bedroom that evening studying for a Civics final, would pass the exam with an A. The following year he would begin taking college courses in addition to his high school courses, earning college credits for the next two years. Then he would receive a full four-year scholarship to Harvard, where he would graduate with a 4.5 grade point average and then continue on at Harvard Law. Projections showed him following his original life path and dying in his nineties of natural causes. Disaster had been averted.

"Poor Max," Helen said. "I'm so sorry for that poor kid. He was finally making progress." She looked emotional and wiped away a tear. "Poor kid. I'm so sad for him." She covered her face in her hands, and then stood to hurriedly go up to her room and shut the door without saying goodnight to Avid.

CHAPTER 54: HELEN GRIEVES

Helen still looked haggard at three in the afternoon, as if she hadn't had any sleep. Avid didn't know when she had woken up because she hadn't come out of her room until just now. While she was dressed, more or less, she wasn't as put together as he was used to seeing her. She was wearing sweat pants and an old t-shirt, no makeup, and her hair wasn't styled. He had never seen her look disheveled before.

Avid was watching a movie on Netflix when she wandered into the kitchen and grabbed the quick drink generator from a drawer. She pulled a mug from one of the cabinets, filled it with water and wordlessly walked over to Avid, who took the items from her hands and made her now-favorite tea beverage, which he handed to her. She nodded thanks, and plopped down on the couch beside him, looking at the television without actually watching it.

Avid didn't say anything to her because he knew she wanted company but no conversation. He returned to watching the movie, monitoring her mood as he watched. She was bereft over Max Richmond. All her work, she thought. Everything she had worked toward, to keep him from killing Joseph, had been futile because four men were dead, the story was all over the news nationwide, and Max had already been taken into custody with James. There was nothing she could do to save him.

Avid couldn't think of anything to say to make her feel better. Explaining to her that it happened the way it had to would not console her. He was not privy to information regarding the disaster that Joseph's death would have triggered, but he knew that the attention the Anomaly had received at the control station, and the crisis mode it had caused, were clear indications that it would have been catastrophic. He didn't need to think about it because the crisis had been averted. He was simply sad for Helen that she could only focus on Max right now.

Vendi popped up on his Alert screen.

"Hey hotshot," she said smiling. "Good job."

Avid smiled back and thanked her.

"I have some information to disseminate to you. Can you talk?"

"Sure." Avid nodded his head and got comfortable. Helen glanced at him when he began speaking to his Alert screen, then looked back at the television, still unseeing.

"Perks for life, Avid. You have the bank account of a Hero now. You also have the right to Hero living accommodations, including furnishings and upgrades. You qualify for a five-bedroom, three bath apartment. Congratulations."

"Really?" Avid liked living in a Hero apartment, but he was just unwilling to pay for one, especially one of the largest they had. This was great news. She was describing more perks than he had ever heard of anyone receiving for a single mission. He was more and more curious about the disaster they'd averted, just based on the way they were treating him now.

"The Mitigators would like to thank Helen for her contribution to the success of the mission. We can't give her perks, but we can give her health care for life. We'll send a doctor to check on her once a year and more often if she needs it. She can also get unlimited psychotherapy. She'll be excited about that. And we're sending her a credit card with a high maximum limit, but the balance will be paid off as soon as she charges anything or takes cash withdrawals, so it will essentially have no limit at all. If she wants to buy a castle in Scotland or her own Caribbean island, that's fine. We'll cover the cost. Tell her we would do more if we could, and if she can think of anything else we can do for her, she should just let us know. Tell her we mean that."

Avid turned to Helen. "The Mitigators are giving you healthcare for life, Helen! And psychotherapy! As much as you want! They really appreciate what you did, so they're sending a doctor to you once a year and whenever you need one. Also, you have a credit card with no limit that they'll pay off for you whenever you charge anything!"

Helen turned to him with a look of astonishment. Then she smiled. "Tell them thank you so much! Ask when can I have my first therapy session, okay?" She flexed her muscles. "Tell them I feel wonderful, and thank you again for the doctor visit! It was all unbelievable!"

Vendi instructed Avid to grab a pencil and write down a phone number. "Tell Helen to send a text message to this number whenever she feels ill or wants to make an appointment for therapy. Also, tell her to let us know whenever she needs anything we can possibly give her or do for her. The number goes to the director of the mid-Atlantic control station, and she'll arrange everything for her. Helen's new physician will be there, and is just as good as the one she saw before, tell her."

Avid got up and fished for a pen and paper in Helen's office, wrote down the number on a Post-it note and stuck it to Helen's computer screen. Then he walked back to the living room, carrying Vendi with him twelve inches in front of his face.

"I put the number on your monitor, Helen. Send a text to that number any time you feel sick or want some therapy. Or anything else, Vendi said. And don't be a martyr. They absolutely want to do this for you, okay? It's the only way they can repay you for everything you did."

"Promise." Helen's mood had lifted considerably now. She was now facing Avid, watching him impatiently for the rest of the information he was receiving, excited for both of them.

Vendi continued relaying her list of rewards.

"You have unlimited visits to Helen with partial clearance to interact, and you won't have to use your perks to do it. You can speak to anyone in Helen's household, including Nelda and her wife, but you're going to speak Hinduese if you try to speak to anyone else without special clearance."

The Mitigators had reassessed their initial decision to make an ancient indigenous language be the on-land default language, deciding that they had over-shot their initial objective out of panic. Hinduese was fine, they all agreed. No more frantic calls to 9-1-1 by the locals.

Avid was happy about his unlimited visits, and turned to Helen to share the news. "I can come visit you whenever I want. I'll still come for Game Night every week, and your birthday, and Mother's Day, whatever holidays you want, and we can travel together when you get vacation time."

Avid turned to Vendi. "Can Helen have free travel and accommodations?"

"Whatever she wants," Vendi said. "Tell her to charge it on her credit card."

Helen had heard the question, and was looking at Avid, waiting for Vendi's answer. He nodded his head and gave her a thumbs up. Helen clapped her hands with delight.

"Can I please leave my stuff in your guestroom? I'll be back here at least every weekend, so it only makes sense," Avid said to her.

She covered her mouth with excitement, then burst into tears. She had been bracing herself for Avid's departure, now that the mission was complete, trying to measure the hole in her life that would be there after he left. This was wonderful news to her. Avid leaned over and hugged her while Vendi stayed silent in the background, watching until they were finished.

"One last thing," Vendi said in a solemn voice. "They told me to tell you that if you weren't male, they would nominate you to be a Mitigator. They can't circumvent the laws so it can't happen right now, but they wanted you to know how much they appreciate you. If the laws change in your lifetime, you'll be automatically nominated."

Avid stared with his jaw slowly dropping open. "Say that again?"

Vendi smiled. "If you were female, you would be nominated to possibly become a Mitigator. Congratulations. You now rank with the Educators. They were extremely impressed with the way you taught Helen—they honestly didn't think it was possible because of her insufficient brain makeup—and they would like to train you to officially teach Advanced Telepathy. That means the Heroes won't mess with you anymore. Good news, right?"

Avid turned to Helen, whose tears had dried while she attempted to read his face. He was too stunned to speak. Helen was getting more and more impatient.

"If I weren't male, she said, they would nominate me to be a Mitigator. Vendi just told me that. Can you believe it?" Avid waited for her to jump for joy because he was nearly unable to contain his own. Instead, she stared at him thoroughly confused.

"What do you mean, if you weren't male? What does that have to do with anything?"

Avid lived in a world where women were in charge. He took that for granted, just as Helen seemed to always expect that leadership roles would go to men. He had to stop and remind himself that his world was different from hers in that way.

"It's against the law to hold a world leadership position if you're male. They set up the laws to ensure that all males are correctly educated before they permit them to be leaders again. The law expires in two hundred and fifty years, so until then 'Educator' is as far as we can go."

"Why two hundred and fifty years?"

"We have an average lifespan of about one hundred and twenty years in my time. Male leadership is still in living memory, and it still will be for quite some time. They don't want that to influence the leadership style of males coming up through the ranks. So, they're waiting for all of us to die and for the next generation to be properly trained before they let men lead again. They probably don't need the full two hundred and fifty years, but they wanted to make sure."

Helen stared at him. "The Mitigators are all *women?*" Helen was trying to process this information and was having a difficult time.

"Yes of course. I thought it was obvious or I would have said something. I mean, they sent you heart emojis and cupcakes. Good grief, Helen."

Thinking back it all made sense to Helen. She had pictured them all as old white men, even though the Mitigator names she'd heard every day when each Mitigator-on-Duty introduced herself were from every culture around the world, which meant they were of every race and national heritage. She was sometimes unable to discern the gender, from the foreign names they all seemed to have, but she *had* thought that Mitigators were all exceptionally...nice...for men in charge. They had never been dismissive, or condescending, or insultingly placating, or impatient and superior. They had never tried to manipulate her into an inferior position in any of their admittedly indirect dealings, or ignored her and made her voiceless. Maybe that alone should have tipped her off.

No. The pregnancy simulator should have tipped her off. She was losing her edge, she thought ruefully.

Vendi was still on Avid's screen, watching the conversation. "I'm going to sign off now. You can explain it all to Helen. You know which information you can't divulge, and I trust that you won't do that. We'll alert you if you get too close to telling her things she can't know. Just keep everything at an overview level without going into much detail, and you should be fine. I'll talk to you later at the control station here. We're setting you up to arrive tomorrow, so clear out your things and pack them for shipping. You'll need to have a meeting with the other Educators, and they'll walk you through the paces and the paperwork. Then, after that conversation you'll be back on automatic scanning. The Mitigators won't be monitoring you live anymore."

"Holy shit," Avid breathed, edging toward a panic attack. 'Educator' was something he had never aspired to in his life. It was completely unexpected and completely out of his scope. He was never going to be able to pull it off. They were crazy to promote him to Educator. What were they thinking? He began to worry and fret. Vendi heard him fretting.

"You have to stop that, Avid. Let Helen fix your self-esteem issues before you show up for training. I mean that. Tell her it's an order. Then come here knowing you deserve this. No more of this whiney baby crap."

"Okay. Will do." He was gnawing at a cuticle. "Thanks, Vendi. Talk to you later."

Vendi grinned, flashed him the two-fingered peace sign, and shut the screen.

"You have to fix my self-esteem, she said. It's an order. They've promoted me to Educator. I have no idea where or when my assignment will be, but I have to go home to the twenty-eighth century for training." He shook his head as if it were all unbelievable.

"You're going to be a teacher? That's so nice! Won't you miss traveling though?"

"It's more than 'nice,' Helen. It's only one ranking below Mitigator. In fact, they draw most of the Mitigators from the Educator pool. Most of the Mitigators we've worked with were teachers at one time. Some of them go back to teaching when their twenty-year terms are up."

Helen read on his face that twenty-eighth century Educators didn't need to go to Dollar General to purchase school supplies out of their own money for their students. They didn't have to secretly pay off overdue lunch fees in school districts that humiliated the children and let them go hungry when their overdue amount was too high. They didn't have to fight for pay raises that would enable them to teach without having to work second and third jobs as restaurant servers or shop clerks. They didn't have to leave the profession and switch to careers that allowed them to pay their bills. In Avid's time they belonged to the Leadership social class, and had everyone's respect, judging from Avid's expression.

Shifting her thoughts on the "teacher paradigm" would take some mental adjusting, but Helen could certainly do that. In fact, it made her heart sing.

"Vendi told me I could give you background information on why the Mitigators are all women."

"Please do." Helen was rapt. She held up one finger, ran to the kitchen for water, ran back, then held out her mug for another cup of tea. Avid obliged. Helen sat down and then nodded for him to continue.

Where to begin? It all began with the very things that he could not tell Helen, so he had to begin somewhere in the middle. Or maybe he could lump it all into a generalized statement that would bridge the gap to the middle part, and then he could begin explaining it all to her from that point on.

"The world's leaders made a mess," Avid began. "It was a very big mess, and someone needed to fix it. Officials from the various governments teamed up and had focus groups with social scientists and all kinds of experts, who figured out that toxic masculinity was at the root of the mess. They'd found that training didn't help, because men usually reverted to their old habits of mess-making whenever they were given free rein to lead, but were not constrained in how they led, or were not constrained enough. It was a combination of deeply ingrained cultural tradition all over the world, and the innate nature of some males to use their alpha position to bully and dominate, and to be entitled and self-serving, and these were precisely the males who sought and won, or forcefully took over leadership roles. That alpha male behavior is pretty consistent in nature for a lot of species, and you see it all throughout world history."

"Makes perfect sense," Helen commented. "Go on."

"So they gave up on an entire generation of men and banned them from holding leadership positions. Then they extended the ban to the generation after that one, and then the generation after that. They passed laws that prohibit men from being in world leadership roles for two hundred and fifty years, like I said. They wanted to rule the world with feminine energy instead of masculine energy for the very first time, because the computer projections indicated that it was the best course of action. If I recall correctly, the projections actually said it was the *only* course of action to get out of the mess and prevent it from happening again."

"So they put all the men in *timeout?*" Helen threw her head back and laughed until she began choking. She gasped for breath. "All the men in your world are in *timeout?* Oh my God. I'm dying."

Her mirth had to subside at some point because it was exhausting her, and because she really, really wanted to hear more. She panted, grinning widely, occasionally letting out a shriek and laughing again. Finally, she calmed down.

"Even past female leaders usually patterned their behavior after the men's behavior, so lots of them exhibited the same toxic leadership traits as the men. What you see here in your world never really gets entirely better, at the world leadership level. Lots of world leaders were psychopaths, by the way. Narcissists, sociopaths, and psychopaths. I learned that from my History classes, but you probably already knew it. If not, you can Google it. New men took leadership roles and followed in the footsteps of the men who led before them. Lots of them were psychopaths and narcissists, like I said, and new leaders emulated them for the next seven hundred years or so, shooting for the same goals of winning and domination and self-aggrandizement, because that's how leaders had usually done it before them. And women tried to emulate them in order to succeed. Most people don't thrive anywhere, under these leaders, except for the people at the top of the heap."

Helen nodded.

"So, the toxicity was systemic. Then it resulted in a big mess. The focus group spent several years running emergency computer projections, looking for a better way to run the world. At about that time a group of Educators took the helm to try and stem the chaos— and really, nobody wanted to take the helm at that point. It was a crazy mess. They teamed with the experts and the social scientists, declared a temporary unified world state with the control stations managing things at a local level in the interim, then stripped all countries of their statehood so nobody had allegiance to any country anymore. We all became one world, following one set of international and inter-time laws.

"Their first recommendation after that was that we have a shift in focus for Educators to educate all the children so the next generations of leaders would know how to lead without making messes. The educational system was completely stripped and rebuilt. The focus group's next recommendation was that they screen all potential leaders for psychopathy and Dark Triad personality disorders to prevent them from successfully advancing into leadership roles, or to remove them if they already held them. In fact, they recommended that the leaders all be empaths instead, which is why you got your cupcakes. They called those leaders the 'Mitigators' because that was what they were put into place to do: mitigate the mess and pull us out of it. It's also a more accurate description of what they do than 'leader'."

"Mommy is in charge now, and Daddy is in the doghouse. I am literally dying."

"True. Sometimes they treat us like we're all their children. That's good and bad. On top of that, they're mostly all teachers, so they have their own set of behavioral modification strategies, if you remember your own school years. They'll loosen parental control when the social norms have successfully shifted and everyone behaves. We're only about fifty years into the first phase of the rebuilding, so the rules have to be strict and they have to strictly enforce them until the behaviors the Mitigators want from everyone are ingrained in the culture. They want to completely overwrite the old world order, permanently. But even with all the rules and the close monitoring, nobody wants to go back to the way it was. It's much better now for everyone, even the men."

"So how did they get the men to agree to this? Didn't they revolt or something?"

"The world leaders all knew what they'd done, but they had no idea how to fix it. They were pretty defiant at first, to be honest. None of them ever thought about changing the world order because that would threaten their own positions, which was really their primary concern overall, not the wellbeing of the people they led. They were all removed from power, and nobody cared whether or not they agreed to it. They all ended up in prison, with only a few exceptions."

"And that's when you call Mom."

"Exactly. There were some peacekeepers who meant well, and had genuinely tried to be reasonable and stop the mess before it happened. Those leaders weren't punished and they're still around working at some job or another, if they're still alive. But most of the old school world leaders are totally shunned unless they're performing community service. They all got life sentences. Now students study them, to learn about their leadership failures and compare them with the new leadership tactics the Mitigators use. We view them the way you view Hitler.

"How far the mighty have fallen, eh?"

Avid nodded. "They all live in one-room windowless apartments and wear uniforms. They can't go anywhere without people staring at them, laughing at them, or taunting them. You aren't supposed to mock prisoners because it isn't empathetic, but the Mitigators don't stop you from tormenting those particular people, so everyone does it for fun. They're notorious and everyone hates them. We all hope they hate themselves, and I figure they probably do because you can't feel good about yourself or expect anyone to take you seriously after you deliberately burn your own house down, like an idiot."

Avid continued his story, describing how the focus group created the founding charter bylaws, and structured the new world order around the same kind of corporate model in use during Helen's time, except that they eliminated the CEO and appointed Mitigators to work together as the Board of Directors.

The Educators had taken over and gone through the process of screening people for leadership roles. They looked for high intellect and emotional intelligence. Nominees had to fall high on the scale for empaths, so people scoring low on the scale were completely excluded from consideration. They looked for extremely smart women who had demonstrated high levels of skill and good judgment in their careers, had strong character, and who demonstrated an ability to punish fairly and stand their ground without buckling under manipulative pressures, such as threats, pleading, or tears, and who reacted to those pressures thoughtfully, and without knee-jerk vengeance. But they also wanted them to not use a nuclear approach, or a "one size fits all" approach to infractions. In short, they were essentially looking for good mothers and good teachers who could be stern but fair.

Things improved immediately. But the world's population still required motivation to move past the mess and keep going.

In the midst of the chaos, society took care of everyone's basic needs, at first viewing it as a response to the state of emergency, and then continuing on with it because the strategy worked. They obtained funds by piggy-backing off the economic systems of the world throughout the continuum. There were no taxes, except for the false corporations the Mitigators set up in the various centuries; these had to pay local governments for their investment earnings in order to remain in place and evade investigation.

This kind of environment could create a potentially paralyzing situation if people had no reason to strive. To motivate people into higher performance and higher life satisfaction, the Mitigators doled out perks as both earnings and reward. They publicly anointed certain roles with "high status" for various reasons. In the case of the

Heroes, their status was a lure, a reward, and a way of placating them for their brutal assignments. In instances where status was more widely attainable, such as raising Dynasty Children instead of your own biological offspring, Mitigators used status as a lure to encourage people to help them advance their goals for civilization. They knew there would always be competitiveness, and there would always be people with a burning desire for success, earning status for athletic achievement, success in the arts, and technological advancements, just as they did in Helen's time. But Mitigators also made certain that people always had something to admire or envy, and then to strive for, on top of all that.

They addressed mental pain and mental illness immediately, and required periodic screenings for everyone, in part because of the trauma they had all experienced during the mess, and in part to prevent the mess from ever happening again. People were not as angry now, as they always used to be. They were not in as much pain.

Once they took on their roles, the Mitigators received continued input from the focus group and used additional computer scanner projections to determine a path forward, based on various scenarios and approaches. They began by putting the Education Project into place and implementing their new education strategy. Then they created the other projects, and assigned Mitigators to lead them based on their backgrounds and interests. In both the smaller groups and the all-encompassing All-Mitigator Group, they had to arrive at decisions through group consensus, by law. Anyone who attempted to insert ego or personal ambition could be ejected from the leadership role altogether, but that hadn't happened yet. They had chosen the Mitigators well.

"So when they organized the corporation, per se, people all self-sorted themselves into the Projects that they wanted to work for. The Mitigators offered huge perks to people who couldn't decide, to lure them to the Projects that still needed staff, so it all worked out. With all of history to pick from, people can usually find a slot that they want, if they qualify. Workers get promotions and raises and incentives and all of that, but the people who are industry leaders and billionaires in your world are just middle management in mine.

"The Historian Project came when I was about twelve years old. That's the project I work for—worked for. It's kind of a division of the Education Project. They're closely aligned. Mitigators decided to create it to supplement the curriculum for the Education Project, and they use what I gather up to teach children.

"I always wanted to be a Historian from the very first moment I heard about the job. But you know what? I think I can move on now. I think I can go back home and teach. Or maybe they'll assign me to a time that I like, and I can teach children in a control station. I'll see what they say. Maybe they'll even assign me to this time period. I'll let you know when they tell me. It's still so new, I'm a little nervous."

"You'll be fine. You'll be wonderful. I'll just give you a therapy session before you leave."

Avid grinned.

CHAPTER 55: EXPOSED

Avid had texted Helen that he was back in her place and time and would be stopping by her house in the early afternoon, before Nelda arrived with Mary. He had a lot to tell her about his new job, for which he had been in training for the past several months. This was his first opportunity to come back for a visit, but he'd scheduled it for less than a week after he'd left because he'd promised Helen he would come back every week for Game Night.

He let himself in with his key, and saw Helen in the kitchen, making a pot of coffee. She looked up and grinned. She wasn't nearly as excited to see him as he was to see her because, for her, it had only been a few days.

He waved away her offer of coffee.

"Oh *Avid*," she said with her eyes twinkling, walking toward him with her mug of coffee. It was as if he'd only left the room for a minute. "I have something to show you, but first I need to make popcorn. You'll understand why, when you see it." She set her mug down on the coffee table, quickly hugged Avid "hello", then returned to the kitchen where she pulled out a microwave popcorn pouch and popped it into the microwave, turning to Avid several times, grinning.

"Turn on the TV please, would you? Then go to the DVR recordings list and play *60 Minutes*. I recorded it last Sunday."

Avid navigated through the DVR recordings with the remote, and clicked *60 Minutes*.

Helen returned with a bowl of popcorn and a glass of water for Avid. She presumed he would like to make whichever beverage he preferred with his quick drink generator, so she hadn't asked him what he would like to drink.

He made himself an iced green tea.

"Okay," Helen said, passing him the bowl of popcorn. "Hit it."

Avid clicked Play, and the recording began.

Helen and Avid sat and watched a news story about the US government openly admitting that UFOs (they were calling them UAPs now) were real and that they were, and had been, zipping about in the skies for who knew how long. Navy pilots had racked up countless sightings that everyone had failed to report because anyone who did was mocked and laughed at.

"They spotted *you* guys, am I right?"

Avid nodded, his mouth full of popcorn. "Mmm," he answered.

"They think it might be China, or aliens from outer space."

Avid shook his head, chewing.

They both turned back to the television and watched the entire segment.

"But *wait!* There's *more!*" Helen pulled up the show *60 Minutes Overtime*, and played it. One of the military people they were interviewing described watching a spacecraft that hovered over the ocean surface, then simply drove straight into the waves and disappeared underwater.

Avid nodded thoughtfully, still chewing.

Helen turned to him and asked with real concern, "What does that mean for you guys?"

Avid swallowed, then burst out laughing at Helen's concern.

"I mean it. What happens now? Are you in danger?"

Avid leaned over and kissed her on the cheek.

"I can't tell you because it's in your future," he said.

Helen sniffed.

CHAPTER 55: THE BEGINNING, AD 2714

The ancient news clip of the aftermath of the Hiroshima nuclear bombing played as the Mitigator stood to the side of the stage with her head down. When the video ended the hall went dark. Then a spotlight illuminated her. She raised her head, stepped toward the front of the stage, and faced the auditorium audience. Her image displayed as a hologram for people in the back, and simultaneously appeared on the Alert screens of the audience watching from control centers across the continuum.

That audience had not yet even completely processed the news clip that played before this one, where Nazis bulldozed skeletal corpses into ditches near concentration camps at the end of World War II. Still stunned, the audience was now confronted by images that were arguably as bad or worse, with the living dead losing seared chunks of their own flesh as they scrambled in confusion, and screamed for help amid smoldering buildings and bodies in the streets.

The Mitigator gave a Namaste bow to the audience with her hands in the prayer position, touching her chin. Then she addressed everyone.

"World War II in the twentieth century was one example of our shameful and ghastly history. I'm sure you'll all agree that our memories are still fresh as to what 'ghastly' looks like in modern times. We could provide examples of our last war and other wars for days…and I can assure you that every war was a failure in some respect, even if we've traditionally viewed the ultimate result as positive, as we did with World War II.

"In the past we had students memorize the dates of battles, and we taught them how many troops died on each side. We taught them who won."

She sighed.

"But 'won' is not the correct word: we only taught them who prevailed, for better or for worse. We commented on the killing of civilians caught in the crosshairs, but thought of the victims in terms of numbers."

She paused and looked to the right and left at the audience.

"I want you to compare these two events side-by-side."

Still images appeared of the two scenes.

"For those of you who recall any of what you studied about twentieth century history, you already know that one of the clips shows you what the 'bad' side did. The other news clip shows you what the 'good' side did. If you do not recall your history, I'll ask you to guess which side was which."

She listened to the audience murmuring, asking each other for the answer because most did not recall their history lessons from the classroom, and the answer wasn't apparent from the images they were viewing.

The Mitigator did not answer her own question and left it up to the audience to decide.

"You have just watched original recordings, taken by contemporary witnesses at the time of the incidents," the Mitigator continued, "so you actually saw the real people who experienced these events. Each one of these people was a casualty number to you before this moment, but now you can see their actual bodies and faces, and imagine them alive and whole. Still, they're nameless, and they mean nothing to you, not really. They're just sad and unfortunate, and the situation you see is untenable but unchangeable because it happened in the past. It lost its impact. Most of you don't even remember the details of the war that did this to them, and most of you don't really care. However deeply you feel grief and regret in the abstract, when you see them in these images, you maintain a comfortable psychological distance because it happened long ago, and you don't really know them. They aren't yours. This didn't happen to you.

"We have just emerged from a war so terrible that the earth is scorched, and will be totally unfit for habitation for the foreseeable future. We cannot complain about our situation because, together, we all did this.

"It's safer here, so we've retreated into the oceans while we use our best technology to decontaminate and repair the devastation that we and our leaders left behind. Now we have to huddle underwater

266

for another few decades and think about what we have done. And in the meantime, the youngest of us have never even seen the sky.

"Many of us still remember what it was like to exist on-land, and those who have had the privilege of traveling back in time marvel over blue skies filled with birds, mountains covered with trees, air so fresh you feel intoxicated, and streams that run clean and carry countless fish.

"Meanwhile, we have lost more than ninety-five percent of the world's population, which either died in the war, or volunteered to resettle in the past until we can return to land. Most will remain there permanently. Billions of people have traveled back in time to the control stations we are now in the process of expanding as quickly as we can. Right now, most people are in the past solely to escape, because we can't return to land yet and there is no longer anywhere to house them all here, as fast as we're building. But if the Historian Project receives approval these refugees are prepared to work as control station staff, filling positions that support Historians from the earliest eras of the human race to the end of the twenty-sixth century, when the final war began. We sent them back and spread them over the entire span of humanity, where they are hiding in the oceans, watching from the sidelines while humanity fights its way toward this, our moment of ultimate shame."

She looked up and ran her gaze over the crowd, intensely. "But this ultimately is also our moment of purpose and hope."

She paused to look over her audience, and then continued.

"We in the present time are now down to just a few million souls to press forward until the repairs are complete, the forests are revived, and bodies of water and the rest of the ecosystems are restocked with animal and plant life we'll import from the past. Imagine us now as a large city, scattered in pieces in the various oceans around the world. Those of us who remain here live in a time of truce, maybe a time of lasting peace, we don't know. We have made every effort to create lasting peace but can't be sure yet that we have.

"But we now know, as we never did before, the importance of lasting peace. What we all have learned is that everyone who fought in the final war, lost that war. We lost, and they lost. We have learned about war, and we have lived through war, and we have lived and died for war, and it is futile. If we do not know that now, after this, we cannot ever survive and thrive and progress, at least not for long. Perhaps we don't deserve to."

A video image displayed the faces of people, many of them familiar: celebrities, athletes, leaders, coworkers, family. The montage displayed happy moments, then shifted to scanner images of them in death, twisted, contorted and maimed. Gasps rose from the audience.

"Have we learned our lesson yet?" She asked, running her gaze over the audience. "Every one of these people is dead because of that war. We can continue on the old path, the path you saw earlier and the path you see here, the path we followed since we began to walk upright tens of thousands of years ago." She gestured toward the death images.

"Or, we can adapt to the knowledge that there is a better way through kindness and compromise, and we can press forward in that direction. We can teach our children by example. Our Educators can shift away from rote learning and memorization to a deeper understanding that includes feelings and insight. They can teach children responsibility, respect, and meaning. When they teach the basic skills of math, reading and science, they can insert empathy, and together we can create a society that rewards that empathy, celebrates that empathy, and nurtures that empathy.

"We can all shift away from personal advancement at the expense of others. We can stop following, deifying, and applauding world leaders and generals who lead us into death and annihilation. We can stop idolizing and emulating the powerful and the ambitious and the greedy, and we can begin idolizing, emulating and rewarding the builders and the healers. We can stop demonizing and dehumanizing our imagined enemies, and provoking them with threats as if we were chest-thumping apes. We can turn our backs on armies and choose peace, and we can view each other as neighbors who all deserve to live and thrive. We all need one another equally. We need to believe that and live it.

"We can teach and encourage our children to build, not destroy. We can immerse them in art and beauty, and humbly ask them to please replace the priceless works of art that we destroyed in the devastated areas...and add their efforts to the artwork we salvaged and saved, and now preserve in the Gallery in the Indian Ocean. We, the ones who came before them, left them with none of it, aside from that, not the paintings, or the statues, or the great cathedrals, or the towering skyscrapers...We did not even leave them the grass and the birds and the trees, except for all the living things we rescued and still care for in our artificial habitats, thanks to the Noah's Ark Project,"

The audience shifted and murmured.

"Our goal for now is to revitalize the planet, and to simultaneously quell the anger, neutralize the greed, and the envy, and the resentment, and the need to get even, the need to be 'better than', and the need to overpower and conquer. We can make a sincere effort to finally lessen the violence in our natures and stop believing that we are superior. We have proven that we are not."

She stood small and slight in that single shaft of light, an awe-inspiring, illuminated sacred goddess, a Spiritual Mother, a kindly aunt. She raised her hands and extended them to the audience, and then lowered them. She bent over into a Namaste bow and then rose upright again.

"It begins with us, today."

She cleared her throat.

"What we propose is a deep dive into the thoughts, feelings and experiences of the people you see in these images, and in all the other images that will confront us in the upcoming years. We propose that we all respect—and honor—their hearts and experiences, and by extension the hearts and experiences of all the people whose images we can never see, for all the events throughout history. We can study them, and we can learn.

"History should not be dry. It should make us cry. We can teach our children to weep over our collective history, not celebrate it. We can redefine the term 'historical achievement' to exclude destruction, exploitation and corruption. We can call war what it is: failure. And we can teach the children how to never repeat our mistakes again. We can change."

A smattering of applause erupted, then was quickly quelled when the Mitigator resumed her speech.

"The Historian Project's efforts will take hundreds of years to complete. None of us here today will live to see them finished. However, we predict that they will ultimately advance human civilization, which is our obvious goal. We have the technology to go backward in time. We are now gathering a team of Historians for this project and are training them to record our history as it actually happened, for us and for the generations that come after us. With your approval, they will begin work within months. After we sort through the events they record, our Educators will then decide how to present those events, and will use the Historians' findings for classroom curriculum. Anything that does not become classroom curriculum will be stored in the Library for anyone to access. Old historical records that count casualties and glorify war will be archived. Hopefully, we will forget they exist.

"Most importantly we rely on the Educators, as always, to form the backbone of the project and teach empathy to our children, whom we depend upon to carry lasting peace into a better future."

She bowed again and rose. She smiled.

"And may we please succeed this time."